CW00734737

# THE
# WITTY
# WOMEN

# THE BOOK OF WITTY WOMEN

## Introduction by Helen Lederer

 In association with

First published in 2024 by Farrago,
an imprint of Duckworth Books Ltd
1 Golden Court, Richmond, TW9 IEU, United Kingdom

www.farragobooks.com

Copyright in the compilation and introductory
material © 2024, Comedy Women in Print

The list of individual titles and respective copyrights to be found on
pages 341–2 constitutes an extension of this copyright page.

The moral right of the contributing authors of this anthology to
be identified as such has been asserted by them in accordance
with the Copyright, Designs & Patents Act 1988.

All rights reserved. No part of this publication may be reproduced,
stored in a retrieval system, or transmitted, in any form or by any
means, without the prior permission in writing of the publisher.

This book is a work of fiction. Names, characters, businesses, organisations,
places and events other than those clearly in the public domain, are either the
product of the author's imagination or are used fictitiously. Any resemblance
to actual persons, living or dead, events or locales is entirely coincidental.

Print ISBN: 978-1-78842-463-9
eBook ISBN: 978-1-78842-464-6

Cover design and illustration by Emily Courdelle

# Contents

# Introduction

Dear witty reader, welcome to this anthology. Conjure, if you will, the pleasure of sampling a box of sweets with different flavours and textures – each of them designed to make you laugh, or at the very least allow a suppressed guffaw. My mission is to celebrate and create parity for comedic women writers, so how lucky am I to be here, at the front of all this mirth. Some stories are from established published authors; others exciting new voices made up from shortlisted entrants to the Comedy Women in Print prize.

From the frankly strange to the satirical and even touchingly true, the joy of the mix will, I hope, place you in a VERY good mood. Kimberley Adams offers a unique approach to funeral planning, while Sadia Azmat contributes a menopausal boss on steroids. There's the death of a hamster through song by Annemarie Cancienne, alongside the imagined world of extreme shopping by Kim Clayden. Jean Ende's account of a family party gone AWOL will have you giggling, as will Wendy Hood's old people's choir.

Paula Lennon channels a narcoleptic biscuit lover, while celebrated author Kathy Lette tackles an irrational fear of the phallus. Comedian and writer Josie Long takes a satirical route into therapy, and there's a pig on the run by R. Malik. A fibbing bird watcher is called out by Jaqueline Saville, while Claire Shaw reveals the consequences of accidental gluing. Kathryn Simmonds offers up a pesky mother-in-law; highly prized author Lucy Vine conjures the delightfully surreal world of canine dating, and there's a minefield of mishaps provided by Julia Wood.

These stories remind us that fun and comedic writing can also move us. Oh, and also – laughing out loud is good for you... Bon appétit!

Helen Lederer

# Sorry, Delivery

*Paula Lennon writes in multiple genres including contemporary crime, historical, and magical realism. With this story, she won the Comedy Women in Print Short Story Prize 2023. She was longlisted for the Historical Writers Association/Sharpe Books Unpublished Novel Award, and was a finalist in the ScreenCraft Cinematic Book Competition. Her Jamaican detective trilogy is published by Joffe Books.*

This wooden bench is cold, hard and hurts my bum. I'm in the drab, bustling lobby of a South London police station shuffling from one cheek to the other trying not to look like I need the loo. It's close to midnight. Around me are people of all shapes, colours and accents, testing the patience of the desk constable whose face suggests he resents his career choice.

Sad drunks, mugging victims, mouthy escorts, they're out in their numbers tonight, filling the air with beer and sweat. Miserable crowd. Not to be judgmental or anything, but I'm quite different from this set of idle losers. I'm waiting for a detective to descend the stairs and arrest me for murder.

Me? I'm Kayla Reilly, a melanin-rich, pocket-poor, fifty-something Londoner, and a delivery driver. I was working in advertising, but my thirty-year experience stood for little when the pandemic hit and I was one of the first to be laid off. That said, my firing could have had something to do with my failure to adapt to modern technology. Forgot to mute the microphone when comparing a client's intelligence to that of a rock. I guess I became that rock. My career sank like one, anyway. So, for the past ten months I've been dragging boxes and packages around the city, building admirable biceps as well as calf muscles I could have done without.

Two days ago, I woke up to a warm, sunny August morning with the birds chirping sweetly in the trees outside my Stockwell terrace, a gentle breeze blowing through the open window and a fat spider two inches from my ear. After I'd done screaming, I showered and slid into my burgundy uniform. I caught a glimpse of morning face in the dressing table mirror and I can tell you it wasn't pretty. Thank god for make-up. My silk bonnet had slid off in the night so my thick natural hair was in a right state. The bottle of shea butter detangler had nothing left to give despite me turning it upside down and squeezing its neck. So, I brushed down my unruly mane, pulled on my peaked cap, popped a pill to stay awake and set out to challenge the rush-hour traffic.

My trusty transit van took me past all kinds on the congested streets of South London: joggers, dog-walkers, old and lonely, young and lonelier. The young kept their heads bowed, adrift in a vast desert with one structure on it: a phone. This particular neighbourhood, Battersea, was the sort where people had time and money, and time to spend that money. Not that I'm the judgmental type, I just see things. As you do. The wheely bins were perfectly aligned; rubbish and recycling segregated for the good of the environment and middle-class consciences. Monster Hummers and Land Rovers took little Tarquin and Tabitha to schools five minutes' drive away. On the busy pavements competing Mercedes baby buggies fought for pole position in a race to Starbucks. Before those babies were even weaned off formula they were trained for Formula 1.

The sun was 11 o'clock high and melting my skin when I pressed the buzzer on a nice detached pad. I hoped the owner was a tea-and-biscuits lady; juicy gossip would be a bonus.

'Delivery for Mrs Magenta Larson!'

No answer and I waited a good while. Five-point-two seconds to be exact. After that I got antsy and plunked the pot plant down. I photographed the front door to prove I'd made the delivery and turned to leave.

The intercom crackled: 'Hello?'

I shackled my annoyance and perked up my voice to psychotic cheeriness. 'Delivery for Mrs Larson!'

The robotic voice made no attempt to match my deranged tone. 'Drop it off, back office shed,' she said.

'It's a potted plant, madam.'

'Stick it by the shed door, please. Thanks.'

My bright smile for the camera hid a whole world of resentment. With both hands I carried the pot across a perfect green lawn, managing to damage a fingernail in the process. I hoped Mrs Larson would glance at her video screen and decide that a woman carrying a Bromeliad in a heavy terracotta pot deserved chocolate digestives, but it didn't happen for me.

Carefully, I placed the pot outside a large she-shed. Being a nosey sort, I stood on tiptoe and peered through the single window. On the walls were watercolour paintings: a mound of green breadfruits with glossy leaves attached to the stems, a Caribbean market scene with buxom women in colourful headwraps and a large montage of Jamaican national heroes.

The surface of an antique desk was cluttered with note-pads and pens. A laser printer stood beside it with piles of printed pages stacked on top. The overflowing bookshelf contained mainly memoirs, biographies and autobiographies of celebrated Britons: Benjamin Zephaniah, Lenny Henry, Doreen Lawrence. Magenta's tastes even stretched to the notorious Margaret Thatcher and the slightly more notorious Rose West. A book propped up against a stainless-steel lamp promised the reader sound advice on how to conduct successful interviews. Clearly, Magenta had a keen interest in other people's lives, whether good citizens or closet criminals.

Also on the desk was a large photo of a woman and man, temples pressed together. With a name like Magenta, I had imagined a glamorous Hollywood type with big hair like Whitney or Dolly. Well, Magenta wasn't Whitney, although they shared the same complexion. I was pleased to see she looked like an everyday woman, like me even. Her natural curly brown hair was piled up in a messy bun and she wore barely any make-up. Her wide grin complemented a wholesome look that suited sisters who decided to get along with time and not rage against it. The man, presumably her husband, looked slightly younger, shaven headed, with a well-shaped salt-and-pepper goatee, and a whole lot of sparkling teeth set in his smooth ebony face. Damn, good for you, Magenta.

As I strolled back to my van, a tabby kitten ran out from under next door's fence, mewing, demanding to be worshipped. 'Hey, kitty.' It purred as I rubbed its plump tummy and squeezed its soft pink toe beans. 'Yes, you're a prince, but I've got a schedule to meet.'

I hopped into my van, ticked off my latest delivery and drove on. At one point I did notice a green SUV in my rear-view mirror, but other than thinking it was a nice shade, I paid little attention to it. While tapping my knee at a stop light I glanced down at my split fingernail, which hurt a bit. The small white card in the passenger footwell caught my eye. *Oh no, the plant care card for Snooty Larson.*

With traffic cameras eager to flash at me, doing a sneaky U-turn was not an option so I had to find a convenient spot to turn around. A supercenter with a gigantic car park lay not far ahead and I headed in that direction.

I pressed Magenta's house buzzer and chirped, 'Sorry, delivery! Me again!'

Not a peep from the robotic voice. This lady really had a nerve ignoring me like she was some best-selling author and I was some stalker desperate for her autograph. I walked down to the shed and peered through the window. The Bromeliad was now inside, cosy in a corner. Magenta Larson was not. Her manuscript pages were scattered on her desk and her notepads had definitely been moved around. I frowned as I pushed the plant care card under the door frame.

As I turned to leave, the tiny kitten rushed over again demanding attention and I poked its soft belly. 'I hope you don't belong to Magenta, cutie, she doesn't deserve you.'

With my shift finished, I phoned my boss to check in. Cherise Wilkins, or Miss Cherry, as most of us called the owner of Cherry Drops, was the caring motherly sort who always wanted to know her staff were safe. She had emigrated from Trinidad as a child and her sing-song lilt was as comforting down the phone line as it was in person. Always ready with a buxom hug that made me lament my B-cups, she paid decent wages and was generous with time off, so an easygoing gal like me was content in her employ.

The next day I followed a pretty similar routine, dropping off packages, gossiping with neighbours, turning down fig rolls. I mean, fig rolls? Gross. I argued with road hogs who weren't worth my time and showed them an upward-pointing digit or two. When evening came, I was glad to get back home to my cosy terrace. Snug in the sofa, channel-hopping, I caught the early evening TV news. I choked and it wasn't the hot pepper on my jerk chicken that made me splutter, though it didn't help. The fine man from the photo frame on Magenta's desk was staring at me larger than life and talking. The bottom of the screen said: DANE LARSON HUSBAND OF THE MISSING WOMAN.

My mind fought to make sense out of nonsense. *Husband of the what in the world?*

'Please call me or the police if you've seen her. I love you, Magenta. Please come home.' His voice was emotional, his lips quivered. Dane came home last night to find Magenta missing and no note explaining her absence.

I felt like I was afloat on a faraway plain looking down on real life. 'Holy cow.'

I wiped red sauce off the sofa that needs tossing out anyway, grabbed my phone and dialled the police. Now I have about as much use for the Old Bill as a supermodel has for Spanx, but I didn't fancy contacting the grieving husband direct. By the time I hung up, Detective Jewell and Detective Barclay were on the way to my home having invited themselves over in the sly way of cops.

I called Miss Cherry, told her what happened and that the cops were coming to interview me.

'Not a good idea talking to them without a lawyer, Kay-girl, you know they're good at twisting things. I'll send my lawyer over.'

'They can twist as much as they like, they won't tie me in knots.' A mental picture of boss lady's happy round face, now lined with concern, invaded my mind and I smiled. 'Don't worry about me, Miss Cherry. A ten-minute conversation and they'll be gone. I'll be just fine.'

I made a half-hearted attempt to get the front room more presentable. I was one of those people who saw no need to keep a show house, and couldn't imagine putting away the washing-up liquid after every use and polishing the taps. Magazines and newspapers were swiftly tucked under the sofa seats and the cushions plumped up. Bottles were cleared off the centre table and hidden under the kitchen sink. I sprayed a dash of air freshener from a rusty can I hadn't used in years and the vile odour reminded me why. Once my eyes stopped watering, I was ready for my unwanted guests.

Detective Jewell was, maybe, mid-thirties with short cropped brown hair which clung to his pink scalp. He was built like the kind who spends weekends brawling after pub closing hours or moonlights as a bouncer. I had a feeling he alternated between both. The bull dragged a chair from the dining table across my polished wooden floor, leaving a marked impression on the woodwork and on me. I ground my teeth. As he sat, I hoped the sturdy chair legs would fold, but they stubbornly held firm. I glanced at his sidekick, Detective Barclay, a small, grey-haired, pot-bellied man. He stayed on his feet, quietly scrutinised the surroundings and rubbed his pointed chin like he was comforting the stubble.

I was hot. Not for the cops, just hot. I fanned my neck with my open palm. Internal heat for women of a certain age was a thing, and such an unnecessary thing. We were going to die anyway. It seemed downright unfair that we had to burn first, for a few decades.

I sank onto the sofa and sat bolt upright, hands on knees. Had to be alert. Cops were a strange breed and once they pinned that badge on, they changed species, to a unique animal that could not be described as warm or cuddly. This pair did nothing to dispel my reservations. Detective Jewell was all steely-eyed and sour. Man, some delivery driver must've lobbed a fragile package onto his lawn and he'd never forgiven them. Wasn't too long before I grew weary of Jewell's unfriendly interrogation technique, and when I'm weary it's hard to maintain my naturally sweet disposition.

'Why all the damn questions?'

'You were the last person to see Magenta Larson.'

'Er, you missed the part where I said I didn't see her, Detective. I only heard her. On the intercom. She told me where to stick the pot plant.'

Jewell's dark eyes sought to penetrate mine. 'How'd you hurt your finger?'

I curled the purple tip into my palm. It throbbed. I winced and hoped he wouldn't make too much of my pained expression. 'Caught it in the plug hole, cleaning the bath.'

Jewell leant forward and as his long sleeve drew up, I glimpsed the beginning of a tattoo on his forearm. All I saw were the letters HA. Following my gaze, he quickly pulled the sleeve down. Not being judgmental or anything, but I could guess what that was about – HARD RIGHT, no doubt. He exchanged a meaningful glance with Barclay in what appeared to be some sort of professional cue since I couldn't imagine this pair dating.

A thought crossed my mind as I watched Barclay looking around my four walls. I didn't want him to get the wrong impression from the things he might notice. See, I'm a popular lady so men bring me things all the time; fancy chocolates, unique wines, expensive perfumes, smart phones. I'm really good at selling them on, once I've removed the anti-theft tags.

'Ms Reilly, I do believe Mrs Larson is the victim of foul play.' Barclay had a surprisingly high-pitched voice for an older man. No wonder he preferred not to speak.

'Oh?' I spoke to be polite as I couldn't imagine what he wanted me to say.

'Thirty years on the job and I trust my gut,' said Barclay. 'It's usually right.'

I glanced at Barclay's extended waistline that strained against the leather belt holding up his trousers. His gut didn't even know when it was full, yet he was taking tips from it. I didn't get why the officers and the husband were so certain Magenta was really missing. The lady was clearly a well-off woman; a Communications Director for a multinational conglomerate, no less. Maybe she was annoyed with her husband and left to *find herself* as only the financially sound can do. Wage slaves, like me, cannot afford to lose ourselves and must wade through the nine-to-five jungle until blessed retirement or death.

'Three days ago, a person paid for the Bromeliad at a florist in West Norwood which is where, I understand, you collected it.' Jewell pushed a phone under my nose with a fuzzy image of a CCTV still. 'Recognise him? He's clearly in disguise.'

Man, he was in disguise all right. Stylish Afro wig, broad moustache, thick lens glasses, upturned collar on a long-sleeve shirt on what was a warm day. This chap was obviously going for a cartoon look – that Family Guy character.

'Cleveland Brown.'

Jewell gave me his darkest glare. 'You find him funny, Ms Reilly?'

'The writers gave it their best shot, but funny? Nope.'

'You and Dane Larson, are you… friends?'

'Whoa! What?'

Jewell imposed social distance between 'you' and 'friends' more effectively than any virus protocol. Me and Dane indeed. The very idea that I would. Well, actually, I would. But I had not, and did not intend to.

'There is no me and Dane Larson, Detective. I've done over fifty years of independence and I enjoy my me-time.' No point telling him about the string of dead-end boyfriends I'd suffered over the years to finally get to the stage of not giving a toss. 'Never met the man, never met his wife.'

Barclay rubbed his much-massaged chin. 'You've had a few rather physical run-ins with people.'

For the first time I noticed a slim manila folder tucked under Barclay's arm. As he read a slip of paper taken from it, a chill ran through me. I should have expected it. Should have known the cops would turn up my criminal record before turning up at my door.

'Now wait a minute. People have stolen my packages and, yeah, I've chased down one or two... convinced them to hand it back without opening my mouth.'

'Leaving them battered and bruised?' added Barclay.

I shrugged. 'Protecting merchandise is work.'

'It's not just in work though is it, Ms Reilly?' said Jewell. 'You have a naturally violent streak. You slugged a man in the gym.'

'He turned off the ceiling fans, Detective.' I rolled my eyes at the blank looks on their faces. 'The magistrate was around my age, she understood.'

'And what did Magenta do to you?' asked Jewell.

'Copied my lipstick colour. I bought it first, I wore it better.'

My fridge broke the painful silence by making a sudden churning noise. Jewell squinted so hard I swear his eyes closed. London Bobbies couldn't find a sense of humour, how the hell were they going to find a missing person?

My toes curled and I stood up pointedly, hands on hips. 'Well, I'm fresh out of Tetley and Jammie Dodgers so...'

Detective Jewell took me by surprise when he rose and changed his tone. He politely asked if I would accompany them to the Larson's place and said my assistance would be appreciated. My mind worked quickly. Daylight would last for at least another hour. An evening out with the detectives or an evening in with Netflix? Lord knows I had fallen out of love with Netflix. Don't get me wrong, I hadn't fallen in love or even in like with the officers. Might get to see inside Magenta's palatial house, that was the box office draw.

'Sure, why not?' I said.

Miss Cherry pulled up kerbside just as we were leaving my house. She was such a dear I should've known she'd come check up on me. Having lost my mom many years ago it was good to know Miss Cherry had my back. She stepped out of her Audi looking smart as always, kitted out in a floral pinafore dress and high heels.

'Hey, Kay-girl. I'm guessing these aren't your body-guards so they must be police, right?'

'Right.' I grinned at her. 'Detectives, this is my boss, Cherise Wilkins. She can confirm everything I told you about my delivery schedule.'

'Kayla's not your girl, detectives.' Miss Cherry offered Jewell a short nod then turned sympathetic eyes on me. 'Sure you're gonna be all right? I can make a phone call?'

'Oh, they're not taking me in, everything's fine. We're going to the Larson house for a bit.'

Miss Cherry frowned. 'Well, keep your hands in your pockets, Kay-girl.'

Jewell looked at her expectantly. 'You think Ms Reilly might take something belonging to the Larsons?'

I glared at him, full of righteous indignation. 'Sir, you said that out loud.' When I 'sir' people it is not a show of respect, but if I swore at the detective, I knew he'd throw the cuffs on.

Miss Cherry ignored Jewell and shook her head at me. 'Next thing you'll hear your fingerprints are all over the house.'

'True talk, Miss C.' I pushed my hands deep down in my jeans pockets. 'I'll walk around the place like this. Won't even lean against a wall or I'll hear "her clothes fibres were found all over the scene".'

Detective Jewell's neck flushed deep pink beneath his collar. 'You ladies watch too much television,' he snapped as he opened the car door and waved me in. 'Mind your head now. Wouldn't want to dislodge any other stereotypes you've got floating around in there.'

A posse of cops were swarming around outside the Larson house, like they were holding their annual police convention. No surprise there. The surprise opened the front door and my eyebrows went right up like they were on stilts. She was a stunning young woman, her hair a long straight Brazilian weave with red streaks. She was dressed – if you could call it that – in a Kente cloth bra and denim batty rider. My grandma would say God gave up being a tailor and passed the sewing machine to Satan.

Detective Barclay appeared unbothered by the sight, while Detective Jewell's eyes widened. Jewell's shoulders must have widened too, as try as I might I couldn't see past them and get even a half-decent look inside the Larson palace. So annoying. Dane emerged from behind the sultry glamour puss. He wore a loose vest and long shorts he must have rushed to find. His hand brushed against her waist as he eased her aside and stepped out into the humid night air.

'I'll show you to Magenta's shed, officer,' he said.

'Just a minute, sir.' Jewell stopped him. 'Who's this?'

My eyebrows stayed up as I waited for Dane to explain the presence of a half-naked African princess at what was bedtime for a lot of people. Not to judge the woman or anything, but I just knew she had 'Actress /Influencer' on her resume and spent a lot of time online. Even when she was in Dane's bed.

'My niece, Detective Jewell, Alicia Todd.'

'Your... niece?'

There it was again, the Jewell specialty. More distance between those two words than there was between William and Harry.

'Magenta's sister's daughter. We're not actually blood relatives.'

As Jewell shuffled in his pocket for a notebook and pen, I could barely keep the scepticism from my face. Must be hard to find your missing wife when your head is buried in a sweet young thing's double-Ds. The police had got it right after all. Magenta Larson was not just missing; she was dead. Meanwhile Dane was faithfully following the script for murderous husbands. Crocodile tears, check. Lost and miserable look, check. Emotional, pleading tone, check. Younger mistress, check with bells on. Almost without exception, husbands like Dane not only knew where their wives were, but had put them there.

Alicia tossed back her fake hair like she'd grown it and not forked out a couple hundred quid to get it. Her light brown Jezebel-eyes were on me and I stared right back. In those eyes was a look that held a dark secret and I guessed the secret was that she and her lover had got rid of Magenta together.

Detective Jewell questioned Alicia who spoke in a soft voice I could just imagine whispering in Dane's ear. She said she was at work all day teaching yoga classes at the sports centre next door to Dane's business consultancy firm. Said she only broke for an hour for lunch when she went for a walk over Battersea Park. Well, that was convenient for this pair of abductors, the park being no more than a short drive from the Larson home or a good run for the physically fit, like Alicia Todd.

'When last did you see your Aunt Magenta?' Jewell's pen hovered over his notebook.

'Would've been around eight yesterday morning.' Alicia flicked her mane again. 'I got up and went jogging. Came back, showered, changed and had breakfast.'

I wondered what she had for breakfast. Not a decent fry-up for sure. Probably hot lemon, a sprig of lettuce and half a tomato that she couldn't quite finish because her sunken stomach was full.

'When I left for work Aunt Magenta was loading dishes into the dishwasher. Haven't seen or heard from her since.'

'Do you live here, Miss Todd?' asked Jewell.

'No, I sometimes spend a couple of nights a week here. Still live with my parents in Kennington. You know what house prices are like so I'm saving up. And it's good to have somewhere to crash when things get too heated at home.'

'Can you think of anybody who'd want to hurt your aunt?'

To my surprise the homewrecker had the nerve to turn her caterpillar lashes on me again. 'She's the delivery driver, isn't she? Why don't you ask her?'

'You talking to me?'

'I was speaking to the detective.'

'Just answer my question, Miss Todd,' said Jewell. 'I'll deal with Ms Reilly.'

'No, I can't think of anyone who'd want to hurt her.' A thin line creased Alicia's otherwise smooth brow. 'She's a people person, Detective. Loves meeting new people, and always said one day she'd pitch a book proposal to literary agents, about unsung Britons.'

'Anyone else around here yesterday morning that we should know about?' Jewell's voice hardened as he stared at Dane. 'Wouldn't like to think there was another person you forgot to mention.'

The adulterous couple shook their heads in unison. I was outraged that Jewell didn't press them any further. Beautiful people say, 'It wasn't us' and cops say, 'We know, just kidding! Carry on.' I decided to stick my oar in.

'So, aren't you going to ask him where he was?' I said.

'I never thought of that.' Detective Jewell gave me a look that could cut steel. 'We've already spoken to Mr Larson, Ms Reilly.'

Dane glared at me. 'I was seeing various clients all day, inside and outside of the office. Some turned up, some didn't. I can account for my time, Ms Reilly.'

Yeah, the Yorkshire Ripper could account for his time too. Didn't dare say it out loud.

Dane hovered in the background as the detectives checked inside Magenta's shed. Played the part of angelic husband quite convincingly. Answered their questions and became suitably distraught: reddened eyes, downcast lips, looking more victim than villain. Alicia stood beside Dane rubbing his bare upper arm like he had eczema, only she wasn't holding no calamine lotion. I glanced at the detectives to see if they were paying attention to her possessive behaviour, only to find Jewell staring right at me.

'Ms Reilly, you say you came back right away, dropped off the card and left immediately after?' said Jewell.

So, one cop was paying attention… to me, a complete stranger with no motive. Like that made sense. He must think I had some kind of grudge against Magenta. Carrying a grudge is no hardship for me; in fact, I consider it a labour of love, but murder as the end result? How sick is that? I wanted to throw my head back and scream out loud in frustration, but I knew I couldn't show any signs of being unhinged, even though screaming at the sky was something I did on a daily basis, when I got a bit crazy, without caring who was within earshot.

'Not more than half hour passed between my first and second trips to the shed, Detective, I swear.'

A furry four-legged vision crept before my mind's eye and I swallowed the air that expanded in my throat. The second time I saw that tabby kitten it was no longer podgy. And that meow was more of a feed-me meow, not a play-with-me meow. Time had certainly elapsed between my delivery of the plant and my return with the card. How much time, I wasn't sure. Two hours, three? I'd had a nap in the supercentre car park. Not on purpose. Narcolepsy made me sleep at unexpected times of day and now I recalled catching forty winks, except forty winks could have been four hundred and forty winks. Surely when I was asleep, I was asleep, not wandering around playing Michael Myers?

'None of our officers found any plant care card, Ms Reilly,' said Detective Barclay.

'I bet they found all the buy-one-get-one free pizza cards though,' I said.

Jewell shot me a dark look. 'You'll have to do better than blaming my team.'

'I didn't see a card either,' said Dane, casting an accusatory look in my direction.

He was lying, of course. The green SUV sitting on his driveway looked exactly like the one that had followed me. Maybe he'd been in the house with Magenta and killed her as soon as I left. Now he could use me as the mug to take the fall. I thought about explaining narcolepsy to the cops, but details of my unpredictable condition were shared only with those people closest to me.

'Well, Ms Reilly?' said Barclay. 'Care to refresh your memory?'

'My memory is not thirsty, sir. I told you I never even met Mrs Larson.'

Perspiration pricked every pore in my upper body and although I was sure it was just an inopportune hot flush, I knew the cops would see it as a sign of panic. I wiped my brow with the back of my sleeve. 'Can I go now?'

'You won't mind if we borrow your delivery van to run a few tests?' asked Jewell.

'OK by me, and I know Miss Cherry won't object.'

'Do that, Detective,' said Dane. 'Please do everything you can to find my wife.'

Jewell took a phone call, didn't say much, but his eyes bored into me as he ummed and ahhed. He tucked his phone away. 'My colleague tells me that your personnel records indicate a complaint was made two weeks ago from this very address, about you being rude. Would that surprise you?'

Well, it did, but I wasn't about to tell Jewell that. 'Detective I get reported if I smile too much, if I don't smile enough, if I take too long to park, if I take too long to leave. It wouldn't surprise me at all.'

'If we find out you're holding something back we won't go easy on you.' Jewell fixed me with a cop-look I guess was designed to coax a confession out of me.

I shook my head. No way was I going to admit there were a missing couple of hours I couldn't account for. 'Wish I could be of more help, Detective.'

Next morning, I gazed out my front window with a degree of sadness and anger as I viewed the spot that had once held my transit van. Not so much because I missed my vehicle, although I did. More because my neighbours had parked their battered Volvo there. Man, I hated the sight of that piece of junk. Detective Jewell had promised I could have my van back within twenty-four hours, which was fine since it was my day off anyway and I didn't plan on going further than the nearest patty shop.

*News at Noon* was on TV and I munched my saltfish patty as I watched. The earnest female anchor said the police had few clues and were asking possible witnesses to come forward with information. 'The last person known to have visited Magenta Larson at her Battersea home was Cherry Drops delivery driver, Kayla Reilly, who police say is cooperating with the investigation.'

Flaky pastry stuck in my craw. That low-life detective had put my name on blast hoping someone would say they'd seen Dane and me together. And the thing is somebody probably would. People will say and do anything for clout nowadays. I closed the curtains and didn't go near my windows for the rest of the day. In between watching B movies, I obsessively checked the internet for updates on Magenta, afraid to pop down to the pub in case my name was on everybody's mind and worse, on their lips.

At nightfall, primetime TV broke horrific headline news. Magenta Larson's body had been discovered with stab wounds in a skip less than a mile from her home. No other details were given. Shocked, I scoured social media sites and found a grainy video posted by a local resident, from a surveillance camera fixed outside his home. The short clip showed a person heaving a suspiciously large object into the waste container.

Recognition dawned. My hands shook and my shot glass fell to the floor sending white rum seeping between the wooden planks. Even though I was seated, my legs went all rubbery as if the bones had taken a walk and left the flesh behind. That person on video was a woman and although distance blurred her face I knew who it was. Me. That was my uniform, my cap and, damn it, that vehicle in the shadows was my transit van. This was insane. OK, so sometimes I do act a little insane and I've been known to hurt people, but why would I have done this – and to her? I stared at my shaking hands almost expecting to see blood dripping from my palms.

I dragged myself to the bathroom and splashed cold water on my red hot face. I could practically see the steam emitting, fogging the mirror, but nothing could remove the video image imprinted on my mind.

I knocked back a rum cocktail to calm my nerves and then another to calm the ones that I'd missed. The third was just to make sure they were all fully sedated. It was only a matter of time before Jewell and Barclay turned up on my doorstep to read me my rights. To spare myself the humiliation of having chunky steel bracelets clapped onto my wrists I took a cab to the police station.

As I sat shuffling cheeks on the hard bench, I listened to indistinct male voices arguing all around me. My mind conjured up images of being forced into grey sweats and tossed into a dark cell with one of the men. That would be awful; blue suited me better.

I felt I needed professional help to get through this interview and pulled out my phone.

'Miss Cherry? That lawyer you mentioned, can you call them? Yeah, at Lavender Hill nick. Thanks, you're an angel.'

I decided to take a selfie, just in case I got beaten up and my lawyer had to prove I was in one piece when I arrived. My finger automatically pressed the gallery icon instead of the camera and I stared at the image of a white front door. The Larson's front door with the terracotta plant pot beside it. When I took the photo I hadn't given the image more than a cursory glance, but now I did. The stained glass panel at the top of this door had geometric patterns – a mish-mash of squares, triangles, rectangles with a bluish green tone. The door that Alicia had stood beside last night had hexagonal patterns and a reddish purple tint.

You could have knocked me down with a feather. Well, actually, I'm allergic to feathers so I would only have sneezed my head off rather than fallen. Dane and Alicia had replaced the front door. And the only reason they could have for changing it was because of blood stains, Magenta's blood. In a violent struggle the door had been damaged and smeared in her blood. That person caught on CCTV was not me, it was Actress slash Influencer, Alicia Todd. Clearly she was even more slasher than influencer, and when all the slashing was going on I was fast asleep. They stuck me in the SUV. They stole my spare uniform and van, then dumped Magenta where a security camera would see it all to frame me.

In my Eureka moment I jumped up and declared, 'It wasn't me!'

The lobby fell silent. Even a toothless drunk stopped spewing obscenities to shoot a dazed look my way. The desk officer stared at me as if he just remembered my presence and reached for his phone.

I took off running. Technically, I was never in custody so I couldn't be charged with escaping custody, but I didn't think Detective Jewell was one to worry about technicalities.

I was a fugitive. Couldn't take the risk of hailing a cab so I stayed in the shadows and ran all the way to the skip. Yellow caution tape circled the giant container and two cop cars with flashing blue lights were parked on either side. The cops wouldn't know the significance of a discarded white front door even if they came across it, and had no reason to link it to Magenta. Intense frustration overcame me. I wanted to see inside that skip, but it was being watched more closely than a Russian oligarch watches his teenage wife.

Jewell needed to know about the evidence and I had his direct number, but I was not about to let him trick me into turning myself in. Instead, I phoned the harassed desk constable who, to his credit, answered on the third ring rather than rip out the phone line.

'Tell Detective Jewell to make Dane Larson show him the old front door. Magenta Larson's blood is all over it. Oh, don't ask stupid questions. Dane Larson murdered his wife. Search every skip in Battersea. Search Alicia Todd's house.'

One click cut him off mid question. There was another thing I needed to do: take a trip to the Cherry Drops premises. Alicia must have set the stage for this frame-up weeks ago. She phoned in the complaint about me being rude, just so she could point her perfectly manicured talon at me as the murderer. Miss Cherry would have kept a record of the complainant's name, phone number and address. People were always complaining, but boss lady never told us who the moaners were. Said anonymity saved us from animosity. Didn't stop us from guessing though, and booting those moaners to the end of the delivery queue. Whoever had called it in was a killer and I was going to nail them.

The half moon threw long shadows across the entrance to the industrial park, home to giant rectangular warehouses and heavyweight businesses. Standing outside his security hut was the night watchman. The bright light from his hands told me he was watching something, just not any of the buildings.

Nothing and nobody was going to keep me out of Cherry Drops tonight. After waiting a while I scrambled over the back wall and dropped down into the yard landing with an undignified thud. The watchman looked over in my direction and I scuttled behind a disused car. My heart palpitated as he came within a metre of me.

'You absolute idiot,' he said.

That was a bit harsh. Idiot, maybe, but not absolute. Thinking the jig was up, I was set to leg it when a crackling voice chuckled on the watchman's tablet and he chuckled too.

'Name a fruit you *must* peel to eat,' he mumbled in disdain. 'Apple? Seriously?'

He turned and walked away taunting the dim-witted contestant. I wiped sweaty palms against my jeans, then retrieved the spare key from its hiding place inside the old car.

Visibility was poor inside Cherry Drops, but turning on the fluorescent lights was a no-no. I squeezed past corrugated metal shelves and concrete floor space packed high with boxes, barrels and parcels, careful to avoid a row of forklift trucks used to move the loads.

At the rear I quietly climbed metal stairs leading to the mezzanine floor which held the administration office, kitchen, break-out room, bathroom and storage room for dry cleaning. As I made my way to the office I peered over the safety railing at the boxes and packages below which looked like an array of dark hills and valleys. All was quiet.

The computer monitor took its own sweet time to start up and, as I'd learned from the IT chap who desperately fought to hide his disgust last time, slapping it on each side wouldn't help. The screen cast a soft glare on the window and with no way to darken the effect I sped up my search. Had to stay awake, get this done and get out. No complaints from the Larson address. I searched their individual names instead: Magenta Larson, Dane Larson, Alicia Todd, but still came up blank.

Frustrated, I opened a filing cabinet of manila folders and retrieved my bulky personnel file. The frivolous complaints were thick like a slab of beef, the notes of gratitude thin like strips of lettuce. Still the whole sandwich amounted to a nothing burger. Nothing from the Larsons or Alicia. Then it hit me that maybe there never was any complaint. Maybe Detective Jewell made up the complaint allegation on the spur of the moment to throw me off-guard, see if I'd take the bait and confess to having met Magenta.

Suddenly, I became aware of a distinct smoky odour. I was feeling sleepy but knew this was no dream, something was burning. I grabbed the small fire extinguisher and rushed down the landing towards a glow of light reflected on a wall. In a corner of the break-out room, crackling flames rose from a waste bin and a man stood with his broad back to me. The flames were at knee height and he seemed to be trying to contain the spread, as if the fire growth had caught him by surprise. My foot nudged a stool and the man spun around.

'Kayla Reilly, the last person to see my wife alive.'

Behind Dane Larson the glow of yellow and red flickered, illuminating him in the darkness. From head to toe his was a demonic silhouette: luminous white eyes, glimpse of canine teeth, pointed goatee, heaving chest. No getting around it, the man looked good.

'You were the last person to see your wife alive.'

'I told Detective Jewell to keep you under surveillance, but he said he'd handle the case his way.'

'Give it up, Dane. You can walk out of here without causing more harm. I'll put out the fire.'

'You'll put out the fire? I should knock you out and let you burn right here.'

'Stay back! Don't do anything stupid.' I turned the extinguisher nozzle in his direction and hoped I looked like some fearless gladiator.

'You killed my wife,' he said.

I frowned, confused at that firm declaration. Until now it had never crossed my mind that Alicia could have acted alone. I brushed the thought away. If she couldn't be trusted to put on pants, she certainly couldn't be trusted to carry out a murder single-handedly. No, Dane Larson was smart. Crazy smart. The suggestion of innocence was a clever trick, meant to unnerve me. He nearly succeeded.

'The police are onto you, Dane. You removed the front door, that was your mistake.'

'What?' Flames crackled behind him. He turned and stamped at the fire again. 'Magenta's house keys were missing, I changed the door.'

'Who changes a whole door, not just the lock?'

'A panel broke while it was being drilled. Easier to replace a door, than fix a panel.'

'Save that line for the detectives, but they'll have found the evidence by now.'

'Locksmith and carpenter too?' he sneered. 'Aren't you the talented little all-rounder?'

He gave up on the flames and edged towards me, hands obscured in the semi-darkness, and I feared he held a blade.

'I said stay away from me, you brute!'

I pressed the lever, once, twice, expecting a plume of white foam to emerge and burn his eyes, but unlike in the movies nothing came out. He lunged for my arm and I took a step back. Using all my strength I swung the extinguisher at his temple and connected with a pleasing thud. Dane Larson went down heavily near my feet and closed his eyes. At any other time I'd have celebrated my good fortune to have landed this one, but no one wanted to land a wife-killer. Well, no one except Alicia.

I finally got the extinguisher to work and doused the billowing flames in foam leaving soggy half-burned pieces of paper. I felt around in my pocket for my phone, but found just empty space. Must have dropped it when I scaled the wall.

The clanking of shoes on metal slats sent my heart plummeting. Someone was coming up the stairs. It had to be the night watchman and I was pretty sure he'd hand me over to Jewell without a second thought. Silently, I ducked into the clothes storage room. At the front was a rail of dry cleaning, multiple uniforms hanging fragrant under flimsy plastic sheaths. The back rail held unwashed uniforms awaiting collection. They stank. I backed up as far as I could into the dirty clothes and held my breath against the funky smell of dried sweat. The footsteps neared and my spirits lifted as the new arrival came into view.

'Miss Cherry!' I was so relieved to see her that when she clutched her ample chest I forgot to be jealous.

'Oh my god, Kay-girl! You nearly scared me to death, you OK?'

'Ssshh!' I whispered. 'Get in here! Where's your phone? Call the police.'

'What happened?'

'Dane Larson killed his wife and tried to kill me. I'm not sure if he's got a knife. He was burning some papers in the break-room.'

'He's here?' Miss Cherry pulled out her phone. 'You triggered the silent alarm and I thought we were being burgled. Why'd you come here?'

'Ssshh! Get down, I think I can hear him.'

Physically exhausted, I leaned against the musty uniforms, trying my best to stay awake. A blouse fell from the rack leaving the matching trousers. As I retrieved it I noticed a torn epaulette, which I remembered tearing. This was one of my uniforms, stolen weeks ago. One sleeve was covered in specks of blood and I was pretty sure I never bled over it. No way did I put it here, but how was my stolen uniform hanging with all the others? How likely was it that Dane Larson had found the right room and right place? I'd never met a man who could find a laundry basket without directions and a torch.

I stared at boss lady as I retreated onto the landing. If I had triggered a silent alarm it would have alerted the night watchman as well as Miss Cherry. He would have turned up long before she set one stiletto into her car, let alone drove the two miles to get here.

'Cleveland Brown,' I whispered.

'What?'

I waved the blouse with the dangling epaulette at her. 'You put this here and I'm guessing that's Magenta's blood on it.'

'What are you talking about, Kay?'

'You're not here because of any alarm. You told the cops someone made a complaint about me. You forgot to make a note to back it up, didn't you? That's why you came here. To plant a complaint from Magenta's address.'

'You're wrong, Kay.' She slowly followed me out of the room, her face incredulous. 'I never lied to any cops about you.'

'You never just called them either, did you?'

The uniform slid to the floor and I held only the wire hanger. With speed I fashioned the hanger into a dagger while my eyes roved over her face.

'Kayla, behind you!' Miss Cherry shouted.

I spun around and there was Dane hobbling closer with one hand against the wall to steady himself, blood trickling from his temple.

I stared at him in confusion. 'Don't you dare!'

'He put the uniform there, Kayla,' said Miss Cherry. 'Who knows how long he's been in here? The storage room is easy to find.'

'I did not kill my wife,' he murmured, in obvious physical pain. 'Believe me.'

In his face I thought I saw earnest pleading eyes, but then again millionaire TV pastors had a similar look when begging for your last penny.

I picked up my uniform and held the fabric to my nose. The odour was a light scent with essence of guava, sea salt and coconut milk. It might sound like the remains of a spicy sauce, but it was actually an island perfume that I was pretty familiar with. Despite being no probability expert, I knew the chance of Alicia Todd and Cherry Wilkins wearing the exact same perfume must be a few million to one. Motherly Miss Cherry, who had often listened to me pour out my heart about narcolepsy and sympathised with my predicament, was a killer. You couldn't trust anybody nowadays.

'You murdered Magenta, Cherry.'

'You, you killed my wife?'

Cherise pursed her lips and seemed set to argue, then changed her mind and shrugged.

I edged towards the safety rail, self-preservation firmly on my mind. 'Well, I'll just leave you two to talk it out…'

'Don't move, either of you.'

A shiny gun appeared in Miss Cherry's hand and I stared at it, mesmerised. The clothes hanger dagger slipped from my moist fingers and pinged onto the floor.

'I followed you that day, Kay-girl. Knew you'd take a real long nap at some point. Nearly missed you, you'd pulled into the supercentre and I drove straight past. Had to double back double quick.'

I thought about leaping over the guard rail to the ground far below, but I figured hip replacement surgery at my age was a bad look and besides the NHS had a backlog.

'You barely parked before you were snoring away like a freight train.' Cherise shook her head. 'Had to haul you into the back of my van. Locked you in though, so you couldn't be molested by perverts.'

'I appreciate it.'

'Then I took your van and drove back to her house.' She smiled at me. 'Was a right headache getting you back into your vehicle later. Like you gained ten pounds in your sleep.'

'Tell me about it,' I mumbled. 'What did poor Magenta ever do to you, Miss Cherry?'

'Magenta didn't have to die, stubborn woman. She was writing about me, about how I made my investment money to start Cherry Drops. I told her not to because I'm a respectable businesswoman and haven't done sex work in years. I refused to give her my email address, so she phoned me.'

'I'd fight her for that, but murder?'

'Don't get cute. She said she was going to write my story anyway for a book called Unsung Britons. She said "sue me".' Miss Cherry gave a dry chuckle without mirth. 'Ain't nobody got no time nor money for that, Kay-girl.'

Miss Cherry was once a sex worker? My imagination tried its level best, but could not stretch that far. I fought to get my mind back to what was really important, that gleaming gun she was waving around. 'But everybody knows that's not you now. No one would care how you started out.'

'Well, there was the little matter of an unsolved murder, a John who didn't pay me. Magenta was asking too many questions about him, getting too close.' She gave a deep sigh. 'I was right, too. Found a whole lot of notes in that shed of hers.'

My exhausted brain tried to process what I thought I knew about Dane and Alicia. 'But... the Larson's front door?'

'Hmm? What about their front door?'

I just knew Miss Cherry was not faking that puzzled expression. I glanced at my bloodied victim who was clutching the wall, his blazing eyes staring straight at Miss Cherry as if I didn't exist. Man, I'd made a mess of his temple, but with a bit of Dettol and a plaster it wouldn't look so bad. I hoped he wouldn't hold it against me.

'Oh god, I'm so sorry, Dane.'

'Dane will have to join his non award-winning wife, Kay. You bludgeoned him to death and I caught you in the act. Shot you to try and save him, but it was too late.'

'Why frame me, Cherise?' I moved closer to the guard rail, sideways like a crab. 'We always got along, you and me. Why?'

'Why not you? I sure as hell didn't want it to be me. Magenta phoned here a couple of weeks ago determined to schedule an interview. I warned her not to call me again. I figured the police would eventually find out about the call, so I got in first… told them she called to complain about you. Sorry about that, baby.'

Miss Cherry did look apologetic. I last saw that look when she'd mistakenly added two teaspoons of sugar to my coffee instead of one.

'Really? You'd see me go to prison for the rest of my life and you're sorry?'

'Aww, don't make it all about you, Kay-girl. Your narcolepsy would've saved you. Your lawyer would've said you were mentally disturbed or something. Got a lighter sentence. They'd give me life because there's nothing at all wrong with me.' She cocked the gun. 'And I have history that won't stay buried.'

'You killed my wife!'

Dane rushed at her and as they struggled for control of the gun I took off. The only thing on my mind was: *I'm not dying tonight.* I sped along the landing and bashed on the locked window, but the watchman was now at the far end of the complex still fixated on his tablet. I leapt down the stairs two at a time. As I reached the bottom, a bullet flew close to my ear. Dane came plunging over the guard rail and smashed into a box beside me. I had no idea whether he jumped or was pushed but I could see he was hurt pretty bad.

Having managed to avoid my conscience for ten years my first thought was: *better him than me.* Unfortunately my pesky conscience caught up with me when I paused to look at Dane. I grabbed him and staggered across the floor to the nearest huge box which housed a refrigerator. Too dark to see what great features the manufacturer promised, but I was sure the list didn't include 'Suitable to hide behind in case of flying bullets.'

'Stay down, no groaning,' I whispered. 'Pretend you're avoiding a Jehovah's Witness.'

Crouching low, I moved away from Dane and dodged between the hills and valleys, afraid my heavy breathing would give me away. With the gun pointed straight ahead Cherise descended the stairs, high heels clicking, a picture of poise. Fancy that, she had nice ankles and pretty good calves. I could see her being a sex worker all right. Didn't even need to pick a new stage name. Not that I was judging her, of course. She strutted purposefully towards Dane's hiding place. They weren't called killer heels for nothing and I had to stop the killing.

Beside me was a forklift truck stocked high with goods. I pressed the controls, set the vehicle in motion and watched as it beeped its way down the aisle, veering off at an angle like a drunk driver. Cherise did an about-turn and pursued the forklift. She shot at it twice in quick succession. I sprinted in the opposite direction, bashed the big yellow button that controlled the electronic roll-up door, and scrambled under it before it raised more than a metre. A bullet pierced the steel as I exited on the other side. I covered my head with my hands and ran blindly.

Another two explosions followed. I felt extreme pain as I hit the ground and waited for death to claim me. I heard the thundering noise of pounding feet and a series of loud voices. This couldn't be Heaven because God wouldn't put up with boots on his daisies, which meant Hell sure was festive at night. Maybe it got quieter in the daytime when even the Devil demanded peace.

'You all right, Ms Reilly?' Strong arms pulled me to my feet.

'Detective Jewell, I'm not dead!'

'No, you're not.'

A bullet had grazed my upper arm and blood smeared my sleeve. Behind me lay Miss Cherry sprawled out face down, her chest oozing red liquid onto the concrete. One of the cops took her pulse and waved frantically at his colleagues. 'She's still with us. Get an ambulance.'

'Dane Larson's inside, he's badly hurt,' I said.

'I'll get him.' Detective Barclay and two other cops headed into the unit.

'Got a phone call from Mr Larson telling me he'd seen you enter the building,' said Jewell. 'I told him not to follow you.'

At last I understood Dane's presence on the scene. 'He must've seen flames and thought I'd set the place on fire, that's why he was inside there.'

'He still shouldn't have gone in, but no one listens to sound advice these days.' Jewell retrieved Miss Cherry's gun and slid it into an evidence bag. 'I blame the movies.'

'Blame Peppa Pig. Never listens to authority figures.'

Jewell stared at me as if I was a loony. I had to concede to being a bit loony. Who in their right mind says pig near to a policeman? There was time to redeem myself yet.

'Cherise killed Magenta Larson, Detective. Check the waste bin, I think she was burning Magenta's notes. She's killed before.'

'We'll check it out.' Jewell managed a small smile. 'By the way, the plant care card was in the fruit bowl. Alicia.'

'Why that little...'

'You're not a bad investigator, Ms Reilly. You may want to consider a change of profession.'

I gave him my best side-eye. 'To what? Bullet stopper?'

Detective Barclay and the cops appeared carrying a bruised and limping Dane Larson between them. Dane and I shared a look. No, not the *look of love*, come on. The relieved look of two people who had escaped death and were grateful to be out of its sight-line.

A familiar feeling overcame me and in an instant my eyelids grew heavy. I weaved around unsteadily on my feet. 'Detective Jewell, I know this will sound strange to you, but I'm about to fall asleep.'

'Bored?'

'Narcoleptic. Don't get excited now, I'm talking involuntary sleep not narcotics.'

'I know what narcolepsy is, Ms Reilly. Here, I've got you.'

As Detective Jewell grabbed my good arm, his unbuttoned cuff rolled up and the last thing I saw before I drifted off was the tattoo on his forearm: HAVE COURAGE BE KIND. Oh boy, one day I'll learn not to be so judgmental.

# Double Date

*Lucy Vine is the best-selling author of* Hot Mess, What Fresh Hell, Are We Nearly There Yet?, Bad Choices, *and* Seven Exes, *with book 6 scheduled for summer 2024. Her books have been bought in 17 territories and optioned for TV/film.*

God, I'm gorgeous. Look at me! I'm, like, *ridiculously* beautiful.

I turn around again, watching my firm bum move in the reflection of the patio doors, and move closer to study my face. Even in the blurry bifolds, you have to admire the symmetry.

Everyone always compliments my features – even strangers on the street stop to tell me how pretty I am. My best friend Ava says my eyes are the most beautiful she's ever seen and she's going to steal them one night when I'm asleep and give herself an eye transplant.

Sometimes I think she might be a little bit jealous of me. She does talk about how I look *a lot*.

I blink in the glass, thinking about Ava, listening for her movements upstairs.

She really shouldn't be jealous, because she's pretty, too. I've got big, brown eyes and short, sleek dark hair, but she's fair and blonde, with piercing, Siberian-Husky-blue eyes.

The only thing I *will* say is that she sometimes doesn't make that much effort. Like, around me – around the house – she seems to only ever wear leggings or pyjamas. And *sometimes* when we go out, I can tell she hasn't even brushed her hair or had a wash.

But, then, she doesn't want to take me to bone town, LOL! I'm sure today, for Curtis, she'll put on something nice.

I examine myself in the reflection again, studying every angle.

Blurry, but gorge.

This dude is one lucky fucker.

I can't believe Robert didn't want me.

Don't think about Robert.

Today is about Tommy. Tommy and Curtis. The guys Ava and I are going on a double date with in a few minutes. Tommy is my date, Curtis is hers – she found them on a dating app.

I give her a shout to hurry up because we're going to be late if we don't leave soon. I hear her stomping around upstairs, on the phone. She'll be speaking to Sophie, the third in our best friend trio. She doesn't live with us, but she's always here.

I sigh, turning around again, wishing I could check myself out in a proper mirror. We don't have any full-length ones in the house, for no reason except we haven't got around to buying any. Ava lived here before me, so she'd already decorated and put up all the tiny, useless mirrors too high for me. She's tall – like crazily, excessively tall – whereas I'm tiny and dainty. 'Cute,' as she would say, but I'd love to have her height. Being tall must be like having a superpower.

Ava and I have been living together for nearly three years now, and she is the best person I've ever known. Before her, I was living with Robert the arsehole and when he dumped me I was completely lost. She took me in, helping me through those months where I was a hopeless, quivering, broken mess. Sometimes – when I think about how lovely and kind to me Ava has been – it feels like she rescued me.

She is my knight in shining armour. My saviour. My confidant. My best friend.

I itch my nose, feeling my stomach rumble. I can't tell if I'm nervous about this date, or maybe just hungry. I'm always hungry.

Ava rushes in at last, all flustered and flappy, but looking really great in skinny blue jeans and a green blouse. She's still on the phone and waves at me apologetically, before frowning into the receiver.

'What d'you say, Soph? *Something About Mary*? Did I *what*?'

She shakes her head at me now, rolling her eyes. Sophie is an absolute filth-bag and it's clear she's said something rude.

'No, I did not have a pre-date wank, you're disgusting,' she sighs, pulling another face at me as I try not to giggle. 'I'm nervous enough as it is. Trying to get myself in the mood to masturbate takes about three hours and involves feverish mental images of the Green Giant fucking me from behind in a maize field.' She pauses. 'Yes, the sweetcorn guy.' I hear Sophie howling on the other end of the line before she asks something else. 'Oh, I don't think there's a name for it, but I'm sort of holding on to some ears of corn—' she frowns as Sophie interrupts. 'No, I don't know what the difference is between a husk and an ear.' She waits again. 'Or a cob, no. Maybe they're all the same thing?' She tuts. 'Why are there so many weird words around sweetcorn?'

She makes eye contact with me and I pointedly – passive aggressively – go and stand by the front door, glaring crossly. I hate being late.

'Look, I have to go,' she says, pouting at me. 'Eliza's getting annoyed.' She smiles now, raising her eyebrows. 'But at least we're in it together for this, whether it's terrible or fun. And you never know, maybe we'll *both* fall in love.'

She finishes up the call at last, throwing the phone into her handbag and yanking on her favourite coat. I try not to react but I'm not really a fan of that one. It started off camel-coloured but has morphed more into a kind-of dirty Labrador hue.

'Sorry, sorry,' she cries. 'I'm ready, I'm ready!' She hesitates by the door, looking down at me nervously. 'You ready, Lizzy-loo?' She asks this in a cutesy voice and I try not to cringe. I hate that nickname. My name is *Eliza*. But I don't want us to fall out right before we meet a couple of strangers, so I just smile.

'It's only ten minutes to the park where we're meeting them,' she tells me, checking her watch and pulling awkwardly at her top. She turns to face me again, grinning as she towers over me. 'I'm so glad you're coming with me,' she says with relief. She pauses, staring at me. 'God, you're so beautiful, I love you sooo much.' She reaches down, stroking my face and I lean into her hand.

*You're beautiful, too*, I tell her silently, wagging my tail. I wish she could hear me.

She tells me every day how beautiful I am. I wish I could say it back, just once.

She slips on my harness and we exit out of the front gate. I'm eager to get there. I have to admit I'm excited to meet Tommy. I've never been on a *date* before! Imagine if he's really gorgeous! I mean, he'd totally *have* to be. He'd need to be super-hot to keep up with me. I want someone on my level – I know my worth.

Ava hasn't told me anything about Tommy's looks or breed, and I don't want to sound shallow, but I *do* have a definite type. I like a sort-of bad boy, fully grown Andrex puppy, y'know? He's got to have that cuteness but with an edge. That playfulness but with a brooding, serious side. And I have to admit, I do like blondes.

'Slow down, Eliza!' Ava laughs, skipping a little to catch up. I glance up at her anxiously and she gives me a treat. She looks worried and I lick her hand affectionately.

'This is a good idea, right?' she murmurs to me or herself. 'He sounds nice enough. And he's got a dog, which means he definitely isn't a serial killer.'

Why would anyone murder cereal? What a weird thing to say.

I flatten my ears, getting low as a squirrel runs across our path up ahead.

Fucking squirrels, I hate the pricks. They think they're so cute and clever, but I'm the one living in a nice warm house, with a nice warm human, while they're nipping about trying to find nuts or whatever. They want to try getting themselves domesticated.

Although, I remind myself, humans can be cruel, too.

An image of Robert's face flashes before me – of him shouting and hitting me, locking me outside in the rain – and I stop short on the pavement. Sometimes memories of him overwhelm me and I have to take a second.

Ava knows everything that happened with my previous housemate, Robert, and I think she gets it. She's always patient when I have these episodes.

'You OK, girl?' she says now, softly. The sound of her voice calms me and I feel my heartbeat return to a normal pace.

*I am, thanks to you*, I tell her and we resume walking.

Ava starts muttering to herself again and I catch Steven's name.

I haven't heard her mention Steven in *ages*! To be honest, I'd forgotten all about him! He was living with Ava when I first moved in. He seemed OK. He would sometimes feed and walk me. But they broke up and he moved out quite a while ago now. Ava's been single for a couple of years.

I guess this date is bringing things back up for Ava, just like it has for me.

As we approach the park, I feel my heart thudding against my ribs. In the distance, I can just about make out a dog waiting by a tree with his human. That must be them.

Tommy and Curtis.

Since I can see them, that means – unless Tommy's, like, a blind shih-tzu or something – he can probably see me, too. Eek!

We move closer and I can feel Ava's anxious energy coming off her in waves. It makes me feel stressed, too.

He's closer now and I can say for sure, Tommy's no shih-tzu. He's well-built with sturdy shoulders; a hot bod. He's handsome! He looks like a crossbreed, like me, so that's a tick. I know it's such a cliché, but you never want one of those fancy inbred pure breeds, do you? They are sooo dumb and so, like, up their own arses.

I lift my head up, trying to appear taller as we make our final approach. I'm still barely up to Ava's calves, but we all have our flaws, don't we?

'Hello!' I hear Ava call out nervously. 'Curtis?'

'Yes, hiya!' the man greets her. 'Ava?' he adds unnecessarily and she nods enthusiastically. 'And this is Tommy,' Curtis announces proudly. Ava bobs down into a squat, offering a hand for Tommy to sniff. He's got a red bandana around his neck and it trails along Ava's arm as he snaffles hungrily around her. She often smells like treats.

'He's lovely,' she tells Curtis with delight, turning her head slightly to gesture at me. 'And this is Eliza.'

'What a sweetheart,' Curtis says a little patronisingly. 'What a beautiful face! Those eyes! She's so *pretty!*' Ava beams at this, though we both hear it a lot.

Politely, I turn slightly to offer Tommy my lovely bum, but – to my absolute horror – he walks away without even a cursory sniff.

My mouth drops open in shock. Oh my god, the *rudeness*. I am dumbfounded into silence, watching my date trot back to Curtis's side, refusing to even look at me. I glance up at Ava for her reaction, but she looks distracted, only smiling vaguely back. Can't she see the literal red flag – slash bandana – this idiot's waving?

Curtis shrugs, 'Sorry, Tommy's a little shy!'

He has a slight lisp, adding a ch sound to his esses.
*Schorry, Tommy's a little schy!*

His accent is familiar, too. It's the one everyone has
on *The Only Way Is Essex*, a show Sophie comes over every
Sunday evening to watch with Ava and me. We curl up
under a blue blanket, me warm between them, their soft
hands on my back.

We don't need anyone else, do we? I don't need this
rude boy Tommy, and Ava doesn't need Curtis. She won't
like him anyway. He doesn't look anything like a green
giant and his dog is a knobhead.

I glance over at Tommy again. He's still sulkily staring
in the opposite direction. He looks pissed off to even be
here, stuck with this lame date.

*How dare he! I'm beautiful! Everyone says so.*

'Here, Lizzy,' Ava says now, handing me a treat. It's a
crunchy one, which I'm sooo not in the mood for. I hope
she's got the softer, meatier stuff on her as well or I am *out
of here*!

We move off and into the park as Ava and Curtis
exchange boring small talk about work. I study her, watching her mouth move. She lightly licks her lips as she speaks
about the kids she teaches.

*Nobody cares about your work, don't be boring!* I scold
her. Honestly, I love the girl, but who cares about teaching?
I didn't go to school and I'm doing great. I spend my days
lying around on sofas, being pampered and fed. *Occasionally*
I have to chase a ball around the garden because Ava likes
throwing it, and it's important to make an effort to be kind
to your friends, right? But that's it! My advice would be
to definitely not bother with school and just find yourself
an Ava.

We make our way around the green space, sniffing shrubs and greeting other passing dogs. Obviously, I wee as much as I can – but not because I'm trying to impress Tommy! I couldn't care less what Tommy thinks! But I also know he would've been totally blown away because he could barely squeeze out a scenting.

Otherwise, we studiously, aggressively ignore each other.

Every now and again I check in with Ava. She's smiling a lot, giggling. She's saying something to Curtis now and he throws his head back, laughing. There's something unfamiliar on her face and I move closer, sniffing the air around her.

'Hey pretty girl,' she leans down as I approach, flattening my ears back with her hand even though she knows I don't like it. I cock my head, trying to focus as she straightens back up.

What's different?

I notice Tommy watching Curtis too and we make fleeting eye contact for the first time. He narrows his eyes and his tail comes down a little.

What a dick.

After an hour or so, we make our way to a nearby café, where the nice lady behind the counter brings over a bowl of water. I go to drink, as does Tommy, and we glare at each other across the rim, daring the other to go first. After a few seconds he turns on his heel, scurrying back to Curtis, who laughs and pats him gently.

*Humph*, I think, glaring at Ava's date. I can't believe he's encouraging this rudeness towards me. Always judge a dog by their friends, that's what I say. If Curtis isn't willing to call out Tommy's toxic masculinity, then they're both wrong'uns.

Ugh! I desperately want this double date to end. It's been a complete disaster.

Tommy's been acting like he's better than me since the moment we met. He hasn't even given me a chance! Not that I want one.

*For the record, I can do sooo much better than you,* I glower under the table at him before settling in to rest on top of Ava's feet. Through her boots I feel her toes wriggle uncomfortably against me.

She can't be having fun either, surely? I vaguely tune into their conversation. They're bantering stupidly about the difference between a latte and a flat white. What kind of chat is that? This is the worst date ever. I just want to go home, get dinner, climb onto the sofa and nuzzle into Ava's side. We can even watch *TOWIE* a day early if she wants. Sophie won't mind. All they ever do is talk over it about how much they hate everyone anyway.

I stand up, turning restlessly on the spot.

*Can't we go?* I urge Ava, looking up at her beseechingly. She doesn't even look my way, too busy talking and teasing Curtis over something else mind-numbingly boring.

Why does she look so different? What is it? I can't... Oh.

That's it, that's what's different.

I feel my tail start wagging, hard.

She's happy.

She's lighting up this café with her happiness. She even *smells* happy, which she hasn't for a long time. Not properly.

I try to think back to the last time I saw her like this – it's been so long. She hasn't been bright and alive like this since before Steven left her.

She was so sad after he'd gone.

47

There were so many nights where we huddled together on her bed, and she cried soft, silent tears into my fur. When I felt the wetness on my neck, I would turn and gently lick her hand, knowing it was all I could do. Sometimes the lick would help. Sometimes she would sob even harder and pull me closer into a tight hug. It was uncomfortable but I'd let her do it for a minute or two.

I felt so helpless back then, watching her suffering, unable to do anything.

But today she is different. She is happy again.

My tail freezes mid-wag. No, she can't be happy. Curtis can't be the reason she's happy! I look over at Tommy, aghast. I hate him and his big dumb face and that big dumb red bandana. He looks back at me balefully. What if Ava and Curtis fell in love and got married? He and Tommy would move in – I can't live with *him*! This is terrible, I have to stop it! What can I do to stop this happening? I could growl or bite or bark until everyone goes away. I could… I have to…

I regard Ava again, taking in her rosy cheeks and her busy hands as they wave around while she talks.

Oh god.

I really *do* want her to be happy. She's done so much for me; rescuing me from that place where Robert dumped me, when he decided he didn't want me anymore. She's given me so much in the last few years, don't I owe her this chance to glow like this all the time?

I sigh, picking myself up off the floor reluctantly and moving closer to Tommy. His head jerks up from atop his front legs as he looks up at me with surprise. His big stupid eyes are wide and curious.

That bandana is ridiculous, I want to rip it off him.

I wag my tail slowly, and he watches suspiciously.

*You dick, I hate you*, I think and then give myself a shake, trying to let go of the resentment. I peek up at Ava again, bathing for a moment in her radiant joy. I have to try to make this work, for her sake.

I turn back to Tommy, sniffing him and then lowering myself to the ground at his side.

'Oh my god, *look!*' I hear Ava squeak from above us. 'She likes him! How cute is that?'

'He totally likes her, too,' Curtis enthuses, as Tommy shoots him a withering look. Curtis reaches down, offering us a palm each and I catch the distinctive whiff of a treat. I accept it begrudgingly, as does Tommy, and our eyes meet again. This time neither of us look away and I feel the beginnings of a truce settling between us. We lie still, side by side, and for a few minutes it is OK.

I could cope with this, I acknowledge, side-eyeing Tommy, who side-eyes me right back.

So, I will have to make some adjustments, that's to be expected. I peek over at him again thinking how handsome he is, underneath the silly bandana and big ears.

Why doesn't he fancy me? I mean, it's so *rude.* I'm beautiful! Not to mention amazing and fun and great at jumping. What doesn't he like about me?

The café door opens and there is a perceptible shift in the atmosphere. Ears up, I scan the room, looking for the cause.

A new dog has arrived, tall and wide, black haired and intimidating. He has a big, dark, spiky collar around his neck and wrapped around his midsection is an ink-black coat with the name 'Karl' in thick lettering across his back.

Mean dark eyes dart around the room, glowering balefully at every occupant.

Beside me, Tommy is staring over, a little bit of drool leaking from his bottom lip.

I know that look. I usually *attract* that look, dammit.

Oh my god. Oh my *god!* That's why Tommy doesn't like me! That's why he didn't want to sniff my bum! It's why he's been ignoring my attempts at flirting all day and why he didn't seem to care how great I was at scenting everywhere.

I never stood a chance. I was never in with a shot because he… because Tommy likes… his type is… Tommy likes *goths*.

A new understanding of him floods me and I beam across the inches between us. He looks bashful, trying to tear longing eyes away from Karl across the room.

How adorable. He's in love. Maybe I should try and set them up? I could be Tommy's friend; I don't have to be his girlfriend. We could all be pals.

I glance around at our small group, huddled together around this corner table. Tommy staring in wonder across the room at his crush, Ava and Curtis making goo-goo eyes at one another over their coffees.

This could work, the four of us. This could be OK.

When we finally leave, Tommy gives me a friendly sniff goodbye. Our noses touch and I wag my tail at him.

*I'll see you again soon*, I think, listening as Ava and Curtis shyly arrange a second double date for the four of us. It won't be a *date* as such for me and Tommy, but I can be a great wingwoman for him *and* for Ava.

Back outside in the fresh air, I consider this new life we might be about to have.

So maybe it'll be Curtis on the sofa watching *TOWIE* with us on a Sunday night. Maybe I'll have to share some of my toys with Tommy.

But it could be nice, too. It might be fun having more people to snuggle with, to stroke me. Having Curtis around might mean more fuss, more treats. It could be handy, too, having Tommy with me to chase the ball when Ava's desperate to play – he could share some of that emotional and physical labour of having a human around.

And Ava would be happier. She would be the smiley, shiny person I remember from the early days with Steven, before he left.

Plus, there are still so many of Steven's things around the house that Curtis could have.

I don't know why he didn't take them with him when he moved out.

Maybe he was too tired?

Steven got so tired before he left. He used to take me for walks with Ava; the pair of them would laugh and tease each other as I ran around the park chasing things they kept accidentally throwing. Then he got too tired and couldn't go far without getting out of breath. He would sit on the sofa with his duvet, looking like a hollowed-out version of himself. He smelled wrong, too. There were suddenly lots more people in the house. Family, friends, but also strangers I didn't know in uniforms that smelled like cleaning products. They helped him stand up and go to the bathroom. They put needles in him and gave him pills he had to take. Everyone – even Ava – started moving around him in a strange, frightened way.

And then he was gone. And Ava was sad.

But she's not sad anymore.

Beside me, Ava swings the lead happily as she rifles through her bag for her phone. We're only a few minutes from home but she will want to brief Sophie on the double date.

'Hellooooo,' she says down the line when Sophie answers, pure joy in her voice. 'I just left,' she cries. 'It's over! I can't believe I went on an *actual* date.' She pauses, listening and then laughs. 'God *no*, he was awful. But I've been a bit cowardly and pathetic, and agreed to a second date.' She glances down at me, rolling her eyes. 'He put me on the spot as I was trying to escape. Plus, Eliza liked his dog Tommy so much, I felt like I had to say yes just so they could hang out together again!' She shrieks a laugh. 'They were so cute and awkward to begin with but then they made friends.' She shakes her head, though Sophie can't see. 'No, honestly, it's definitely not a go-er, Soph. He was nice enough but he also asked me no questions at all and there was absolutely no chemistry. At one point I was so desperate for something to say, I started talking about the coffees!' She shakes her head as I stare up at her in wonder. 'But I don't care, I'm so happy I did it, Soph. I'm so fucking proud of myself.' Her voice wobbles a little as she continues. 'I really didn't think I would ever be able to go out on a date again after losing Steven. I really didn't. It felt for so long like it would be betraying his memory.' She takes a deep raggedy breath. 'But I did it! And now I can see a future for myself again, for the first time since we lost him. Curtis might not have been the one for me, but I'm starting to believe there might be someone out there. You never know, I might even love someone again one day!' She grins down at me as we walk, eyes shiny and wet. 'And I think it's OK, too, if it doesn't happen for me. I was lucky – I had Steven – and now I've got you and I've got Eliza. You guys are enough for me.' She waits again, listening to Sophie speak. 'I know, I know, I'm a cheese ball.' She sighs. 'I better go, I'm nearly home. But I'll see you on Sunday for TOWIE? Love you.'

We stop outside our front door as she hangs up the phone, searching for her keys. Inside, I hop up on the sofa to digest everything that's just happened.

'You rest down here, Lizzy-loo,' Ava tells me nicely, throwing down her bag on the side table. 'I'm going straight up to bed. I didn't meet my soulmate, so I think I deserve some alone time with the Green Giant...'

*Have fun*, I tell her, meaning it.

# Unbound

*Jean Ende is a native New Yorker who is trying to exorcise her background by writing short stories largely based on her immigrant Jewish family. Her stories have been published in over a dozen print and online magazines and anthologies and recognised by major writing competitions.*

As soon as I noticed that Aunt Rachel wasn't wearing her girdle, I knew she didn't have long to live.

Of course it took a few minutes for this to sink in since, from the neck up, she looked the same as always. With her quivering hand, Aunt Rachel had applied dark red lipstick, sparkly blue eye shadow and thick foundation, all of which seeped into her many facial crevasses.

Maddie, Aunt Rachel's aide, took her to the beauty parlor under the train tracks every week so her little blonde football-helmet hairdo was dyed, teased and shellacked into place. I had no doubt that Aunt Rachel's hair was now completely grey or white – after all, her eightieth birthday was approaching. But I knew she'd go to her grave without my ever seeing her natural colour. Growing up, I'd watched

Aunt Rachel's hair morph from the palest blonde to the peppiest ginger to the deepest ebony, a new shade every few months depending on the covers of fashion magazines, her planned wardrobe and the whims of her stylist.

Maddie answered the doorbell as soon as I rang, took my coat and gave me a quick hug. 'I'm glad you're here today, Sarah. Your aunt's out of sorts, feeling uneasy. Try to cheer her up.'

As usual, Aunt Rachel was in the living room, sitting on the plastic-covered yellow silk club chair, her swollen feet propped on the matching ottoman, a cane leaning against the chair. The TV played softly but she wasn't paying attention to it. As I walked through the door, Aunt Rachel cried out, 'Saraleh!' using the diminutive Yiddish pronunciation of my name, a nickname no one else used anymore. 'It's so good to see you. How are you? It's been so long.'

'I was here only a few weeks ago, Aunt Rachel,' I told her.

Actually, it had been closer to two months since my last visit but I figured she wouldn't remember. I bent over to give her a hug and noticed there'd been a change. Beneath Aunt Rachel's flowery housecoat oozed the physique of Jabba the Hutt, her ample body, unrestrained, was covered by only a thin cotton slip and pooled over the sides of her chair. I didn't know whether to gasp or giggle.

Rachel is my oldest living relative, the last remaining member of a tribe that believed, with Mormon ferocity, in the absolute sanctity of proper underwear. The Jewish matron version of the blessed garment is a one-piece boned corset that kept everything exactly where the good Lord intended it to be. That meant no jiggling or wiggling in the back or bouncing in the front where proudly encased cleavage thrust forward with the rigidity and determination of the figurehead on a mighty ship's prow.

For my mother and aunts and most of the women in their neighborhood, the best place to buy a good garment was Fleisher's Corseteria. With the onset of puberty, many of my contemporaries were taken by their mothers to a place like Fleisher's where stout Russian matrons stuffed hips and busts and bellies into sturdy, womanly-shaped sausage casing. That may be why so many of my friends were early feminists – it doesn't take much exposure to a good garment to make you want to burn your bra.

'Well, you look comfortable,' I said, trying to be discreet. But my aunt knew when something as important as her attire was being criticised.

'She stole my girdles!' Aunt Rachel yelled, pointing towards the kitchen where Maddie had retreated. 'Now I can't get properly dressed.'

I couldn't imagine the type of fetish that would lead anyone to break into an old lady's underwear drawer, rummage through the stained, stretched-out, faded garments and find something worth stealing. I was sure Maddie had no part in such a caper.

I glanced around the living room; there were better things in this house to steal. On either end of the engraved marble coffee table were multi-colored cut glass bowls, each overflowing with cellophane-wrapped hard candies. In the middle was a gold plated vase filled with embroidered silk flowers. On the weeping-willow-print wallpaper that covered the walls, gilt-encrusted frames held pictures painted on velvet: sunrise (maybe sunset) over the water, roses in bloom, stooped old men praying at the Wailing Wall in Jerusalem. On every surface – ebony-stained fireplace mantle, walnut credenza, end tables and mahogany TV cabinet – were silver-framed family photos.

I made the trip to the Bronx to visit Aunt Rachel as often as I could. She had always been my favourite relative. Aunt Rachel had two sons: big, rowdy guys she called 'my hoodlums' and I believed I was the daughter she'd always wanted and never had. Growing up, if I wanted to play with make-up, get a doll more expensive than my mother thought I deserved, or learn important life lessons like not mixing gold and silver jewelry, I headed around the corner to my Aunt Rachel's house.

I never visited my aunt without slowing down when I drove past my old house, close to where the rest of the *misboucher*, our extended family, had lived. They'd fled the Holocaust, arrived in the Bronx from various parts of Eastern Europe and established their own *shtetl* filled with sturdy red-brick, two-family houses. Parents and children lived upstairs, in-laws or unmarried relations occupied the small downstairs apartments. My widowed mother had died five years ago, most of her generation was gone, their children moved away.

Immigrants from other areas, Asian, Caribbean and Hispanic families, now lived in these buildings. Kosher butcher shops had been converted into bodegas. People bought frozen bagels instead of fresh.

'So, how have you been?' I asked Aunt Rachel, unable to think of a proper response to the disclosure that she'd been the victim of undergarment theft.

'How could I be?' she answered. 'I'm an old lady. But I try to keep myself up.' She patted her hair and struck a glamour pose, one hand behind her head, the other on her hip.

I told Aunt Rachel she still looked like a model. She'd told me the story many times (too many, my mother would say) about how when she'd arrived in New York from the area now known as Lithuania, the young men called her 'The Russian Princess' and said she could get a job as a model or a movie star. (My mother would point out that Rachel never revealed who told her that).

Suddenly Aunt Rachel paused and looked at me blankly. 'Where do you live? Do you have a job?'

I'd left the Bronx for Manhattan after college, stayed there for five years and moved to Brooklyn a decade later when I got married. I told Aunt Rachel I still lived in Manhattan. Brooklyn was a foreign country to people in the Bronx.

'Oh, that's right, you're near the museum,' she said.

I wasn't sure which museum I was supposed to be near, but that seemed to satisfy her. I said I made TV commercials, because it's the only part of advertising I thought she'd understand. There's no way to explain market research.

Most of my generation had jobs our parents didn't understand. We'd given up explaining that a bank vice president wasn't second in command of the entire firm; a hedge fund manager had nothing to do with shrubbery.

'Are you hungry, Saraleh?' asked Aunt Rachel as she dug into the candy bowl, scattering its contents while she searched for her favourite flavour. 'Myself, I don't eat much anymore. But young people need to keep up their strength. Go tell Maddie to make you something.'

I was glad to retreat to the kitchen since Maddie and I were old friends. She took care of my mom during her final years when she was trapped by senility and her mind withered away while her body functioned. I couldn't have got through those years without Maddie. She had friends who wanted off-the-books income and Maddie scheduled their shifts, made sure there was someone with my mom twenty-four hours a day.

My mother took too long to die.

I'd like to remember the strong, intelligent woman who raised me, but I can't forget the helpless, confused person she became. I try to remember the woman who introduced me to the joys of literature and theatre, even though we lived in a TV-obsessed family and people teased her about being a bookworm. But my most vivid memories include adult diapers, vacant looks and watching my mom stare fixedly at a TV tuned to a Spanish telenovela. I let the aides choose the channel. I knew it didn't make any difference to my mother.

During those years, when I made daily phone calls and visited every week, I spent most of the time talking to Maddie, enjoying the slight lilt in her speech. She told me about her husband who led a church in a part of the Bronx I didn't know, her children who were doing so well at school and at their jobs. I never knew Maddie's age – older than me, younger than my mother. 'Island women age differently,' she'd say with a laugh when I tried to guess. Maddie was tall and thin and always wore a shiny silver cross on a long chain around her neck. She had the flawless skin my friends and I fruitlessly tried to achieve with expensive facials, a figure that looked like she spent countless hours with a personal trainer.

My mother would sit at the table with us, smile pleasantly and hum a tuneless tune. Sometimes she'd pat my hand. Sometimes she didn't say anything for the whole visit. Sometimes I wasn't sure she knew who I was, or who she was.

I never doubted that she would have hated the woman she became.

There are no old men left in my family. Fathers and uncles died shortly after they closed their businesses, their reason for living gone.

When our mothers started to fade, my contemporaries didn't move back to the houses in which we grew up, we didn't ask our parents to live with us, although we often had extra rooms. We all remembered hearing complaints about mothers and mothers-in-law who lived too close. Instead, we hired people to care for our parents and maintain our childhood homes, we called and visited and took pride in respecting our parents' wishes not to be sent to nursing homes. When my mother died, my cousins immediately hired Maddie to care for their mom.

Of course, Maddie won't be around when I reach Aunt Rachel's age. My friends and I worry how our children will cope with us. We obsess about our physical ailments, have personal trainers, dieticians and contacts with the top doctors in the top hospitals. Our portfolios include lifetime care policies.

The dementia boogeyman haunts us. We do crossword puzzles. We stockpile pills.

I went into the kitchen and helped myself to a glass of the seltzer in the fridge. 'What's with Aunt Rachel's new casual look?'

'She's too fat for her girdles. So she hid them. Now she blames me and just wears a slip and panties, which I've been suggesting for a while.' Maddie shook her head. 'I've looked all over and can't figure out where she put those girdles. Last month her cane disappeared, just around the time the doctor said she should walk more, she needed exercise. It's probably next to her girdles. I found your uncle's old cane and told her to use it. She knows if that cane disappears, I'll get her another one. Canes are easier to replace than girdles.'

Maddie took half a roasted chicken out of the refrigerator and cut it into bite-size pieces. Then she got a container of macaroni salad and added a hefty scoop to the plate along with some lettuce and a cut-up tomato. Two slices of bread popped out of the toaster.

'Did she say she doesn't eat?' asked Maddie. 'Let me tell you, that woman has a healthy appetite. She thinks if she puts some saccharine in her coffee it makes up for the muffins she gobbles between meals. She insists I pour half a bottle of low-cal dressing over a few lettuce leaves and says she's on a diet. The doctor isn't happy with your aunt. No siree. Her pressure is high, her diabetes isn't under control and we don't even mention cholesterol anymore. But she won't listen. She says her husband worked his whole life so they'd have enough money to eat when they got old. Now that she's old she doesn't plan to starve herself. Take it from me, she's in no danger of starving.'

Maddie put silverware, a paper napkin and a plastic glass of seltzer on a tray. She went into the living room and set a TV table in front of Aunt Rachel. I followed, carrying the lunch tray. Rachel's eyes lit up when she spotted the food. Then she glanced at me.

'Saraleh,' she beamed. 'It's so nice to see you here. I miss you so much. Where do you live now? Tell me, do you have a job?'

'I've been in the kitchen talking to Maddie. I live in Manhattan. Near the museum. I make TV commercials.'

Aunt Rachel nodded and got busy cramming the food into her mouth. It wasn't a pretty sight. I walked around the room looking at the items on display. 'That's Dessie,' said Aunt Rachel, pointing to a nearby photo with a fork that almost slipped out of her trembling hand. 'Look at that million-dollar smile. Everyone says she looks just like me.'

Desiree Rosenblatt-Schwartz is one of my cousins' children. I thought she was about four, maybe five or six, it's not easy to keep track. They're a fertile bunch. She's a pretty little girl with big brown eyes and hair coaxed into blonde ringlets. Unfortunately, her parents taught her to give an ear-to-ear grimace every time they asked for a smile. The whole family oohed and aahed over this performance, conditioning little Dessie to stretch her lips further and further apart while everyone applauded.

If my child did anything like that, I'd call an exorcist.

I spotted the picture of me, my husband and my son among the family photos. 'I'll bring you another picture of my family next time I visit,' I said. 'My boy's really grown since that was taken.'

There were numerous photos of Aunt Rachel's sons, pictures of their Bar Mitzvahs, weddings, vacations with their wives and children. 'How are the boys doing?' I asked.

'Knock wood, they're all fine.' She interrupted her eating to tap her fist on the chair leg and then resumed her lunch. She took a piece of macaroni off her fork, eyed it suspiciously, then popped it into her mouth and gobbled up the rest.

'This is new, isn't it?' I was looking at an ornate wooden frame with a picture of a smiling couple in a gondola.

'Bring it here, let me show you, let me show you,' Aunt Rachel called as she jumped up and down. I handed her the photo; she pressed a button hidden in the frame and it played 'O Sole Mio' while she clapped her hands.

'Really cute,' I said and put the frame out of reach as soon as the song ended.

'They were here last week and brought that,' said Maddie. She was busy wiping up the macaroni Aunt Rachel had dropped onto the carpet.

'That's Howie and the *shiksa* he married,' Rachel explained. 'She's a nice girl, she converted. Morris and I went to Passover at her house a few years ago and she tried really hard. The brisket wasn't bad, but those matzo balls.' Rachel shook her head.

I'd heard this story before. It's a Passover saga as familiar to me as the four questions. Howie's wife is a gourmet cook. She makes her own bread, has a freezer full of homemade stock, a garden where she grows her own herbs and she slices and dices with lightning speed. I wouldn't be surprised to hear that the cloth covering her dining room table came from her basement loom and the Seder plate was baked in the adjoining kiln. But despite all of her Cordon Bleu courses she'd been defeated by the task of producing soft, airy matzo balls.

'It's just not in my DNA,' she'd admitted with a smile.

'Come here, Saraleh,' said Aunt Rachel. She'd finished lunch and was watching Maddie take away the dishes. I waited for her to ask me where I lived and worked.

Instead, she took my hand and whispered, 'You want to know how I make my matzo balls? I never had my own daughter, you're my little girl. I'll tell you.'

The sacred formula was being passed to the next generation. And I was the anointed one. 'Sure, I'd love to know.' I tried to sound humble.

I'd never tried to make matzo balls. Why bother? I can buy them at any deli. I left it to the *shiksas* to validate their conversions by producing the authentic foods of The Chosen People. But I know lots of gentile girls married to Jewish guys who want to please their mothers-in-law. And Aunt Rachel's matzo balls were always terrific. I grabbed a pen and paper, ready to write down the recipe. Aunt Rachel glanced around, making sure Maddie was gone.

'You go to the store and buy a box of Manischewitz instant matzo ball mix,' she said. 'You follow the directions carefully but instead of water you use seltzer. So it's fluffy.' Aunt Rachel laughed so hard tears ran from her heavily mascaraed eyes.

I stared at her for a second and then started to laugh too. The famous matzo balls came from a mix! Who would have guessed? This from a woman who grated her own beets to make horse radish and assured anyone in the kitchen at the time that a little blood from skinned knuckles enhanced the flavour.

I knew I'd never reveal this recipe. Why share it with the *shiksas* who were born with straight noses and the ability to accessorise? Anyone who can regain her size 4 dress size within a month of giving birth deserves to eat matzo balls that can be used to play pool.

Maddie returned from the kitchen. 'So, where's dessert?' Aunt Rachel said. 'My niece is starving.' She waited until we were alone and looked directly at me. I braced myself. Did her famous gefilte fish come from a jar?

'Where do you live?' she asked. 'Do you have a job?'

I almost said I lived in Bora Bora, in a grass hut, wore a sarong and gave lap dances to tourists. But I didn't want to make fun of her, she was still my beloved Aunt Rachel, still deserved my respect. 'Manhattan, near the museum,' I muttered. 'TV commercials.'

It was time to change the topic. 'So, are you excited about your birthday?' I asked.

I vividly remembered that by the time my mother reached her eightieth birthday she was too far gone to have a party. 'If you make a fuss it'll confuse her, frighten her,' Maddie cautioned. 'She gets nervous when she hears loud noises, sees excitement. Why don't you go out with your family and celebrate for her? She'd like that.'

Maddie was right. I knew that. But I didn't go out. No one celebrated my mother's eightieth birthday, or any of the birthdays that came after.

'Maybe I'll have a birthday party, and invite everyone,' said Aunt Rachel. 'It's my house. I can do whatever I want.' Then she lowered her heard. 'But how will I look? Bad enough Maddie takes my girdles, she's probably upstairs stealing the rest of my clothes.'

I looked at my aunt in her shapeless housecoat and worn slippers and immediately saw the amazing outfits she had worn over her sturdy corsets, her affair dresses. (A Jewish affair has nothing to do with sex, it refers to a large catered event like a wedding or Bar Mitzvah.)

The dresses were usually made from jewel-toned taffeta or stiff brocade, the bodices were clustered with bugle beads, small hollow plastic tubes that came in all colors and sizes. They bounced back and forth and up and down with every movement. Catering hall personnel watched that patrons didn't slip on beads that fell off during a particularly vigorous hora.

There were also peau de soie shoes, each pair died to match a particular dress and then carefully placed in plastic bags and stored in the enormous walk-in closet in her bedroom, under its designated dress. I remembered precariously trying to walk in my aunt's shiny high heeled shoes with one of her Ziegfeld Girl hats perched on my head.

Aunt Rachel had been famous for her hats, enormous creations with peacock feathers and beads, lots of netting and silk flowers. Each year, when friends and family gathered to celebrate the high holidays in our synagogue, the congregation waited with bated breath to see what she'd wear. And what would her rival, Bessie Shapiro, wear? Were there any new fashion plates who planned to compete for the most spectacular hat of the holiday season?

The hats came from *Bertha of the Bronx, Fine Millinery*, in large round boxes with black and white stripes. Bertha knew which synagogue each of her customers attended and made sure no one arrived at services in a hat too similar to the one worn by her neighbor.

My mother was smaller than Aunt Rachel. She wore simpler dresses, and the hats Bertha made for her weren't elaborate. My mother called her wardrobe tasteful. I called it boring. My mother had bad feet and wore orthopedic shoes during the day. For affairs she had silk flats dyed to match her dresses.

When she died, I gave all my mom's clothes to Maddie who kept what she wanted and gave the rest to her husband's church. I assumed my cousins would follow this practice. The church ladies would be in for a surprise when Aunt Rachel's wardrobe appeared at their bazaar.

I walked into the kitchen where Maddie was filling a plate with bran muffins while the water boiled for tea. I took a piece of fruit from the bowl on the Formica counter. 'What's the deal with the birthday party?' I asked.

I long ago learned that Maddie was the best source of information about anything happening in my family.

'The boys are thinking about having separate parties. You know they'll go all out and try to outdo each other. They still refuse to be in the same room. Of course they hide their fighting from their mom. They know she wouldn't stand for it. Each of them calls me at the beginning of the week to find out when the other one will be here so they won't meet.'

Like most family feuds, this war dates from some hazy incidents that occurred years ago. Allen was the brother who got better grades, now he made less money than his sibling and felt no one respected his intellect. Kenny believed no one appreciated his achievements. Five years ago, when he was called to read from the Torah at his nephew's Bar Mitzvah, the lights had flickered and he'd stumbled over the text. He was certain Allen had manipulated the lighting to make him look like a dumb kid again in front of the whole family.

Of course, they also fought about how to manage the estate their father had left and how to take care of their mother.

'Allen keeps track of every penny.' Maddie shook her head. 'Always asking if there's a cheaper way to do something, making sure he's not contributing more than his share, that someone isn't walking off with something from the house he thinks he should get.

'Kenny gets furious if his opinion is being ignored, but sometimes he doesn't have an opinion until after his brother has announced his plans. Then he wants the opposite.'

'What do you think should be done about her birthday?' I asked.

'I think she'll be disappointed if there's no party,' Maddie said. 'But too much carrying on won't be good for her. There should be limits so she'll be comfortable, like she is at home. She gets tired faster than the boys realise.'

I thought for a minute. 'How about doing it here?' I asked. 'We'll only invite family and the closest friends, just enough people to fill the living room. The little kids can run around in the backyard if they get cranky and make too much noise. I'll hire people to set up, serve and clean,' I assured Maddie. 'You won't have to do a thing.'

Maddie knew that was a lie. Nothing happened in this house without her involvement. But I knew Maddie would do what was best for Aunt Rachel, just like she had always done what was best for my mother. I wondered about her devotion to my family. Did she really care about us? Did she just need the money?

'You think you can convince the boys to go along?' asked Maddie.

'Yeah, I think I can.'

I'd tell Kenny it was the least expensive plan. I'd tell Allen it was the most intelligent choice. I'd ask both of them if they wanted to make her sick. (We all responded well to guilt.) I'd make sure their wives knew Aunt Rachel was no longer wearing her girdle, they'd understand and explain to their husbands that the situation was critical.

When I went back into the living room, Aunt Rachel welcomed me profusely, asked where I lived, what I did. I ignored the questions.

'I had a terrific idea,' I announced. 'We're going to have a birthday party for you right here. With a cake big enough for eighty candles.'

I could see the idea of a giant cake pleased her. 'You're a smart girl, Saraleh,' she said. 'If the boys give you any trouble just leave it to me. I can still take them over my knee.'

Then she looked into her lap. For a minute I thought she was going to ask me to take her to Fleisher's for a new garment, but she just shook her head. I realised that if Aunt Rachel had wanted a new girdle, she would have asked for it. Long ago. She didn't want to be bound up anymore, but she wanted to remain a fashion plate.

'Don't worry,' I said. 'There's a great dress shop near the museum. I'm sure I can find something for you, something perfect for a Russian princess.'

The plans for the party came together quickly.

I negotiated a one-night ceasefire between my cousins. They were now competing over who would buy their mother the best, most expensive present.

I hired a catering company and arranged a buffet luncheon and an elaborate birthday cake, making sure to order enough food to feed many more than the number of people invited, just like my mom and my aunt would have done. I asked Maddie to stock up on Tupperware so everyone could take something home.

After a futile search of plus-size dress stores, I found a shop that sold clothing formerly worn by opera singers. I started to look through racks of ball gowns and was approached by a Wagnerian clerk wearing hi-top sneakers. When I explained what I was looking for, she pointed to a small, tufted chair. 'That'll take a while to find. Sit down and be patient,' she said and disappeared through a doorway in what I'd thought was a solid wall.

Just as I began to wonder if the saleswoman had given up on my request, she emerged, almost hidden behind a dress that looked like it was proceeding through the store by itself. It was burgundy taffeta, empire style. On the front panel, emerald and sapphire-colored crystal pigeon eggs were clustered in a geometric pattern outlined in gold braid. Faux ermine pelts dripped from the armpits to the sequin-flower-studded hemline.

I gasped, then shook my head. 'It's magnificent but it won't do. I need a dress for an old lady. A fat old lady. My aunt could never get that on, much less walk in it.'

The saleswoman snorted. 'It's perfectly appropriate for the elderly woman you described,' she said as she handed over the garment and walked back into the wall.

I held up the dress and examined it carefully. It was lighter than I'd imagined and wider than it looked. There were sturdy horsehair seams in the bodice to hold erect even the most formidable breasts, a thick inner lining of soft silk to avoid chafing a wearer's saggy sections, and velvet laces in the rear to create a flexible fit, eliminating the stifling clamp of a zipper-closing.

'Perhaps you'd like to add this to the ensemble,' said the saleswoman as she re-emerged from the wall holding aloft what I immediately identified as a royal sceptre. I wondered what this woman expected my Aunt Rachel to do with it. Then I realised it looked just like Uncle Morris's cane, if the staff had been dipped in sparkling gold paint and the curved wooden top unscrewed and replaced with the crystal knob from their downstairs bathroom door.

'Doesn't this look like something fit for a Romanov?' asked the saleswoman.

I smiled and nodded and told her she was right. This was the perfect dress. When the show's over and the fat lady sings, she isn't wearing a girdle.

All the plans went smoothly until the day of the party when a tractor-trailer accident on the BQE tied up traffic for hours. By the time I got to Aunt Rachel's house the caterers were already setting up and I could hear her sons arguing. I ran upstairs and heard the boys arguing in their mother's bedroom. The lady of the hour was nowhere in sight.

'I thought we were going to have something small and tasteful,' yelled Allen. 'Don't expect me to pay for this circus.'

'Doesn't matter what I expect, you always find a way to wiggle out of paying your share. If you had your way, we'd celebrate Mom's birthday someplace cheap and boring. And dark,' yelled Kenny. 'But don't get mad at me today. I didn't make these arrangements.'

'I thought you couldn't pull this off, too complicated. But you allowed it to happen, didn't you? Gave a blank check to our dear cousin Sarah, the little sister we never wanted. The sophisticate who thinks she's the only one in the family with any taste. The saint who believes she's the only person on Earth who knows how to properly care for an elderly mother.'

'Wait a minute. I thought you were supervising Sarah's plans.'

I walked into the room, prepared to defend my actions. Didn't they realise that if not for me Aunt Rachel's birthday would be a disaster? I was prepared to remind them that, even as kids, I was always smarter than both of them.

Before we could start in on each other we heard a loud bang, the commanding noise a bronze-tipped sceptre makes on ceramic floor tile when it's wielded by an angry monarch. And out of her large, walk-in closet, came a Russian princess, well, maybe a tsarina, followed by Maddie trying to tie the back laces while my aunt kept moving.

My cousins and I froze.

Rachel strode to the center of the room, lifted the sceptre and thrust it to the floor again. She frowned. This time all anyone heard was a dull thud, the noise made when the tip of a cane is pounded into thick shag carpet.

'ENOUGH!' she yelled. 'Allen, Kenny, have some respect for your cousin who comes all the way from Brooklyn to visit me almost every month. If you weren't so busy avoiding each other and fighting about nonsense that happened years ago, you might have helped her with the party. And you, Sarah, if you want to someday get promoted and make TV commercials instead of just doing research you need to learn to show up on time.'

Wide-eyed, the three of us turned to Maddie. 'She knows?'

'Sometimes she has good days,' said Maddie, patting the neat bow she'd just tied. 'But never mind that now. Just look at her.' We turned and stared.

The dress had been perfectly altered at a local drycleaner's shop. The track-lighting created dazzling ripples on the material, the jewels twinkled, the fur pelts had been tamed so an observer longed to stroke them.

'You look beautiful, Mama,' said Allen.

'Amazing,' said Kenny.

'Wow,' I said. 'You really could be a model.'

'Oh, don't be silly, I'm just an old lady,' said Aunt Rachel with a nod and a smile and a wave of her hand. It was the exact gesture I'd seen on TV whenever Queen Elizabeth stood on her balcony and waved to adoring crowds.

'Now help me get ready.'

Aunt Rachel checked her make-up while Kenny followed her directions to the hatbox on the very top of the pile on the highest shelf. I expected one of the hats she'd worn to *shul*, but the tissue paper didn't reveal a hat that could be worn to a religious event. The box held a glittering tiara which fit like a crown on her freshly styled hair.

Rachel took a deep breath and nodded to us. 'Now children, let's all go say hello.'

There were about twenty-five people noisily gathered in the living room when we finally descended the staircase, Aunt Rachel in the lead, one hand on the stair rail, the other carrying the sceptre aloft. Kenny, Allen and I trailed behind. We were halfway down when the crowd spotted us. The room went silent.

I thought, I've made a horrible mistake, they think she looks like a joke. I was about to burst into tears.

Then someone started to clap and, within seconds, the applause was rocking the crystal chandelier. Everyone was yelling, 'Mazel tov! Happy birthday!' Aunt Rachel gave her Queen Elizabeth smile and wave and entered the room. 'I don't know why everyone is making such a fuss,' she said. 'But I'm glad you all stopped by.'

The party was a huge success.

There was twice as much food as needed.

Someone's teenage son had brought his tape deck and *Fiddler on the Roof* played on a continuous loop while cousin Howie demonstrated how his photo frame played "O Sole Mio."

The two women who were wearing the same dress each assured the other that the outfit looked better on her and tried to stay on opposite sides of the room.

The giant birthday cake was bedecked with enough buttercream roses to allow each child to have one to eat and one to smear on clothes or furniture. The towering '8' and '0' candles, which turned out to be sparklers, missed setting Rachel's heavily lacquered hair on fire as she bent over and tried to blow them out.

Little Desiree was on the verge of dislocating her jaw by repeatedly giving her million-dollar smile when Rachel asked if she wanted to try on the tiara. Delighted, the child twirled in front of the mirror until she started to throw up. The tiara was whisked back to the rightful head and the toddler was cleaned up.

Angela, the matzo-ball-impaired matron, hugged my aunt and suggested that, on this auspicious day, she impart some of her wisdom, like her matzo ball recipe.

'I'm glad you brought that up. I never wanted to hurt your feelings, dear,' said Rachel. 'But your matzo balls aren't fit to eat. I know it's a challenge for a shiksa, even a convert. Maybe you should try a mix.'

The woman blanched. 'I've never used a mix in my life,' she said.

Rachel shrugged and walked away.

I was nearby, happily eavesdropping. Angela turned to me. 'There was no reason for her to be insulting. Your aunt really does think she's some sort of Russian princess.'

'Well, there is the legend that when Tsar Nicholas II and his family were executed one of the daughters, Anastasia, escaped because the jewels hidden in her corset deflected the Bolsheviks' bullets,' I said. 'And Aunt Rachel has always been very particular about her undergarments.'

Howie's wife looked at me, didn't say a word and turned away. I saw her walk over to her husband and whisper into his ear, and then they both left the party. I knew that within a week the story would make the rounds of the family. And I knew that, of course, no one would think Aunt Rachel used a mix, they'd assume she was just trying to be supportive to poor Angela.

As the crowd thinned, Aunt Rachel pulled me onto the sofa beside her. 'So, Sarahleh. It's so nice to see you. Tell me, how are things? Where do you live? Do you have a job?'

I stared at her, confused, shocked. What was going on? Was she senile? Pretending? What had happened to the rational-sounding woman who had scolded my cousins and me when we were upstairs?

Aunt Rachel didn't wait for me to reply. 'Just look at my boys, how well they get along,' she said, pointing across the room where Allen and Kenny had their backs to each other. 'Even when they were little they were always good friends. I'm so lucky to be surrounded by my loving children, my boys and my Sarahleh. I thank you for this dress,' she said, stroking the fur. 'I want you to have it when I'm gone. You can wear it to a formal party at the museum.' She sighed, closed her eyes, and started to snore softly. I didn't disturb her.

I found Maddie and told her about our conversation. 'What's the truth?' I asked. 'How much does she understand?'

'She's old, she gets confused, but she loves you. That's what's true,' said Maddie. 'I'm going to suggest she go to bed, she's had a long day.' Maddie patted my hand. 'It was a good day. You did a good job.'

Aunt Rachel didn't bother saying goodbye to anyone, she just allowed Maddie to support her up the stairs. The boys and I explained that she'd asked us to thank them all for coming, that she was too tired to do it herself. Everyone said they understood. Each family grabbed a doggie bag with filled Tupperware containers as they left.

I drove home tired and satisfied, curious about how Aunt Rachel would greet me the next time I visited.

Three weeks later almost everyone was together again… at Aunt Rachel's funeral. A brain aneurysm. Fast, painless. Everyone said they envied her. 'Leave it to Rachel to leave on such a high note,' they said. 'I hope I go that way.'

Jewish funerals require a closed casket and a simple white shroud for the deceased. I was very glad I'd found the right dress for her birthday party and Aunt Rachel wasn't denied a final opportunity to show off.

I bought a hat for the funeral, the first formal hat I'd ever owned. I was sorry *Bertha's of the Bronx* was no longer in business; Bertha would have known what I should wear. I wound up with a black straw dome with polka-dot netting. Not as elaborate as any of Aunt Rachel's hats, but, like my mom, I've never been grand enough to carry-off her style.

Of course Maddie was at the funeral. Both Kenny and Allen acknowledged her contribution to Aunt Rachel's life when they spoke. I'd done the same thing at my mom's funeral. I saw one of my cousins, whose mother was slowing down, approach Maddie. I hoped she'd negotiate a substantial raise for herself.

Within a month, the boys had sold Aunt Rachel's house and divided up her possessions. I imagined her in heaven, sitting on a cloud as fluffy as her matzo balls, watching what was going on and laughing.

I brought the birthday party dress to my home in Brooklyn. It makes the other clothes in my closet look drab. I'm thinking about getting some brighter things the next time I go shopping. I'm also considering a new hairdo, maybe I'll get a few highlights.

Desiree got the tiara, she really does look like a young Aunt Rachel. She'll look even better when she outgrows her willingness to provide million-dollar smiles.

After some intense discussions, Allen and Kenny divided up the good jewelry and the objets d'art. It won't be long before they each claim they were unfairly manipulated and the other one got the more valuable share.

All of my women relatives took home the photos of their own families along with the elaborate frames in which Rachel had displayed them. They also helped themselves to Rachel's pricey cosmetics and perfumes. There was little demand for her dresses, hats or shoes. A few things were scooped-up by fans of vintage clothing or to restock children's dress-up boxes.

When the relatives finished gleaning, a few young men from Maddie's church showed up with a truck and took away the rest of the clothing and furniture.

No one ever found Aunt Rachel's girdles.

# Jenny Bean, Calamity Queen

*Julia Wood is an author of non-fiction and fiction. Her short stories have appeared in numerous anthologies. Her novel,* The Adventures of Jenny Bean aged 49, and a Lot, *was long-listed for the Fiction Factory First Chapter competition in September 2022. Julia is a member of Leicester Writers' Club.*

**https://playingsillybloggers.blogspot.com//**

**July 3rd 2022**
**Party preparations**
**Days till party: six**
Welcome to my blog. I'm Jenny Bean. Yes, that's right, Bean. As in the legumes that make you fart in front of your boyfriend and blame the cat. Or do I mean fart in front of the cat and blame your boyfriend?

I live in Leicester, in a place called Clarendon Park. It's a friendly neighbourhood, great community spirit. We borrow each other's houmous. We swap home-improvement tips over the fence and the Ocado drivers spend more time around here than they do with their family. Unless you park in someone else's spot and then someone might chuck a falafel through your window.

Anyway – guess what? *#JennyBeanisshavingaparty!!!* That's right. Next week, in fact, on July ninth, which is the Saturday nearest to my birthday which falls on the sixth. I am, in fact, having my fiftieth, except that I am fifty-two because my fiftieth, so desperately looked forward to in 2020, had to be cancelled.

So, I rather think I deserve a good old-fashioned booze-up, as well as an opportunity to make a ninny of myself in person instead of on Zoom, where something interferes with the Wi-Fi mid-ninny-making. I have booked Clarence's, a new bar and restaurant in town, because it is GLAM! I love to be glam. Oh, and all right, it's also because it sounds like Claridge's, where I used to go with my parents when we stayed at the flat in London years ago.

I have realised as I revisit this hash-tagged phrase that I have misspelt it, so it says Jenny Bean is *shaving* a party. Well, I will be shaving but which bits of me I'm shaving – that's between me and my Ladyshave.

Actually, I did think about having a beard party because I thought it might be rather fun and would save me from the double chin problem in photos. I was going to go as Brian Blessed. I even bought a Brian Blessed beard from Amazon, but then I decided I wanted to fem up more. (Sorry, Brian, no offence, I still love you. In case you're reading this, MWAH! ☺)

Anyway, I am having an eighties-themed party, so dig out those legwarmers, deely-boppers and crimpers, guys! People can come as a famous person from the eighties, or a famous character, or even a famous craze. When I'm having a bad bloat day I consider going as a Rubix Cube.

I am having a Queen tribute band – booked months ago. They're called A Kinda Magic and are playing from Queen's seventies and eighties catalogue. I am going as Madonna, circa "Like a Virgin". I do love Madonna. She's been wafting her bosoms around the globe for decades, without a care. I admire that.

Right, let's get to it. What have I been doing in preparation for such a momentous occasion? First of all, of course, I have been checking and double-checking the food menu. I've never used Bellend Catering before, but their menu looks interesting. I chose all vegetarian, as I'm doing my bit towards saving the planet with couscous.

Then there is the all-important guest list, making sure all the invitations have been sent, checking I haven't missed anyone out. Because that's super-important, isn't it, making sure no one gets excluded? My old Nemesis from boarding school, Henrietta with the Vendetta, neglected to invite me to her party when I was thirteen. It has left me with a profound sympathy for the undergirl.

There is my boyfriend. I'll just say that again in case you missed it. THERE IS MY BOYFRIEND. Ooh, I'm coming over all Bridget Jones.

His name is Ben Carter. *Doctor* Ben Carter. I sometimes refer to him as Clap Man – no STD reference intended – since we met clapping for carers and bonded over a good banging session. Sadly, the banging to which

I refer was restricted to ladles and pans, but we have made up for it since.

I know it's a cliché but we get on so well. We have the same sense of humour, the same taste in music and well, what can I say? He is The One. I have great plans for him. All will be revealed in due course... ☺

I have close family and loved ones of course – so that's my sister, Fiona, and her wife Polly; my crazy mother who has thankfully, stopped clit-banging postmen (her words, not mine, don't ask ☺). Then there's Sprig, the landlord at The Swans, where I play my weekly gig (it brings in a bit of extra income to support my other job playing silly bloggers).

There is my next-door neighbour and fellow menopau-see, Cassie, and a few former work colleagues from Wilson's Upholsters, in the days before the pandemic, when I was their personal assistant.

Oh, and there's everyone on Facebook, because I pan-icked that no one would turn up, so I put it on social media. What could possibly go wrong?

## July 4th 2022
### Preparations
### Days till party: five

Another preparation I have been making is getting back into yoga. Until six weeks ago, I hadn't pulled on a pair of leggings or pulled mercilessly at a TheraBand until my triceps caught fire, since before the pandemic. But, you know, a girl can never be too fit and healthy for a night of alcoholic debauchery.

Besides, call me a shallow bint, but I want to look good. I have spent the past few years locked up and sweaty, binging on Green and Blacks until my knicker elastic pinged its way into outer space; yelling, 'bugger my cholesterol!' every time the voice in my ear said, *Jennifer, you need to get healthy.*

So, today, I go along as usual, only I'm running late due to a printer malfunction with Mummy's party invitation. My mother is rather old fashioned and insisted on a 'proper' invite, but my printer and my computer have stopped talking to each other. I do hope this is not a bad omen.

Therefore, I go to the eleven o'clock class instead of the ten o'clock one. It's the same instructor, same venue, so, I surmise – all will be fine. The class turnss up, with our mats and our squishy balls (this is not a euphemism, they are for exercise purposes only).

The instructor comes in. Uh-oh. It's not Trisha, my usual instructor, who is toned but *shapely* with a modestly rounded belly, and not much younger than I.

This one is dressed in lilac leggings and crop-top, swishy hair like she's in a conditioner ad; body that looks as if it has been photoshopped. Her body is, of course, a living testimony to her dedication to the art of twisting herself into positions no human is designed to attain while managing not to either fall over or break wind.

Anyway, we're sitting there on our mats as she puts on the music – sort of hypno-trance floaty music with drums and swirly stringy bits.

'Morning, guys!' she says.

She looks around, smiling, nodding at various people, who say hello or give her a little wave. Then, she says, 'Welcome to Advanced Yoga.'

Well, this is the bit where I want to do an Iron Maiden and run for the hills. *Advanced?* I'm fifty-two. The only advanced thing I do these days is to get older, which is a gradual and gentle sort of advancing. I consume *easy* drinking wine, I'm starting to like *easy* listening music, I sit in an *easy* chair... get the picture?

Trisha arches her back, showing off her toned body.

'Let's do some stretches before we get started.'

*Onwards and upwards, Jennifer,* as my mother would say. We do the stretches, Happy Cat/Angry Cat, Child's Pose, full body stretch, so far so good.

'Now,' Trisha says, 'drop your head forwards, and walk your hands along your body, into Down Dog.' She does it herself as she talks us through it and she's talking in rhythm with the music. 'OK. Lift your right leg up, towards the ceiling, that's it. Point it up, towards the sky. Now, bring it down, circle it. Then, lift it up, one-two-three...'

I am just about coping with this uncomfortable move when she says, 'Now lift your left arm and take it back towards the person behind you. That's it, now circle the leg, take the arm, and one-two-three, bring it forward, back again...'

The woman next to me is at least half my age and does this with ease and composure, but as I try to follow the moves, there's a loud crunching sound. Pain shoots up my back. I fall onto my belly.

'Aargh!'

Trish comes over.

'Are you OK?' she says. 'You're new, aren't you?'

'No,' I reply, grimacing. 'I am not new. I am *old*.'

# July 5th 2022
## Preparations
## Days till party: four

I cannot *move*. I have my chiropractor on speed dial for emergencies like this, but he is currently in the Seychelles on the proceeds of my middle-aged exercise mishaps. I am aware that this can be triggering for my abandonment issues – I was abducted by a mad woman in Milton Keynes when I was seven. I still can't look at a concrete cow without having a panic attack and wanting my mother.

But this is Serious. If this doesn't get better super, super soon, I am going to have to cancel my party. Again. I spend all day on my sofa, with a hot water bottle, feeling desperately sorry for myself and planning my big, dramatic party cancellation speech on Facebook. (I'm a Cancer with Leo rising so believe me, I can do Emotional, and I can do Dramatic).

But it's not just the party I'm upset about. It's my plan. I can't tell you about it on here yet in case it gets back to Ben. He doesn't read this blog as blogs are not really his thing. Besides, I like to keep my work (i.e. this blog) - and my private life separate. So, The Plan is top secret for now.

Anyway, I'm lying there composing my letter of resignation from my party, which (trigger warning for the cheese intolerant) contains a paraphrase of lines from "Careless Whisper."

'I am truly sorry, but I am unable to move without great, mind-obliterating pain and I shall never dance again because my guilty feet have totally lost their rhythm and it is not easy to pretend; I am a fool…'

Before I can finish, I fall asleep dreaming I am at a motorbike rally. I wake up, to find Brexit sat on me, purring. He is a big Persian Tom, so when he purrs it feels as if there is an earthquake.

And yes, I admit it. I have a cry. Not with the pain, as I am out of it on Codeine, but with despair. I am going to be miserable Cinderella who can't go to the ball yet again, who has been abandoned by her chiropractor in her hour of need. This is far too much post-lockdown trauma for one girl to cope with.

So, I drift off again, with Brexit paddling my chest. Next thing, I wake to the sound of tweeting. No, not the social media sort of tweeting. A bird sort of tweeting.

Brexit has brought me a present. It's a blackbird. Before I can think what to do next it escapes from The Deadly Jaws of Doom and is torpedoing into my chandelier, causing shards of glass to fly off, onto the floor.

Without thinking, I leap off the sofa, and there is a huge crunch – no, not the crunch of broken glass but the crunch of me, standing up straight. Yes, that's right. I stand up *straight*. My chandelier, on the other hand, is ruined. The blackbird, thank god, flew out through the casement window with a bit of arm-waving on my part because I can move again.

Who could have imagined Brexit would save the day?

## July 6th 2022
### Preparations
### Days till party: three

It's my birthday today. I am now officially fifty. Well, actually, I'm fifty-two but during lockdown, life was on pause so I'm not going to count those two years. ☺

I checked my phone to find fifty messages, all from Ben. They all say the same thing. 'Happy Birthday, love you, Beanie.'

'Love you Doctor Carter,' I write back, with a flurry of pink heart emojis. I am overjoyed. Unlike me, Ben is a little reserved. Well, unless he is in one of his Viking role-play games; then he can wield an axe and shout 'AAAAHHH!' in a battle charge without a glimmer of self-consciousness. Still, he's not generally one for big romantic gestures, so this has made me one *very* happy woman.

And guess what? My party is back on! I checked this morning and yes, I can still move. I'm a bit sore, but I can walk, and carry things, like bags of cat poo and cat litter. So, although I don't want to undo Brexit's good work, today is SHOPPING DAY. It's next on my to-do-before-party-day list: get myself a fabulous dress to complete the Madonna look. I have the veil, the long white lace gloves, and of course the Boy Toy belt, the myriad bangles and the crucifix. So, it's dress, here I come, because *non desistas, non exieris*, Jennifer. It was the school motto. It means, *never give up, never surrender.*

I gingerly get myself ready. I pull on my jeans that used to fit before lockdown and are still rather tight. A loose crochet top covers my bloat, side-effect of the otherwise excellent G.I. Diet. No, you haven't fallen down a rabbit hole and landed in an episode of Foyle's War, and no, I haven't turned cannibal, I'm still saving the planet with couscous.

The G.I. Diet is a high fibre one. It stands for Glycae-mic Index and works to stabilise blood sugar and avoid cravings for junk. Suffice to say, I am now back down from a size sixteen to a fourteen, which is kind of OK, I guess. I am, after all, a middle-aged woman and my body should reflect that.

So, Wee-Away pad tucked neatly into my gusset, deodorising function carefully set to Medium (I'll explain later), I slip on my ballet pumps, pick up my bag, and off I go into town, reliving my mourning ritual for shops that no longer exist. Dorothy Perkins. R.I.P. Topshop. R.I.P. Miss Selfridge. R.I.P, etcetera.

Zara, my favourite, is still here but I can only ever afford anything in the sales. Still, my old trusty ballgown friend, TK Maxx is still here, so I head in there. I look through the dress rails and find a white frilled chiffon one. It's strappy, knee-length at the front and long at the back, with more ruffles than a Dallas convention. Dare I wear something this frilly?

As I'm pondering this, a woman is staring oddly at me. Maybe I have chocolate on my face, or I've smudged my mascara?

But then – shock horror – she says, 'How far gone are you?'

I allow my jaw to drop in horror.

'Do you know what sex it is?' she says. 'Boy or a girl?'

'It's trapped wind.'

Well, I have never seen anyone look so embarrassed or move away so fast. But, because I was distracted by this incident, and because as a windy woman, bloat is something I'm self-conscious about, I walk, flustered, towards the exit. How can I have a fiftieth birthday party when I look *pregnant*? It looks like my plan to go as a Rubix Cube might be back on... either that or cancel the wretched party.

So, I'm once again playing out a scenario of announcing: *party cancelled due to trapped wind*. I am, in fact, so preoccupied that I don't notice the alarm in the shop going off until the security guard is marching towards me. I look down to find a coat hanger three-pack of thongs hanging off my crochet top. *Oh, not again.*

He looks me up and down as if he has already decided I am guilty, then says, 'Could you come with me, please?'

I'm struggling to extricate the wretched thing from me, and when we get into the room for thieving delinquents I am lamely saying, 'I can explain.'

'You see, this looks like shoplifting to me,' he says.

I detach the coat hanger. I place it on the table. I look him straight in the eye. I say, in a calm and hormonally neutral tone, 'I am a middle-aged woman. What would I want with a thong? I like my knickers as I like my men – the strong, sturdy type.'

He goes wide-eyed.

'I like pants I can *trust*. Thongs, you never know where you are from one minute to the next, do you? They wander all over the place. It's like having a skipping rope between your legs.'

He blushes. 'I know you, don't I?'

I give him a bewildered look.

'You tried stealing an elasticated Velcro baby stroller a couple of years ago. I never forget a face.'

'What?' Clearly my attempt to diffuse a tricky situation with humour is not working.

'I'm a super-recogniser. I used to work for the police.'

Oh, marvellous. Just my ruddy luck. 'I didn't steal it. Velcro is *very determined*.'

'Give me one reason why I shouldn't call the police.'

I do that rapid blinking thing, otherwise known as flirting, and say, 'Please don't prosecute me. I'm having my fiftieth birthday party today. It got cancelled because of lockdown. You can come if you like.'

He looks tempted, so I say, 'You could go as the bodyguard – you know, from the movie with Whitney Houston. You wouldn't need a costume.' I look at him beseechingly.

He shakes his head and looks like he's not sure what to make of me. At this point I get a tickle in my throat, so I cough, causing a small bladder leakage. This gives rise to a gush of vapour which floods the room with the smell of Country Roses. He starts sneezing and complains it's set off his hayfever, but at least he lets me off with a caution.

I am, however, barred from entering the shop again. Not that I can ever go back after that Wee-Away malfunction. I can only conclude that the dial on the deodoriser got knocked when I was flustered by that woman accusing me of being pregnant. It does happen from time to time, but Wee-Away are still the best stress incontinence pads in the world because you can, 'Wee-Away without a care, with Wee-Away,' without worrying that your gusset will smell like a 1980s phone box.

What is more they are neat and discreet, so you're not feeling as if you have a thirteen-tog duvet stuffed in your pants and walking as if you have just lost your virginity to a pop-up bollard. I am sponsored by them on this blog, so I should know. (Wee-Away, that is, not pop-up bollards.)

However, this is my situation right now. I look pregnant. I have no party dress and I have only two days until the Big Day. And I am barred from TK Maxx. It does not bode well.

## July 7th 2022
## Preparations
## Days till party: two

Things can't possibly get any worse, I think with naïve optimism, when I get up this morning.

No, they really can. I have a spa day today with Cassie, who is my best friend and neighbour. We have been the best of friends since she moved in next door to me over ten years ago. We bonded over a pile of unpacked boxes, a bottle of Chardonnay and a DVD of *Desperate Housewives*. We share the same naughty sense of humour and a love of Queen – the band, that is, not the monarch. The spa day is her birthday present to me. I'm looking forward to a day of pampering and relaxation to take my mind of my party stress.

We head off to Ratcliffe's Gym and Spa. Ben and I have a joint membership. He still uses it but I haven't been back since before the pandemic, so I get the *oh-I-thought-you-had-died-or-emigrated* looks from the staff as we head through the turnstile into the lounge area.

'What do you fancy doing first?' Cassie asks, as I stare longingly at the chocolate flapjacks.

She sees where I'm looking and nudges me. 'Self-indulgence later, punishment now.'

'Punishment?' I go wide-eyed. 'I came here for pampering.'

She raises an eyebrow. 'I need a swim,' she says. 'I have abs to maintain.'

Cassie is a serious swimmer. I mean a fifty-lengths-a-day kind of swimmer. I shake my head. 'I fancy a massage first. I'm still a bit sore still from that yoga escapade.'

'Cool,' she says.

'I can join you afterwards,' I reply. 'When you're almost at the end of your swimathon.'

She grins. 'OK, see you in a bit.' She gives me a little wave and heads into the changing rooms.

I enter the massage area nervously and speak to a masseuse called Mandy, who asks me if I have any issues or areas I'd like her to focus on.

Mandy is petite and looks super-fit, so I blush slightly while saying, 'I injured my back during a yoga class a couple of days ago.'

She recommends the stone massage, which sounds perfect, as I've heard about these but never had one.

'If you'd like to undress down to your pants and lie on the table, on your stomach, I'll be back in a few minutes when I've heated up the rocks.'

'OK.'

Rocks? I undress and lie nervously on the table.

When she comes back, she's wheeling a trolley and I'm relieved to see that they are in fact, stones and quite small.

She says, 'I'm going to start with a deep tissue massage to relax your muscles.'

She kneads various parts of me. At first, I'm wincing from the soreness but then it starts feeling soothing and like it is releasing tension.

'Are you OK?' she says. 'Say if it's too much.'

'No, I'm fine.' The truth is, I am not fine. My muscles are relaxing, but my heart is racing. She places the hot stones all down my back and shoulders in a wiggly line. In the reflection in the side mirror, I look like a miniature version of Stonehenge.

I try thinking of waterfalls and spring meadows with buttercups, but my heart is palpitating and no matter how many slow yoga breaths I try it won't go back to normal.

She's talking to me in a soft voice about what my plans are today, and do I have shopping to do, and 'Isn't this weather muggy, that's global warming for you, we'll all be extinct before the next general election, good thing if you ask me, get rid of the Tories.'

While she's jabbering on about the wretched state of the world, I can feel my arm turning numb; my chest feels tight.

'Oh my god! I am having a heart attack! I'm dying!' I clamber up, causing an avalanche of stones. I stumble out of the massage room into the foyer, clutching my chest. I pass out next to the vending machine.

I come round to find I'm lying on the floor in *just my knickers*, surrounded by paramedics. A black hooded figure is walking towards me. I scream.

One of the paramedics covers my exposed bits with a blanket, saying, 'I think you are having a panic attack.'

Next thing, Ben walks over, pulls down his hood and says, 'Oh my god, Jen, what's happened?'

I pretend to faint again, just to avoid the embarrassment.

## July 8th
### Preparations
### Days till party: one

It is the day before my party (OMG!!!). I am having to play whale music and drink lavender tea. I should have known something like this would happen. The problem is, I haven't been to a big event since before the pandemic, and although I was going to have my party last year I had to cancel at the last minute for the same reason.

I had a major panic attack in Waitrose car park after finishing the party shopping. I had to do box-breathing over the bonnet of someone's Range Rover.

Too much time spent staring at Matt Hancock and baking sourdough bread had obviously turned me into a semi-recluse. But this year, I am chomping at the proverbial bit for a good old knees-up.

Oh god, oh god. Why couldn't I have just stayed in the room? Why do I do this to myself? Do I have a subconscious desire to run around in public topless, or something? And in front of my boyfriend, for crying out loud!

The thing is, my bosoms have rather a history of wanderlust. I ran out into the garden in my bra during a hot flush a few years ago. Still, at least I was fully clothed from the waist down that time. (I am not Madonna, who does it on purpose and is therefore not embarrassed about it).

I was witnessed by Cassie, her husband, Clive and their two children, sporting an escaped nipple. It didn't go far, just a few centimetres, but that's all it takes to render life unbearably awkward. This time, it was two feral bosoms in the foyer, and I wasn't even conscious.

But Ben? He's only ever meant to see me in this condition in a sexually alluring and romantic setting involving candles, James Blunt, and a nice vintage Malbec.

It's not as if he hasn't seen everything before. But with nudity, or even semi-nudity, context is everything. *At least I had my knickers on.* That's what I keep telling myself. Ben is a doctor. He is used to the human form. So why do I feel too embarrassed to speak to him?

He has called me *three times* today already and it's only ten o'clock in the morning. I can't face him. I just can't.

What am I going to do? And now I'm having doubts about my plan. What was I even thinking? I must be deluded or mad or both.

The spectres of Richard, Total Bastard the First and Simon, Total Bastard the Second hover over me like something out of a bad version of a Shakespeare play. Total Bastard the First ran off with a lap-dancer from Kirkby Muxlow with and I quote – 'legs that go all the way up.' Total Bastard the Second turned out to be married to a Brazilian beautician with a twenty-six-inch waist and a chateau in the Dordogne, so it's not long before I'm on a self-doubt trip.

Ben is a catch. He's a doctor; he's clever; he's dishy, a sort of Hugh Grant with a stethoscope. Oh, and he's six years younger than me. You know the saying – *if it's too good to be true, it probably is.*

He only got together with me because we were in lockdown, and he was desperate. What does he see in me? I know he sent me fifty 'love you' messages but men can change very quickly, especially if you do something stupid to lose their respect. So that's it. He is going to break up with me. I can feel it in my water – or my wind, or whatever.

I can't have a party without my boyfriend. What would I say to people, 'we're not together anymore, he saw me lying on the floor *topless*, next to the vending machine, I mistook him for the Grim Reaper, leading to irreconcilable relationship difficulties'?

Oh, and just when I think my world is falling in, I get a phone call about tomorrow.

'Can I speak to Jenny Bean, please?'

'Speaking,' I reply.

'It's Sarah here, from Bellend Catering.'

'Hello.'

'Your order is all ready for tomorrow. I have 100 vegetarian samosas, 100 cheese and red pepper roles, 100 tofu with spinach…' She continues down the list and all seems fine, until she says, 'And 1000 boxes of couscous.'

Well, I almost drop my phone. 'No, that's not right. I didn't order a thousand of anything; it was a hundred of everything.'

'Oh, we have you down for a thousand.'

'Well, can't you cancel it?'

'I'm afraid not. The order has been put through. It's automatic, on our system. It wouldn't have been me that put it through. It would have been one of our order team.'

Now I am really losing it. 'Oh, for crying out loud! Bellend by name, bellend by bloody nature!' I hang up.

What in the name of the Crap Party Fairy am I going to do with a thousand boxes of cous-cous, build a life-sized sculpture of the Wailing Wall? I am doomed. I am under the curse of the Crap Party Fairy. My phone rings again. It's Ben. I let it go to voicemail.

Bollocks.

## July 9th 2022
## Party Day ☹

I woke up this morning, head full of my doomed relationship, a Wailing Wall of couscous, and that dress in TK Maxx. I can't do anything about the first two, but I can do something about the third thing because, *non desistas, non exieris,* Jennifer.

A plan is forming, was in fact forming as I was waking up just now. There is a black suit of Ben's in my wardrobe, which he wears to the opera when it's formal dress (we both love a bit of Puccini). I push away the ache in my heart at the thought of his name (I still can't face speaking to him, and hearing those words – 'I'm sorry Jen, but I don't think this is working.').

Anyway, I put on the suit, and dig out my Brian Blessed beard and wig. It even has a bald patch in the middle to reflect his current age. I tuck my shoulder-length blonde hair under the wig and fiddle about with it until I'm satisfied it looks natural. Then I attach the beard.

I'm glad I bought this stuff now. I have the height. I once played God in a school play, so I can do the voice. I practise the stature and I deepen my voice and yell into the mirror, 'Gordon's alive!' until I am so hoarse my voice has dropped an octave.

Yes. I am ready to take on Mr Super-Recogniser. I know, you're all screaming, 'She's gone mad!' Well, maybe I have, but I need a dress – I need *that* dress. Yes, I could make one, but I want a bought one for my special day. And yes, I could ask Cassie to get it for me but she might get the wrong one.

Therefore, I must disguise myself completely in case Mr. Super-Recogniser, who is a face and apparently, a baby-stroller recogniser (is there no end to his talents?) is also a voice-recogniser.

So off I go, on the bus, asking the bus driver for a ticket into town in my Gordon's Alive voice. People are staring as I sit down, and I feel self-conscious. *Please let this not go spectacularly wrong.* The bus heads off down London Road into town.

I am just disembarking when a little boy comes up to me and he says, 'Are you Flash Gordon?'

Oh no.

His mother smiles at me and she says, 'He just wants you to say, *Gordon's Alive*. Oh, and can he have your autograph?'

Well, what do you do in a situation like this?

I don't have children of my own but I adore them, and far be it from me to ruin a small boy's expectations, so I say it, as passionately and as Brian Blessedly as I can muster in the middle of a busy street on a Saturday.

'GORDON'S ALIVE!!!'

People are staring and pointing.

The kid looks at me suspiciously, and he says, 'That's not how he says it in the film. He says in in a sort of low voice, like this, "Gordon's Alive".'

His mother tuts at him, 'Alex, don't be cheeky. Ask the nice gentleman if he will sign your comic.' She looks at me. 'He's wanted to meet you for months, he loves all the old films and comics, gets it from his dad.'

So, like the worst, most deceptive woman who ever tottered the Earth, I repeat the well-worn phrase in the gruff version, and sign his Flash Gordon comic. Next thing, other people are coming over and crowding around me.

'Is that Brian Blessed?' a middle-aged man says.

'No, it can't be,' a woman replies. 'What would he be doing in Leicester?'

I use this slight diversion as my chance to run off, waving bye-bye to my 'fans' as I do so.

By the time I get to the entrance of TK Maxx I have convinced myself I am going to get arrested for forging a famous autograph, and I'm so hyper-twitchy when I walk into the shop, I'm expecting to get thrown out for being on drugs.

It takes me a lot of searching to find my dress and I panic that it's been sold. I feel even more self-conscious dressed like this than I did with the pregnant look. I keep checking for a resurgence of the 'fans' but fortunately, the ones that had accumulated around me by the clock tower have not followed me in here.

I search the hangers. Nothing. So, I get down on all fours and crawl manically under the dress rails like a toddler on the red Smarties. I can see it under a row of zebra-print onesies. I pull it out, emerging triumphantly. My next challenge is to wrest myself free from a coat hanger that seems to have an attachment disorder. What it is with me and coat hangers?

Finally, I extricate my dress – and myself – and stand in the queue to pay for it. My beard is itchy, my hair is sweaty under my wig. This time, thankfully, no one gives me a second glance. When I hand it over, I don't want to attract any more unwanted attention from Brian Blessed fans, so I speak in the muted Gordon's Alive voice. 'Can I have a bag? I forgot mine, sorry.'

I get funny looks again, and then, as I am leaving, I realise to my utmost horror, that Mr Super-Recogniser is standing in the doorway. I pull my beard up so it covers my nose. I catch a glimpse of myself in a mirror. I look like a hedge on legs, and I can't breathe without strands of beard going in my mouth but he's looking my way, staring. I pretend I'm distracted by an item of clothing. Unfortunately, I'm in the baby clothes section, so remembering my track record with baby strollers I move away.

I keep my head down as I leave the shop, but I can feel his eyes on me. I glance backwards and he shakes his head with a half-smile playing on his lips. Is he revoking the ban, or about to arrest me for impersonating a famous actor? No ruddy idea. But I'm sure he recognised me.

It is only when I arrive home, remove my Brian Blessed disguise, and sit down with a cup of coffee that I realise: *I signed the comic as* Brain *Blessed*. Ruddy marvellous. I can't bring myself to check my phone yet. So I do what I always do when I'm procrastinating. I go to my piano and sing one of the songs to which I changed the lyrics. I started doing this in lockdown when I was bored. This one uses the melody from the Jennifer Rush, "The Power of Love." I wrote it so I could woo Ben with music from my window.

'I'm still you're ladle, and you're still my pan, and I still want to bang you, so badly Clap Man.' I add in the word 'still' because my feelings have not changed.

After that I muster the courage to go and check my phone. There are five messages from Ben on my voicemail.

I listen in dread.

Message 1 – 'Jen, it's me. Talk to me. Have I done something wrong? Call me back.'

Message 2 – 'Jen, it's me again. What's happening? Are we OK? You're not answering my calls. Am I still coming round later?'

Message 3 – 'Jenny, I don't know what's going on with you, but call me back when you get this.' The phone clicks abruptly.

Message 4 – 'I don't know why you're avoiding me. I'm trying to get hold of you, I've been worried about you.' I notice he is sounding increasingly irate.

Message 5 – 'I'm not sure what to say. If you don't talk to me, I can only assume you want to break up.'

NOOO!!!

I hit the call-back button with the ferocity of the desperate woman I am. I have no idea what I'm going to say to him, my thoughts are racing: 'Knickers, semi-nudity, heart-attack, shame, knickers, semi-nudity, panic-attack, shame, knickers, semi—'

'Jen?'

I realise I have just uttered those words out loud. Oh. My. God.

'What's happening?'

'I'm such an idiot and I don't know why you want to be with me, I'm a boring, bloated, topless, feckless, hopeless, shameless—' I stop because I can't think of any more words that end with 'less.'

'Jen, you are never boring. Ever. You're clever, you're witty, you're talented. You speak the Queen's English, and you have excellent taste in wine. And you cook a mean prawn paella. I'm just a comprehensive boy with pushy parents and a nerdy interest in science.'

He means I'm posh, which I'm not sure is a good thing. I've always tried to play down my poshness. I blame the industrial revolution. My great-grandfather was big in stockings. I can't help my Pony Club childhood, my boarding school education, or my habit of calling my mother 'Mummy.' My sister does too, and she's a socialist. Besides, there's little money. It all went on Mummy's escort habit. (After Daddy died, back in 1989, she was lonely).

'Oh, and I think you're really cute when you say "bollocks".'

Well, that's it. I burst into tears, at which point he says, 'I'm coming round.'

When he gets here, with the help of a whisky stiffer than a stay-pressed trouser leg, I have calmed down a bit. I tell him about my embarrassment at what happened in the foyer and how I felt I couldn't face him.

'Oh, Jen, you silly thing. I don't care about all that. I was just worried about you.'

'Does this mean we're OK?' I ask him. There's an icy feeling in the pit of my stomach; so much depends on his answer – my sanity, my heart, everything.

'Of course, why wouldn't we be?' He pulls me into his arms.

Several hours and many vigorous bonking sessions later I am getting ready for my party. My back is sore again, but I have it under control with heat gel and excitement.

Ben is putting on his Boy George costume, while I pull on the fingerless lace gloves and place the veil over my head, fixed into place with a diamante tiara. Saucy red lipstick, check. Mole above my lip, check. Boy Toy belt, check. My hair is blonde so no need for a wig. Well, actually it is more of a muted blonde, sort of Gwyneth Paltrow if she were locked in a cupboard for a few years and no one remembered to dust her.

The slight problem is that my bosoms shrunk a few years ago so I have a job summoning them for the corset-bra. Well, what's a girl to do? Tape some iron filings to them, put a magnet in my bra and hope the law of mutual attraction works? Try and find a quick Levitation for Bosoms class on Zoom?

Still, when I'm done, I manage to impress Ben.

'Wow!' he says. 'Have we got time for another quickie?'

I laugh, 'No, you'll smudge my lipstick.'

'You'll smudge mine.'

'Oh, I do love a man in make-up.'

'Bring back the gender-bender age.' He grins.

'I can't see a bloody thing in this veil.'

He laughs.

I bought it from LOROS by Design in town. It's a full, gathered wedding veil, the sort you might wear if you were on the Wanted list for some terrible crime and had the sudden urge to marry.

We head off in our taxi. I'm fluttery and nervy. I hold his hand in the cab. My palms are sticky, my hand is shaky, but he doesn't seem to notice. I could murder a large Highland Park, but I don't drink whiskey, it gives me heartburn.

'Are you OK?' I ask him, my mind still on Vending Machine Gate.

'I'm fine.' He doesn't look fine. He looks shifty. I feel worried again. I need tonight to go well. I'm taking a big chance but that's something I learned from living through a pandemic. *Don't wait for opportunities, create them yourself.* Margaret Thatcher would be proud.

To distract myself I check through my catering order on my phone. I realise to my horror – I *did* order a thousand boxes of couscous! I must have typed in an extra nought by mistake. I think it must run in the family, typing extra noughts. During the pandemic when my mother ordered Polly Filla for the house so she could 'block the gaps, save the NHS, save lives', she managed to order three hundred boxes instead of three.

Oh, and it appears they are called *Blend* Catering, not Bellend. Not to self: *overdoing the anti-wrinkle serum will lead to* slippage *with the varifocals.* Like having a menopausal brain isn't bad enough. Oh, my giddy aunt, as Mummy would say. I could have sworn Sarah said 'Bellend' on the phone.

It's me who's the bellend. *Blend* Catering will be there, and I now shall have to eat humble couscous. Ruddy marvellous.

When we arrive at the venue, there doesn't seem to be anyone around and I start panicking.

'Oh, please don't tell me I got the day wrong,' I say to Ben, as we get out of the cab. I lift my veil, so I can see where I'm going.

'What are you like, Beanie? We're early. You do realise that?'

'It's seven o'clock.'

'What time are people meant to be arriving?'

'My family should be here now. They're coming earlier than everyone else. I don't know, it's a bit *quiet.*'

'Stop panicking.'

Bad advice. I am totally panicking. I was brought up as a catastrophiser. It's part of our family system. Only last week Mummy had a meltdown when Fiona spilt a drop of Aqua Libra on the Axeminster.

A long black limousine pulls up in front of the entrance. I glance at it, but the windows are tinted so I can't see who's inside.

'Do you know who that is?' I ask Ben.

'No, why would I?'

Next thing, a figure emerges from the limo. It looks like a guy, wearing jeans and black trainers, but he has an Ocado bag over his head. He's accompanied by another guy, who's guiding him. He lets himself be led up the steps, into the building.

I turn to Ben. 'What was that all about?'

'I haven't a clue.'

'You're up to something.'

'No idea what you mean,' he says.

I don't believe him. We go through the main doors into Clarence's foyer. I look around, at the Lincrusta walls, the high ceilings, the chandelier that's bigger than Jupiter. Yes, it's suitably glam for a grand old dame, I think to myself, glad I chose this place. I am just nervous in case anything else goes wrong.

I go to the reception. I lift my veil and address the lady behind the polished wooden desk.

'I'm Jenny Bean. I've booked a party for this evening, a fiftieth. It's in the Byron Room, upstairs.'

'Ah, yes, go on up. The catering people are here, sorting things out.' Oh god. It should be me with an Ocado bag over my head.

'Thanks.'

I ascend the mahogany staircase. Ben walks beside me. He squeezes my hand as we climb to the Byron Room, which is on the first floor.

'You OK, Jen?'

'I'm fine.'

When we get into the room, I look around, checking the layout. The bar – I have my priorities in the right order – is to the left in an alcove. There are wooden tables dotted around the edges, a large space for dancing, and a stage the width of the room. There's a banner with 'Kinda Magic!' on it in sparkly blue letters and another banner above the stage, saying 'Happy 50th Jenny Bean!'

I look again. No, it does not say that. It says, 'Happy 50th Jelly Bean.' *Right, Jenny. Deep yoga breaths. You are calm. You have got this, it's all under control.*

Bollocks to that. *#needwinenow!!* I head for the bar, where I get myself a large glass of Malbec. My sister, Fiona comes over. Ben lets go of my hand and stands back slightly.

'Happy birthday, sis!' Fiona says, giving me a big hug. She is, as is my sister's way, looking elegant without trying, in a black sleeveless polo neck and a short orange crop. She sees me trying to work her out.

'Annie Lennox,' she says, touching her hair. 'It's a wig.'

'Ah, yes, of course.' My sister has always been a big Eurythmics fan.

'How's life on dry land?' I ask her.

'OK. But the flat is very *still.*'

'Still?'

'We've got the hammock but it's not the same.'

'You're missing the houseboat?' They sold it after the pandemic and bought a flat.

'I am. Polly isn't. She says it made her seasick when we had rumpy-pumpy.'

I laugh.

Fiona is looking across the room. 'Happy Birthday, *Jelly* Bean? I take it you've see that?'

'Yes. I've seen it.' I feel like throwing another shit-fit because I am so stressed you could hire me as the National Grid. My sister is not the most observant of people unless she is editing the proofs of her book, *Plato, A Thoroughly Modern Thinker*, so if she's noticed it, it's obvious.

'You should complain,' she says.

'It's an easy mistake to make I suppose, it sounds similar.' I spy Sarah moving around arranging the food on the tables. She is putting out the couscous, mountains of it on plate after plate, until there's a whole table filled with it. Oh god.

Polly comes over, shuffling along in her Smurf costume, in footwear that looks at least six sizes too big, bits of her pink pixie crop jutting out of the white plastic hat.

'Happy Birthday, old fart,' she says.

'Thanks,' I reply absently, my gaze still on the misspelt banner.

'Hi, Ben,' Polly says.

'Hello,' Ben says, smiling.

She steps back. 'You look so much like Boy George it's freaky.'

'Thanks,' he replies.

'Yes, hello, Ben,' Fiona says. My sister is a Philosophy research fellow at Oxford University, so she talks to Ben about Plato while Ben talks about platelets. I consider whether I should take the banner down before more people arrive. It's going to cause issues with my plan – and it will be on all the photos. But right now, I have other concerns. Mummy should be here, and she is not, which is worrying me.

'Where's Mummy?' I ask Fiona, when there's a pause in the conversation.

'Oh, she's going to be late. Did she not call you?' Fiona says.

'No – oh, I don't know.' I search in my bag and pull out my phone. There are two missed calls from her, and a voicemail.

I call voicemail. Mummy's agitated voice comes on. 'Oh, Jennifer, darling! I am so sorry. I can't come to your party. I've dyed myself blue!' The phone clicks dead.

I'm about to press call back when Polly says, 'She's had an accident.'

'Oh god, what kind of accident?' My heart starts racing. I hope I'm not *actually* having a heart attack this time.

'Blueberry juice,' Fiona says.

'What?' I reply.

Ben erupts into laughter.

'The juicer kind of... *exploded*,' Polly explains.

'Oh, for crying out loud!' I say.

Ben gives me a bemused look.

My mother has been obsessed with blueberries ever since she read in *Health and Wellbeing Magazine* that they help stave off dementia.

Privately I've been worried about this for years with her. I regularly ask her who the Prime Minister is, to which she always replies curtly, 'Boris Johnson, *unfortunately*. I'm not going doolally, and don't ask me to count backwards from a hundred in even numbers because you can't do it either, which means we must both be crackers.'

'The thing is,' Fiona says, 'she was wearing her Margaret Thatcher costume when it happened, so she's a bit cross.'

'Maggie Thatcher costume? So, how can she have dyed herself blue then?'

'Wrong shade of blue, apparently,' Polly chips in, giggling.

Sarah is making her way across the room wheeling a hug three-tier trolly that's at least two foot taller than I.

I lift my veil, steeling myself for the sheepish apology I am about to make. I go over to her and hold out my hand.

'Jenny Bean,' I say to her.

'Sarah Hardy.' She shakes my hand. Then she looks at me and says, 'I did check through the order. It definitely says one thousand boxes of couscous.'

'I know. It's my mistake. I'm really sorry I was so rude. I've had a lot on my plate.'

She looks at me and erupts into laughter.

Realising the silly pun, I laugh too, and no, before you ask, no, I don't get a little leakage since I have the Wee-Away pad firmly set to Low in case I give anyone else the full Darling Buds of May experience.

'Where do you want the rest of the couscous?' she says after composing herself. 'There's no more room on the tables.'

'I don't know.' I have visions of giving large party bags, not just to my guests but to everyone in the street I can find or selling it as wedding confetti.

It is then that I have my brainwave. 'Take the rest to the food bank.'

'Are you sure?'

'Yes.' I have always felt guilty about coming from affluence and so I regularly donate to food banks and homeless charities.

'Oh,' she says. 'And it's Blend Catering, not Bellend.'

I blush and mutter, 'I know, sorry.'

Next, the door opens, and a group of people comes in.

I stare at them. They are all dressed the same as me. Oh hell. This is not part of the deal. One of them, a lady about my height and build, is coming over. Even her hair is the same colour as mine – Gwyneth-Paltrow-left-in-a-cupboard-blonde. I'm about to say, 'This is not a Doppelganger party,' but she speaks first.

'Is this the fiftieth party for Jenny Bean?' the voice behind the veil says.

I nod, relieved she at least has my name right.

'You put it on Facebook, thanks for the invite. I'm a such a *huge* fan of your blog, I read all your posts, every day. You brighten up my life so much.' Then, she says, 'I'm wearing Wee-Away too. The Creosote odour. My husband likes it because I remind him of his newly varnished shed.'

Before I can reply to this bizarre statement, I see the figure from earlier, who had emerged from the limo.

No, it can't be. It just can't be.

I pour myself another large Malbec because, 'It's my birthday and I'll drink if I want to; you would drink too if it happened to you.'

To my delight, my mother walks in. I rush over.

'Mummy! You made it!'

'Yes, darling, I made it.'

I look her up and down. Her face and neck are blotched with blue patches as well as her Margaret Thatcher wig and her white blouse.

'Oh, yes. You *are* quite blue, aren't you?' I say to her.

'I can't seem to get it all out.'

'That's your karma for voting Tory,' I reply, archly.

'Do you think I could book myself into the dry cleaners?'

I smile at the twinkle in her eye.

'Anyway, happy birthday, darling!' She gives me a hug.

'I'm so glad you made it,' I tell her.

We chat about her chess-playing and she says, 'This is my first outing since before the pandemic. Unless you count that sofa trip to Stratford-upon-Avon to see *Hamlet* earlier this year.'

'Which trip?'

'The one when the bus broke down on the way there. By the time we got there Polonius had already been stabbed in the arras and Ophelia was having a nervous breakdown with the Bouquet Garni.'

I chuckle. Mummy is on form tonight.

She looks at the banner. 'You do know that says, "happy birthday, Jelly Bean" don't you?'

'Yes, Mummy. I know.'

'Are you taking it down?'

'I don't know. I'm menopausal. I can't make sensible decisions anymore.'

'Jennifer, darling, you are the only member of this family who *can* make sensible decisions.' She pauses, then pulls out a shortbread tin from her bag. 'I still can't decide what to do with him.'

My eyes widen. 'Roger? You've brought him with you?'

Roger was Mummy's chess and opera companion, who sadly died from Covid in 2020.

Mummy nods. 'Don't worry. I'm not going to scatter him here. He doesn't like modern music. But he gets lonely left in the house.' She taps the tin fondly and puts it back in her bag. I give her a hug because I know how much she misses him.

We chat for a while longer about how wonderful it is to be out and how pleased Mummy is to be vaccinated and how she wishes Roger could still be here because he was the first companion since Daddy whom she didn't pay, and because, 'he loved a good party.'

More people start arriving. I go to greet them, glass of wine in hand. Cassie and Clive are here. Cassie has come as Joan Collins, Clive as Sue Ellen. Side-by-side, they look like a polyester Hadrian's Wall.

Sprig comes in, dressed as Suggs from Madness, and gives me a present – a lovely new book of sheet music for my gigs.

'You're not performing tonight then?' Sprig says, giving me a funny look.

'What do you mean?' I reply.

I notice Ben looking over. *What* is going on? I get another icy feeling in my stomach. *Please let tonight go OK.*

Next, A Kinda Magic come on stage, and I'm blown away by how much they look like the real thing. The lead singer - *oh, my days, he is handsome.* He has resurrected my teen crush on Freddie Mercury. I feel weak at the knees and like I'm sixteen again.

They launch into the first song of the night, 'Who wants to Live Forever?' The wine is kicking in and I'm feeling relaxed at last. Once I have had alcohol all is well with the world and nothing can go wrong.

The trinity of Madonnas start dancing and so do Cassie and Clive. My mother, never to be outdone, joins in, as do I – as they play 'Another one Bites the Dust.' They really are milking the mortality theme tonight.

When they start playing 'Big Bottomed Girls,' the trinity of Madonnas leave the dance floor, looking offended. I don't know. It's never bothered me. I have a big wide horse-riding arse, legacy of my posh background. No sense of humour, some people.

I keep staring at them, trying to make out their identity but they won't remove their veils. It is then that things start to get a little bit weird.

'Freddie' is talking into the microphone, 'Jenny Bean! Happy birthday! Come up here, Jenny,' he says.

Perplexed, I head towards the stage. The only problem is, so do the other Madonnas.

'Freddie' is looking down at us, confused. 'Which one of you is Jenny Bean?'

'I am,' I shout, at the same time as the three lookalikes. Next, one of them jumps up onto the stage and grabs the mic from Freddie. The other Madonnas follow her, piling onto the stage.

'Good evening! I'm Jenny Bean, and this is my party!'

Well, I can't believe it. I pull up my veil and rush up after her, trying to snatch the mic away, but she pulls back. I make a grab for her veil, but she moves away. Now the stage is swirling with Madonnas. It's making me feel quite dizzy. They are circling around me chattering excitedly. One of them says, 'Can I have your autograph?'

I lean close to her, yelling into the mic, '*I'm* Jenny Bean!' I seem to have slipped into my Brian Blessed voice, so people look confused. Even Ben doesn't appear to know what to do. My mother has turned a funny colour but maybe that's just the Tory blueberries.

I charge at her, force the mic from her hand, and I say, as Un-Blessedly as I can, 'This is my party! You need to leave!'

'You can't prove it's not my party,' she says. Then, she pulls back her veil. Oh. My. God. She really is the image of me. Same eyes, same hair, everything.

'Are we related?' I stammer out.

She doesn't reply. Tipsy, my inhibitions desert me. I look at her, then at the crowd.

'*She* is wearing a Wee-Away pad that smells of *creosote*! I always wear Country Roses. Make her wee and you will find the truth!' I shout.

There's a big whoop from the crowd, followed by a roar, and Cassie shouts, 'You tell them, Jen!'

Having been revealed as a wearer of stress incontinence pads that smell of newly varnished sheds seems to have done the trick. She says, 'I just wanted to be you for a day. Is that so wrong? I'm not mad. I'm not a stalker. I just want your life *so badly*.'

I'm unsure what to say to that so I look across the room at the other Madonnas. 'Who are those people?'

'They're fans,' she says. 'Like me. You're a celebrity blogger. We came together. We hooked up on Facebook after you put out that invitation. We just wanted to meet you. You said you were going as Madonna, so we thought would too.'

Well, I can't think what to say to that. I feel guilty. I don't deserve fans, especially devoted ones. Yes, I have a huge following on my blog, yes, I have a Matreon (specialists in female-related content), and I get lots of comments etcetera.

But a celebrity blogger? I'm just a middle-aged woman with flatulence issues and a leaky bladder.

A security guard is coming in, weaving his way through the crowd.

'What's the problem?' he says. 'I understand you have gatecrashers?'

'I reported them,' Ben says. 'It's my girlfriend's party. Those three are not invited.' He points out the intruders – Creosote Crotch and the other two.

The trinity of Madonnas look at me, waiting on my word.

Creosote Crotch lifts up her veil and says, 'I'm sorry, we'll leave if you want.'

The security guard look at them. 'Please come with me—'

I hold up my hand. 'It's OK. It's my party. They can stay, as long as they don't cause any more trouble.'

'Are you sure?' Ben says.

'It's fine.'

'Could you please get off the stage, the three of you?' the security guard says.

They do as he asks. I can't help it. I don't like excluding people. Blame Henrietta with the Vendetta.

As they are getting down, Ben comes up onto the stage; the guitarist puts down his guitar and leaves.

'Oh, what *now*?' I moan to Ben.

Before he can answer me the figure from earlier enters the stage and picks up the guitar. It really is him.

The room goes swimmy. I drop to the floor.

I wake up to Brian May, standing over me and I'm muttering, 'Are my knickers on show, did you see my knickers?'

He doesn't appear to hear me and helps me up.

'Can you get a glass of water for this fine lady?' he says to Ben.

'Course,' Ben says.

He turns to me. 'Are you OK?'

I nod, speechless.

My mother, Cassie, my sister and Polly rush up onto the stage flapping and fussing.

'It was the shock,' I reply, staring at Brian in disbelief.

'I don't look that bad, do I?' He smiles. I wonder if I'm dreaming.

I am helped to the side of the stage, while Brian picks his guitar up and they launch into "Happy Birthday." The crowd joins in. Of course, the inevitable happens – I start crying because I am overwhelmed by all the excitement.

'Did you do this for me?' I say to Ben.

He puts an arm around me. 'I just have contacts in the right places.'

They finish playing and the crowd cheer. I sense that now is my moment.

Brian is looking at me and I'm staring back because this is so surreal and I can't believe a member of Queen is actually at my party, *in person*. I consider asking him to autograph my gusset but decide that's a bit cheeky, even for me. *Focus, Jennifer, focus.* Ben. This is about Ben. *Non desistas, non exieris.*

'Can I have the mic?' I ask nervously.

'Sure.' He hands it to me.

I drop to my knees in front of Ben, my heart racing.

'Benjamin Christopher Carter, I know I'm a mad sweaty woman with a brain that has more holes than a pair of fishnets, but I love you. Please marry me.'

He stares at me, open-mouthed. Oh hell. Have I got this wrong? The room has gone silent. What on earth I was thinking? I'm not sure how much longer I can stay here, on the hard floor, begging for a chance at wedded bliss.

'Can you hurry up and make a decision? This posture is playing hell with my Housemaid's Knee.'

He grins from ear to ear and laughs.

'Yes! I'll marry you!'

Well, it's all I can do not to faint again.

I stand up and pull him into a kiss. The crowd start cheering again, and my mother says to Ben wryly, 'You do know what you're taking on, don't you? She's completely bonkers. It runs in the family.'

Fiona, Polly and all my friends are coming up to me, congratulating me. I even get a hug from Brian May.

What a day this has turned out to be! Fancy proposing to my boyfriend, and in front of one of my idols. And it's not many people who can say they started the day as Brian Blessed and ended it as Madonna.

# You Can't Get There From Here

*J.Y. Saville writes prose and scripts in the north of England and wanted to be Douglas Adams when she grew up. Her short fiction has been published in more than forty places in print and online, performed live and on radio, and made into short films.*

Ian scrolled idly down news headlines while he finished the last few mouthfuls of toast and marmalade. He'd promised himself an unplugged weekend in the Lake District, and he'd have stuck to it too if the helpful lady who'd checked him in to the B&B hadn't given him the Wi-Fi password as she handed over his room key on Friday. After that, it would have seemed rude not to use it. Or so Ian told himself as he poured one last cup of tea and lingered at the breakfast table, thumb sweeping wars and natural disasters off the top of his screen. He didn't intend to click on the one about the seafront hotel fire. Why spoil his own holiday with an article about the spoiling of someone else's? Then the helpful lady – Janette, he thought she'd said but he wasn't confident enough about it to call her that – startled him and his thumb jerked.

'Finished?' she asked, reaching for his plate.

'Just draining the pot.'

Ian placed his hand over his cup in case she hadn't got the hint not to take it away, smiled at her and glanced back to his phone. *Good job I didn't really go to Brighton*, he thought as he caught the opening paragraph about road closures and falling masonry. The line about the lab technicians' conference didn't filter through until he'd hit the arrow and returned to the main page.

'Oh, no no no no no,' he muttered as he scrolled frantically. Why couldn't it have kept his place?

'Something wrong?'

He looked up at Janette's politely concerned face, then round at the empty room.

'Sorry,' he said. 'I'm holding you up.'

'Not at all. There was only you and the couple from Worcester this morning.' She gestured to where a couple in their fifties had been sitting both the previous morning and when Ian had come down to breakfast half an hour earlier. 'The guys from Peebles wanted an early start so they skipped breakfast. It'll just be you in the morning: Sunday night stays out of season are pretty unusual.'

'Right,' he said, standing up while he turned his attention back to the phone. How many pages of headlines had he swiped past, earlier?

'Sure you're all right?'

'Yes, thanks.' And then, 'No, oh bloody hell no.'

'That doesn't sound like "all right" to me.'

'I'm fine, really,' said Ian. 'But I might have to go home.'

He raced up to his room and paced while he thought things through. The hotel in Brighton hosting the lab technicians' conference he'd told his wife he was attending had caught fire in the early hours. It was currently a safely-evacuated smouldering hazard with a large cordon and several fire engines around it. The annual conference, the BBC helpfully pointed out for any wives who chose to check, had been brought to a premature close. Ian opened his suitcase and prepared to pack.

He was just tucking his deodorant into his slippers when it occurred to him that he'd never actually told Patty he was staying in the conference venue itself. He could plausibly claim that he'd wanted to be able to avoid the other delegates and booked his own B&B. All he needed to do was brazen it out.

'Hello?'
'Patty, don't worry. I'm OK.'
'Now I'm worried. What have you done?'
'I haven't done—'
Patty's phone made three beeps to signify Ian had hung up. Or lost the signal. Whatever had happened, it must be serious if he was willing to jeopardise his peculiar annual fiction about the national conference.

'Damn,' said Ian, looking at the screen. He wasn't sure when he'd lost the signal. This was why he didn't usually ring Patty when he was away; it's hard to pretend you're in a conference centre on a major throughfare when you're suffering rural connectivity.

The lack of connection was part of the appeal. Six and a half years ago Ian had turned forty and had a bit of a wobble. Not the full sports-car-and-affair job, not even career recalibration like the woman next door, who'd cast aside twenty-two years of secretarial efficiency and become a dog-groomer. Ian had had a mild bout of existential angst that happened to coincide with his annual invite to the dreaded technicians' conference. Ordinarily he chucked the flyer in the recycling and made his excuses to his colleagues but that year he announced his intention to attend. Patty was surprised but when the weekend arrived, she drove him into the centre of Leeds and dropped him near the station. Up to the point where he got off the train at Manchester Piccadilly he fully intended to go. Maybe not to all the sessions he'd signed up for, and certainly not to the gala dinner, but he meant to go to the hotel and wear a lapel badge for a bit before he spent the best part of the long weekend mooching around Manchester on his own. Then he saw Windermere on the departure board, and how could he resist?

'Patty, can you hear me?'

He looked at the screen again, but whatever hint of a connection they'd had, it had vanished. And, he noticed with alarm, he only had 13 per cent battery. He wasted a little bit more of it navigating through the stuff he never normally looked at, to see if he could confirm his suspicion that it was the BBC news app that had tipped him over. He pulled on his fleece and the coat that had probably been described in technical outdoorsy language in the shop but was basically a serviceable grey and red anorak. Hopefully he'd be able to find a spot outside that had decent reception but was also sheltered from the biting wind.

'Patty, are you there?'

'I am. Your conference has burnt down.'

Damn, did that news-bearing tone mean she hadn't heard any of the last call?

'The conference centre has, yes,' Ian said. 'I'm not staying there though.'

'No?'

'No. I'm in a B&B, so I'm not really affected.'

'Yes, but there's no reason for you to stay now, is there?'

How had he phrased it a few minutes ago?

'Some of us fancied carrying on. In the pub.'

God no, he hadn't put it that badly. Had he?

'I mean,' he tried again, but Patty cut him off.

'There's no reason we can't go to Helen's fiftieth now, is there?' she said. 'I know you would have wanted to if you hadn't already arranged to be away.'

Oh crumbs, Helen's fiftieth. Of course he wanted to go, apart from anything else she was the only other woman who'd ever been rash enough to go out with him. After three increasingly disastrous dates she'd brought her friend Patty along for moral support as she tried to let Ian down gently on the fourth. Patty had been spelling her name with an i at the time, trying to claim she was named after Patti Smith, but of course you can't hear the difference when you're introduced. Ian had immediately mentioned Peppermint Patty from Peanuts, who her parents had genuinely named her after, and the rest was baffling history.

'Ian? Are you still there?'

'Yes. We should go, I'll—'

'I'll pick you up.'

He was about to ask where, and why, and some more of the questions pinging around his head but a sheep wandered closer and opened its mouth as though about to bleat. Ian cut the connection. The battery symbol flashed red in the middle of the screen twice, then the screen went black. He hadn't packed a charger, hadn't been planning on using his phone much and preferred to travel light. The sheep ambled off up the fell in silence.

Patty tried ringing her husband back a few times before she concluded that his battery must be dead. She assumed he wouldn't have taken the charger with him and indeed when she checked his bedside drawers there it was on top of three dog-eared Peanuts paperbacks and a clothes brush he never used. He claimed he hardly used his phone. While it was true that he rarely answered her texts and never phoned anyone for a chat, he would sit engrossed in his screen for ages when he thought she wasn't looking. She'd worried about it for a while, then checked once when he left it on the chair arm. She found the library app open at a book about otters, which he no doubt thought she'd laugh at. To be fair, she probably would laugh. But only in an affectionate way.

She looked in the cupboard on the landing to make sure his binoculars were missing, and since they were she concluded he must be in the Lakes as usual. It was of course possible that he had really gone to the conference this year, and the binoculars were for a newly-acquired voyeuristic streak but she had known Ian for twenty-seven years. She was willing to bet a full tank of petrol that at that moment he was somewhere not too far from Keswick, watching a lesser-crested something-or-other in chilly isolation. When she'd had another cup of coffee she'd head off over the Pennines and fetch him.

Ian finished packing and looked at his watch. Ten past nine. He didn't know what time the buses were on a Sunday, he'd only looked up the ones he needed on Friday and Monday. He didn't know what time the trains from Penrith were either, but he needed to get there as soon as possible. Why would Patty want to pick him up in Brighton? Did she think he'd had a shock? Was it cheaper for her to drive down and fetch him than to pay for a last-minute train fare? Actually, it probably was, and since bills and the household budget were very much Patty's domain, that made some kind of sense. It was frustrating that he was going to end up paying for a night in a B&B he couldn't use. Patty would have asked for her money back, but that wasn't Ian's style.

He rang the bell in the hallway, waited a moment then knocked on the Staff Only door, just as Janette pulled it open, startling them both.

'Ah, sorry,' Ian said, stepping back. 'I need to go, I'm afraid. Not sure what time the buses are so I'd best be off.'

He glanced around as one final check for a hitherto overlooked stand of bus timetables but the hallway remained empty of timetables, tourist attraction leaflets and adverts for local restaurants. That was probably why Janette was so keen to pass on the Wi-Fi password, then her guests could find all that out for themselves without cluttering up her hall table.

'Two nights, that's a hundred and fifty pounds. Just pop your card in there.'

She handed him the card-reader but Ian didn't put his credit card in.

'I booked for three though,' he said.

'And you've had to leave early.' She shrugged.

'But it doesn't seem fair.'

'I had other rooms free, it's not like you made me turn someone away.'

'But you were expecting two hundred and twenty-five.'

'It's all right, I hadn't booked a Caribbean cruise on the strength of it. I thought you were in a hurry.'

Janette nodded at the card-reader and Ian completed the transaction feeling simultaneously relieved that he hadn't wasted seventy-five pounds, and somehow as though he'd fleeced her. He put his room key on the table, picked up his suitcase and walked out into thin drizzle.

By the end of the lane, Ian had already shifted the case from one hand to the other and back again. A rucksack would have been more appropriate and far easier to handle but deception didn't come easily to Ian and he also had a tendency to overthink. That first time, when he'd been heading to central Manchester, he'd taken a small suitcase thinking it would be a short walk from the station and easy to wheel. The seasoned deceiver would no doubt have said the following year that half the delegates used rucksacks and since he was more comfortable with one, he would too. It's not like he was taking a suit. But Ian had got it into his head that going to a conference required using a suitcase, and so he carried one on local buses and over uneven ground, to out-of-the-way guest-houses in the Lake District. Similarly, he daren't pack his sturdiest walking boots or his waterproof trousers. As the rain got heavier, he wished he had them with him now.

It was a little over a mile from the B&B to the village bus stop. He had an idea that as in the Yorkshire Dales, you didn't necessarily have to be at a stop to flag a bus down, but he always felt safest with a bus stop and he thought this one had a timetable fixed to it so he'd at least know how long he had to wait. He'd just worked out that the answer to that was twenty-four hours and thirty-seven minutes, when a car pulled up and the passenger window descended.

'I remembered after you'd left,' Janette called from behind the wheel. 'There's no buses on a Sunday.'

'I'd just discovered that,' said Ian, leaning down to the open window and dripping onto the passenger seat. 'But thanks for coming to tell me.'

'No, you ninny, I came to offer you a lift. Where are you heading?'

Ian was somewhat distracted by the revelation that the word 'ninny' hadn't entirely died out as an insult, but he managed to say Penrith after a pause.

'Hop in,' she said. 'Stick your case in the back, I'm not sure how to open the boot.'

It took them a couple of miles to get through the pleasantries, the thank-yous and the not-at-alls, the praise for the breakfasts and the comfortable bed. Then Ian said, 'Why don't you know how to open your boot?'

'Because it's not my boot.'

The first thought that shot into Ian's mind was that she'd stolen the car, then he almost laughed out loud at the absurdity of the idea and realised she must mean it was her husband's. Ian hadn't caught his name but he seemed to spend all his time on the fell so he very likely didn't use it much. How nuts would you have to be to steal a car to give a stranger a lift to the nearest town? Although if he was a stranger to her, she was also a stranger to him – he knew nothing about her except that she ran a bed and breakfast. To Ian, letting a succession of unknown people sleep in your house seemed a very odd way to make a living.

'I think this way might be quicker,' Janette said, turning up an unmarked road and doing nothing to reassure Ian.

'When you say it's not your boot…'

'My sister left her keys with me in case the car was in anyone's way.'

'Oh, your sister,' Ian said, relieved. 'So she won't mind you borrowing it?'

'She'd kill me if she knew. Don't scratch the paintwork with your case when you get out, will you?'

The way they were hugging the hawthorn hedge, Ian thought his suitcase was unlikely to make much difference.

'Let's hope she doesn't keep too close an eye on her mileage,' he said.

Janette glanced across uncertainly. He wished he hadn't said anything. His dad used to keep an exercise book in the glove compartment and note down the mileage after every trip, something to do with having a dodgy fuel gauge.

'I'm sure she doesn't,' he said.

Janette shrugged and turned left. The road looked strikingly familiar.

'That's right,' she said, 'I shouldn't have gone ahead over the cattle grid, you need to bear right. I'll turn round and try again.'

'Look,' said Ian, 'it's very kind of you but really…' He trailed off as she executed an awkward three-point turn. There wouldn't be a bus from anywhere near here and he wasn't sure if there was a local taxi service. If there was, he didn't know its number and he hadn't noticed a phone box. Janette was his best chance of reaching Penrith station this side of midday. She grinned at him.

'OK, no more short cuts. What time's your train?'

'I don't know. I wasn't planning to catch one till tomorrow.'

'That's interesting. Most people look it up on their phones these days, and I know you've got one because you were reading it at breakfast.'

'Yes well, that's rather the problem. I ran the battery down before I had a chance to look at timetables.'

'Hence you didn't know about the bus?'

'Precisely.'

'Where are you trying to get to?'

'Brighton.'

'Oh.' She was quiet for a moment. 'So when you said you need to go home you meant leave, not literally going home? You live in Yorkshire, didn't you say?'

'Yes, near Leeds. I am going home, it's just that I need to go home from Brighton.'

The sidelong look Janette gave him made Ian aware of quite how crazy that sounded. His concerns about her purloining her sister's car to give a strange man a lift to town on a wet Sunday were nothing compared to what she was probably thinking about that strange man right now. He thought for a moment and then reflected that she'd drop him in Penrith in a few minutes and he'd never see her again; he didn't like to go to the same B&B twice.

'I told my wife I was going to Brighton for a conference,' he confessed. 'And now the conference centre's burnt down and she's on her way to pick me up.'

'From Brighton?' Janette looked scandalised and delighted in equal measure. If boredom had played any part in her decision to come to Ian's assistance she must be congratulating herself on uncovering this extra source of entertainment.

'I guess so. The battery ran out before I could clarify. It'll be cheaper than me buying a same-day train ticket, I should think.'

'Wow,' said Janette. 'I bet you wish you picked somewhere closer.'

'Oh no it's a real conference,' Ian said as she drew up outside Penrith station. 'Some of my colleagues are there.'

'But not you.'

'No.' He undid his seat belt but felt strangely reluctant to get out of the car. Some of that would be the horizontal rain.

'Shall I check train times before you get wet?'

'Oh that would be great, thanks.'

The phone Janette fished out of her pocket looked so old he was amazed it could connect to the internet. Unless... Did National Rail Enquiries have a text-messaging service?

'You're OK as long as it isn't due in the next five minutes,' Janette said, huddled over the phone in concentration. 'It's not the quickest, and I can't see what I'm doing on this piddling little screen.'

Ian opened the window a crack so he could listen for approaching trains but all he heard was the whistling wind, and he got a wet head.

'Right, Penrith to Brighton... That's over an hour away,' she said. 'Hang on, what about Windermere station?'

She prodded at the screen for a while longer. Ian's hopes flailed towards this unexpected lifebuoy, only for it to be snatched away a moment later.

'It sets off a bit sooner but it still ends up being the same train into Brighton, after all the changes. You don't seem to be able to get there before four o'clock.'

'Four o'clock?'

'What time's she picking you up?'

'We didn't get that far, but if she's already set off... Early afternoon?'

'What if I drove you to Manchester?'

'You can't drive me to Manchester,' said Ian, wondering at the same time if that might be his only hope.

'No, you're right. I think we've missed that one already and it only gets you to Brighton an hour earlier. Unless you know someone with a helicopter you're going to have to ring her up and admit you're not there.'

'If I was going to ring her, I'd say I'd meet her at a station partway up to save her some time.'

Janette grinned.

'That's a great idea. Why don't you?'

'My phone battery's dead.'

'Use mine,' she said, holding it out.

'She won't recognise the number.'

'You could text her first to say it's you on a borrowed phone.'

'Who do I say I've borrowed it from? I'm not a very good liar, I'm afraid. I can't say I've made friends with someone at the conference, it just doesn't sound all that plausible.'

'What's the conference, by the way?'

'UK laboratory technicians' annual gathering.'

Janette nodded at him with a smile that said yes, that fits.

'Tell her the truth,' she said. 'The phone belongs to the owner of the B&B.'

'Why wouldn't you have let me use your landline? You're bound to have one. And a payphone would betray the area code.'

'You've got an answer for everything, haven't you?'
'Besides,' said Ian, 'I can't remember her number.'

Patty was stuck in traffic on the A65. She didn't mind
that much though, since she was in Wharfedale and the
views were pleasant. It wasn't the absolute quickest route to
Keswick but it felt more direct and it was certainly scenic.
If Ian could have a weekend break, surely she could allow
herself the scenic route on her way to fetch him. She wasn't
sure how to go about finding him once she got there, he'd
stayed at a different place each time, but surely even Ian
would have managed to borrow a phone charger or locate
a phone box by the time she reached the Lakes. Although,
this was a man who'd apparently never realised that paying
for a bed and breakfast with his credit card would make it
show up on the statement that his wife checked over each
month with a pile of receipts and a red pencil.

The first year, Patty had seen the unexpected payment
and worried about cloned cards. Who clones a credit card
and only uses it for a weekend in Borrowdale, though? She
checked the dates and realised Ian must have diverted from
Manchester. For about five minutes she thought he was
having an affair, that he'd found someone willing to sit
silently outside in the cold on the off-chance they'd see
some rare bird that he wouldn't be able to confidently iden-
tify if it landed on his rucksack. Someone who wouldn't
insist on country walks on well-made paths only, and
complain about muddy boots in the car. The thought made
her feel as though her insides had been replaced with cold
custard. Then she remembered this was Ian, it wouldn't
occur to him that straying was a possibility. She looked at
the payments in pubs, none of them enough to have been a

meal for two. He'd obviously just needed a little me-time, she knew he'd had an unsettled few months. She waited for him to confess but to her surprise he didn't, and he even claimed to be going to the conference again the following March. He kept up the same charade each year and she played along, not wanting to spoil his fantasy adventure. In a way it was a shame it had come out like this, but maybe next year she could book a boutique hotel and go with him.

'Where shall we head for?' Janette said.

'Sorry, what?'

'You need to charge your phone. Where's your best bet for getting a charger?'

'I don't know,' said Ian. 'Look, I've caused you enough trouble already. I'll get the train home from here and explain when I get there.'

'She'll be in Brighton by then though, won't she? Your wife. What's her name, by the way?'

'Patty.'

'Like Patti Smith?'

'Yes,' said Ian. It seemed simpler. 'I guess so, but I can ring her from home and—'

'She'll have wasted all that time and petrol.'

'I know. And she'll have to come back to Leeds to get me before we go to Helen's, we'll miss the party.'

'Who's Helen? What party?' And then before Ian could answer, Janette added, 'Do you fancy a coffee? It's not as though we're about to rush off, is it?'

They settled themselves in an empty café that had been open about five minutes.

'My treat,' said Janette. 'I thought today was going to be another dull, wet Sunday. Thank you for scuppering that.'

'It's still quite dull. And wet, and most definitely Sunday.'

'This isn't dull, it's intrigue and cloak and dagger and a quest. You still haven't told me why Patty thinks you're in Brighton.'

He opened his mouth to answer but Janette turned to the counter and called, 'You don't have a phone charger we could borrow, do you?'

'What sort?'

Ian fished his phone out.

'The little USB one,' he said.

'No, sorry.'

'Worth a try,' said Janette, turning back to Ian.

'You don't have one back at the B&B, do you?' he said.

'What do you think?' She held her phone out to him and he saw the round charging port; Janette's charger would have a connection like a miniature headphone jack.

'What about your husband's phone?'

Janette laughed, which Ian took to mean he didn't own one.

'Your sister?'

'My sister would never use anything so vulgar as a charging cable,' she said. 'She has tables and shelves and things that do induction charging. Besides, I don't know the alarm code for her house.'

'Oh.'

'Seems to think I'd go in and use her stuff without asking. Can't think why.'

Janette grinned and Ian couldn't help but laugh.

'Go on then,' she said. 'Why Brighton? What party? And who's Helen?'

Ian opted to refer to Helen as a family friend rather than an impossibly sophisticated mature student he accidentally asked out when he was nineteen. Her fiftieth birthday party somewhere in Cheshire was an easy enough answer. The annual conference, on the other hand...

'You do know most people pretend they're on a work trip as the cover for an affair, not so they can go hiking in the drizzle?'

'Patty's a bit of a fair-weather walker. And only when there's a proper path and a car park. Preferably a tea room for afterwards.'

'I see.'

'It's sort of become a tradition. If I could go any time I know I wouldn't get round to it, whereas if I always go on conference weekend it gives me a fixed date and duration.'

'Which is how come you were going to miss your friend's birthday.'

'It's not actually her birthday until Thursday so I thought she'd be celebrating next weekend but that clashed with something her daughter's doing for work.'

'Unless her daughter's really pot-holing in Wales, or kayaking off the east coast.'

'Yeah, OK.'

'Where could you feasibly meet Patty?'

Janette laboriously looked up the Brighton to Leeds service on her phone and read out the calling points north of London.

'Peterborough, Retford, Doncaster, York. Any of those any use?'

'I wouldn't have thought so,' said Ian. 'Have you got a map?'

They found a pristine road atlas in Janette's sister's car and tried to work out the most likely route from north-west Leeds to Brighton. It didn't go anywhere near any stations on the list.

'The M1 isn't *that* far from Doncaster,' said Janette, measuring the paper distance with her thumb.

Ian glanced at his watch.

'She'll be further south than that already.'

'Even if she has to cut across to Peterborough, it'd still be a shorter journey than going all the way to Brighton.'

'How the hell am I going to get to Peterborough before her?'

'I'm only trying to help,' said Janette.

'Yes, sorry. Thank you.'

'You say she's going to pick you up in Brighton and then go back up to Cheshire for your friend's party?'

'That seems to be the plan.'

'If you manage to get in touch with her soon, you could say you'll get the train to Cheshire and she can pick you up at some station near where your friend lives. Hopefully she won't have gone too far south and she'll just have to cut across to the west.'

'Genius,' said Ian.

'What's the nearest station to your friend's house?'

'I don't know.'

'Look her up in the atlas and we'll look for stations nearby.'

'I can't remember Helen's address.'

'Oh, OK, we'll have to wait till you've charged your phone.'

'Why would I write addresses in my phone? It's in the book next to the phone in the kitchen.'

Janette put her seat belt on and reached for the ignition key.

'You study the pages for Cheshire and see if anything jumps out at you, I'll start driving.'

'You don't know where we're heading.'

'We're heading to my cousin's house in Kendal to see if he's got the right sort of phone charger.'

Ian peered at the page with Chester on.

'Oh look, there's a place called Puddington.'

'When I said to see if anything jumped out, I meant more sort of places you recognised. Somewhere you remember stopping for petrol or something.'

'Bunbury!'

'Ian...'

'Sorry. Don't you ever look at maps for the funny names?'

'I know there's not much that passes for entertainment where I live, but I've never been that desperate.'

Patty pulled into the car park in Keswick. She hadn't heard her phone make a noise, but she was still disappointed when she checked it and there was no text or missed call from Ian. What the hell was he playing at? And how was she supposed to find him? Even outside the main tourist season there were surely too many middle-aged men with binoculars and precision-engineered walking coats for her husband to be memorable. That was even assuming he'd been to Keswick itself. She logged in to the banking app to check the credit card account, but the last thing that had been processed was what looked like a bus fare on Friday, probably from the station to wherever he was staying. Nothing else from the weekend would appear until Monday. Why couldn't she have a normal secretive husband who was covering for an affair? Then she could go by herself to Helen's party with a clear conscience. She checked the time: too late for elevenses, strictly speaking, but it seemed like a good way to kill time.

Janette's cousin Will was just as amused and intrigued by Ian's predicament as Janette had been.

'And you haven't got your friend's address in your phone?' he asked as he filled the kettle. Ian's phone would take hours to charge fully but he reckoned twenty minutes might be enough to tide him over, which Will insisted was long enough for a cuppa.

'No,' said Ian. 'Why spend all that time typing it in? It's not as though I can send her a letter from my phone, is it?'

'True,' said Will. 'It wouldn't half come in handy at times like these, though.'

'Couldn't you ask Patty for Helen's address, once your phone's back on?' suggested Janette. 'Say you were heading north to meet her partway but you've just thought you could divert and save her some trouble, only you can't remember what station you need.'

'Oh, that's a point,' said Ian. 'I could... No, I couldn't.'

Will made an exasperated noise as he placed the teapot on the kitchen table.

'I told you he had an answer for everything,' said Janette.

'I'd need to have gone a completely different route from London,' Ian pointed out. 'Otherwise I'm not saving either Patty or myself any time. And if I'd already bought a ticket to Leeds then I bought another one to... wherever it is I need to go in Cheshire, I'd waste a load of money too.'

'So you need to pretend you were heading there straight from Brighton but you didn't get a chance to tell her sooner?'

'Exactly,' said Ian. 'So I'm stuffed, because I can't think where Helen lives and I can't contact Patty until I can tell her where I'm going.'

He put his head in his hands. He'd already taken up too much of Janette's time, not to mention petrol, and now here he was in Will's kitchen drinking his tea and using his electricity. He ought to have come clean to Patty hours ago and saved everyone the hassle.

'What if you got it wrong?' said Will. 'Best intentions and all that, but you misremembered.'

'Eh?' Ian looked up. 'Misremembered what?'

'Pick a station, any station. Tell Patty that's where you're headed. She says that's half an hour away from Helen's, you've still saved her the trip to Brighton.'

'Oh, that's brilliant,' said Ian. 'I'll go to Macclesfield. I don't think that's nearby but you're right, it's nearer than Brighton. I'll text her now.'

He typed awkwardly with the phone resting on the radiator shelf while plugged in at the skirting board.

'Now I'm going to be cheeky,' said Will when he'd finished. 'You're the tallest person who's been in my house in weeks. If I give you a stepladder and a lightbulb, could you illuminate my stairwell while your tea's cooling down?'

*Finally borrowed charger. Will save you a trip – pick me up at Macclesfield. Ian xx*

Patty read the text three times as she sipped her hot chocolate. It was endearing the way he still put his name at the end of every text message, as though the photo that

flashed on her screen might not be enough to prompt recognition. And frankly who else would be asking her to pick
them up in Macclesfield? Why was *Ian* even asking her
to pick him up in Macclesfield? Surely he'd realised she'd
have set off to fetch him shortly after they last spoke? She
rang him to ask but there was no answer. Pointless leaving
a voicemail, she'd told him years ago that they cost fifty
pence to fetch – probably true at the time – and he'd never
listened to a single one since.

'I'm glad you've finally got that back bedroom redecorated,'
said Janette as they came back into the kitchen. Will had
given them a quick tour once Ian had replaced the bulb.
Ian hadn't been particularly interested but Janette was so
he trailed around the house after her, making vague appre-
ciative noises about feature walls and accent lighting.

'My phone's probably charged enough by now,' he said.
'So I can get out of your hair.'

The station wasn't far away, he could easily get there
without having to ask Janette for a lift.

'I'll give you a lift to Lancaster,' she said, 'save you
a connection.'

'What?'

'I'll come with you for the ride,' said Will. 'I'm not
doing anything else.'

'No, really,' Ian began as he switched the phone charger
off at the wall. He glanced at the screen and forgot what he
was going to say next. 'Oh no.'

'What?' Will and Janette asked together.

'I missed a call from Patty.'

'So?' said Will. 'Tell her you were at the toilet and you
didn't think answering it was a good idea.'

'I never go to the toilet on trains.'

'Of course you don't,' muttered Will.

'Quiet carriage?' suggested Janette.

'Good idea,' said Ian. 'She's texted me as well. Oh, damn! I didn't say what time I'd be there.' He opened the message. 'It just says Macclesfield. With a question mark.'

'Well there you go,' said Will. 'You've picked the wrong station, she's asking why there when it's miles from Helen's.'

'Unless...' began Ian.

'Unless what?' asked Janette.

'We got cut off this morning. What if she was saying she'd pick me up at Leeds station and save me the bother of getting all the way home on public transport on a Sunday? And now she's at home wondering why the hell I'm on the way to Macclesfield. With nothing to wear to the party.'

'Oh.'

'You've torn it now,' said Will.

'I'll have to ring her back.' Ian stared at his phone as though it might suddenly conk out again and save him, but it steadfastly remained lit up and ready for action. He'd hit the button to return the call when a thought occurred to him. 'Where am I?'

'Kendal,' said Will.

'No, I mean she'll ask – oh, hello, love.' He gestured frantically to Janette as he spoke to Patty. 'I'm on the way to Macclesfield. I think we've just come through, er...'

Janette made hurry-up gestures at her phone as she tried to look up the route of Ian's supposed train.

'Why are you on the way to Macclesfield?' asked Patty. 'And how is it saving me a trip?'

'Isn't Macclesfield near Helen's?'

'No.'

Will peered over Janette's shoulder, covered his mouth and boomed, 'Milton Keynes your next station stop.'

'Oh,' said Ian, 'I'm nearly in Milton Keynes. Wherever that is.'

'No you're not,' said Patty. 'It's too quiet for you to be on a speeding train, for one thing. And for another, you haven't had time to get down to Milton Keynes yet. And it's not on the way to Macclesfield.'

'It is if you're coming from Brighton,' said Ian, wondering whether 'get down to Milton Keynes' was like 'going up to London' in that it had nothing to do with geographical direction.

'But you're not—' Patty sounded unsure, which Ian found unsettling. 'You haven't been in Brighton, have you? You've got your binoculars.'

Will and Janette were both watching him as though he was a particularly gripping episode of Corrie. They must be able to hear every word in the quiet kitchen.

'They have birds in Brighton,' he said. 'Gulls, mainly.' Hang on, what did she mean? If she didn't think he was in Brighton was he right about her picking him up in Leeds?

'No, wait a minute,' said Patty, sounding much more like her usual self. 'You're not on a train. Which means someone was pretending to be a train announcement.'

Will waved at the phone and grinned. Ian slumped and covered his eyes. Time to come clean.

'That was Will,' he said.

'Who on earth is Will?'

'Janette's cousin.'

'Ian...'

'B&B landlady.'

'So you're still at the bed and breakfast?'

'We're having a day out,' called Will. Janette tapped his arm crossly and he laughed.

'I'm on my way to Macclesfield,' said Ian. 'Where were you planning to pick me up?'

'At your bed and breakfast,' Patty replied.

'But...' Ian paused. 'How do you know where that is?'

'I don't,' said Patty. 'But you always stay somewhere near Keswick during conference weekend so I headed there and hoped you'd have found a phone charger by the time I arrived.'

'How do you know..?'

'Oh Ian,' said Patty in a way that he would have bristled at from anyone else. 'If you ever looked at the credit card statement, you'd know it has business names and locations on it.'

'Ah.' All that pretence for nothing. He could have had his waterproof trousers with him. In a rucksack.

'So where are you?'

'Kendal,' said Ian.

'Kendal? What are you doing in Kendal?'

'Having a day out,' he said. Patty made an exasperated noise in reply. 'Don't worry, stay put and I'll see you in Keswick for lunch.' Patty murmured agreement and hung up. 'She knew!' he said. 'And I still don't know exactly where I'm meeting her.'

'Oh, I love it,' said Will. 'You can come again, Ian. Best laugh I've had all week.'

'My name's Janice,' said Janette. She looked annoyed. He ought to look up the timetable and head for a bus. On the other hand...

'Do you think you could give me a lift to Keswick, Janice?' said Ian. 'It seems I have to get to Cheshire from there.'

# Fake It Till You Hate It

*Sadia Azmat is a British stand-up comedian, writer and published author of* Sex Bomb. *In 2018, Sadia launched her critically acclaimed BBC podcast 'No Country For Young Women' which was named as one of the Best Audio 2018 by the* Observer *and Apple's Top Picks 2018.*

It's London, so it's grey. Only a glimmer of sunshine peeks through from beyond the clouds. Shamaila, short and brunette, is sat at her desk in the advertising agency, hunched over her laptop. She's 32 years old and single. As an Asian this means she has failed.

She doesn't really fit the usual stereotypes. She hates spicy food, isn't into Bollywood or mango lassi (the mass industrialisation of milk has a lot to answer for – can't say PETA never warned us). The truth is, what makes it decidedly harder these days, is that there isn't really anything that distinguishes what is quintessentially Indian. Is that a bindi or just a smudge of chocolate you rubbed on your forehead?

Shamaila went the academic route that was expected of her. She graduated with honours and holds an MBA in

Business, did the travel thing and landed herself a successful enough role as a Marketing Executive.

But she hates advertising. She can't abide any of it. It wasn't until she was in her second year that she knew it wasn't for her, but she couldn't drop out, she hadn't quit anything in her whole life. Despite a whole host of dropouts who do go on and achieve great things – Tom Cruise, Al Pacino and Mark Zuckerberg to name a few – she wouldn't have been able to deal with the uncertainty. Girls like her always have to have a plan. To deviate from said plan – no matter the quality of it – would open her up to a life less ordinary but equally a life that she would have absolutely no clue how to live. To defy expectations is glamorous but can also often be foolhardy. They say pick your battles but she just wanted a quiet life.

She got into advertising because – until she'd found out what it stood for – she had liked the idea of communication. But she'd realised it was all about sales, and it never sat right with her, to mislead innocent (or foolish) people. She tries to operate ethically but in marketing that's the equivalent of selling someone in a wheelchair a Peloton bike and letting them pay in instalments. Advertising is like the mob: once you get in, it's hard to get out. Not to mention having to consider a whole new identity.

The phone rings. It's her manager, Henrietta.

Henrietta is a white supremacist. She fired her last intern for sending a department-wide email about diversity awareness. Her issues with people of colour manifest not in the outright exclusion of them – that is too easy – but in the hiring and then swift firing of them. Think Liz Truss and Kwasi Kwarteng, that is just one example of what really is an epidemic.

Henrietta's more than stern; she wants a legacy for being a bitch. Even when she tries to disguise it with her fraught smiles, they convince nobody. If anything, they're more proof of how inhuman she is. She's in her fifties, curly burnt-red hair that doesn't quite go with the rest of her ensemble, and perplexed about being single. This is a middle-aged menopausal white woman who doesn't even own any cats.

Henrietta's been in the marketing game for two decades and she didn't get there out of any fondness for connectivity, no, she got there by sleeping around. She's slept with *so* many executives that she gives a whole new meaning to the Fortune 100. Despite the G-string of goodwill Henrietta's created, however, mutterings in the office regarding the fact that nobody of colour ever lasted more than two weeks had got back to the CEO. Shamaila is sure that's the only reason she's managed to cling on to her job.

Shamaila isn't stupid. She knows the score. *Turn up, do the work, keep your mouth shut.*

Shamaila's phone keeps ringing. She takes a deep breath. 'Hello'.

'Hi, Shamaila, have you got a second?' Less of a question, more an expectation.

'Sure.'

'Look, I've got a talk in two weeks and the usual Black girl we have can't make it, something about a lump in her breast, I need you to step in. You don't have to worry too much about prep — the main speakers will bear the brunt of it, we just need you for… aesthetics'.

*'Henrietta, I think it's time you stopped talking to me like I'm some livestock and actually get over yourself. You're a sick*

*woman who treats everyone like they're beneath her. You're not even that good at your job, you can go and find some other sucker cos I quit!'*

Well, that's what Shamaila *would* have said. It's not that she especially needs the job or the handsome fee. She had enough income from the smaller jobs ticking over – but marketing is a small world, and she can't risk word getting around. She was just like one of the tiny gadgets or campaigns she was hired to promote. Without the branding, she wouldn't exist. If she didn't deliver, rumours could circulate that she's having a breakdown or even worse, developed a conscience and so she replies, 'Sounds good, I will be there'.

These jobs didn't usually get to Shamaila. She was able to separate herself from the task to go through the motions. But this particular job made her feel dirty. More than Christina Aguilera's version of dirty – filthy on an internal level. She couldn't get out of it and it drove home that she was feeding a system that dehumanised not only her but literally all of humanity.

She'd made her peace with this all before. It didn't matter if people didn't see her as more than just a brown girl, she knew she stood for more than that, that's what counted. If she spent all of her time trying to reeducate ignorant people there would be no time for spa days.

Shamaila wrestled with her conscience that it isn't her fault, and that everyone starts somewhere, she didn't get in this game to change the entire industry, it was the laws of the jungle. She just wanted a place in it, it couldn't be solely on her terms. Besides, everyone has had a terrible boss.

Why should *she* have to suffer and be disadvantaged after all the effort she's put into making a career? The voice in the back of her mind chastised her: *Erin Brockovich wouldn't have taken this.*

She wondered whether she was the problem. Maybe if she did actually stand up for herself, or what she actually believes, she could be happier.

The following day Shamaila sat in Caffè Nero with the girls. It's lunchtime and the café is dimly lit with soft jazz playing in the background.

Shamaila confessed, 'I think it's time I moved'.

'Your avoidance issues just went up a notch,' Bushra comments as she casually she takes a bite of her mozzarella and tomato panini. She isn't emotional in the least – always practical and level-headed. She bakes for a living which helps her see everything in purely a measured way.

'This wouldn't happen in America,' Shamaila protests.

Bushra sniggles: 'America? You're kidding, right? They have fewer workers rights than Brits! They literally lay people off without any notice'.

Khadija, a doctor, gets involved sarcastically saying, 'I'll come America with you, I've heard they're huge fans of Muslims there.'

'I just don't want to be where I'm not wanted,' Shamaila proclaims to no one in particular; a feeble war cry.

'I've been making do. I just can't look myself in the mirror anymore – they don't have filters,' confesses Shamaila, lowering her gaze.

'Self-love is overrated, this is because you don't have any dick in your life, isn't it?' Bushra decides.

'Not everything is about dick you know,' Khadija chimes in. It's a sore spot for the present trio.

'How did three Asian women in their thirties manage to stay single? It's unheard of,' Khadija reflects.

'We're friendly, no criminal records', Bushra jokes.

'I can't put my finger on it, but somehow I'm sure it's the fault of the white man,' Khadija quips.

'Well, I blame Tinder – it's basically killed the arranged marriage and people started arranging their own,' Bushra declares flippantly.

'You mean hookups,' Shamaila hits back.

'Touché.'

'So are we going to America or staying here?' Khadija's bored.

'We?' Shamaila exclaims.

But before Khadija or Bushra can answer, Shamaila's phone rings. *Please not Henrietta again.* But when Shamaila looks down at the screen, she sees it's the CEO of the company.

He never calls.

'Girls, I've got to run back to the office'.

'Is everything OK?' Khadija asks, but Shamaila's already grabbed her jacket and shot out the door.

Shamaila runs back into head office out of breath. 'Stephen, what's happened'?

The whole company of 67 people are sat gathered in the big conference room.

Audrey, the secretary and longest serving member of the organisation is sniffling uncontrollably in thirty-second intervals (it's difficult to discern if the tears are of relief or of grief).

'Shamaila, I'm sorry I had to announce it to everyone.'

'What's happened'?

'It's Henrietta.' Audrey's sniffle is a high pitch and she's now in a flood of tears.

Stephen continues, 'She's no longer with us'.

Shamaila's jaw drops and she's confused. She sinks, almost falling, into the empty seat beside her.

She mumbles, 'What? What happened?', staring into space.

'Treadmill. She fell and sustained injuries. They did the best they could.' Stephen consoles. 'The thing is it doesn't end there, she left behind a list of tasks.'

Shamaila stares at Stephen blankly, her cheeks flushed. He looks down at a solitary A4 piece of paper left on the table.

Shamaila is shaking, even from the beyond Henrietta is ordering her around. 'Is this some sort of joke'?

Stephen, 'No. It's deadly – ah, it's serious. There's a few miscellaneous items, but she's asked you to arrange her funeral. It's all spelt out from the outfit she wants to be cremated in, to the music and even down to the speech.'

Shamaila holds herself back. 'I don't get it, how could she have known to leave a list of tasks? I don't think I'm the best person to do this. Isn't there anyone else?' Shamaila looks around the room. It's already dispersed. Audrey looks chirpier and is completing Wordle on her phone.

Nothing makes sense. Shamaila is completely numb. She didn't like Henrietta, nobody *liked* her, though she didn't wish this for her.

At the same time, it wasn't up to her to make funeral arrangements.

Stephen pleas with Shamaila: 'She has no next of kin.'

It hit home that there is *no* one else. Shamaila wonders if she could outsource the task to some independent third party, but no such services exist for the dead.

It is clear from his face that Stephen wasn't asking, he is telling.

The following day, as part of her errand duty, Shamaila visits Henrietta's house. She's visiting to collect some company papers and an outfit for Henrietta to wear at the funeral. But she's also keen to try and find out more about the person behind the monster.

There must have been something about her that was human.

She turns the key in the bright blue door and picks up several bits of post, putting them on the adjacent table.

There's a coat stand with a few different coats on it, an umbrella hanging up and some hats.

She's got the creeps knowing it's a dead person's house, but she perseveres. It's not like Henrietta's going to come back and haunt herself, Shamaila rationalises.

She definitely didn't have cats or any pets, Shamaila notices, wandering around.

She pops her head into the living room. It's weird-looking, all the ceilings are a very dark blue, the curtains are drawn and there's no light at all. Other than the sofa there's very little furniture.

Still no signs of definite humanity.

She heads upstairs.

The bed isn't made, and there's some exercise stuff dotted around. A Pilates ball on top of the cupboard, a yoga mat rolled up in the corner. No pictures. Again, the curtains are drawn.

Shamaila calls Bushra as she picks up a laptop and rummages through drawers in case there are any papers.

'Hi, I'm just at Henrietta's place,' Shamila says as Bushra picks up.

Bushra blurts out, 'Are you gonna hop onto the treadmill?'

'Bushra! Shamaila berates, 'I don't know what I should be looking for. She didn't have *anyone*. You're coming to the funeral aren't you?'

Bushra's in the middle of a pedicure and almost smudges her toes, 'You what? Don't be silly!'

Shamaila says, 'Come on Bushra, it's important to me, it's out of respect. She's no longer here!'

'You didn't like her; she was very racist,' Bushra splutters, 'and how comes she didn't have any family?'

'I dunno, ages ago I heard that she was estranged from her parents,' Shamilia admits, 'so I don't know who told them'. She peers down at her list to make sure it's not something she's meant to have done. It's not on the agenda. *Thank god.*

On the day of the funeral, Stephen's managed to bag a cremation, it was a two-for-one, he's saving the other one. He's also managed to find a distant relative to attend, her aunt Sally, although she refuses to speak to anybody.

Dressed in all black are Shamaila, Bushra and Khadija, though Bushra's outfit of a tight bodycon and high heels is more skimpy than funereal.

'You never know there may be some men that need consoling,' she'd exclaimed when the appropriateness of her outfit is brought up.

Shamaila looks around. She doesn't recognise many of the faces and wonders who they all are.

Stephen is meant to be giving a speech but texts Shamaila: *Sorry I can't make it, could you cover for me?*

Shamaila is stunned. She hasn't prepared anything. She knows that Henrietta would never have done the same for her, but that she can't say no. This isn't because the request has come from Stephen, it's just because she has to. A woman has died.

She's been in marketing long enough to wing it. Shamaila takes a deep breath and makes her way to the pulpit. She takes a sheepish look around, there are less than fifteen people there including her friends.

'How do I begin to find the words, when there are no words to surmise the loss that we all feel of Henrietta's passing. Grief *can be* crippling, she touched so many, with her work, with her rawness...'

A man raises his hand.

Shamaila's a little thrown. 'Are you OK?'

'I just want to say you're talking utter bullshit. She was a bitch to all of us, I for one am just here to make sure she's gone.'

The silence is deafening, interrupted only by some guests uncomfortably clearing their throats.

Shamaila thinks quickly. 'Sir, with respect, none of us are perfect. This is a respectful gathering to commemorate the memory of a person who meant a great deal.'

He grumbles and, before he can show greater signs of disruption, Shamaila quickly continues, 'I think what you're really dealing with right now is grief. I understand it's a horrible thing to have to say goodbye. What I'd like us to do right now is go around in a circle and say one thing that we can all change about ourselves for the better.'

Everyone looks confused.

Trying not to lose the room, and refusing to take no for an answer, Shamaila starts, 'I don't like how I'm a pushover. I am going to be better at doing the things that matter to me rather than people pleasing.'

Bushra joins in, 'It's difficult to beat perfection, but I'm going to try less hard. I think I need to accept myself for the things I'm good at but also the person I am when weaker, as that helps me to grow.'

The gentleman who was heckling confesses, 'I need to give up my gambling habit. I sometimes throw money on the horses even when I know they've not got any chance.'

As the group continues with their self-improvement hopes, the pianist starts to play "My Way" by Frank Sinatra which just about sums up Henrietta's entire life. Once everyone has finished Shamaila says, 'The last wish Henrietta had on her list was for everyone at the funeral, her nearest and dearest, to donate to her special cause: Zombie Squad, a zombie removal business who in their spare time support a whole host of good causes including disaster relief fundraisers, disaster preparation seminars and support emergency agencies.'

The room is aghast and the angry gentleman from earlier is now a lot more relaxed. 'A zombie removal squad – perhaps they can retire now that the battle-axe has gone!'

After a brief pause they burst into fits of laughter. The warmth and high-spiritedness wasn't something that Shamaila could have anticipated, but it's something she's truly thankful for. The vicar stands again and after he says some prayers and final words the coffin is taken away.

The party retires outside to a small garden.

Khadija says incredulously, 'Well done Shamaila, you did an incredible job.'

Shamaila laments, 'No one shed a tear.'

Bushra, 'Yeah but it's hard to grieve, like in public. People are complicated. It's the thought that counts.'

The man from the funeral comes up to Shamaila and says, 'Thanks so much for putting that together, it was lovely. I'm sorry I interrupted earlier, only she was my former employer. She fired me, stole my campaign and make a good amount of profit out of it too.'

So it wasn't just brown people that she had a thing against, Shamaila reflects. Without have much to say by way of consolation, she taps his shoulder and gives an empathetic smile.

The music continues playing and Shamaila reflects on the last few days.

She looks down at her list. She's sorted the funeral. She's started the estate arrangements.

There's still something that feels like it's unresolved.

She turns the page over.

'I really didn't want to keep you around but you were always so dependable. You can do better than marketing, you'll never make it without me now anyway. Henrietta.'

Shamaila smiles to herself; that's the Henrietta she knew, unapologetically cold.

The next day Shamaila walks into the head office.

'Shamaila,' Stephen welcomes her. 'Listen, thank you for holding the fort for me, I know it was a tough gig.'

Shamaila puts an envelope down onto his desk. 'Stephen, I quit.'

'What? Where has this come from?'

'This isn't what I want to do anymore,' she says.

'But you're really good at it, this is just a knee-jerk reaction. Look, I understand the last few weeks have been hard, and this has been a shock to us all. Why don't you take the week off?'

'I'm afraid I've made up my mind,' she resigns.

'How about we talk about your package? Look, with Henrietta's departure I'm going to need someone I can trust.'

It's tempting, it's so tempting.

Shamaila's so used to sacrifice. It's always had to be a choice, happiness or success. Career or relationship. Carbs or looking hot.

This time she chooses herself. She smiles at Stephen and raises her hand to say goodbye. She turns and opens the glass door and walks out.

The girls are all at Shamaila's place for a final get-together. Shamaila has decided to move to New York. She has the best immigration lawyer, and knows a relative there that she's going to stay with until she figures things out. They're stood around a cake as Shamaila cuts it.

'I can't believe you're going!' Khadija says.

'It's time', Shamaila concludes handing her a piece of velvety chocolate cake.

Bushra says, 'You got balls. That's not easy to go somewhere new.'

Shamaila replies, 'Thank you'.

'We got to stay in touch, promise,' Khadija gets upset.

'Come on, do you even have to ask?' Shamaila says.

The three hug and it gets too sickly for Bushra.

'What are you hoping to find?' Bushra alludes to the elephant in the room.

'On one level it's easy, the things that we all want to find. Love, security, peace. But if I know anything it's that things may not turn out the way we want them to, so I'm also trying to stay open to the things that I'm not expecting. Whether they're opportunities, adventure or just myself.'

# Glue

*The author of* The Mother and Daughter Diaries, Sageism *and some terrible parenting books, Clare Shaw has also written plays, radio plays, poetry and endless lists of things to do. She is now working on a comedic novel.*

Standing in my bedroom in my oversized hoodie that reaches to my knees (with a picture of the *Countdown* clock on the back) and my Susie Dent slippers, I am staring at myself in the mirror. Everything behind me looks the same – the Rick Astley poster, my chart of cereal packet designs through the ages, my collage of nineteenth century botanists, but me, I'm looking older and wiser. Because I have just made a decision.

I'm going out without my mother and I'm not only going out all on my own, I'm going to help save the world. Yes, me, Gillian Braithwaite of thirty-one Arcacia Avenue, collector of cereal packets and Rick Astley memorabilia is about to leave the house. On my own, I tell you, without the person I have been glued to all my life as if we are used Christmas cards stuck side by side in a scrapbook made by Matt Baker. In his Blue Peter years – he doesn't go in for glue so much on Countryfile. Unless you count cow dung which can really be quite sticky. I once did some research into all twenty-six types of glue but no one found it as interesting as me so I'll just leave that thought there.

I say I'm going out on my own, but of course I'll be in a group. Me, in a group! Me, Gillian Braithwaite, who was always the last to be picked for netball and who took my mum as my plus-one to the only party I've ever been invited to, is going to be in a group. And not just a group of Rick Astley fans either. In fact, it has nothing to do with Rick Astley, which is amazing and very surprising.

It's all organised: Forest Oak is picking me up on his tandem and I'll take my trumpet and my cereal boxes. I realise that my mother will want to follow behind to make sure I'm safe and I understand that. After all, it's a scary world out there and, as she so often reminds me, anything could happen. And apparently that anything won't happen if she is lurking in the vicinity, despite her bad knee and dodgy back. She follows me to school every day and is always waiting there when I come out again which is a bit embarrassing. Especially now I'm the deputy head. Yes, I am thirty-six and living at home with my mother. To be honest, I never thought there was anything wrong with that. Until I ended up in therapy.

It was Abi, head of history, who suggested it.

'Have you ever thought of talking to a professional about your relationship with your mother?' she said.

'I have a very good relationship with my mother,' I told her. 'So long as she knows where I am and who I'm with, which is fair.'

'It's not normal, Gillian,' she said. 'When was the last time you had a boyfriend? And no, swapping pictures of Rick Astley with the caretaker does not count as a relationship.'

'I've had plenty of relationships. But Mother didn't like Curtis. Or Timothy. Although she quite liked Rupert and we were going to move in together.'

'What happened?'

'He didn't like the idea of Mother coming too.'

'You definitely need therapy.'

I haven't told Mother about the therapy. I have a strong suspicion that it wouldn't be done to take a parent to the sessions with you. So, I told her I had weekly meetings with the school governors and she believed me although the truth is the governors only like meeting with the head as they find it annoying when I insist on scrutinising the minutes of the previous meetings. It has to be done; sometimes there are some very questionable uses of semi colons.

Even before the therapy, I was pretty self-aware. I knew exactly why I hadn't been popular at school and why I couldn't sustain a relationship. It's because I'm a geek and was geeky before being geeky became fashionable and in that respect, I was born at the wrong time. Also, I know I'm geeky in the wrong way. To be fashionably geeky, you need to be obsessed with gaming and IT and wear thick glasses and *Star Trek* t-shirts. But I'm obsessed with Rick Astley and *Countdown* and have twenty-twenty vision. See? The wrong sort of geek.

When I first walked into the therapy room, it wasn't what I expected. It was more like a living room with two comfy chairs, a plush carpet and pot plants on small oak tables. There were candles on every surface and it smelt of lavender, Dettol and Wotsits. Amanda smiled at me with her plump mouth, her straight blonde hair hanging down like curtains. She wore a long green skirt and a pale cheese-cloth shirt. She looked like a folk singer. I half expected her to burst into a ditty about dead sailors.

'Come and take a seat, Gillian.' Her voice was so soft I could barely hear and she ran the words together as if she had been smoking pot. Perhaps she had.

I sat down and immediately noticed an odd echoey sound.

'I think your plumbing needs a look at,' I said and she stared at me oddly. 'Sorry, I don't mean your personal plumbing in your body, I meant your actual pipes.'

'It's whale music,' she explained, forgetting to speak softly.

'Why?' I asked, but she didn't seem to have an answer to that.

'What brings you to therapy?' she said.

'I have difficulty sustaining a meaningful relationship,' I explained. 'It's because I'm the wrong sort of geek. I need to move on from Rick Astley to someone more current. I wondered about Ed Sheeran. Oh, and I probably need to ditch my Sylvanian Families collection. And wear different clothes. Maybe even stop watching *Countdown* on a loop. I need to reinvent myself.'

She looked me up and down, assessing my appearance. Other geeks can wear unfashionable clothing but my baggy jogging bottoms and washed-till-it's-grey Rick Astley t-shirt did make me look a bit disheveled compared to the perfect Amanda.

'What would it mean if you were to change?' she asked me.

'It would mean a trip to Primark,' I said.

Then she asked me about my parents.

'My dad left because he was ashamed of me and my mother follows me everywhere in case I go missing,' I said.

'Ah,' she said and wrote something down as if what I had said was somehow significant.

Over the weeks, Amanda led me into believe I needed to go out on my own and act more like a grown up and that's when I began to talk to Professor Green next door. It started with just chatting over the fence (Amanda had said to take small steps) and eventually I even went round for a coffee. Without Mother. Although to be fair, her surveillance cameras cover both his front and back doors so she knew where I was and was able to monitor when I came out again. He told me about the climate crisis and I began to form my own opinions, some of which were different from Mother's. I could feel the change coming.

So that's where I'm going. On a climate change march. I have a trumpet to blow and a banner to carry although there's no way I can sneak them out of the door without Mother noticing. But Amanda says I shouldn't be sneaking, I have the right at thirty-six years old to go where I want. She doesn't know Mother.

'I'm off to a climate change march,' I say in the firm voice I've been practising. Except it comes out sort of shaky as if I'm sitting on the washing machine on fast spin.

We're standing in the kitchen which hasn't been changed since the seventies, although I'm told orange units and brown linoleum floors are coming back into fashion at last. Mother has just put something in the oven as we gave the microwave away when Mum's friend, Betty, said they are the main cause of Alzheimer's.

'You've been talking to that dodgy neighbour again, haven't you?'

'He's Professor Green. He's a scientist. Hardly dodgy,' I explain in my new assertive tone.

'He has some dodgy ideas about the climate.'

'He's done intensive research, Mum. He's been on Radio Four talking about it all. He's written scientific papers on climate change.'

'Doesn't make him an expert,' Mum insists.

'It kind of does, Mum.'

'I've written on climate change myself,' she says, 'and I've researched it.'

But what Mothermeans is that she's tweeted about it all. And she gets her information from Betty who works at the sandwich shop. I tell her that retweeting Betty's conspiracy theories does not amount to being an expert.

'It's just an anomaly in the weather. It'll put itself right in time,' she says.

'That's not what the scientists say.'

Of course they don't. They're working for the government. And the government want us to be scared. Look at the pandemic.

'The pandemic was real, Mum. People died.' I'm really holding my own in this conversation. Amanda would be proud of me. But Mum isn't shifting.

'Old people and poor people died. People who don't pay taxes. People who are indispensable. Coincidence? I don't think so. And now you're being sucked into this climate crisis nonsense.'

How can she accuse me of being sucked in when she was well and truly sucked in when Betty said she'd seen

Princess Diana in Marks and Spencers. I point this out to her.

'I admit that was a mistake,' she says, and it looks as if I'm winning the argument but then she adds, 'We now know Princess Diana is alive and well and living in Tunbridge Wells. She was spotted buying salami in the delicatessen.'

'Never mind about Diana, we topped forty degrees this year. You can't argue with fact.'

Mum even has an answer to that. 'It's the population getting older that's done it. All the menopausal women giving off heat.'

'What's caused the floods then? Stress incontinence?' I am now being witty. This therapy is reaching more parts of me than I thought possible. But then Mum starts pleading.

'If Betty says it's not a thing, then it's not a thing. It's fake news. Please, Gillian, don't go on this march.'

I realise this has got nothing to do with her views on climate change. She just doesn't want me to go. But then she changes her mind.

'But if you insist. I'll get my bag.'

'No, Mum, I'm going with Forest Oak. He's picking me up on his tandem.'

At this, she turns pale and has to sit down on the bottom stair. I go and fetch her a glass of water.

'You won't be safe,' she says. 'Fetch me the paper.'

But I am now a rebel so instead of fetching the paper, I fetch my banner, although it's something of a blank canvas as I haven't written anything on it yet.

'It looks like a lot of bran flake packets sellotaped together,' she says.

'It is. I'm just going to write my slogan on it.'

'You must have eaten an awful lot of bran flakes. You definitely can't go. You'll need to be within running distance of the bathroom.'

I ignore her and write my slogan in big bold letters: *DON'T BE A FOSSIL FOOL.*

'You've spelt fuel wrong,' Mother says and I explain about the play on words but she's still urging me to fetch the paper.

I am still in rebel mode so instead I give her a blast on my old toy trumpet.

'That's my point exactly,' she says. 'You can be arrested now for making a noise like that. It's disturbing the peace and you're not allowed to block the traffic or be in a noisy crowd. They're going to arrest anyone who blows a trumpet.'

'Arrest?'

'Yes. It's in the paper.'

I put being a rebel on pause and dutifully fetch the paper and listen while Mother reads out a very stark warning.

'See,' she says, 'you'll get a criminal record and then you won't be able to teach anymore.'

Now I'm worried. It's all I have in my life – I'm good at teaching. I mean I know the kids laugh at me but they also respect me because of my enthusiasm for history. I've shown them that history teaches us so much about what we should and shouldn't do in the present. That thought gives me my lightbulb moment.

'But, Mum, I want to be one of the heroes who goes down in history. Protests got the equal pay act. They helped get rid of Apartheid. They got rid of Poll Tax. Look at Ghandi and his salt protest. Mandella. Emily Pankhurst. Martin Luther King. All heroes.'

'All dead,' she says.

I think about my therapy and decide to channel Amanda. I even use the soft and gentle therapeutic voice.

'I understand that you're worried about me,' I begin.

'What? I can't hear what you're saying?'

I go back to my usual voice. 'I won't do anything that risks being arrested so you don't need to be anxious. I understand why you worry so much but that's something you need to deal with yourself.'

'Blow that trumpet and you'll be arrested and then what will happen to me?'

I forget about the therapy and go and fetch the box of old musical instruments. I pull out a biscuit tin and wooden spoon. Still too loud according to Mother so I muffle it with an old vest. Then I realise I can't bang the drum and hold my banner at the same time so I blow a few notes on my old recorder. But even I decide recorders should be universally banned and a prison sentence handed out to any recorder group playing 'London's Burning' in a round.

I try a tambourine but feel like I should be singing out for Jesus so I end up with one maraca which barely sounds louder than a whisper. Then Mother tries an old tactic.

'My back's playing up again. And my knee. Fetch me the emergency number in case I fall on the floor and can't get up.'

'It's 999, Mum.'

'Write it down for me. Of course I might not have my phone in reach. I could be lying on the floor for hours with no water, in intense pain.'

I have fallen for this before. As a child, I missed so many school trips and as for trying to meet up with colleagues socially, she would always have a flare up with her knee, a grumbling appendix or on one occasion a definite case of malaria. But I have been to therapy. I have strategies which I have worked out with the whispering Amanda.

'I'll pop next door and ask Professor Green to keep an eye. Bye, Mum.'

I dash for the door and she tries to run in front to bar the way, her knee and back seeming to have made a remarkable recovery. But I make it there first and I arrive on Professor Green's doorstep.

Five minutes later I am back inside my own house. Mother is frantically dancing along to Abba, looking like Theresa May on crack.

'My doctor said to try and keep it moving,' she says, 'but it's hard.' Her hand goes to her back and then to her knee and she grimaces. 'Still, I'm glad you changed your mind. Only I was thinking, if climate change is a thing, then they'd have Chris Whitty on the telly in shorts and a sun hat with slides about the rise in temperature and advice on where to pick up your free canoe in case of floods.'

'I've come back for my trumpet,' I say defiantly. 'Professor Green told me to. He also said I should break the law if needs be. He's given me some glue. I'm going to glue myself to the bridge. He called me a hero. Professor Green. I mean, wow. Me, a hero.'

'You're not a hero, you're just a rebellious little girl.'

'I'm a thirty-six-year-old woman, Mum. And I want to be a rebel. Must go, Forest Oak is here with his tandem.'

She looks out of the window and points out that it isn't Forest Oak but Arnold Higgins, the butcher.

'He likes to be called Forest Oak,' I say.

'Sounds like one of them toilet fresheners.'

'I think it sounds cool. Like Swampy. Must go. Bye.'

I lean against the wall outside amazed at what I have done. I can hear Mother's voice inside shouting at me.

'Gillian, wait! I'll make you some egg sandwiches and a flask of tea.' Then a pause followed by, 'Swampy. Forest Oak. What next? I might as well call myself Rustic Bush.'

I've done it. I have escaped. I am a new person. I might ditch the old me who has held onto her GCSE revision notes all these years and be someone that embraces the new. I might stop watching *Countdown* with Mother and start going to Green Party meetings. Anything is possible. Although, on reflection, there might be things in those revision notes that could come in handy. I suppose I'm a work in progress. I climb onto Forest's tandem and away we go, wind in our hair, our legs pumping up and down like pistons.

I start to think about Mother. What if she does fall on the floor? What if she's right and protesters all smoke weed, break the law and wear inappropriate footwear? I don't think I'm up to smoking drugs. I don't even drink caffeine in case it affects my ability to solve the conundrum on *Countdown*.

'I'm having doubts,' I shout to Forest.

He reels off a speech about floods in Pakistan and starvation in Ethiopia and islands in the Caribbean sinking.

'My mother says we can't afford to go to the Caribbean anyway.'

Forest laughs and I laugh too. I am being funny again. Suddenly I see myself doing a stand-up performance based on things my mother has said. Live at the Apollo. This could be a whole new career for me.

'There's not much that's great about Switzerland,' I say, 'but the flag is a big plus.'

Forest doesn't laugh so I rethink my career and start moaning about my mother again.

'She thinks global warming's a good thing because we don't need to bother going to Benidorm when Skegness will be just as hot and with better fish and chips.'

He laughs again and I realise that Mother's views are indeed funny. And if I can laugh at them, it will surely help.

'My mother doesn't like me going out on my own,' I say, 'she thinks I'll get kidnapped.'

I laugh. Forest doesn't. 'That's sick, man,' he says.

'No, you don't understand, it's not her fault. You see...'

But we've arrived and there are crowds of people with drums and banners and the atmosphere is electric. People are smiling at each other and there's this intense feeling of camaraderie. I blow my trumpet.

'Sounds like a fanfare for the Queen,' Forest says.

'Shit fanfare,' I say, 'although I suppose it could be for Andrew.'

It seems I am funniest when I have no intention of being funny. Oh well.

I'm thirsty and a bit peckish and regret not waiting for my mother's flask and sandwich but there's a Tesco Express right where we're gathering so I decide to pop in for a can of drink and a bar, not realising that this is where it will all go very wrong.

I choose my items and go to the self-service checkout but as I get my card out, the glue comes out with it and somehow the top comes off and then it all happens so fast. What was once an ordinary self-service checkout station at Tesco Express turns into a scene from *Mr Bean* meets *It'll Be All Alright on the Night*.

'Help,' I call, as I somehow get my hand glued to the bagging area. A young man with a badge declaring himself to be called Gary runs over and somehow I get glued to him as well. 'Unexpected item in the bagging area,' blares out over and over, drawing a great deal of attention. A group of three policemen arrive and I mutter, 'Thank goodness' because I know they have that stuff that can unglue protestors from roads. But they all get out their phones and start laughing and taking photos. I try and pull myself off Gary and he ends up sprawled over the checkout and now customers are abandoning their bumper bags of cheese and onion crisps and their three-for-two on jam doughnuts as they join the police in taking their own videos and photos. I try and hide my face but imagine it's all over social media by now. I can hear the clicks and whirrs of the phones and begin to understand how Princess Diana must have felt when the press hounded her. I have not felt this embarrassed since Mother ran into the school hall when I was taking assembly with a warm vest for me because it 'had turned a bit nippy.' I groaned again at the thought of Mother saying, 'I told you not to go. Next time, you'd better mark my words.'

Eventually, the police manage to unglue me from Gary and the checkout and a policeman who looks as if he's twelve-and-a-half decides it was a planned protest and arrests me for a breach of the peace.

'It was an accident,' I protest.

'Save it for down at the station,' he says.

'Can I have a blanket for my head?' I ask. I don't want Mother seeing this on the six o'clock news.

'You haven't committed murder,' he says, 'although I think Gary is receiving treatment for shock so you never know.' He laughs along with his two colleagues who seem to be enjoying this in a rather unprofessional way.

The next thing I know I am bundled into the back of the van. Forest Oak is already in there.

'I broke a window at the bank,' he declares. 'They support fossil fuel companies. All good publicity.'

He looks at me and I realise he wants to know what I'm doing here.

'I glued myself to the checkout in Tesco express,' I say. 'It was an accident.'

'Good on you. I didn't know you had it in you.'

'No, you don't understand. I've just made a prat of myself.'

'Not at all,' Forest insists.

At the police station, I have to empty my pockets. I pull out a few coins, my bank card, six photos of Rick Astley, a note from my mother reminding me to send Uncle Trevor a birthday card, an ironed handkerchief I didn't know I had (it must have been put there by Mother), a list of things to do with urgent matters highlighted in yellow, another note from my mother with the numbers to phone in case of accidents (111 or 999), two small folded up cereal packets from the variety set, a letter I'd written to Kellogg's but hadn't yet sent and a pencil.

A police woman, clearly experienced in taking statements and sarcasm interviews me.

'I only went in to get a drink and a bar.'

'Course you did.'

'The top came off the glue by accident.'

'Course it did.'

'It was given to me by Professor Green, eminent scientist.'

'Course it was.'

'I would never have had the courage to use it as a protest.'

'Course you wouldn't. Actually, I bet you wouldn't. You teach my niece. I doubt you were involved in this protest at all. You wouldn't say boo to a goose.'

'In that case, I really was involved in the protest,' I say, 'because I'm a new person. I want to be a hero protesting against climate change. The system needs to change and I want to be part of making that happen. And if that means gluing myself to the checkout and someone called Gary, then so be it.'

I am pleased with my outburst. This is more like it, I think. I finish off my mini speech with, 'And I will prove my mother wrong.'

I leave the police station to more cameras flashing and people shouting. I cringe and duck my head. I need time to process what had just happened. I may have just made a fool of myself in Tesco and at the police station. I need to be on my own to think it all through so I run across the road to the park and stride down to the river where I find a bench. I decide to sit and stare at the ducks and swans until the rest of the protest is over. It's peaceful there away from the town centre, with just the sound of the river gently bubbling along and the occasional flap of birds' wings.

I decide it must be glorious to be a swan, just scrabbling about in the weeds, floating along nonchalantly with nothing that could possibly embarrass you. No wonder they seem so superior as if they are looking down at us. They quite simply have no cares or worries except perhaps a passing thought that a member of the royal family might have them roasted for dinner. And even better, when their cygnets reach a certain age, they chase them off and never see them again. I think of Mother chasing me off. If only.

Suddenly, someone is next to me and throwing lumps of bread towards the river. It's Gary from Tesco Express.

'By the way you dropped this,' he says, handing me a photo of Rick Astley. 'Very underrated,' he adds.

'You're a fan?'

'Massive.'

'Sorry about the glue.'

'Not your fault. Anyway, they gave me the rest of the day off. I went to the police and explained it was an accident.'

'Thank you.'

'If ever you want to come round and play Rick Astley records. Or see my collection of train tickets. Sorry. Of course you don't.'

Then he walks away. I know that if I was in a romcom, I'd be running after him but I don't. Because I'm not sure I'd have anything in common with someone who collects train tickets. I mean come on, even I have lines that can't be crossed.

I walk home slowly, knowing that by now Betty and her team of news reporters will have got word to Mother that I'd been arrested by the police and bought shame upon the family. It would, of course, give her even more reason to follow me about and keep tabs on my every move. I need to move out, I decide, but then I've been telling myself that for a very long time. Or at least since seeing a therapist. I decide to phone her.

'Hello, Amanda? Any chance of an emergency session?'

I soon find myself enveloped by the pungent odour of lavender, sipping a bland cup of chamomile tea which manages to taste of absolutely nothing, not even water.

'I glued myself to the checkout and Gary who works there and collects train tickets.'

'And how does that make you feel? Mmmm?'

'Like a prat.'

'Mmmm.'

Amanda does an awful lot of humming and nodding.

'I can't face Mother.'

'And how does that make you feel? Mmm?'

I look up to check that Amanda's actually there and hasn't left a recording which is playing the same phrase on a loop.

'I'm not sure this is helping,' I say.

'And how does that make you feel?"

I want to say, 'Like punching you in the face', but I don't. Instead I try and explain why Mum acts the way she does.

'Then maybe it's your mother that needs the therapy.'

'It is, you're right.'

'So, in summary, you feel like a prat, you don't think this is helping and you believe it's your mother that needs the therapy.'

'That's about the gist of it.'

'And how does that make you feel?'

I go home without booking another session.

I open the front door and let myself in as quietly as I can. Then I creep up the stairs like a burglar.

'Is that you?'

'Yes, Mum. I just need to get changed. I'll be down in a jiffy.'

I lie on the bed. I play Rick Astley's 'Cry For Help' and I sob into my pillow. My phone pings and I glance at it and see Professor Green has messaged me. I have let him down. Only a few hours earlier, I had been an activist, someone who was going to help save the planet. Someone who was part of something that wasn't an online Rick Astley appreciation society. Or a group who post things they've made out of cereal boxes. It was supposed to be a new me.

Mum shouts up again. 'Do you want some bananas and custard?'

'No, thanks.'

Then I look at Professor Green's message.

*You're a hero*, it says.

*Not at all*, I type back. *It didn't go well.*

*It went brilliantly. Look at the Gazette. And the nationals are picking up the story too.*

I switch on my laptop and log onto the Gazette online.

Then I hear Mum knocking on the door. She has bought me a cup of tea and a slice of battenburg. I smile. I love my Mum, I just wish she'd let me grow up. But as Amanda says, that's up to me. I will move out but first I decide I'd better show her the photo in the Gazette.

I turn my laptop to face her. 'A picture taken in Tesco Express,' I explain.

'Oh my,' she says, 'they're doing three-for-two on tins of custard. I must get down there.'

'No, look again. At the headline.'

'*Heroes make us all climate crisis aware.* I can't see any heroes.'

'Look, Mum, it's me, glued to Gary at the checkout. I'm a hero. It says so here.'

I look at my phone as a text comes in. Professor Green is telling me to look at social media.

'I've gone viral. I've got ten thousand likes. There's a petition against me being fined. I can hold my head up. Professor Green says it'll be in the nationals. Maybe TV.'

Mum is looking confused but she looks up at the mention of TV and the national press.

'You mean, you're famous? For gluing yourself to someone called Gary? Is it a new game show?'

'No, Mum. I've helped make people aware of the climate crisis.'

Mum smiles and at last seems pleased. 'Well, that is something. Betty will be very jealous. I knew I was right to encourage you to go on that march. Everyone will know who you are now. That'll stop anyone stealing you.'

Mum is obsessed with someone stealing me. She just can't let it go. It was thirty-six years ago when I was only a few days old. And the woman who took me didn't do me any harm. She just wanted to look after me when she lost her own baby. I was found within a couple of hours but it has affected our relationship for all these years. It is going to be so hard to leave home. I am about to suggest she sees Amanda when a new comment flashes up on my phone.

'Oh my god. David Attenborough supports what I did. I mean, David Attenborough.'

'The dentist?'

'No, Mum. THE David Attenborough. Betty really will be impressed,' I say.

'Don't tell me David Attenborough believes in this climate crisis nonsense,' Mum says. 'He can't get involved. He's a National Treasure.'

'Of course he does. Look.' I show her his comment and then add, 'There are plenty of national treasures calling for action. Emma Thompson, Prince William.'

'I'm not so keen on Emma Thompson, she takes her clothes off rather more often than necessary, but David Attenborough. If David Attenborough says it's a thing, then it must be true. Pass me the trumpet. I might do a protest of my own.'

She blows the trumpet and asks me for some cereal packets to make her own banner.

'What are you going to write on it, Mum?'

'I will write – *IF DAVID ATTENBOROUGH SAYS IT'S A THING, THEN IT'S A THING. TAKE ACTION NOW.*

'Perfect.'

The following week, she has an appointment to see Amanda. She comes back red-eyed and looking exhausted.

'How did you get on?' I ask.

'Betty's right. It's just a lot of chatting over a cup of something very odd tasting. Drugs probably.'

'Chamomile tea.'

'I knew it was drugs.'

But something is shifting because when I tell her I'm buying my own flat, she accepts it.

'I see it's got two bedrooms,' she says, testing the water.

'Yes, but I'm renting the second room out to a friend to help with the mortgage payments. I'll still see you a lot. It's time to let go, Mum. I am thirty-six.'

The friend is Gary. We've bonded over Rick Astley and an interest in the history of trams. And before you ask, we are not having sex. Gary says he finds it too messy and unpredictable. We are just good friends. This is not, as I have said, a romcom. It's a simple story of two women letting the old, unwanted glue finally melt away.

# Care Home Capers

*After many years working as a chartered physiotherapist and university lecturer, Wendy Hood decided to follow her creative passion and completed a full-time MA in Creative Writing. As well as writing, she also loves reading, paper-crafting and making music, and can often be found riding a tandem with her husband or walking along the seafront.*

The staff were rounding up the residents, herding them all into the lounge and encouraging them to take up their positions in the high-backed, wipe-clean seats. Zimmer frames were moved out of the way under the ruse of health and safety to avoid trips, but they all knew that it was really to prevent any chance of an early escape.

'Where's Ethel?' Maureen asked, not even trying to disguise the irritation in her voice. She glanced at the fob watch dangling from her beige tunic, and shook her head.

'Where do you think she is?' Frank answered, easing his scrawny frame onto the chair.

'If I knew that, I wouldn't have asked!'

'She'll be hiding in the toilet, where she always is when she doesn't want to be found.'

'But they'll be here in a minute.' Maureen said, looking at her watch again, as though to emphasise her point.

'Aye, I know. That's why she'll be in the toilet.' Frank chuckled.

Frank took his hearing aids out and shoved them into his pocket, just as the doorbell chimed.

'Here we are!' Matron said in a sing-song voice, as she led the snaking line of children through the aisle in the middle of the lounge to the area, which had been cleared for them to stand. Their teacher bustled around, positioning the children in lines and separating out those who clutched little draw-string bags. These children were placed to one side, and the teacher then proceeded to assemble music stands in front of them.

'Oh no, please don't let it be the violins again.' Charlie mumbled, looking at Frank, but Frank just smiled and nodded because he couldn't hear. 'My ears haven't recovered from the last visit of those bloody violins. I still have nightmares about them. Surely, they wouldn't make us sit through that again?'

As the teacher placed sheets of music on each of the stands she had just assembled, the children opened their draw-string bags and pulled out recorders. There was a collective moan amongst the residents, as more hearing aids were rapidly pulled out and stashed away.

Just as the teacher was starting to announce the first piece, there was a loud clattering sound, as Ethel crashed into the door with her walking frame. Maureen was standing beside her, trying unsuccessfully to hurry her along and shushing her in the process. But Ethel wasn't going to be hurried and she certainly wasn't going to be shushed! She stomped her frame on the floor all the harder for Maureen's efforts.

Frank grinned. Even he had heard the commotion as Ethel made her way slowly and noisily to the chair beside him. *That's my girl!* He thought, winking at her as her portly posterior flopped heavily onto the seat, which made a raspberry-like noise as the air was squashed out of the cushion. Two children in the front row started to giggle, and the hilarity rippled through the choir until they had all lost control. Dark pink blotches blossomed on the young teacher's neck, gradually progressing upwards to redden her face as she hissed at the children, trying to regain their attention.

'Here, Frank. What're they laughing at?' Ethel shouted, which just spurred the children into more fits of giggles.

Frank patted the pocket where his hearing aids were, shrugged and shook his head, then nodded to give Ethel a heads up that trouble was on the way.

'Will you behave?!' Maureen whispered as she waddled over to Ethel's side.

'What was that, dear?' Ethel asked, smiling sweetly.

'You heard!'

Matron nodded nervously at the teacher, giving her the go-ahead to proceed. The teacher stepped forward and cleared her throat.

'Good afternoon, everyone. I am pleased to present to you St Agnes' School choir and recorder group. We will start with a song, that I am sure you will all know.'

'We might know it, but whether we'll recognise it is an entirely different matter!' Charlie muttered, earning him a dig in the ribs from Mabel who was sitting next to him.

A chorus of over-blown descant recorders emitted shrieks across the room, piercing through to even the deafest ears. That pretty much set the tone for the afternoon and things went rapidly downhill from there.

'I'm all for inclusivity,' Charlie grumbled, 'but wouldn't you have thought that they would tell the grunters just to mime?'

'Sshh! You can't say something like "grunters" nowadays!' Mabel said, looking around to make sure nobody else had heard.

'Why not? That what they used to be called when I was at school.'

'Yes, I know, but things are different now. There will be some sort of term like "musically challenged" or "differently gifted" that you have to use so as not to upset anyone.'

'Hmmph. hey don't seem to mind too much about upsetting my ears! You know, I never thought I would envy Frank his lack of hearing, but at times like this it makes you wonder...'

'Oh, I don't know. Even Frank isn't deaf enough to be fully spared from this. I'm sure I saw him wince at least twice in the middle of that last piece.'

'Somehow that makes me feel so much better to know that the suffering is shared!'

'Look, we're getting the evil eye from Maureen, best keep quiet, eh?'

'Spoilsport!'

When the last piece was announced, a flutter of applause broke out in the lounge.

'Hey, for goodness' sake don't clap too hard; we don't want a bloody encore!' Ethel piped up, her voice louder than even she had intended. There were chuckles from the residents sitting nearby and a faltering smile from the teacher, who looked as though she wasn't sure whether to laugh or cry. Maureen and Matron were both keeping their heads down, pretending not to have heard.

When the children had finished, Matron stepped up.

'Well, that was lovely. Thank you so much for coming to entertain us, we have had a thoroughly enjoyable afternoon, haven't we everyone?' She looked around the room at the residents, who were all avoiding eye contact.

'Not at all. It has been a pleasure to come, and we look forward to seeing you all again next term,' the teacher said, smiling broadly.

'Not if we see you first!' Charlie mumbled, earning him another dig from Mabel.

The next morning Frank, Charlie, Ethel and Mabel sat together for breakfast.

'My ears are still smarting from that caterwauling yesterday,' Charlie grumbled.

'Mine too. It was bad enough having to go to school concerts when our own kids were learning to play musical instruments. Why would anyone think that we would want to hear other people's kids making such a din?' Ethel said.

'Yes, how would they like it if we turned up at their school and made such a noise?' Charlie said.

'You know what? I think you might just be a genius, Charlie!' A mischievous smile spread across Ethel's face as she looked around the table.

'Oh no. I recognise that look. What are you up to my girl?!' Frank said, shaking his head.

'Well, perhaps that's what we should do.' Ethel slapped her hand enthusiastically on the table, making the cutlery jump.

'What?' Frank asked, looking worried.

'Have I lost the plot here, or does anyone else not have the first idea what we are talking about?'

'Come on Mabel, keep up. I'm just saying that maybe if we formed a choir of our own and inflicted ourselves onto the school, it might make them think twice about coming back, if they thought it might become a reciprocal arrangement.'

'Don't be silly, Ethel.' Mabel said, 'How could we possibly form a choir? Who would want to listen to us trying to sing at our age, anyway? Half of us are stone deaf, and the other half are probably tone deaf.'

'I think that's her point.' Frank said. 'I can't see Matron letting us unleash ourselves on the poor public though.'

'You'd probably be right, if she heard us beforehand. But if we managed to find somewhere to practice and we just asked her to arrange for us to go to the school as a surprise, I bet she would go for it. You know, if we dressed it up as community engagement and all that.'

'Ethel, my dear, I think you might be on to something here. Do we have any pianists in our midst, who could accompany us?' Charlie said.

'Never mind pianists. Didn't old Fraser say he used to play the bagpipes?'

'Oohh, now you're talking! I believe he did.' Charlie's puffy face lit up at the thought.

'Hang on a minute. Fraser has emphysema. I can't imagine he will be able to play the bagpipes in his state, even if he still had a set to play.' Frank pointed out.

'We could always ask him. It's worth a try, isn't it?' Ethel said. 'Talk of the devil, isn't that Fraser over there?'

They all turned towards the door to see a spindly man, dressed in trousers that looked two sizes too big for him, walking towards a table on the other side of the room.

'Hey, Fraser. Over here!' Ethel yelled, shuffling her chair over to make room for him.

'I thought this table was full.' Fraser said in his lilting Scottish accent.

'There's always room for one more. Go and grab some cutlery off that table over there and come and join us.'

'Why do I get the feeling that you're up to something?' Fraser said, as he heaved a wooden chair from the next table along and squeezed it into the gap that Ethel and Frank had created.

'Probably because she is.' Mabel said raising her eyebrows as Ethel stuck her tongue out playfully.

'Come on then, out with it.'

'We were just wondering if you still had a set of bagpipes?' Ethel asked, smiling sweetly at Fraser.

'Oh my! Why on earth would you want to know that?'

'Just wondering. So? Do you?'

'Well, not here, obviously. I think my son might have kept them though. They're probably up in his loft.'

'He lives locally, doesn't he?' Ethel probed.

'Yes, just a few minutes down the road.'

'Fantastic! Next time he comes to visit, would you ask him to bring the bagpipes in?'

'And why would I do that? Come on, spit it out. What's this really all about?'

Fraser laughed out loud when Ethel finished explaining what she was planning to do, and then the laughing set off a coughing episode, which seemed to go on forever. When he had finally settled, Ethel looked at Fraser and raised her eyebrows.

'Well? What do you think?'

'I think it's brilliant, but I also think that you're all mad! It's years since I tried to play those things, and what, with this blasted emphysema, you'd be lucky if I could get a squawk out of the pipes, let alone a tune.'

'But would you be up for trying?' Ethel persisted.

'For you, my dear, why not?'

'Excellent! Now all we need is a place to practice. Any ideas?'

'How about the church hall just down the road? It's less than a five-minute walk and there's a ramp up to the entrance, so it shouldn't pose any access problems. We should all be able to hobble our way down there. Those who are ambulatory can push those who aren't.' Frank suggested.

'That would be perfect. Does anyone know who we would need to contact to ask if we can use it?' Ethel asked.

'I could ask the vicar on Sunday. I think the hall is free most mornings, so I can't imagine there would be a problem,' Mabel said.

'OK. So, here's the action plan. Fraser, you will ask your son to try to find your bagpipes and sneak them in without Matron seeing. Mabel, you are going to find out about booking the church hall for a few morning practices. Once we have the venue sorted, we can then start to assemble our choir. Everyone agreed?'

There was quite a buzz around the home for the next few days as the word of Ethel's plan gradually spread amongst the residents.

'I managed to persuade the vicar to let us have the church hall on Wednesday and Friday mornings for the next month, free of charge,' Mabel announced when they sat down to dinner a few days later.

'Good on you!' Ethel said.

'Aye, that helpless little old lady routine works every time, doesn't it!' Charlie said, winking at Mabel, who raised her bony elbow, threatening to prod him with it.

'I prefer to think that it is my feminine charm that does it.' She said, batting her eyelids, whilst trying to keep her face straight.

'Package delivered and duly hidden.' Fraser chipped in, with an exaggerated nod.

'OK, don't get too carried away.' Frank said. 'And for goodness' sake make sure you don't try said package out until we are in the church hall. Oh, and even then, could you give me a heads up before you do, so that I can take my hearing aids out?'

'Will do.'

'What about those of us who don't have hearing aids?' Charlie asked,

'Don't worry, I'll bring a packet of cotton wool,' Ethel said.

'Excellent. Now all we have to do is find out who's in. If we each sit on a different table for breakfast in the morning, we should be able to sound out pretty much everyone. Once we have an idea of numbers, we can meet back here at lunchtime, and take it from there.'

'Good idea, Frank,' Charlie said, 'now will somebody please pass me the salt so that I can try to inject some flavour into this concoction. What did they say this was supposed to be?'

'I think it was going to be the hotpot today,' Mabel said, passing the salt to Charlie.

'Isn't hotpot supposed to have lumps in?' Frank asked.

'Yes, but I think they're frightened to give us anything with lumps in now, since the incident with Betty's teeth,' Ethel said, shovelling a forkful of brown goo into her mouth.

'Ah, yes, I'd forgotten about that. Poor Betty!'

The next morning, as planned they all sat at different tables, thoroughly confusing the staff.

'What's going on here?' Maureen asked. 'Why the sudden change in seating arrangements? Has there been a falling out?'

'No, it's just nice to have a change every now and again, don't you think?' Frank said, his face a mask of innocence.

'Hmmm, if you say so,' but Maureen didn't look convinced.

When lunchtime came, Maureen looked even more confused.

'What happened to changing things up?' she asked.

'Oh, that was fun, but you can get too much of a good thing, you know,' Charlie said, a grin spreading across his face as Maureen walked away, shaking her head. 'OK, how did we all get on? I signed Whinny up, but Betty is out because of her teeth. Joe didn't want to come without Betty, and I couldn't get any sense out of Geoffrey.'

'Well, Maud and Isobel are up for it,' Ethel said, 'but I didn't get any other takers.'

'I got Pete,' Fraser said.

'And Dotty and Doug are both in. What about you, Mabel? Any takers?'

'I'm afraid not, Frank.'

'Well, that's not a bad turnout. It looks as though we have ten in the choir and one musician. That should do nicely,' Ethel said, taking a bite of cheese sandwich.

Wednesday morning came and Mabel, who was a favourite amongst the staff, was dispatched to have a word with Matron.

'There's a new club for us oldies that they're starting in the church hall, so a few of us would like to go along and try it out if that's OK?'

'Oh, that sounds nice. If you could give me a list of who's going, I'll send Maureen along with you to make sure you get there safely.'

'Really, there's no need. We have it all worked out. Frank will push Pete in his chair and I will walk with Ethel to make sure she doesn't cause any more damage with her walker.' Mabel grimaced and looked at the floor. 'You know, I think she really does feel bad about that. I'm sure she never intended to break anything, but those things can be difficult to steer sometimes you know...'

'Hmmm, I'll have to take your word for that,' Matron said, folding her arms.

'Anyway, Maud, Isobel and Fraser will walk together to keep each other upright. Charlie will help Whinny with her sticks, and Doug will push Dotty's chair, so I think we have it all covered. Maureen could watch us from the door, if it would make you feel better.'

'Well, it sounds as though you have it all worked out. I'll ask Maureen to keep an eye out. What time are you going?

'Erm, in about half an hour. We'll be back in time for lunch though.'

Mabel gave the rest of the gang the thumbs up as she walked through the lounge, and everyone made their way to their rooms to get ready.

'What a rickety rabble we must look!' Fraser said as they set off, with Maureen standing in the drive, watching as they hobbled their way down the street.

'You have brought the pipes with you, haven't you?' Ethel asked.

'What do you think those knobbly bits are under the blanket on Pete's knees.'

'I didn't like to ask!'

'Well, now you know.'

The five-minute walk stretched to ten by the time Fraser had stopped a couple of times to catch his breath, but they finally made it to the church hall.

Frank and Charlie arranged blue, plastic chairs in a semi-circle, whilst Fraser took his bagpipes from Pete, then they all sat down.

'OK, whilst Fraser gets his breath back, and sorts his pipes out, let's see if we can come up with a programme. What songs do we know?' Ethel asked.

'I used to sing in a band when I was younger, you know,' Whinny chirped up, 'We were called Warbling Whinny and the Wailers.'

'Were you really? What sort of songs did you do?' Mabel asked.

'Oh, whatever was popular at the time. It didn't last very long, so I can't remember much of what we did. My memory isn't so good nowadays, you know.'

'Tell me about it!' Charlie muttered.

'Right, come on. Focus everyone. What songs do we all know?' Ethel said, clapping her hands to get their attention.

'How about Amazing Grace?' Mabel suggested.

'Good idea, and I used to be able to play that one too.'

'Actually, that's a good point, Fraser. Maybe our starting point should be what songs you can play? If we don't know all the words, we can probably find them on the netty-web thingy and print them out, but music might be more difficult to find,' Esther said as collective nods of agreement went around the semi-circle. 'Have you got your breath back?'

'Aye, I think so.'

'OK. Hearing aids out and earplugs in!' Charlie said, as he and Ethel got up and dished out small balls of cotton wool.

Fraser assembled his pipes after shaking the dust off, took as big a breath as he could muster, and blew into the blowpipe. The drones spluttered to life, and an unearthly screech split the air, causing everyone to jump, before the noise whimpered out as Fraser collapsed into a coughing fit. It wasn't quite the start they had hoped for.

'I think I might be a bit rusty.' Fraser shrugged sheepishly when he had recovered his breath sufficiently to be able to speak.

'You don't say!' Charlie said.

'Why don't you have another try?' Mabel suggested.

'Give me a minute.'

'OK, well, whilst we're waiting for Fraser to catch his breath again, should we perhaps see if we can come up with a name for ourselves?' Frank said.

'Good idea! What about Amazing Disgrace?' Pete suggested.

'OK, any other suggestions?'

'I know! We could give ourselves a really modern name, like a lot of the groups do nowadays, when they go acoustic. We could call ourselves the Redwood Residents Unhinged!'

'I think you might mean unplugged, Whinny. Unhinged is something quite different.'

'I don't know Frank, I think she might have got it right the first time!' Charlie said with a wry smile.

'I'll tell you what, why don't we just keep it simple for the time being and call ourselves the Redwood Care Home Choir? If we come up with something better later on, we can always change it?' Mabel said, and everyone nodded in agreement.

Several minutes and three attempts later, Fraser shook his head and admitted defeat.

'I'm sorry, I just don't have the puff for this anymore. Perhaps I could play the piano instead?'

Disappointment rippled around the room, with much tutting, head shaking and muttering.

'OK, never mind. Let's just concentrate on the choir for now. Does everyone know at least the first verse of "Amazing Grace"?' Ethel asked, to which there were lots of nods. 'OK, then let's just give it a go. Can you give us a starting note please and then count us in, Fraser?'

Fraser pressed a key on the piano, and counted to three. They all joined in with the first bar, and then gradually they all stopped until Charlie was the only one left singing.

'Bloody hell, Charlie! Where did that come from?' Ethel asked, as everyone looked at Charlie in utter amazement.

'I thought you said that you were a grunter?' Mabel said, eyebrows raised.

'No, I said that they used to call people who couldn't sing grunters when I was at school. I didn't say that I was one of them. I was a choir boy, actually... That is, before I was trained operatically.'

'An opera singer! Wow! You've kept that quiet.' Mabel shook her head in disbelief.

'I was trained to sing opera, but I only ever did amateur productions. I worked as a plumber. My dad was quite strict when I was a lad, and whilst he was quite happy for me to sing with the church choir, he didn't think singing was a fitting profession for a bloke, so he got me an apprenticeship with a mate of his and it never occurred to me to do anything else.'

'Well, it's quite obvious that you can sing, Charlie, so would you mind sitting this one out so that we can hear what the rest of us sound like?' Ethel asked.

Fraser gave them their note again and counted them in. Once again, everyone except Charlie started singing. They managed a few bars before stopping, and this time everyone looked at Frank. Ethel pointed to her ears, and Frank fished his hearing aids out of his pocket.

'Sorry, folks.' Frank said, 'I forgot to put my hearing aids back in after Fraser stopped playing.'

'Yeah, we noticed.' Pete said.

'Oh. Was I out of tune?'

'Just a bit!'

'OK, let's try it again,' Ethel suggested.

After another few attempts, it was clear that the hearing aids didn't make any difference to the fact that Frank was completely unable to hold a tune. His voice resembled the noise that the drones on Fraser's bagpipes made. The reason why Whinny had been nicknamed 'Warbling Whinny' by her former bandmates had also become patently clear, along with the reason why they only lasted a few months and never managed to get a gig. However, they had also discovered that Charlie was a potential superstar, and Maud, Dotty and Doug also had very decent voices. Ethel's voice wasn't exactly what you would call melodic, and her range was limited, but within that range she could at least keep on key. Nobody else really stood out as being particularly good or bad.

'You know, I've been thinking,' Charlie said to Fraser the next day, as they watched the custard congealing in lumps whilst Ethel tried to coax it out of the jug onto the pudding.

'That sounds dangerous,' Fraser said.

'If I'm right, the main problem that you have with your bagpipes is your lack of puff, yes?'

'Yes, but to be fair, that's a pretty big problem when it comes to playing the bagpipes.'

'OK. Bear with me here. What if someone else could blow into the blow pipe for you. Someone like, er, Frank, say? Would you be able to play them then?'

'I'm not sure,' Fraser said slowly. 'I don't know how that would work. The blow pipe isn't that long. It might be a bit of a stretch for Frank to reach it if I'm holding the pipes.'

'It would be worth a try though, right?'

'Well, I don't suppose it would do any harm. Why not?'

'I was hoping you'd say that. Why don't you, me and Frank go down to the hall half an hour before everyone else tomorrow, and we can give it a try?'

'Sounds good to me. As long as Frank is up for it, we'll give it a go. Oh, and we'd better take Pete with us so that he can carry the pipes under his blanket again.'

On Friday morning, the four men set off half an hour early, as planned. Fraser assembled the pipes, and they tried several different approaches to try to solve their problem. Frank was a few inches shorter than Fraser, which was one thing in their favour, but it still wasn't an easy task. They tried Frank standing on a chair behind Fraser, leaning over his shoulder, but the drones got in the way, and nearly gave poor Frank a hernia. Then they tried sitting down, but that was a complete non-starter. It was like a game of geriatric Twister with props!

Eventually, they found that the best approach was probably the simplest one. Frank simply stood huddled beside Fraser, the difference in their heights working out just right. By the time the rest of the gang arrived, they had actually managed to get a whole verse of Amazing Grace squeezed out.

Now that Frank had been found another job, the choir was already starting to sound much better. Charlie had worked out a lower harmony line for Ethel, which Isobel and Maud would support her with, so that she never had to go out of her range. He had also written a special descant line for Whinny, so that she was only augmenting a few key bars in the piece. Pete, Dotty, Doug and Mabel would sing the tune, and Charlie would join them in the first two verses and then he had written a harmony baritone part, which he would sing in the last verse. He played through the new parts on the piano one at a time, and gradually, line by line, it started to take shape.

By the end of the third rehearsal, they had added a second song, Danny Boy, to their repertoire, which featured Charlie as the soloist, with the choir humming harmonies and Fraser providing a piano accompaniment. It had actually moved Mabel to tears, for all the right reasons, which was quite something, considering where they had started from.

'I thought the idea was that we were going to reap revenge on the school to discourage them from torturing us again?' Frank said at the end of the practice.

'It was,' Ethel agreed. 'But that was before we realised what we might be capable of. Who would have thought that a bunch of wrinklies like us could produce a sound as beautiful as this?'

'Who indeed?!' Mabel said, nodding.

Persuading Matron to arrange for them to perform at the school had not been an easy task, until they had finally given in and allowed her to attend their final rehearsal. After that, there was no stopping her. She had virtually planned out their first world tour, before they managed to reign her in.

The morning of the concert arrived, and the atmosphere at the breakfast table was subdued.

'Is anyone else nervous?' Mabel asked, pushing her cereal around in the bowl.

'Are you kidding?' Ethel said. 'Butterflies have nothing on whatever is flying around in my stomach!'

'You're right there,' Charlie said. 'That'll be the porridge. It does that to my stomach too! I would stick to the cereal in future if I were you. There's a limit to what they can do to destroy that.'

'It'll be fine,' Frank said. 'Let's face it, we have nothing to lose. Either it goes well, and we do ourselves proud, or it doesn't go well, in which case we achieve our original objective. Win win, you see?'

The school hall was a sea of purple and grey uniforms and innocent faces, eyes wide with anticipation. Fraser stepped onto the stage and put the blow pipe to his lips, and a pitiful whimper came out of the drones, before he broke down into a fit of coughing. The looks of surprise on the children's faces soon gave way to sniggers and then full-blown giggles, as Fraser stepped to the side and the choir walked on. Charlie played a chord on the piano, and gradually the giggles subsided as the teachers shushed the children. The choir started with the first verse of Amazing Grace, but Ethel couldn't quite reach the notes so was woefully flat, Whinny's unrestrained warbling was a sound best avoided, and Frank's monotone groan drowned out any semblance of tune. Charlie's one-handed playing on the piano couldn't quite keep pace with the choir, and the result could perhaps most generously be described as a cacophony. One or two of the smaller children at the front put their hands over their ears, and gradually more followed suit, whilst more giggles erupted. Matron looked as though she was about to have an apoplectic fit. They hadn't run this part of the programme past her...

After the first verse, Charlie stepped forward and waited until the children had settled down.

'That wasn't great, was it?' He asked, and all of the children shook their heads in unison.

'So how about we try something different? You see, Fraser here used to be very good at playing the bagpipes, but now he can't blow very hard, so he needs somebody to help him with that. And Frank here, well, he's not very good at singing. I don't know whether you noticed that?'

The children giggled.

'Also, I'm not very good at playing the piano, am I? But, that's OK, because nobody is good at everything. However, Frank has a very good pair of lungs, so he can give Fraser a hand with the bagpipes, and I can't play the piano well, but I can sing, so perhaps I would be better in the choir. So, now that we know what people are good at, and what they might need help with, shall we try again, and see if it sounds any better?'

The children nodded enthusiastically, and Frank stepped out of the choir and joined Fraser on the side of the stage. They started with the bagpipes playing one verse of Amazing Grace, and then the choir joined in. The choir sang the next verse on their own, and the bagpipes re-joined them for the final verse. When they had finished, the children were in awe. Everyone clapped hard, and when Charlie caught the eye of the teacher who had brought the children to the home, she gave him the thumbs up.

The rest of the concert went better than any of them could have hoped, and the mood in the hall was buoyant when the final applause had finished.

'Can we make a deal?' Charlie asked once the children had been dismissed, and the teacher had come to offer her congratulations on their performance.

'What did you have in mind?' the teacher asked.

'If you bring the children to the home again, could you perhaps consider something a little more mellow than violins or recorders? Or, even better, maybe you could just bring them for afternoon tea, and perhaps a game or two of dominoes, rather than a concert?'

'On one condition,' the teacher replied.

'And what's that?'

'That you bring your choir and musicians to us again for a Christmas concert.'

'Done!'

'And if it isn't too cheeky, could I ask another favour?'

'Of course.'

'Could you come and audition the children to find out who would be best in the choir and who might be better given another role. You see... I'm completely tone deaf, so your point about finding the right role for the right person was well-made, but wasted on me because I really can't tell.'

Charlie and the teacher both burst out laughing, and a beautiful partnership between the school and the home started that day.

# Hapless

*From Nova Scotia, Canada, R. Malik has spent decades insisting to friends, family and fraught strangers alike that she is, in fact, funny. She is thrilled to finally have proof in middle age that someone, somewhere, agrees with her.*

Hapless: [adjective] unlucky, luckless, unfortunate, wretched, deserving or inciting pity.

He meant well. He always *meant* well…

A small crowd had formed around the miniature structure that was, '…leaning somewhat *SEVERELY* to the right!' Or at least that was how he had phrased the message sent off earlier in the day to the builder who had hired him on as an apprentice. But what the Goode People of Goodee Village (a term they preferred over the more commonly used, 'Those peasants of that hovel, what'sit called?') were currently seeing was that the tiny extravagant abode, resplendent with diminutive, useless turrets built to house the disgruntled but otherwise unharmed, very large pig that lay pinned underneath, was no longer merely *leaning* somewhat *SEVERELY* to the right.

196

'Ridiculous thing damn near killed Master Builder's prize pig when it collapsed!' A witness informed some newly arrived onlookers. 'If the grunter (the Goode person nodded towards the beast making sniffing sounds like an insulted aristocrat) wasn't so incredibly fat (and here his eyes seemed to brighten just a little too much at the thought) as to be impossible to crush, well, we'd all be having a feast tonight.'

The crowd nodded solemnly, each conjuring up silent fantasies of how the delicious poor swine could be put out of what surely must be anguish and misery, even if it was too thick to know it.

The unfortunate apprentice who had been at the centre of the scene was feeling woefully responsible for the situation at hand, even though he had followed the Master Builder's building instructions meticulously, or so he had thought. The apprentice was young and boyish still, even though he had outgrown that rank over a decade ago. Being lanky, he looked taller than he actually was, but he was more than just a collection of elbows and knees. He was blessed, so he kept being told by the ladies with the pin-straight hair, with a thick mess of unruly curly locks that had a habit of slipping willy-nilly over his surprisingly handsome face. Surprising for someone so gormless, is what most people thought. Why the two were considered to be at odds is a complicated calculation that never ends up looking good for the one making the judgement. His eyes, according to the same value judgement, were disconcertingly clear and bright, something that perhaps the villagers should have paid more attention to.

Currently hair and eyes and elbows and knees were all being carried along at rapid uncoordinated speed reminiscent of a baby giraffe being chased by peckish hyenas. People of the town called him Happy, his real name long forgotten from disuse. Even his aunt and uncle who had raised him from orphaned childhood called him that now. And though they rarely thought of why the villagers had started calling him that in the first place, he could never quite get beyond it. Happy, you see, was the sunnier version of 'Hapless'.

Ah yes, hapless. Ever since he had slipped out of the womb and accidently onto the floor atop a very surprised and justifiably piqued family dog, he seemed destined to trip over sticks, fall into wells and set his beautiful locks on fire with a frequency that hinted at divine intervention. But the nickname of the nickname wasn't just a kindness. As a child, throughout it all, somehow, miraculously, the boy had managed to keep an air of optimistic *laissez faire* with each and every mishap. If he had indeed been born under an unlucky star, then he had also been blessed with the ability to see the beauty of the distant twinkling light. But... sadly, unfurling into adulthood can have a way of making one forget to look up to take in that luminous sight.

And so it was that right now Happy wasn't thinking of distant stars or looking on the bright side. He was thinking, 'Oh geez, oh geez, oh geez' as he dashed to find his missing employer. The errand boy had come back saying that the Master Builder had been busy but that the message had been delivered. Two hours had since passed and still no word had come.

The man Happy was racing to find was the richest person in that village and all the surrounding ones for miles. No one understood why he chose to live in a village so poor and so far away from any town of note.

(The only note that the Village of Goodee could lay claim to was the one a severely disgruntled traveller had carved on the door of the tavern between agonised trips to the latrine that said, 'DO NOT EAT HERE _UNLESS_ YOU ARE DYING AND WANTING TO SPEED UP THE PROCESS.' The villagers hadn't been quite sure how to take that since it didn't _absolutely_ say not to eat there, what with the qualifier and all. So, in the end they had left it, misguided in the notion that any publicity was better than no publicity at all).

In regards to the Master Builder, the general thought among most was that he could afford to live anywhere he wanted and in grand style at that, being a builder in high demand. The five-foot-tall magnificent edifice that his beloved pig currently lay trapped under was in fact a near exact replica of a building he had just completed for an even more wealthy and notoriously powerful couple widely referred to as, 'The Birds' (for their soaring wealth). The Birds commanded the largest landholding in an adjacent county.

Happy ran up the lane to the Master Builder's house. The Builder had designed it himself and it declared to the trees and the hedges and the stone walls that surrounded it, to the sky and to anyone in view, 'I am better than you. Deal with it.'

He raised his hand to knock on the intricately carved door when he realised that it was ajar. He paused for a moment, not knowing if he should go in. He decided to use the heavy knocker, but when after some moments no one came, he hesitantly pushed it open and peeked in.

'Um... hello?' This came out as a squeak. He took a breath and tried again, louder, trying to keep the panic out of his voice. 'Hello? Master Builder Sir? Anyone? It's me, Happy?'

Uncharacteristically, no one came. The Master Builder had several household staff including a Man's Body who was mostly there to answer the door in a decent suit, a Housekeeper and a Cook. They were mere lowly locals, untrained and unqualified to be of any true quality; hired only because more experienced people could not be enticed, no matter how high the compensation, to move to the hovel of Goodee Village. But still, somehow they fulfilled (at least marginally) their purpose of illustrating that the householder was clearly a person of certain means.

Happy took a few steps into the entrance way. 'Hellooooo?'

Nothing.

He looked around, uncertain what to do. To the left was the Master Builder's study. Normally the door was locked when unoccupied, but now it was wide open. Happy had been in it once before and had been in awe of all the books that impressively lined the walls. When he'd asked if they had all been read, he had received a diminishing look that had made him feel foolish for the question, though he wasn't exactly sure why. He was just starting to learn that he wasn't very good at understanding people and their layered motives. This recognition had marked Happy's first tentative steps at moving beyond the lingering naivete of childhood.

Happy stood just past the doorway and scanned the room. It was exactly as he remembered it save for the fact that it looked as though the place had been looted. The desk drawers were open, contents strewn on the floor. Piles of paper lay scattered in disarray. A chair, felled sinisterly on its side. What had happened here? Robbery? Something worse?! Happy felt his anxiety building. He started slowly backing out of the room until it occurred to him that were there any threat still lingering on the premises, coming at it backwards probably wasn't the wisest option. He spun around, hands in the air, in case any grappling with strangers was, gods forbid, imminent. It was not. Half crouching (were he to pass out from fright, he would have half the distance to fall), he continued back into the entrance hall with his hands now curled into very unfamiliar fists like a reluctant pugilist with arthritis. He would have felt supremely foolish if he hadn't been too busy feeling supremely terrified instead. He edged his way around the foyer to glance in the large welcoming room where the Master Builder normally took his visitors. Happy held onto a smidgen of desperate hope that perhaps the Master Builder was in there taking a nap, and that the state of the study had to do with something perfectly innocent like an impromptu cockfight which, upon explanation, could be something they could share a laugh over, ha ha. He tried not to think about the reason he had come running over. The Master Builder would not be laughing at that.

The welcoming room was empty and undisturbed. Happy tiptoed down the corridor to the back of the house which contained the kitchen and the servants' quarters. He thought he had heard a noise from that direction and forced himself to not follow his instinct to run the other way. As he neared the pantry, he heard hushed voices. One was female, the other lower, gruff, and he recognised it as the distinctive voice of the Man's Body. He put his ear to the door.

'What if he comes back?'

'He won't, I'm telling you...'

'How do you know? Once it all settles down, he—'

'Woman, I'm telling you he won't! Not if he doesn't want to be strung up from the nearest tree, he won't. And either way, he's not going to miss a pie or a sack of grain, is he?'

Happy took a deep breath and opened the swinging door. The Cook and Man's Body each held sacks brimming with the household's food supplies. One of them held a large bundle of dried meat. They turned in surprise.

'What are you doing?!' Happy asked, shocked, even though it was quite obvious what they were doing. 'Where's Master Builder? Does he know that you're taking his jerky?'

The two servants assessed the situation then turned back and unabashedly continued their pillaging. Their behaviour confused Happy and he didn't know how to proceed. So, he did what people do in those circumstances which was to stammer incoherently.

'Boy, you're babbling gibberish!'

Happy knew this to be true. He shut his mouth and then tried again. 'Puh-please, can you tell me what's happening? Where's Master Builder? His study...?' He pointed weakly in its direction. He then remembered the pig. 'I really need to talk to him! His beloved pig is trapped! Its new house fell on it!'

At this the two servants looked at each other in amazement then burst into laughter. Happy felt indignant and hurt on the pig's behalf. He was just about to awkwardly not say anything when the Cook spoke instead.

'Two in one day! What are the chances of that?'

The Man's Body was still laughing so hard that he couldn't catch his breath to respond.

Happy was puzzled by the comment. 'Two? Two what?'

'I'll tell you what!' The Man's Body bellowed gleefully. 'Two of the Master Builder's buildings falling down on the same day! The same building in fact, just two versions of it!'

At this the Cook let out a high cackle. The apprentice on the other hand was trying hard to figure out what they were saying and the implications... They seemed to be intimating that The Birds' newly built estate had also collapsed. The reality suddenly dawned on him. They would have had a staff of at least...

'Was anybody hurt?!' Happy's eyes were wide with alarm.

'No, no... they're saying no one was harmed. But the ham for the feast didn't make it!'

At this another loud whoop of laughter and the two held onto each other for support as they ahahaha-ed their way into convulsions.

'And the Master Builder? Do you know where he is?'

The burly man managed to get a grip on himself and ran his hand through his sparse hair. 'Who knows? He ran like a bat out of hell when he found out. First he went into his study and tore it up looking for something...'

'Coin,' Cook interrupted.

'Coin I daresay that he had stashed, but I'm guessing evidence too that he stupidly had lying about, of him pilfering from the building funds.'

Happy looked aghast at this and the two noticed. 'What? You can't say that you hadn't heard the rumours?'

Happy shook his head no. He hadn't. He didn't pay attention to gossip.

'Get your head out of the dirt, boy! Your precious Master Builder, it turns out, has been getting paid for quality but has been using the dregs and pocketing the difference. He's been putting lipstick on a pig and managed to get away with it. Until now.'

The cook had stopped looking amused and now her brow furrowed. 'Thank the gods no one was hurt! I heard that The Birds' own little daughter had been in that room just moments before. Can you imagine...' Her voice trailed off.

The man nodded with a far-off look. He addressed Happy once more. 'So, you can imagine then what trouble the scoundrel's in. They'll have him locked up or strung up. Either way, his life is over.'

Happy stood dazed by the information. The two servants had turned back to their task at hand, or rather flasks in hand as containers of wine and spirits were tucked into the already full sacks. Happy could no longer fault them. They were right. The Master Builder could never come back here and the stores of supplies were of no use to him now. But still, when he was offered up something to take with him, he couldn't bring himself to accept, foolish or not.

The pig eyed the too near crowd nervously. The two-leggeds were looking at it differently than the one who often brought it the delicious treats. That one satisfyingly scratched the itch behind its ears and made sounds that seemed quite friendly. Plus, it was almost as round as the pig and that promoted a certain amount of camaraderie. Then there was that other weird-looking one that was all up and down with no round to speak of who had been showing up lately with food. That one was all right too, although a bit distracted it seemed, but he always took the time to give some gentle pats on the back. The pig wasn't sure what the point of the pats was exactly, but they seemed innocuous at worst and hinted at some sort of mysterious yet sincere conveyance at best. The pig could live with that.

But now, now there was a conveyance of a completely different sort. These two-leggeds were staring at it with strangely glassed-over eyes. Some had expressions that showed their teeth that wasn't at all like when the food-bringers showed theirs.

The pig made some grunting sounds and tried again, in vain, to move from beneath the debris. A sudden poke on the rump area made it emit a frightened high-pitched squeal.

'There's good eatin' on that!' The short squinty-eyed villager who had just stuck her bony finger into the pig's hind quarters declared to the rest of the throng. The rest of the throng didn't need to be told.

The word had been travelling that something had sent the Master Builder scurrying. The word in these parts was not always reliable so the possibilities were being considered cautiously. This is what saved the pig. The villagers had stood around for a time after Happy had run off, unwilling to become involved in anything that was not of direct bene-fit to themselves. One small child had wandered away from the pack and had unsuccessfully tried to move a piece of wood off the pig that was the same size as it was. A parent had quickly put a stop to that charitable nonsense and had carried the foolish child away. When the word confirming Master Builder's absconding had finally arrived, there had been a sudden galvanising of effort heretofore not seen. Many hands make for quick work as they say, which in this case was not necessarily in the animal's best interest.

The crowd was just nearing the point where the pig could be freed when Happy arrived back at the scene. His heart lifted when he saw all the effort the Goode people of Goodee had put in to alleviate the suffering of the poor creature. 'Thank you! Thank you! Goode people!' He exclaimed. He was aware that not everyone in the village had always behaved in the best of ways in the past, but people could surprise you, he thought. He ran over to the pig and gave it a soft pat-pat on the back.

'We'll have you out of here in no time now,' he said soothingly and started removing the remaining building fragments with all his earnest might.

The villagers looked at each other, trying to silently have the conversation as to what to do next. They knew that Happy worked for the Master Builder and in a sense then was an extension of the man himself, at least as long as there was a chance that the Master Builder could still come back and cause unspecified grief to anyone who dared harm his precious pig. The villagers were of a sort that naturally bestowed on anyone with a certain amount of wealth and arrogance a power over them that needn't have actually existed. Aside from the several handfuls of people who worked for the Master Builder and their families, he had no real sway over the fates of others. But somewhere along the way the village had started to view him as not just Master Builder but as their Master and looked to him to guide them as such. The Master Builder who had always felt that he should have been born to a higher station and that something had gone wrong at the last moment, happily took on the position of Lord of the land, such as it was.

'Don't stop, don't stop!' Happy encouraged the crowd. 'Nearly there! Excellent work!'

The people exchanged disgruntled glances, but several men stepped forward and helped to shift the last of the debris still fettering the pig. The pig, freed at last, heaved itself up, shook off the dust and splinters and then made a break for it off down the road. What happened next would be a blurry memory for Happy, and the word would have as many accounts as persons who took part.

First, the pig fled, yes? Yes, all could agree to that. But after that there was some divarication, but the generally unbiased version is that the Goode people, reasoning abandoned, took chase. Happy, a sudden inkling dawning that there may be other motives at play in the great interest the villagers were taking in the pig, frantically followed behind. At first glance it looked as though the villagers were out for an organised, healthful run. This of course was before the mayhem broke loose. One of the smarter locals thought to look back and discovered Happy was in hot pursuit. Taking one for the team, he did a sudden stop, drop, and rolled into Happy's path. Happy went tumbling forward, head-over-arse and rolled into the closest runner ahead of him. The pack was running shoulder-to-shoulder and as the next person started going down, flailing arms, legs akimbo, it was enough to unbalance the people on either side who indecorously went down with her. The noise made two others turn back to look and suddenly off kilter, they went down as well, in the path of several running behind them who also… and so it went until there was only one lone runner who was far enough ahead of the pack to escape the fray. The villagers that weren't so bright turned on each other for getting knocked down. Those who didn't find themselves in the middle of a tousling match tried to break up the ones who did.

Happy tried to navigate his way out of the chaos which ended up being more complicated than one might expect. The grappling had turned to fisticuffs and Happy managed to catch not one, but two misdirected blows before finally extricating himself. By then those who weren't physically fighting were getting into heated debates as to what to do with the pig. Everyone agreed that it was going to be eaten, of course, but how and when to slaughter, communal feast or to be privately savoured, modest sprigs of rosemary vs a heady bouquet garni, these were all impassioned points of contention. The solitary runner who had been at the head of the chase had come to realise that even if he were able to catch up with the pig, there was no capturing the affrighted porker all on his own. So, he too had stopped and was now yelling expletives, trying to focus the others on the task at hand. These went mostly unnoticed except by Happy who heard some words that made his ears turn slightly red.

The pig had by now gotten far enough away that it could no longer smell the hostile seeming two-leggeds but could still hear quite a hullabaloo. It finally let curiosity get the better of it and halted so it could turn around to see what all the commotion was about. The two-leggeds still seemed hostile but this time towards each other. The pig wondered if it was mating season, a time when creatures always seemed to lose all sense of decorum. Regardless, it was glad for the reprieve from the chase. So, the question was, now what? This was answered quickly enough when it became apparent that some of the two-leggeds had taken up interest in the pig again and were pointing fingers with a thrusting motion in its direction. The animal started to get a prickly feeling all over and regretted having stopped. It was just about to turn around and start hoofing it when it saw that a single gangly figure was jogging in its direction. It smelled like the OK weird one. Happy reached the pig and gave it a reassuring pat. He turned around and yelled to the crowd who had quieted down and were watching him.

'It's OK everybody, I've got the pig now! Thank you for your help!' He paused and then added, 'I'm sure Master Builder will be very grateful when he hears about it.'

And so it seems that perhaps Happy *was* smarter than people thought.

Happy took off the dusty handkerchief from around his neck and tried tying it around the pig's. He had hoped that he could use it as a lead but it was far too small for the much fatter neck. So, instead, Happy talked to the pig as he gently tried to veer it in the optimal direction. Although clueless as to what the two-legged was saying, the pig was still able to intuit its goodwill and was glad enough to get away from the others who, frankly, freaked it out. Happy walked slowly with a, 'Here pig, pig, pig' and the pig, well, padded along.

Happy had no idea what to do next. He was trying to wrap his brain around the current situation. The Master Builder, his mentor, had turned out to be a complete fraud and ne'er do well. He wasn't coming back; couldn't or he'd be in for it. That also meant that Happy wasn't going to get paid and he really needed that money. He had promised it to his aunt and uncle to pay for repairs to the wagon wheel that Happy had accidentally damaged when he had been repairing the other bit to the wagon that he had accidentally broken the week before. His aunt and uncle were kind sorts for the most part but had come into the reluctant role of parenting unexpectedly and late in life. Let's just say they weren't naturals at it and never did manage the art of patience and forbearance. And patience and forbearance are what you need a great supply of when you're raising a child called Hapless.

Happy looked down at the pig. The pig looked up at Happy. Happy was startled by what looked to him like a smile on the pig's face. He didn't know they could do that! The pig continued to smile at Happy and Happy, a sucker for a nice smile, grinned back. Then he had the disconcerting thought, *What on earth was he going to do with an orphaned thousand-pound pig?*

Happy glanced over his shoulder and was dismayed to discover that not only hadn't the crowd broken up and gone their respective ways, but they had instead continued, at a slight distance, to follow in pace behind. When he turned back around to properly assess the situation, they had all abruptly stopped in their tracks, innocent faces aglow with nonchalance. Sudden philobotanists one and all, they keenly stared at roadside bushes and earnestly pointed up into trees. They verily brimmed with insouciance as they expounded heartily to no one in particular, the joys of taking in the fresh country air. There was a humming of a jaunty tune.

Happy wasn't buying it.

Looking at Happy now, you'd think it an ironic nickname. He was not only on his last nerve, but that one was already packing a travelling bag to flee to the Riviera.

He needed to get the pig somewhere safe, but where? He thought of taking it home to his aunt and uncle's place, but they were every bit the Goode people of Goodee who enjoyed a ham feast as much as the rest. He looked back at the pig who had stopped smiling and was now waiting patiently, *trustingly*, for Happy to make his next move. This touched the young man in a way that surprised him. He shook his head to clear it. 'It's just a pig,' he said out loud and then immediately felt bad for it. He avoided looking the creature in the eye. 'Come on pig, pig, pig.' Happy mumbled. He was grateful when the pig didn't hold the comment against him and followed along.

Happy and the pig quickly made their way down the dirt road. When Happy next looked behind, the crowd was still no further away. This time when he turned his head, the villagers ingeniously managed, at lightning speed, to set up a tableau scene of 'Fruit in Bowl on Table' and were miming sketching and painting it with intense, single-minded concentration. Upon closer inspection, the table was the old baker's toothless cousin who someone had thrown a cloak over, and the bowl was an upside-down hat, replete with real fruit. Like it or not, one had to give the Goode people of Goodee Village credit for their out-of-character lateral thinking.

Happy stepped up the pace. The pig trotted next to Happy, who felt sad. He wasn't overly familiar or comfortable with the emotion. Happy, not the pig. The pig as of yet hadn't experienced a wide array of emotions, but confusion was one it could now add to the growing list.

It was a beautiful day. The sun shone. It was not too hot. It was not too cold. There was a pleasant breeze that reminded your skin that you were surrounded by an active and participatory universe. Butterflies lazily fluttered about in a way that made it seem like their bodies were too heavy for flight, but yet they persevered. Unlike the bees that seemed quite steady in their flight paths although technically, they should have bumbled about like butterflies.

The world is a confusing place, thought Happy. He couldn't have known that he and the pig were on the same page, so to speak, about that.

The hastily contrived plan was, for the moment, this: Take the pig to his aunt and uncle's without anyone seeing (including his aunt and uncle) and hide it in the small barn beside the house. Man and pig were currently free of the madding crowd thanks to the fortunate reappearance of the errand boy who had earlier conveyed the news to and from the Master Builder. The boy had been heading on an unrelated errand but Happy had made a point to stop and talk with him. He had made exaggerated responses to innocuous chit chat, throwing his arms up in the air as if to exclaim, 'WHAAA??? I can't BELIEVE it!' causing the boy to be extremely perplexed. But the youngster was fond of Happy who had always been nice to him (unlike some grownups of the village), so when Happy had bent down and with whispers asked for the favour of keeping their conversation a secret, the boy had agreed with no qualms. Happy straightened up and the boy went on his way, darting past the villagers before they could stop him. Happy pretended to not see the people down the road and turning sideways, instead spoke very loudly and directly to the pig.

'Did you hear that pig? The Master Builder has come back! What a surprise, eh!' He bent down and rubbed its head, feeling somewhat guilty for the lie. 'Let's get you cleaned up so you look nice and neat for when you see your Master.'

Happy very carefully did not turn his head but could see out of the corner of his eye some reorganising of expectations ripple through the halted throng. There was muffled muttering and some terse words were heard but slowly, one by one, the crowd started to begrudgingly disperse.

Happy and the pig had made their way to the shelter of the barn where they now dwelled in the throes of a dilemma. Or at least one of them felt they were in the throes of a dilemma. The other was just pleased to be lying down.

Happy, with a certain fortitude, resolved to face the facts squarely. Somehow, somewhere along the way, without intent, he had become emotionally attached to the pig. He felt the significant weight of it; not so much as a burden, but as a mother kangaroo affectionately feels the presence and responsibility of her joey in her pouch. Happy had no idea what a kangaroo was. But had he had the good fortune of ever coming across such a one, he surely would have experienced some very curious feelings of kinship indeed.

In light of this, the situation was exceedingly worrisome. There was no getting around the fact that if Happy wanted to be caretaker of the pig, it would need to be fed.

Happy looked at his new companion who was beside him making contented snuffling sounds. It really was a very large pig, even as far as very large pigs went. And very large pigs ate *a lot*.

Happy let loose with a deep and loud sigh. That's an interesting sound, thought the pig. I wonder what it means? In an act of congeniality, the pig attempted to mimic the sound. Happy looked at it, alarmed. He'd never heard it make *that* sound before! Maybe it was hungry. Maybe it was starving. When was the last time it was fed?

Happy looked out the small window to the garden beyond. Should he try to find a turnip? He thought that maybe they could spare one or two but that wasn't going to go very far. The family farm was a meagre one, being of rocky soil and barely producing enough food for them alone, and sometimes not even that. He thought of the Master Builder's land and the huge farm that was part of it. What was going to happen to that now that the Master Builder had fled? It could easily produce enough food to keep the village fed if only people gathered and worked together... Happy paused in his thoughts. He had a certain fondness for his fellow villagers, he really did, even if they didn't always... well, weren't always... the nicest, or the smartest... They did what he supposed was their best. But even with his generosity of spirit, he suddenly understood that when it came right down to it, they were more of an instant gratification lot rather than big picture thinkers. Once the fields had been scavenged for the already existing harvest, that would be the end of it. No more sowing, no more reaping.

This needed thinking about...

Two hours later the pig was semi-dozing and Happy sat with his arm over its back with an idea that had taken dubious form. That it was an unconventional plan, he would have been the first to admit. Some with a decent vocabulary might have gone in for 'audacious'. But for good or for bad, it was the only plan he had and time was not on their side.

In the Master Builder's dressing room, the pig gave a disgruntled low pitched, 'Oof'. Happy could hardly blame it and felt that really, considering the peculiarities of the given moment, it was being a pretty good sport all in all. After trying a few shirts, and then a pair of billowy pyjamas, each one *almost* fitting but just not quite, Happy had lucked upon an especially roomy dressing gown that fit the pig more generously, it not having buttons but a fabric tie instead.

Happy couldn't help but wonder if the Master Builder's fondness for the pig wasn't in part due to their similarities in rotund shape and size. In the builder's earlier life, much of him had been solid muscle born of hefting large pieces of wood and hewing heavy stone. But over the years as the word 'Master' had been added to his title, there had been less time spent building and more time spent lazily bossing other people to do all the heavy lifting for him. As his stature had grown, so had his waistline.

Happy stood back and surveyed his work. The pig looked quite splendid, he thought, in the brocade dressing gown and silken multi-coloured cravat. On its snout rested some dignified spectacles. Happy had tried putting an unlit pipe in its mouth but the pig had quickly put the kibosh on that. 'Yes', said Happy both to himself and the pig. 'Yes, this *could* just work!'

Let's pause here for a moment, shall we, to check in with the pig? We know that it had recently had the new experience of the feeling of confusion. So, we're bound to be forgiven if we were to think that surely this poor woebegone pig, now trussed up like an over-educated gigolo, would be feeling not only confused but unnerved and quite possibly in the throes of some existential angst.

It turns out, no. Quite the opposite, as a matter of fact. Although the experience of clothing was completely foreign to it, it took to it like a pig in... well, you know. It found itself quite enjoying the feel of the luxurious fabric on its usually bare body. It realised with a start that until now it hadn't recognised that it often felt chilled. What a revelation that it didn't *have* to feel that way! And those strange things on its snout. If the pig had had the lexicon, it would have used the word 'magical'. Suddenly, things that had been in hazy soft focus were amazingly crisp and clear! It was as if it was seeing the world through new eyes! How unexpected. How wonderful!

Happy heard voices coming from downstairs. He had known that it was only a short matter of time before the villagers figured out that he had been bluffing and they would come plundering, and with sharpened knives.

OK, he thought, this is it.

'Ready?' He asked the pig.

The pig gave an amicable 'groink', which Happy took as affirmative. Happy led the way, and the pig, now in the habit of following the two legged, did just that.

Downstairs, the scene was unfolding thusly: about a dozen intrepid villagers stood as a gaggle inside the front foyer. They had connived to make haste before the rest of the Goode people who remained manacled by misguided loyalty caught on that they were missing out on the fun and profits. But now that they were here, a certain degree of fear had arisen. They had never before been inside the grand house or anything like it for that matter, and they found the largeness of it, with its high ceilings and lack of free roaming livestock, unnerving. They huddled and in hushed tones looked to each other for guidance;

an ineffectual endeavour it turned out. It was as this one multi-headed entity that Happy came upon them as he apprehensively descended halfway down the stairs. The pig for the moment remained out of sight on the small landing, hidden behind Happy and the curve of the staircase.

Happy let loose with a little cough. The cabal looked up and seeing that it was Happy, shrunk in on itself as if trying to hide behind one another. Both his connection to the Master Builder and his tendency towards honesty and steadfastness made him unfathomable and therefore at the moment to be viewed with suspicion and unease.

'Hello, Goode people,' said Happy.

The Goode people squinted at him.

'I'm glad you came. *We're* glad you came.'

*We?* The villagers looked around confused.

'As you may have heard, the Master Builder has, uh... taken a leave of absence.'

The villagers nodded, warily.

'And I expect that this news has come as quite a shock to everyone and left people feeling...' and here Happy took a moment to find the *mot juste*: '... adrift...'

The villagers glanced at each other, a bit embarrassed. It was true.

'Well, I just want to tell you that we need not worry! The Master Builder's esteemed and very wise cousin from the south heard of the troubles and has unselfishly agreed to come and take over the estate!'

Indecipherable grumbles arose from the ensemble. Could there possibly be any truth in the matter? They eyed the open door to the study and the imagined treasures laying in wait. So close! The villagers were not at all pleased by this turn of events.

One woman spoke up from the middle of the pack where perhaps she felt shielded enough to brave it. 'How do we know yer not lyin'?'

This statement rallied the others who added their disgruntled voices with assorted, 'Yeah!'s, and, 'Good point!' And one muttered, 'Anyone know where the toilet is?'

Happy decided that it was now or never. With shaking knees, he stepped aside to reveal,

'Sir Porcine everyone. Sir Porcine, the Goode people of Goodee Village!'

There was a sudden sharp intake of breath from the collective. The pig let out a snort. The villagers now emboldened by curiosity, stepped closer and peered at the peer suddenly in their midst. Could it be that what Happy said was actually true? They looked at the bespectacled face, the elegantly attired form. Grudgingly they had to admit that there *might* be something in it? Yes, it was sullenly agreed; It *was* indisputable that this was someone of impeccable taste and means. And yes, they thought forlornly, as they continued to stare, there *was* undeniably a familial resemblance between the stranger and the Master Builder. Upon further study, why, they seemed more like brothers than merely distant cousins!

And so started the great shuffling of feet, the averting of eyes, the looking at empty wrists and declaring, 'Oh would ye look at the time! Had no idea it was so late, expected at home...' etc... And out they ran before the new Master could memorise their blushing guilty faces.

The sun was setting. Without denouncement it bathed the Village of Goodee in its soft golden glow. Happy sat amongst vast rows of cabbages as the pig contentedly ate its fill. It had certainly been a strange day. Happy surveyed the estate's farm and thought, 'I could manage this.' After a short while, he raised his gaze from the fields, up to the brilliant orange and red hued sky. My gods! his heart spoke softly. How absolutely beautiful!

The pig, feeling sated, shuffled over and settled down comfortably next to Happy and received some gentle pat-pats which it was coming to quite like. For the first time, the pig took a long, close, bespectacled look at the two-legged. Maybe it wasn't so weird-looking after all, it decided. And then with a well-deserved yawn and a snuffle, it drifted off happily to sleep.

# Poets Rise Again

*Josie Long is a writer and a stand-up comedian. She won the Best Newcomer award at Edinburgh Fringe Festival and has been nominated three times for Best Show. She was born in Kent in 1982 and studied English at Oxford University. She currently lives in Glasgow.*

'I would give anything, *anything* if I could have grown up with a father who loved me, and with a mother who wanted me around. It's like people look at me and all they can see is this idea of me, that I have this charmed life, but it's not fair, it's not fair.' She starts crying again and Naomi squeezes her arm. She passes her a little package of tissues and it takes a long time to open them. We both sit, watching her try to get the little plastic flap up and then try to pull a tissue out, and then loudly blow her nose onto it and put it on the desk so, so close to my god damn arm.

'I'm sorry, I know to you it's just poor little rich girl, I know, I'm sorry, I have felt guilty my whole life. I just can't cope.'

Naomi looks at me but I swear to god I am going to start laughing just out of nerves and I shake my head so

she starts up. 'We know. It's so hard to' – she pauses and
flashes me a look like help me out and I flash back like babe
I am out of my depth also – 'It's so hard to change your circumstances in life...' Naomi swallows back something like
disgust, 'for everyone. That's what people don't appreciate'.

'Thank you. I can't help that I've been fortunate. I'm a
good person.'

That tissue is nearly touching the hairs on my arm,
I swear.

'I'm not a bad person.'

OK, time for me to speak for the first time.

'We know. We don't think that.'

'At all.' Naomi chimes in, thank you, in sync.

After two hours we both hug her and she leaves. We
wave to her, not smiling, not anything, just calm as the
school nurse giving you an injection, as she passes by
outside the office. Our first customer. Three. Thousand.
Fucking. Pounds. I can't stop laughing. We're jumping up
and down. She's just the first of ten bookings this week.

I go home, get changed, kiss my mummy on the forehead and go straight back out to meet Nems. We are going
for dinner and we are not going to think about the money.
I order us cocktails and a bottle of wine. I don't want there
to be any time in the meal where we have less than two
drinks each. Yes, we are paying the supplement for cheese
or steak or lobster or whatever fancy shit costs the supplement, thank you. We are going to get port, dessert wine,
grappa, fuck it.

'Naomi, this is the beginning,' I say for a toast. 'When
you started this scheme, I will admit I had my doubts. I had
my doubts...' I'm trying to make this something we can
remember; I want it to be official. '...but look at this. We

are fully fledged, we have taken our maiden voyage and the world is ours!' We are so loud that people are staring at us, but I think they'd be staring at us anyway. Unfortunately, my new money is as good as yours, mate. And we look fucking beautiful. Two bright birds of paradise.

We are eating little butterscotch puddings and drinking hot liqueur coffee cocktails, when Nems looks so serious and leans in.

'This isn't even it, you know? This is just the first floor, the entry level. Yes, we can get this money absorbing all of their feelings and yes, we can build up our client base, and yes, we can run retreats and workshops and you can bet yes, I am going to be adding two zeroes onto everything we do when we go to Kensington and Chelsea and Richmond, trust me. But this isn't even it. I am talking about getting these people to give it up. Properly give it all up. And thank us for it.' She downs the last bit of drink and winks at me and we both crease up. Got to be dramatic when you do these things, otherwise what life are you living?

And that is how the plan was made. In between dessert and the hot mint tea where I spent most of the time looking into the water to see if there were bugs in it so we could get it for free. She says we don't need to do that do we, but I will always love a bargain. I gave a card to a sour-faced old couple as we left. She did a double take like she was trying to suppress real terror as I came over. Then she did some kind of facial dance as she read it. I watched her all the while so I could give her the warmest smile I could, and then I walked out like I was prime minister. Like I was a cruise ship. Stately as a galleon, I thought to myself.

Confidence is something you can practise. You can practise at home, in the mirror. You can practise to yourself as you go to bed at night. You can develop your persona for public speaking and you can use it whenever you need to. That's what was drummed into us. When we were in sixth form, Nems and I were in the debate team. The legendary year where our school, our shitty school, our school, Our Lady of Perpetual Help, cleaned the fuck UP. Without over-bragging, with perhaps just a lovely bit of bragging, me and Nems *were* the debate team. It was our pair that won the three competitions. The b-team: Elaine Nicholson and Clara Stevens (I will never forget their full names and I will only ever call them their full names) were deadwood. We carried those timid little mice as they stumbled their way alongside us.

Our sixth form was the only time where Our Lady even had a debate team. It coincided with the reign of Mr Hunter on the history department. He was involved, I now think, in one of those teach-first, fuck-off-later schemes. He wore a cravat and a hat to school. He was probably twenty-five but that was just 'old' back then. He had per-manent red cheeks but was otherwise very pale. He looked like a porcelain doll but one with a trimmed beard and styled moustache. He was short, five foot five maybe, but he had presence. And he loved to speak. And he loved the idea of getting us to fuck over the private schools. And we loved that too. It was an instant bond. He would sit with us in the library with *The Economist*, and *The Guardian* and *The Telegraph*, telling us what it all signified. Cramming. Giving us practice topics and cue cards. He wanted us to win so much that once he screamed at little mouse Elaine after she couldn't remember her points and she nearly lost us our place in the rotary final. Which of course me and Nems then smashed. It was a joke with us that the school had to build a trophy cabinet for our trophies. Each one we won he'd say 'they'll have to put a new shelf up now, girls'.

Extra-curricular is what got me into Cambridge, I have no doubt. It got Nems into Durham and it got Mr Hunter into whatever graduate scheme he disappeared into. And I tried debating once I got there, but it wasn't the same without her. Or him. I didn't want to do it on my own. I couldn't win.

It got us in, but after that it just left us there. And when I arrived there, I needed a break. It had taken all of my strength to be the prize pony, and still look after Mum at home, and earn, and hide it all. And that's the opposite of what the rest there were doing. I know I should have got there and kept swimming but I was exhausted. They hit the ground running and I hit the wall and that was that. Nems did better, because she always does. Some people have magic to them. It's like they breeze through life and it works for them. It's like they are playing a better version of this game. I am not one of those people. And sometimes the allure of it makes me want to be with her, hang onto the coattails, and sometimes it makes me want to punch her.

But all of this, it makes me treasure her. I would follow her to the ends of the earth for making this work. She sorted the office, rent-free, for a year. All we had to do was give a presentation to the board of the charity that runs this place. Put up a new shelf, girls. And it's not even her main hustle. She did this for us. For me.

It's not even much but I have really made it work for us. The room is dim, so we made it cosy. We put up pictures of people who they would find inspiring but not threatening. Malala, Martin Luther King, Buddha, Stacey Solomon. Our desks are to one side, totally artificial, we don't do admin here really, but we want to give the impression of us as busy, smart people taking time out to help. It's like a therapist's room, but with softer furnishings. 'It has to feel as safe as the womb,' Naomi declared when we were working out the decor. We aren't doing the lord's work here. We are taking their money. Make no bones about it. We don't have the time in our lives to make them understand, and even if we did, it wouldn't pay enough to compensate us.

First time we tried to flex into the new idea we lost a client over it. It's not an easy shift and we tried it too fast. A fifty-year-old, twice-divorced dad. He looked so good for it though, he looked styled every time he came in. In good shape. Everything about him screamed money and he thought it did the opposite. Scruffy hair, in excellent condition. Beat-up backpack that I Googled and cost four hundred pounds. I counted thousands of pounds that made him look so understated. He skateboarded in the first time he came and that alone made me want to try it out on him. It was his first time seeking any sort of help, and he had been coming for a month. He had come on to each of us separately, so I think he had his own goals too.

He was talking, at length, about how angry he was that his first ex-wife wanted to use their house in France all summer. He didn't even want to keep the place on. It was a burden. The magic word!

'OK,' I said, 'just as a thought experiment...' (thought experiments are, after all, the heart of a debate) 'playing devil's advocate here. What if you just gave it to her?'

I'm hoping I know what's going to come next, and it does.

'Give it to her? I would sooner cut my balls off and post them to her. No, she's the last person on earth I would give it to.'

'Then give it to us,' Naomi says. It hangs there for a second and I look at Naomi. We are way out on a little limb, but you never know.

He laughs. He sits up on the sofa. He looks at us like he is trying to figure us out, and then something clicks and he regains his composure. My blood runs cold. He starts speaking to us in the false, jovial way he did that first time he met us, that we had gently worked at getting him to shed. That way he uses to assure us that he is absolutely the same as us and that he is not racist or sexist or classist, he is exactly on a level with everyone. The way my posh boyfriend at uni would talk to cab drivers, the only time in his life he said mate and talked about football. He leaves the session early, and when I send him his next appointment reminder, he politely cancels. A week later Naomi sends me a link to a song he's put up on his godawful Soundcloud about trust. The thrill, the fear, the abject terror of being rumbled. But thank god someone like him would never want to make that humiliation public. It was a warning shot to do things with a much lighter touch.

The next time we pitched it as a kind of Cognitive behavioural therapy style thing, to try, just to try, just to see if it helped things feel easier. We asked Olivia, who had spent every session saying she wanted to branch out on her own, just to try diverting the support her father gave her each month, just for a couple of months, so she didn't have to feel beholden to him. We arranged for her to stay in Naomi's sister's spare room. She managed two weeks before we got a phone call, direct from the man himself.

We tried and tried and I was starting to feel like it would never happen. 'They don't actually want to lose out. They just want it hidden, not taken. They want the stuff, not the guilt. We know this.'

Naomi's eyes light up. 'So we have to better link the guilt to the stuff!' I see her again at school, first hand up every single time. Prefect, head girl, every possible little badge. Every single pat on the head she could get, then taking the piss out of it all with me on the bus home. She looks at me like, 'We know this. This is a game to work out how to win.'

We spent a week drawing up the rules. We had to make it very clear that we were to tell them that we were just administrating the takeover of assets. Not because we wanted the money. If we want the money then they think we are envious, and they all hate that. If we want the money then they want the money too. Or at least they want the money to make sure nobody else gets it.

The first try, we get a Range Rover.

I am not even joking. We get a car and its previous owner is fucking elated to be getting the bus. He keeps calling us saying he has 'never felt so normal'. He emails us an anecdote about the conversation he had with the lady sat next to him. I think it had been years since he'd spoken to a stranger who wasn't a waiter. I don't even dare look up how much it is worth. He fucking signed it over to us, and he laughed as he did it. He signed it over to Nems because I can't drive, but that is a moot point, and as I pointed out to her, it makes her my de facto chauffeur.

A week later we drive it to Imogen's holiday home in Cornwall, as she is no longer going to be using it this summer. She is going to a caravan park and she's so excited she's started an Instagram about it: @myrealsummerfamily.

Six hours driving, with me and Nems in the front laughing and bopping away and Mummy in the back asking questions. Mum is tense in ten different ways. The last time we went away somewhere, I was tiny. I don't even know when she last left London that wasn't just a day to visit some old family up north somewhere. 'Which friend from university, Naomi? Which friend is this? Have I met them? And they're not needing it? They really don't need it? And you are sure about this? And this car, oh you've done so well for yourself.'

Mum falls asleep, smiling and contented. She's pleased with me by extension. It goes without saying that this is the biggest house I can remember setting foot in. Imogen has organised for the chef to come. When she mentioned it, I flashed a look at Nems and she smiled to confirm that yes, neither of us had a clue that these places came with staff, and that yes, we had narrowly avoided the fuck up of Imogen knowing that too. If we don't understand how things are done, we can't be a safe pair of hands.

We stay for three weeks. I want to get used to it. Every morning the chef, Maureen, puts on coffees and we sweep downstairs and drink them looking out at the bay. Nems wears sunglasses in the house and calls me Dahhling. Mum can't get into it, and evenings she's in the kitchen trying to help out, determined that she won't have anything done for her. The chef, Maureen, is about her age and by the last week she's just given up and mum just cooks with her then they sit up chatting together.

The little cove that belongs to the house is pretty, but you have to climb down to it so mum mostly sits out by the pool and waves at us. I don't know if I've ever seen Nems in water but one night after dinner, we get overexcited and jump into the sea, screaming and yelping at the cold and how it takes your breath away. And I can't stop saying 'But it was so hot today!' like I will not believe how the night works, and Nems is just flat out laughing at me and trying to float so she can look up at the stars. So many stars it's like there's a VIP room for stars I didn't know about; and fresh air, and water. I have to check myself because I'm in it, and I'm staying in it.

After we get home, it is like we have brought something back with us. We buy so many new clothes, and our focus is on the quality of the fabrics and what to wear alongside each other. We update the website. We spend a week looking for venues to host our retreats, and every single one we show up at treats us like the real deal. They look us up and down and nod their heads and take us on tours like we should be going on tours.

I come up with the best idea during a session with Amelia, mid-divorce from a Tory MP. The more she says his name the more I remember the sex scandal but I try not to let it register on my face. We weren't doing well with her and out of nowhere I say, 'I know what it's like to be where you are, because, believe it or not, I was in your position once.'

Naomi raises her eyebrows like *OK girl you enjoy yourself, let's see where this goes.* She's used to me improvising and I think she likes the challenge. We are getting good at this so let's see how much fun we can have, she's thinking.

'Before I met Naomi at Cambridge...' I can't resist getting in anti-Durham jabs when she can't fight back.

'OK,' Naomi says, licking a smile off her lips.

'Before I met Naomi, there wasn't a single part of my life that felt real or authentic to me. I never fit in at school, and when I was home for the holidays, I don't have to tell you how lonely that can be. It doesn't matter how beautiful the place in Capri is, does it?'

Nems has moved to looking concerned, holding her pencil and I know she is loving this.

'I didn't know what a normal life was, I just knew that I wanted it, that I wanted to... step away from the loneliness and the frigidity and the dysfunction of the world around me. I didn't want to feel guilty anymore and I wanted to build my own life, for myself.'

Amelia is staring at me with a kind of devotion, like I've converted her.

'Are you a buddhist, Amelia?'

We talk a bit about how the world you can see is the world you create, but how she could create an entirely different one. We talk so gently, on tiptoe, about how having less is having more. About how giving is receiving.

The next week Amelia is on one. She emails me every day, just me, which Nems cannot get over. She wants to make a plan. She wants to try and convert some friends too. She wants to come on the retreats and she thinks I should write a book. I strategise with Nems about how to handle this flood of engagement. I think she wants a project; Nems thinks she just wants a friend. Either way we want to encourage her and lead her to her own ideas. Her own ideas being the ones we need to give her.

She has been paying us a retainer for four months when one day she tells me that she needs to get rid of everything. I lean back at my desk and cover my face. I didn't think we would get here for years, and I always thought it would be an older guy out to get revenge on his children or something. I didn't think it would be her.

We arrange an emergency session with her, just to test the waters. We both wear linen dresses because I want her to think of it like a religious experience. When she arrives in reception, I hug her and act like I'm trying not to cry. In reality I'm barely keeping a lid on all of this. We are so close to stepping up and we know it.

In the dim light we talk to her about unburdening herself and what that would mean. About how whatever we would administrate would then become a part of our organisation, which as she knows, is set up on buddhist principles to help as many people as is possible. We talk about how she could potentially (keep it far off and uncertain please) run retreats for us. I talk about her spirit. She goes through her various sources of income. Her assets. She is sure she can't remember them all, and she is sure that her soon-to-be ex wants to get his hands on whatever he can. She spits his name.

'Your spirit is so bright,' I say, stroking her hand.

The thing that strikes me is how hard it is. We have to split into two teams for her. Nems is on the new life and I'm on the old. Every time Naomi organises her a holiday or tries to talk to her about a regular job, I swear to god this woman bounces onto her feet like a cat. Everyone wants her on a board of something, everyone wants her at their summer house. We are only trying to get her just to normal, not even like we are trying to make things hard, but the money saves her every time. She can't fail downwards. I feel like if she went to prison it would have a tennis club.

I make a little more progress but it's slow and it does my head in. There is another reason I didn't finish my law degree, and it's because it's dry as the Sahara Desert. It feels physically like my will to live is being scraped out, even when I know the prize is winning the lottery. The ex-husband's maintenance can be diverted to our organisation. We can work on getting the house signed over to us. Same with some of her passive income. We can meet up and talk about her savings, too.

At the next session she says she admires nurses, so we set a nurse's income as her ideal budget to live on. We can administer it from her maintenance and help her learn to live on it. Only after she leaves do I see that Nems is almost shaking with anger. She's never usually the one to get annoyed so it almost frightens me to see her like it. I hadn't been thinking; her mum is a nurse.

'She wants to play dressing up? Fuck her. Fuck her.'

But then we start to laugh because what the fuck have we created? We are paying her not to be a nurse.

'When is she going to catch a fucking clue though?' she says after a minute.

The two or three or honestly god-knows weeks pass by where I'm losing the plot because all I can do is sit with mum and try to make her comfortable while we wait all day, every day, for a cancellation at the free clinic. The whole time I'm stroking her hair and trying to make her more comfortable on the plastic leather chairs that make you sweat and slide slowly off. I can barely sit still; I just keep thinking there's something I can do. I keep going back to reception, like a fly diving against a window.

I keep thinking about the shock after I tried to take her to a private clinic. Walking in like 'this is it, we VIPs now' and sitting in the reception and being brought a coffee and a water each. The reception done up somewhere between a hotel and a spa and quiet and empty. And then the doctor so attentively telling us everything we already know. And then showing us the treatment options where the scale of the money felt like they were adding zeros for fun. And trying to work out how I can tell Nems that we've got to speed shit up and knowing she wouldn't risk it, and knowing she is right that it wouldn't work but this desperate feeling like I'm in a horror film trying every key in the door and it won't open.

All this money coming in and I can't even speed up her getting an ID. I tried to get myself on health insurance but even with that they won't touch me because of her status, and because I can't prove this income is forever. I'm dropping the keys on the floor and the murderer is walking up behind me.

And all the while I'm having to text my fucking 'friend' Amelia who is upset she's having to budget to buy food, and upset that she's realised Waitrose is expensive and upset that buying a coffee eats into your money and I want to call her and shout at her. I try to find it funny but it's one too many things for me to process. I am just about keeping my head above water, there can't be another thing.

And of course, the other thing decides it's the perfect time to ring the doorbell, doesn't it! Naomi calls me in to the office and I have to go. We sit next to each other with Amelia's sister on speakerphone. How am I this I'm stunned she found us? We are not hiding, that's part of the point. At first, Cordelia just asks us about the retreats, about if we offer counselling. I look at Nems and I can feel us building up to ace this. She smiles at me like we have nothing to fear here. She is appropriate and charming and she talks about our duty of care, about confidentiality. I can almost hear Cordelia eating it up, until she speaks again.

'I need to check that she's been honest with you...' she says, in a way that I can't divine. That's the hard part, it's like we are learning a different emotional language. The reservedness, the curtness, the friendliness even, the rules are all different. They sound like politicians. They are the politicians, I guess.

'My sister struggles with her mental health. She's bipolar, OK? She's had several psychotic breaks, OK? She's struggled with addiction. With... you bloody name it, OK?' She sounds angry but not with us and I think about Amelia, who has only ever really been sweet and earnest and alone.

'The whole family has struggled, my father can't cope with it anymore. Anyway. It looks like she's on another bender and I need to know what your organisation is doing to help her.'

I take a breath and I dive in, aware of how I am pronouncing every word. 'At our organisation, our sole focus is on making our clients feel happier and more able to live a life that is authentic to them and their needs. It's a therapeutic organisation, but we are here to provide coaching on a more practical level too.'

'And are you aware of her medical history?'

Naomi jumps in. 'No, that's not something that she's chosen to disclose to us.'

'Right, but you're counselling her, don't you have a right to her medical history?'

I hear Nems swallow. 'That's not how we operate.'

I hear a click on the line and I brace myself for something.

'What are your credentials, actually? Where did you qualify?'

I look at Nems and she looks at me like 'how do we play this?' And I don't know. I don't know. It's like everything has slowed right down and I remember when at uni they asked me 'Where did you go to school?', and I didn't even realise I wasn't answering their actual question until it was too late.

'We understand that you're worried about your sister, but we are here to work with her and part of that contract is that we maintain her confidence, and that we take her side in things.'

Did I say that or did Naomi? Where did it even come from?

I do not have the space in my mind to worry the way Nems is. It just seems clear to me now. We have to make sure the family don't get in our way, so we get her to cut them out. And I am genuinely sure that's best for her too. When Amelia shows up looking fucked and wired saying she can't pay for counselling any more it doesn't stress me. I tell her there is always money. There has to be.

I just want to be with my mum, none of this feels real or important anymore, it is just something we have to finish so that I can pay to get her treated. When Amelia calls and says she can't cope and she's crying and ranting down the phone it sounds like I'm listening to a car radio that isn't tuned in.

I almost hadn't noticed the change in Naomi until she starts at me, immediately one morning, like she's attacking me while I've barely made my coffee. I am still putting the pod into the new machine, I am still choosing my creamer sachet, it feels uncivilised to have her come at me like this:

'Don't you feel any sympathy for them?'

I don't know what to say. I don't feel anything.

'She's going to lose their home!' Naomi keeps going, she sounds so desperate.

'Yes.' That's all I can say.

We both sit there, staring each other down. Heavy nose breathing. Nothing.

Shrug.

'She's got kids!'

'Yes.' I say, shaking my head. Yes. So?

'They've had to leave their school.'

'Plenty of people we know had to move school when their parents got evicted. That's what being normal is. How else will she ever know?'

'Oh come on, it's not because of her though, is it?'

'It is... It isn't... Look, honestly? I don't know. It sort of is. It is true enough. My mum is fucking dying. She is dying. And fuck, she slept on the sofa of that flat for ten fucking years so I could have a room and what have I done to show for it? What happens if we don't do this?'

Now Naomi is silent. She's annoyed and she keeps shaking her head, trying to form the right thing to say and then stopping.

'Nems, we won't ever fucking catch up with them. Life is too fucking short to play a game that is not fair. It is not fair. We couldn't educate ourselves out of it and we can't do it just taking little bites.'

'Stop giving me a little speech. It wasn't supposed to be this... or... I didn't think it through, OK? I just thought about us pulling it off. But this woman is sick, she's really not in her right mind and her kids are going to get hurt. It's too... I don't want to be a bad person, I need to be able to look myself in the mirror here.'

Ah fuck you, I think. Fuck your jammy little life. Fuck you, at Christmas, with your nice parents. I am trying not to cry and it's making my throat and my neck ache and ache and ache. If I try hard enough, I can push it all back down and I can feel calm and numb.

'She is dying. We are all disposable and nobody gives a shit.' Am I giving a speech? I don't know.

'We don't need to go this far, is all I'm saying.' She knows I'm not going to change my mind. 'I want to step back, let's just go back to what it was. You said it yourself, all they want is to pretend, they only want to be tourists, and they don't really want to lose anything.' She takes a breath and stands herself up straighter.

'So, let them pay us, pay us well to give them a guided tour, why does it have to go this far? We could actually do some good, we are making good money.'

'Good money isn't enough to do fuck all.'

She knows I'm not going to change my mind and I have not seen her this distressed, maybe ever. She packs up her laptop and she takes a few personal things off her desk and she walks out, she won't even look at me, and I'm glad because I don't want to look at her. Pathetic little mouse.

I remember at school, right in the middle of our GCSEs a girl, Michelle Crook, stole a bottle of brandy from her dad and brought it in. After an exam the three of us sat out and drank it in the wasteland behind the school. We were rolling drunk. Screaming laughing, vomiting, rolling drunk. And then somehow we were back in school, in the headmaster's office. In that way when you're drunk that you've suddenly arrived in a new scene, lurching in. And I turn my head to see Naomi is sober and her uniform is smart and she is wriggling out of it. Brushing the dirt off her shoulders and readjusting her posture and walking out of the office and I am too paralytic to do anything but watch her go. She doesn't look back and the door shuts behind her.

It turns out that Nems should have warned me in her little speech that our legal standing wasn't as safe as we had thought. I shouldn't have dropped out of my law degree, it turns out. And of course, I didn't take into account what money can always do, because it is starting to be very clear that I won't ever know that.

Amelia's brother-in-law works for the *Times*, I do now know. And that he must have made it his pet project to look into us. I used to hate that she thought I was her friend but it hurts just as if she was when I find out that Amelia chose her sister over me.

I didn't take into account what someone who has always wanted a cause will do once they get one. How Amelia contacted every single one of our clients. How Amelia contacted her old friends to write about it. How Amelia convinced her ex-husband to speak in fucking parliament about it, talking about dishonesty like butter wouldn't melt. Amelia making it into an online campaign. Amelia on *This Morning* making Holly Willoughby cry. She really worked hard to fight injustice when she was personally affected, credit where it's due.

And then it's just something hitting me every day. Nothing is a surprise but every blow lands. The charity kicks us out of the office. Naomi will not speak to me.

The arrest. The newspapers. The legal fees that eat up every penny of money I have ever made.

Mum dying.

Losing the flat. Losing my waitress job. The trial.

On the steps of the court, I see Nems with her family all around her and she won't even look at me. I walk in on my own, trying to go over what I want to say, prepping my points. I think of the day we won the national schools final. This House Believes We Are All Middle Class Now. Won by Our Lady of Perpetual Unfairness. Can you imagine. This house believes in absolutely nothing at all. This house believes nothing means anything anymore.

# Ways With Mince

*Kathryn Simmonds has published three collections of poetry and a novel. Her writing heroes include Muriel Spark, George Herbert and Victoria Wood. Like Alan Partridge, she lives in Norwich.*

Dear Rosemary,

Please don't crumple this up – I know you're angry with me, but I just want to give you my side. I started this letter twice already, but I couldn't seem to make the opening right, so what I'm doing is just explaining things, as if you and me (should that be you and I? I'm a bit foggy on grammar) are sitting down together having a heart-to-heart. That obviously takes quite a bit of imagining after last weekend.

The first thing to say is, I'm sorry. I wish last weekend had never happened, honest to god. I wish I'd said to Mike, *you visit your parents, love, I'll have a go at the flaky garage door* – because that's been on my list for months, and Mike's never been handy, so I just look at it flaking away, saying to myself, 'Get that sorted, Sue! Please, just sort it out!' Those thoughts can go around in my head for weeks. I don't expect you're a procrastinator, Rosemary. I think you're a get-the-job-done type. I wish I was like that. Or I wish I had a Roy who'd get the job done (or more like, get someone else to!).

Anyway, that Saturday morning I actually got as far as B&Q, all ready to look out some sandpaper and a tin of primer, and then I thought to myself: No, Sue, this isn't right. You go and visit Rosemary and Roy, even if you don't fancy it. Because they are Mike's parents and you are Mike's wife and you should support him because marriage is a team game (I read that somewhere, 'Marriage is a team game').

Besides, I'd always kept this flicker alive, this little hope, that one day there'd be the breakthrough visit, the one where you and me I have a proper relax, lean on the kitchen island with a glass of Pinot and leaf through your recipe books. Maybe share a little giggle about some of Mike's funny ways. It's silly really, but I always thought there might come the day when things would change, when I could be the daughter-in-law you wanted. Well, not wanted exactly, but you know what I'm getting at.

So anyway, I ditched B&Q and the garage door, and flung some things into a bag, and I said to Mike, 'It's all right love, I'm coming with you!' And mentioned my line about marriage being a team game, thinking that might give him a smile, but he just sort of nodded and went back inside to double-check the bathroom window was locked (which it was. I think he's got a fear of very thin burglars. In all honesty, you couldn't get a squirrel through that window, even a fat one, and it jams. Another job for my To Do list!) So, there it was. Decision made. We were making the visit together. Team Sue and Mike! It was clear that Mike was a bit relieved actually, because it meant I could drive and otherwise he'd have had to catch the train.

Well, the drive down was lovely. I took the B-roads, passed some bright snatches of countryside, and I was definitely feeling positive. I'd also asked Mike – in a nice way – if he wouldn't mind chipping in a bit more conversation-wise during our stay. Roy's fond of his cross-word isn't he, and Mike is Mike, and that leaves just you and me, and sometimes I think we both feel the strain. I know I do. I love Mike to bits, of course I do, but while I'm getting this all down, I might as well say that I've had a few bleak moments. It must be the same with any marriage I suppose - it must be the same for you when Roy's banging on about the council bypass again – but here's something I've never asked: do you think Mike could be on some sort of spectrum or other? And if so, is it too late to get him looked at? Not that I'd change him, Rosemary. That's the way he is, the strong silent type. Well, the silent type. It's just, perhaps he could be tweaked?

Despite the pleasant drive, I did feel a bit knotted up when I saw your front door looming. It might sound silly, but I'm never completely myself when I'm in your house, always a little on edge. Still, I was determined to make the best of it, and when you opened the front door and we walked into the hall, there was that delicious waft of cooking and I thought, Ooh, moussaka!

You must know how much I love your moussaka (remember all the times I've asked for the recipe?) and the rich, meaty aroma was filling up the house, winning the war against potpourri in every room. It lifted my heart, Rosemary. Gave me something to look forward to.

You greeted Mike first, fussed him a bit, and then it was, 'Come in Susan!' and in I came, and you asked if I had a new scarf on, and that was nice, and quite a surprise too because you don't often tend to notice what I'm wearing. So, a good omen.

We had our usual pre-lunch sit down and a cup of tea. A chat about traffic, Roy always takes an interest. Then Mike and Roy had a whisky (or did Mike have a couple? He can be cheeky when there's a bottle out!) A bit more chit chat interspersed with the usual little pockets of silence.

It has a certain quality I've noticed over the years, the hush of your front room. When Mindy was still around, she offered a bit of background noise, what with her yappy hellos and the intermittent growling, but then she couldn't shake that flu and we were back to the creak of leather sofa, weren't we? Mike's never been what you'd call a conversationalist, that's always been my department, but when you're chatting for two there's more space to fill and sometimes when you're snatching about for something to say, you snatch the wrong thing. I snatched the wrong thing several times, Rosemary. I'm sorry. I want to say now that I didn't mean what I said about your new outdoor sculpture looking like recycling (I could see you were affected – I can always tell by your top lip). I had no idea you'd had it commissioned by a local craftsperson. It was just something to do with the rusty tones of the metal. A bit scrap-metalish, maybe? That's all I was getting at. But rust is a lovely colour. Some people have rusty hair, don't they, and you can get it in the box-dyes, I'm sure I've seen it. Rust is very sought-after really – except on a car (ha ha!). Anyway, what do I know about art! And then, somehow I was digging myself in even worse, and I tried to send Mike a look he might respond to, like HELP ME, but he just sat there staring at his phone, mute as a doorknob, bless him. So I tried to get us on to the subject of Her Late Majesty, because I know you loved the Queen, your eyes get that shiny far-away look, and she was a wonderful lady, and so many years dutiful service, she was all about duty wasn't she. Doing the right thing. Grinning and bearing it. And there must have been quite a lot bearing it, especially with her family. It does make you wonder what Christmas afternoons were really like at the royal estates, doesn't it! But even her Majesty couldn't save the day.

(By the way, I hope you didn't take offence when I said that thing about Princess Anne, because that sort of slipped out too, and it was only a joke. Something to lighten the mood.)

You disappeared soon after, off into the kitchen. Didn't need any help. Quite a bit of clanking, though I'd like to say again that I'm always more than happy to offer a hand, despite you liking to do it all yourself. Then it was your voice ringing out, 'Lunch! Lunch!' And then a pause, 'Lunch! Lunch!' Funny how you always say that twice. Like some sort of programmed announcement. 'Come through please!' And through we went.

The kitchen/diner looked immaculate as ever. I should say again I love what you've done with the sink area and that extra large mixer tap was definitely the right choice. And the tiles you've chosen for the backsplash are lovely too aren't they, really special. You'd think they were from Andalusia, not John Lewis. Well, it all looked very pretty with your white cloth on the table and the good cutlery, and I have to say, I sat there feeling quite calm, because food does that for me, calms me down, and I wasn't even thinking of the garage door or the other jobs I was going to get done at home. And then you sang out, 'Make a space, Michael!' like you always do, even though the space is already there and the mat is on the table waiting for the dish. It must be a habit from when he was little. The salads were out, and you'd done something with cous cous (all one word?), really shows what a detail person you are, Rosemary, keeping everything on theme. And finally you set down the moussaka still bubbling from the oven, cheesy brown topping, a little frill of aubergine peeking from the rim of the dish. Tell you what, I could have gobbled it up all in one go!!

Those TV chefs go on about how they love to feed people, how food is their way of loving their friends and family, and over the years I've tried to convince myself that your way of loving me is by not feeding me. I know you pride yourself on keeping trim, looking after your health – and you're looking after mine too, that's what I tell myself. That's what I told myself as you served up the gorgeous layers of spiced meat and béchamel and the smallest portion came my way.

Even so, it tasted wonderful, Rosemary! (Are those fresh oregano leaves? I can't find them in Asda. I've experimented at home but I just don't have the touch, it all turns into a big sloppy mess. Last time I tried adding a cinnamon stick, as suggested by an old Delia Smith I found in the library, but that was a disaster. Mike pulled his *What's happened this time* face, and to be honest I couldn't blame him). I never did much Home Ec at school, and it's harder to get the hang of it when you're older, even if you watch all the shows.

The other thing I've noticed with the TV chefs, they're big fans of eating, aren't they? I mean, look at Nigella crouched in a silky dressing gown, face lit by the fridge, giving us her *Aren't I naughty* look. Whereas, for someone who's so good at cooking, you have such restraint, Rosemary. Such self-control. The thing is, I'm not a rude person. Wait to be offered, Mum always said; don't dig in. But the problem is, I never am offered. When second helpings come around, you'll always say the same things, 'Now I know Susan is wise enough not to be tempted!' Or simply, 'A moment on the lips, isn't that right, Susan?' And I sit there and smile and watch Roy lick sauce off his chin.

But the truth is Rosemary, I'm a big build and I need my calories or my blood sugars drop. They do, and my stomach makes an awful racket when it's empty, like a bear waking up from hibernation, and I didn't think you and Roy would welcome that sort of soundtrack all afternoon. And here's the other thing, that particular weekend I'd forgotten my snack bag. I usually bring emergency supplies you see, crisps, bananas, Bounty bars, to help me through – but I'd forgotten them, what with the last-minute rush back from B&Q, and it was too late to nip out for a multi-pack of Hobnobs. So I had no option. I *had* to ask.

You'd just finished serving Roy and the spoon was still hovering in mid-air, and before you could do your line about a lifetime on the hips, I took my chance: 'Actually Rosemary, it was so tasty. I'd love a little bit more.' (I remembered too late your feelings about 'tasty'. It seems to affect you the way other people flinch if they hear the word fart. Words are funny like that, aren't they? All those little squiggles giving us different reactions.)

Anyway, I made my request.

It was like watching one of those grabbing claws in the arcade, wondering if it'll move to the right position and you'll strike lucky. The spoon stayed in the air for a long moment, and then you said, in an extra quiet voice, 'Oh. Well. I see,' not looking me in the eye, and sure enough another spoon of moussaka plopped onto my plate.

But it was such a little spoonful, Rosemary, and the giving of it seemed to have cost you something. Conversation died away altogether, and even my questions about your recent sunshine break in Kefalos went nowhere. I nudged Mike under the table but he didn't take the hint, kept refilling his wine glass and didn't seem that interested in the food.

Still, I did enjoy that little extra plop of moussaka. It was so ~~tasty~~ delicious, and all that lovely flavour packed in there. I tried to eat slowly, make it last.

Then it was washing up, a look at Roy's terrarium, and some more sitting.

Tell the truth, I don't know what Mike looks at all the time on his phone. Some of it's cycling, he seems to have lists of all the fixtures, who's won this and that. And he checks the forecast a lot for his angling, he likes looking up the latest on lures and what, and that's fair enough, but we weren't fishing were we. It was just us in your living room and no one was going anywhere.

Eventually tea time rolled around (sorry, supper! I always forget). Sandwiches and salad. No pudding. It took the edge off, but about half an hour later I was hungry. Not a passing idea of hungry, but an actual groaning space in the stomach hungry.

Now, if I can be honest, your 'No food after 7.30 p.m.' rule has always been a bit of a bugbear, Rosemary. I realise you're attached to your anti-bacterial spray gun, and you like to have the final wipe-down, but I need to eat. Ask Mike. He sees me all hours, slicing gherkins, poaching eggs.

I tried to mention it to Mike, whispered to him about toast. But he knows how you are about crumbs (you have such a bond the two of you, don't you?) and he was brought up with the 7.30 rule, so his body must have learned to adapt over the years. Maybe that's it, Rosemary. I've just never adapted.

In hindsight I should have held out, but by bedtime I was famished. That moussaka was taunting me as I lay awake: *'Sue, have a little taste... Sue, she'll understand if you're hungry... Come on Sue, the house is quiet now.'* I tried to control myself. Turned over in bed and buried my face in the duvet. Mike twitched and spluttered in his sleep, possibly having one of his snorkelling dreams, and in the end I had to get up.

The landing was dark. I knew which floorboard creaked and I told myself I'd just go downstairs and have a couple of crackers. Maybe an apple. But that was me fooling myself. We all fool ourselves sometimes, Rosemary. There was the dish in the fridge under Clingfilm. It was heavy and cold but that beautiful smell still came off the thick meaty filling. I stood and stared at it for a long minute. My heart was pumping high in my neck like I was about to do a smash and grab.

All the cutlery was in the dishwasher, and I didn't dare open it in case it jangled, which is why, when you walked in, I was eating moussaka from a spatula (it isn't my habit to eat from cooking utensils, I want to clarify that now). I'd only had two or three mouthfuls when the kitchen light snapped on. I nearly jumped out of my skin, the dish went flying, lamb mince everywhere, aubergine splattered all over.

Your face was a dangerous shade.

'What are you doing?' you said. Well it was more of a screech, wasn't it? And 'That was my mother's!' The dish was cracked in two, wasn't it. That's the hazard of tiles, there's more of a give with linoleum. We were both shocked. I tried to apologise, explain, but I don't know what I was saying, just that I was hungry, and you didn't seem to hear properly, only shot me a look and said, 'You should have got yourself a Bounty bar then.'

You were already wringing out the floor cloth, wouldn't let me help, though I wanted to, I really did, but you wouldn't have it. So I went back upstairs, passed Roy and Mike on their way down, coming to see what the fuss was. I got into bed and just lay there, my mind swirling round and round like a big pot of béchamel.

Next morning you could have cut the tension with a knife, though not a bread knife because that was out of bounds to me by then, along with the bread. No buffet-style breakfast, it was you at the counter with everything laid out. I watched you do the slicing. I was starving to be honest Rosemary, because I'd barely managed any moussaka, and exhausted because of the all-night worry. It was the thinnest slice of toast you served me, practically see-through, and I'm sure you know I don't get on with that very bitter marmalade you like. But I ate it up. And then, there we were, Roy with his golf shoes on and Mike in his lycra saying he was off for a cycle. And that left the two of us.

I was on the sofa, you in the armchair with the Gazette. I'd complimented the new fire guard. Nobody was mentioning anything about moussaka. I thought of Mike gliding along on his bike, and Roy whacking across the fairway and truthfully, I didn't know how we'd get through the morning. Then I had a thought.

'I've brought *Mamma Mia!*,' I said, because I'd spotted it in a charity shop, and I know you like Meryl Streep, so I'd bunged it in the bag.

There was a twitch from the paper. 'I don't think so,' you said. Then a horrible silence. Then from inside the Gazette a sigh darker than the rain clouds gathering over the back garden, 'She's done some terrible rubbish.'

If I'm honest, Rosemary, I'm not really a *Mamma Mia!* fan either, but I chose that film because I remembered you'd said something complimentary once about Meryl Streep, and your compliments aren't given lightly. In all truth, I'm not really one for films at all. I prefer a good book. Proper long thought-about stories. *The Mill on the Floss*, that's one of my favourites. I've read a lot, Rosemary, I'm in two different book groups, you probably don't even know that about me. I get a lot of time for reading actually, being married to Mike.

After another silence you folded the paper on your knee, and I knew it was coming, twelve years of the unsaid, like an inside downpour. You glanced out of the window, as if you were talking to yourself, and said in a lemony sort of voice, 'I should have made him see sense.'

The room began to pulse and I had a queasy feeling in my stomach, like I'd eaten a bad egg. Still, I tried to be polite. 'Not the weather for golf, is it?' Followed up with a nervous laugh.

'*Michael*,' you said. 'I should have made *Michael* see sense.'

I tried playing innocent. 'Oh, Mike's all right, he cycles in all weathers.'

Then you turned and looked at me full on. You took your tortoiseshell reading glasses off and I felt something bad was coming. And it did. 'It's not easy seeing him married to you.'

My legs felt watery, even though I was sitting down.

I think I said, 'Why?' But I didn't want to know why. You had me trapped Rosemary and there was nowhere to go.

You didn't answer directly, started on about Jennifer instead, what a lovely girl she'd been, how serious Mike was about her (I knew about Jennifer, skinny audiologist with a nasty streak. Dumped him in a Travelodge when she knew he couldn't drive). And then you said you couldn't believe it when he turned up with me. Thought it would never last. Thought he must be on the rebound, didn't interfere, knew his feelings had been hurt, realised he might want someone to talk to (someone to talk to! Mike!!).

None of it felt fair, Rosemary because I've tried, I really have. Researched your holiday destinations. Took pains with Mindy – even when she kept having those accidents on me (there's still a bite scar on my little finger). But on you went saying some pretty mean things, and the meanest was that I wasn't good enough for him, that's what you said to my face, Rosemary. You said, 'It was clear to me and his father that Michael should have made a better choice.' And that's when I told you to wind your neck in, and you said how dare I speak to you like that, and I felt proper shaky and ran upstairs.

I was panicked, Rosemary. Couldn't seem to calm down, my hands were all shaky and when I looked in the bathroom mirror my face was ashen. I knew Mike had a half bottle of brandy in his spongebag (helps him get off to sleep when he's been playing too much Minecraft) so I dug it out and started sloshing some into the bathroom beaker. I added water, but what with not having had a proper breakfast, it affected me, Rosemary. I'm not saying I wasn't angry – furious actually – but brandy is not my drink, and in fact I'm not really a drinker. Certainly not the way Mike drinks anyway. He must get that from Roy.

I remember there was a soft drizzle coming down outside, I sat on the edge of the loo and watched it with a far away feeling as I took big glugs from the beaker. Your voice was coming in and out like a wave. You must have been shouting from the bottom of the stairs. I heard you, but the voice seemed to come directly from inside my mind, the way it has so many times, accusing me as I reach out to buy tinned peas, or cut the nose off a wedge of brie (I didn't know cheese could have features before we met.) Only this time it wasn't the petty domestic comments, it was the full treatment. I remember coming out of my trance and standing at the top of the landing and there you were shouting up at me.

'Wasn't I allowed to be a grandmother? Wasn't I allowed to get something out of this arrangement?'

And I shouted down that me and Mike couldn't have kids, surely you'd worked that out, and you shouted up how you weren't surprised, what with me being so enormous. Well, that was a match to dry tinder. So then I was raging, wasn't I, raging.

(I'm sorry I swore at you then Rosemary, and I'm sorry for the language that followed. Thought I should do a blanket apology because I can't honestly remember all the details, things might have got quite creative. But you must agree that it wasn't fair, the things you were saying. And anyway, that boat has sailed long ago. Why would you even mention it?)

Up and down we were shouting, weren't we:

'Mike's infertile, it's nothing to do with my eggs!'

'How can I believe that? Look at the size of you!'

'Ask him!' And I started saying how he's always been out all hours on his racing bike where he doesn't have to speak to anyone, how it's warmed up his sperm, what with all that lycra chaffing away. And I might have given you too many specifics, but it's the truth, heat has an effect on the body, it affects me, makes me sluggish, which is why I never wear my fleece in the office. But your responses were not kind. Of course, I was shouting and swearing and probably slurring a fair bit, but to suggest he was on his bike trying to get away from me, that I was always yakking about nothing, well that was unfair.

What I shouldn't have done was retaliate. What I shouldn't have done was come charging down the stairs accusing you of trying to starve me on every visit, torture me at every meal – lamb tagine slow cooked with apricots, and pavlova piled with double cream, and me only ever getting a taste. What I shouldn't have done was open the fridge and cupboards and start tearing through them, taking bites out of whatever I could – cheddar, ham slices, digestives. Cornflakes flying about all over. All that Nutella, it went everywhere didn't it, like a dirty protest. I shouldn't have blamed you for making Mike the way he is, and I should never have threatened you with your own anti-bacterial spray gun.

I shouldn't have done that, Rosemary. It was wrong. But I was in the heat of it, and I couldn't calm down, I just couldn't, it felt so unfair, and all the pain I'd had with things you didn't know anything about, because Mike always wanted everything private. But I was shaking with all the rage and the hurt.

And suddenly Mike was standing there in his lycra and Roy wasn't far behind, both of them dripping with rain, and I was crushing cheese straws in my bare hands and you were sobbing.

It's a picture I can't get out of my mind.

Roy tried to calm things down, didn't he? Mike was shouting, actually shouting, (Mike!!) 'What have you done to her!' and it took me a minute to realise he was talking to me, not to you. It's a deep love that mother-son love, isn't it?

Off you went upstairs with Roy, the rain still thrashing at the windows, then Mike went up there too, and when he came down, he gave me this look I can't describe. Beyond disappointment, beyond coldness. And before I knew it, we were packing. I stumbled about through the blur doing what I could. Had quite a head on me, by then. We got the bags in the car, still being rained on. Mike told me to get in while he went back into the house. So I sat there for a while watching rain smear the windscreen. To be honest, Rosemary, I must have been over the limit. Well over. And Mike must have known that, but it didn't seem to occur to him. I drove off, but I had to stop at a Little Chef fifteen minutes later, have a black coffee and an all-day breakfast to sort myself out.

Sometimes I wonder what Mike would do, if he was a driver. Would he let his emotions out on the road? My dad was like that if he got riled up, lurch to a dead stop at the lights, whoosh into fifth gear, cut other drivers up left and centre. (You'll be pleased to know I didn't take after him! I always drive carefully no matter what's happening, and I drove along smoothly as I could, despite my banging head). But Rosemary, it was deathly quiet. Mike just zoned out – didn't even tell me what lane to get in, or thank the other drivers if they let us through like he does sometimes (it's quite sweet really, that little 'thank you' wave, his way of sharing the responsibility of the drive). He stared straight ahead. Didn't fiddle for Five Live, didn't reach for his 'Best of Level 42'. Just me and him and the traffic, me asking now and again if he wanted a fruit pastel, him never wanting one. I thought about swinging by Sainsbury's on the way home to get us something nice for tea, but deep down I knew a couple of Mediterranean chicken fillets wouldn't fix anything. Even if they were *Taste the Difference*.

That was a terrible night, Rosemary. Awful. We shared the bed, but he put his headphones on. Then he was up extra early, and he's been working late almost every evening. He's not talking to me, Rosemary. Well, he's often not talking to me, but this time it's deliberate.

I didn't mean for any of this to happen.

He's off on his bike somewhere now. I know it would help if you gave him a ring, softened the situation somehow. Do you think you could, Rosemary? Could you find it in your heart?

I finally tackled the flaky garage door. It was a long slow job, and even after I'd done my best with the sanding, there were still little flaky edges of paint coming up. It made me think, it's like being married, being there with a pot of primer, pasting over the flaky bits. But is it enough, Rosemary? Maybe the day comes when you have to take the entire door off – even if you don't know where to get a new one – and stand there and look into the darkness with all the muddle inside. I don't know if I'm ready for that.

When some time has passed, perhaps you and Roy would like to come over to us for a meal? A sort of peace offering? I can't cook like you, you know that already, but I'm trying. I really am. I've got a new recipe book, *Ways with Mince*, everything step-by-step. Actually, I was leafing through and there on page 19 what did I find? Moussaka! Doubtless it won't be up to yours, Rosemary. But I'd like to give it a try, if you'll let me.

What I wanted this letter to say is that I'm sorry; honestly I am. Perhaps when enough time has passed, things won't look so bad. Perhaps one day we'll even look back and laugh.

Your ~~affectionate~~ daughter-in-law,

Sue xx

# The Art of
# Genital Persuasion

*Kathy Lette has written twenty books, including fourteen bestselling novels, the first of which was* Puberty Blues *and the latest of which was* Till Death – Or A Light Maiming – Do Us Part. *She is published in over seventeen languages. Her books have been made into films, TV series and an opera. She also works as a TV presenter and travel writer.*

When judging penises, it's probably not the most appropriate time to make small talk. That's the only bit of advice I can pass on, if you are unsuspectingly called upon to undertake such a task – as was I, one bleak London day when I was abducted to a theatre in Shaftsbury Avenue by my best friend and told that now, for once and for all, I would be cured of my 'irrational fear of the phallus'.

Phobias are as common as freckles. Heights, snakes, spiders, commitment, crowds, work… Well, I suffered from a phobia which was a little harder to explain away, especially to prospective boyfriends. I was penis-phobic. Successfully brainwashed by the nuns at Our Lady of Mercy All Girls

School not to be a 'fallen woman' (the nuns failed to point out that women didn't actually 'fall', but were invariably *pushed*) – I'd only seen one or two male appendages in my entire life. And they'd terrified me. Especially during my late teens when they'd been unsuccessfully prodding and pushing at me in a cold car on some dingy back road accompanied by male cries of 'Is it bloody IN yet?' or 'What are ya? Frigid?' (When will sexologists realise that the problem is not women faking orgasms, but men faking foreplay?)

Did this penis-phobia cramp my style in later life? Well, put it this way: the Pope took to ringing me up for tips on celibacy.

Collette Kennedy, my best friend since primary school, on the other hand, was a penis-aholic. 'My name is Collette Kennedy and I am addicted to dick. I'm ad-dick-ed!' It was a love of word play which cemented our friendship from day one in year three when she asked me what reptiles were good at maths? I looked at her curiously and kept braid chewing. 'Adders,' she'd replied.

But it was the reptilian species known as the 'trouser snake' which now sparked her interest. A run-in with a lousy boss, a bad hair day, a hangover, a rejection by a casting director... could all be alleviated by taking the Phallic Cure.

Collette had thespian tendencies. Lesbian tendencies would have been preferable to her rather formal, academically inclined family, but um, sorry, absolutely no chance there. Collette giving up men was as likely as Prince Andrew getting a job in a day nursery. Her main stage roles had been limited to that of 'buxom wench number 2,' but she'd been murdered once or twice on *The Bill*, so had already written her Oscar acceptance speech.

My career choice was the antithesis of Collette's. I, Judith Jenkins, was studying to become a lawyer... Although all I'd experienced so far in my pupillage was a severe case of subpoena envy. The barrister I worked for gave me nothing more intellectually arduous than menial filing... And he seemed to require an awful lot of papers to be put away under 'x', 'y' and 'z' mainly as it clearly required a *lot* of bending over.

'What pins, Jenkins! Let's make the word of the day "legs"... Why don't you stay late tonight and we'll spread the word!' had been today's sexist comment de jour... Which I why I leapt with such alacrity to join Collette for lunch while she judged some competition or other at a theatre in Soho.

Collette was forever telling me to stand up to Rupert Botherington Q.C. She maintained that the reason I found men intimidating was because of my penis phobia. Demystification of the male was her mission... I just hadn't realised my conversion course would start that very day.

'Oh, goodie. I love judging competitions. What sort is it? Scones? Flowers? Pumpkin carving...?' I chirped as the taxi belched its way through Covent Garden.

'Ah, no... An audition.'

'Of course. Great.'

It wasn't until we strolled onto the stage that the horror hit me.

'Penises?!' I read the promotional poster. 'You want me to judge penises? Are you mad!'

'*Puppetry of the Penis* auditions. It's the cure, Judith. To your phobia. Surely you've heard of these Aussie guys? They perform a kind of genital origami. Anyway, the show is so successful the producers urgently need more puppeteers... And, as the producers are all gay, they booked me and some other actresses to judge the boys' performances from a heterosexual point of view. And I took the liberty of signing you up, also.'

'Um... I know I'm training to be a cutthroat lawyer, but this is taking the term "naked ambition" a little too literally Collette. ...I mean, saints preserve us!'

'And don't give me any of that shy convent shit. You know how I loathe that miserable God with his white beard and wagging finger.'

As Collette dragged me toward the other four female 'judges' already sitting behind a desk, my shoes left skid marks visible from outer space.

'WARNING: these craft ideas are for amateurs. Do try this in your own home...' One of the puppeteers greeted me with a wink, as he strolled out from the wings. I made a mental note not to visibly react to the fact that he was stark bollocking naked.

Sitting behind the desk, I made another mental note: kill Collette and sell her internal organs on the internet.

As more naked men wandered onto the stage, my eyes darted about like pinballs in a wonky machine. Unlike Collette, I'm not all that comfortable with public nudity. I've been to a nudist beach only once, in Greece. Gritting my teeth, I tried to shed my swim suit and divebomb face down onto the towel in one deft movement – which merely resulted in a grazed chin, a cracked rib and a bit of seaweed up my freckle. Mortified, I lay rigid on the sand, fantasizing about putting my clothes back on. Then, just to be really kinky, I fantasised about other people putting their clothes back on as well. So, you can imagine how I felt about this undress rehearsal.

Clipboard in hand, I perched one bottom cheek precariously onto my swivel chair. As the twenty or so male job applicants trooped about on stage in their birthday suits, I tried to put a positive spin on things. There are, after all, some good things about being nude. First off, you never have to buy anyone a drink – 'I'm sorry. But my money's in my jeans pocket.' Nor is it likely anyone will ever steal your barstool. Having a dress code which reads 'clothing optional' also does away with all that boring 'I've got nothing to wear!' angst.

But then the contenders started to audition. I wasn't quite sure where to look. I glanced at my clipboard for help. The score sheet comprised a list of boxes to be numbered from one to ten.

**Facial looks**

**Body**

**Appendage**

**Comedy skills**

It was not unlike the kind of questionnaire Collette no doubt handed out to a prospective boyfriend, really, I thought, trying to calm my mounting anxieties. The term 'mounting anxieties' only made my anxieties mount more... Feigning nonchalance, my eyes slid down the list till they snagged on the last category which read:

**Tattoos, Piercings/Other.**

'Other?' I gasped in a piercing whisper, 'What could they possibly mean by "OTHER"?'

What was left of my mind boggled and my heart beat out a drum solo against the wire in my bra. Overcome with timidity, I decided to concentrate on **Personality** and made eye contact with each contestant in turn to ask some basic questions. But eventually, having exhausted queries on hobbies and star signs, I had no choice but to slide my eyes slightly southwards…

All the applicants had serious *pecs appeal*. Judging by their muscled physiques, these blokes were of the *excuse me while I do the six hundred metre butterfly, climb two alps and abseil back down for some dressage and parachute formation before lunch* types. Next to the boxes marked **Bodies**, the all-female judging panel enthusiastically scribbled their **10/10** scores.

I would also have given the candidates high marks… except that my hand was shaking so badly I couldn't write. It was palsied with terror because the time had come to look at the men's appendages. I'd heard of clubs for 'Members Only' but these auditions seemed to be taking this motto too literally. Besides which, it was my lunch hour and I was decidedly worried that what I was about to see might put me off my ham and cheese baguette. With trepidation, I lowered my gaze even further…

If *I* was nervous, the candidates were more so. As the female collective gaze lingered at groin level, the men before me deflated faster than a pump-up plastic lilo at the end of a beachside holiday.

'At least we know that the art of *shrivellry* is not dead!' Collette whispered to me. But as the director put the train-ees through their puppeteering paces, all the candidates rose heroically to the challenge.

In the next five minutes, the 'wow' factor of balloon animal shapes definitely paled into insignificance. Those well-known party tricks usually performed with balloons, were now recreated with penis, testicles and scrotum. The fleshy origami on display included the 'Atomic Mushroom,' the 'Hamburger', the 'Lockness Monster,' the 'Windsurfer,' the 'Baby Bird,' the 'Boomerang' and the 'Eiffel Tower.'

Collette dug her elbow into my ribs. 'Well, what do you think?'

'The only apt word for such a spectacular performance is "Outstanding", really,' I told her, breathlessly.

Collette giggled. As did I. Only I couldn't stop. The laughter started to effervesce up in me like champagne. Nervous laughter I suppose, mixed with relief that this pit of 'trouser snakes' weren't the carnivorous, venomous, aggressive creatures I'd feared, after all. And my laughter proved contagious. Soon we were all guffawing, judges and job applicants alike.

The barrister I worked for had inveigled me into a drink after work on my first day, only to dragoon me into a lap dancing club. The atmosphere had been predatory and sinister. Men watched from the shadows in eerie silence as scrawny, naked young women acted out their ersatz sexuality. But this naked experience was the opposite. With cheery rascality and matter-of-fact humour, the naked men before me were happy to satirise their own sexuality. And there was not a whiff of sleaze, exploitation or baby oil.

'You see?' Collette prodded me again. 'It's nothing more than fear of the unknown. Blokes get to ogle naked women on a daily basis – magazine centrefolds, internet porn, advertising. Naked women are used to sell everything from toothpicks to tractors.'

'The true meaning of "ad nauseum,"' I agreed.

'Exactly! But when it comes to the male appendage, women just don't often get to look it in its eye. I figured once you got to scrutinise a few scrotums they'd no longer threaten you. So, what have you gleaned?'

I glanced back at the performers. What I'd gleaned is that penises, like snowflakes, are each of them different. There's the lean, slinky, kinky ones. The thick, succulent types. The low-slung gunslinger sort. The stubby button mushrooms. The round-heads. The hooded eyes. The meat and two veg, packed-lunch variety. And women like them all. We judges admired every different shape and size. All this male angst over size when it's attitude women are really interested in. Women like a male member which says 'G'day! God, am I glad to see YOU! That is, with your consent.' And we certainly appreciate an appendage trained to do theatrical tricks for female entertainment. At the end of the auditions, we applauded heartily; and it was clear that the candidates on stage also looked pretty pleased with the way things had gone.

'Now *THAT'S* what I call a standing ovation,' I told Collette as we left the theatre, hooting with laughter.

That afternoon I didn't skulk, but strode back into chambers. Rupert Botherington Q.C's reprimand for being late was compounded by a threat to report me to our Head of Chambers; except that this warning was followed by a salacious wink and a suggestive purr. 'Of course, you could always placate me by letting me know just exactly where those legs of yours end...'

Instead of wilting, I found myself imagining him naked, his scrotum comically stretched into a wind surfing sail. I then told him that these legs he so admired were now going to walk me to his Head of Chambers to file a report for sexual harassment.

*Puppetry of the Penis* is referred to by the puppeteers as 'the Ancient Australian Art of Genital Origami'... But I prefer to think of it as the Art of Genital Persuasion. When the aptly named Botherington then got his #MeToo moment, my ham and cheese baguette had never tasted more scrumptious.

# Go Your Own Way

*Kimberley Adams, a lifelong writer who only recently let her words loose on the public, is now the published author of several short stories, and has been listed in many well-known writing competitions. As a Geordie, Kim is surrounded by warm, funny people. Throw in spectacular scenery, and writing inspiration is never hard to find.*

'You'll look ten years younger, Nana, I promise, just like on that programme on the telly.'

'You will, Nana Mary, you'll look lush,' said my bestie Shania, like she was some expert stylist from a glossy magazine, which is maybe stretching the imagination a bit too far as Shan's idea of Haute Couture is the top shelf of Sports Direct.

'Only ten years? At my age you'd better make it twenty, otherwise it's not worth the effort. Oh, and by the way Shania, that programme makes them all look worse, the one last week ended up looking like a Cockerpoo in lipstick.'

'Nana! You can't say that.'

'Well, I just have Donna, pet. Call a spade a shovel I do. So, you two, are you sure you've done this before?'

'Aye, Nana, millions of times. Shan, just keep that phone still so I can see the video.'

My best friend Shania is not known for her ability to keep still. Ever.

'Video? What do you need a video for if you've done it so many times already?' demanded Nana, with more than a tinge of suspicion creeping into her voice.

'Just following the lines of the brow, that's all, Nana.'

Channelling my best soap opera acting skills, I smile confidently at her before delivering the all-important line.

'You won't regret it…'

Cue, dum-dum-dum-dum-di-dum-dum-dum!

'And what do you say this thing is called?' she asks, sounding more than a little worried.

'It's called mic—' began Shan, but I managed to cut her off in her prime with a swift poke in the ribs with a ruler.

'It's just putting your eyebrows back like what they were when you were young, Nana,' I butt in, as Shan glowers at me, rubbing her side.

'I swear down, Don, if you've clicked me shell-suit I'll not be happy. It's original vintage you know, all the rage in the eighties. The Grinch found a box of them in the back of Pound Xpress, he throws nowt away, says everything will make a comeback eventually – what goes around comes around and all that.'

'Shan, pet,' said Nana, 'I remember them the first time and all I can say is don't get too near a naked flame, or you'll go up quicker than the Kings Head when Ozzie the Optic didn't pay his protection money. Anyway, back to the eyebrows, Donna, I plucked them all out in the 1960s in an attempt to look like Twiggy and haven't had any since. I'm quite happy with my eyebrow pencil.'

'Who's Twiggy, Nana Mary?' Shania raised a non-plucked, non-microbladed eyebrow.

'A model in the sixties,' replied Nana. 'Gorgeous she was, still is, and we all wanted to look like her, but most of us had more fat on our cookery pinnies than she had on her entire body.'

'Is that why she was called Twiggy?'

'Yes, Donna because she was as thin as a twig.'

'Eeh Nana, you can't say things like that anymore either. It's called body shaming.'

'Body what? I don't think Twiggy was ashamed, and she still gets called that now and I bet she doesn't mind.'

'Well maybe not, but it's just not the done thing to call anyone out on their appearance anymore.'

'Only on the sly to your mates,' said Shan, tapping the side of her nose and bursting out into peals of laughter.

'Eeh pets, it's a different world for you lot than it was for me. We'd strived for years for freedom of speech, and now you're telling me we can't say what we want to say anymore. How does that work then?'

'I know Nana, it's not easy for us either you know, things change, and different things trend every day, it's hard to keep up.'

'Trend? What's that when it's at home? Donna, Brenda the Bag was telling me that people aren't just he and she anymore. I couldn't take it all in so maybe you'd better enlighten me.'

'Erm, well, it's all very, err, complicated, Nana. I'll explain that another time eh.'

*Like when someone proves the world is flat!*

'So back to the eyebrows,' I say, desperately trying to move the conversation away from a potential inter-generational minefield. 'Just think how much time this will save every morning and you'll be doing me such a favour. Mam says I need to find something I'm good at or she's going to make me go and work with her in Go Your Own Way, and Nana, I cannot work with dead people.'

'Eeh well, just think pet,' she cackled, 'you'd be able to call them whatever you like, and they aren't going to mind at all! So, what's that ruler for, apart from poking Shan in the ribs?'

Between us, Shan and I had managed to acquire a microblade, but the geometry gadget to measure the brows had thus far evaded us. They didn't stock them in Pound Xpress in the precinct.

'Oh, just to measure where to put your brows, Nan.'

'And will it hurt?'

'No, absolutely not, we're going to put some numbing cream on first.'

Truth be told it was a tube of gel to put on mouth ulcers that we'd got from Pound Xpress. Tommy the Tatt said he swore by it, and just to ignore the instructions, which is just as well considering they're written in Chinese. We measured Nan's brows and put dots where they would eventually go, and Shan rubbed in some of the cream.

'Before you start microblading...' boomed the Video, giving me no chance to turn the sound down.

'Blading?' yelled Nan, catching sight of a bleeding eyebrow on the screen, and the blade glinting in my hand. 'What the bejeezus?' She frantically began rubbing her eyes, 'I can't see a thing' she cried, 'I've gone blind.'

She slumped, eyes tight shut, onto the settee.

'Oh my god, you've killed Nana Mary. Quick, give her mouth to mouth or something,' screeched Shan, running round the living room like a demented chicken.

'I haven't killed her. You've blinded her!'

'I swear that I didn't put the gel near her actual eyes. She looks well dead to me,' wailed Shan. 'There's one of those Defroster machines at the library, will I go and get it?'

'Just go and get me Mam, quick!'

Shan ran out of the door to go up the street to our house, and I gingerly lifted Nana's hand, feeling for a pulse. There wasn't one.

'Oh Nana, I *loved* you sooo much. I'm so sorry, I didn't mean to give you a heart attack and kill you, I just wanted you to look nice.'

'Nice?' she shouted, sitting bolt upright and snatching her hand away, almost giving me a heart attack in the process. 'How could anyone look nice after having their eyebrows butchered with a rusty blade, eh? And in case you think this is me talking to you as a ghost, I'm not dead! Just for the record Donna, that is not where you find a pulse, so don't be considering a career in nursing any time soon either.'

'Mam, Mam, what have they done to you?' shouted my Mam as she rushed through the door, Shan in hot pursuit, her face flushed, the nylon shell-suit visibly sticking to her sweaty skin.

'Don't panic, Bernie, I'm fine except hardboard and cardboard here have glued me bloody eyes together.'

Mam spun around and I swear there was steam coming out of her ears.

'What have you put on her eyes?' she demanded.

'Erm, just some numbing cream, Mrs Dobbs, but a hundred percent I didn't put it on her eyelids,' whimpered Shan, pulling at her suit and looking more uncomfortable by the moment.

'Go and get some warm water and towels and be quick about it.'

Ten minutes later we were all sat having a cup of tea. Nana's eyes were fine; true to her word, Shan had only put the gel on the brows. In her early days Nana had been in a dance group called Troupe Romano with her brother and sisters, and the lure of performance had never quite left her. This was a fine example of one of her theatrical dying swan moments. Her eyebrows back in place, courtesy of her stubby, well-worn Rimmel pencil, she was as right as northern rain. Shan however was not. Running up the street to get Mam had made her so hot that the bright blue dye out of the ancient shell-suit had seeped onto her skin and had turned her into Papa Smurf.

'Oh my god Donna, what if this doesn't come off?' she wailed, scratching at her blue arm.

'Never mind, pet,' smiled Nan, 'Donna can always microblade it off for you!'

Mam had her face on. The one that made clear her disappointment in me.

'Donna, me and your dad are so proud of you getting your place at University, the first ever Dobbs to go.'

Nana preened up like a peacock on a promise, and Papa Shan did the fingers down her throat gesture from behind a cushion.

'But,' continued Mam, 'I told you that you couldn't sit on your lazy backside for months while you waited to start your course.'

'Err Mother, I did say I should be going on a gap year, or six months at least.'

My head had been full of the wondrous possibilities of world travel, of life beyond Lockley, my village on the outskirts of Newcastle. Maybe follow the Asia trail, experiencing the smells and sounds of street life in Thailand from a Tuk Tuk. Or perhaps become a boho babe in Ibiza and do early morning yoga to the rising sun, but the reality was that I had been offered two weeks in Brenda the Bag's semi-derelict caravan in Skegness. It was all we could afford.

'Well, you could have gone to Brenda's van,' said Nana belligerently. 'The club house is great, bingo on every night.'

'I know Nana, but Skeggy isn't exactly experiencing the cultural diversity of another part of the world, which is what a gap year is all about.'

*That and a copious amount of hedonistic partying, of course.*

'Donna pet, I don't even know what a gap year is. I started work when I was fourteen and only got time off when I produced your mam and her sister, and then it was straight back to the pickle factory for me. Your mam and Auntie Terri still hate pickled products to this day, I'm sure it affected my milk.'

Shan at this point was stuffing the cushion in her mouth. I'm not sure whether it was in an attempt not to laugh, or to stop herself from being sick.

'I told you to find yourself a temporary job, or some voluntary work,' said Mam, still wearing the face.

'I have tried, Mam, I promise, just there was nothing that used my particular skillset.'

'Skillset? And pray do tell, what are your skills? I'm agog with anticipation.'

'Well, you know, err, writing.'

'Donna, I know you want to be a writer, but I think you have a long way to go. Quite frankly, in order to write you need actual life experiences to write about, so taking any job should help in that respect. Anyway, I've made my decision, you start with me at Go Your Own Way on Monday. I've cleared it with Mr Papadopoulos, he's fine about it because he's not paying you.'

'Not paying me? What kind of job is that?' I ask incredulously.

'Just let's say you will be paid in experience, which will help you become that famous author you talk about.'

'But Mam, I just can't work there, even if I got paid shedloads... but that might help,' I said expectantly.

'No pay – end of discussion,' said Mam firmly.

'But the stress of it all might kill me.'

'Well, you'll be in the right place, won't you? And you'll get staff discount. Donna, all you're going to be doing is making the tea and answering the phone. You're good with people, especially those of the older generation, just look how you fitted in with the Library Volunteers, they all love you.'

'Aye, they do,' said Shan nodding, 'and most of them are ancient and deffo potential customers, no disrespect Nana Mary.'

'Cheeky young whippersnapper,' cackled Nan.

'Please don't tell me I need to wear that ridiculous uniform?'

'I'd wear that jumpsuit, it's pure belta,' said Shan enthusiastically.

'Point proven, Shan,' I muttered sarcastically.

'Well, I think it's very practical,' said Nan. 'Non-iron as well eh, Bernie? Marvellous for jumping out of planes. It reminds me of Anneka Rice, although she looked bet... erm, just it's very unforgiving on some legs, if you know what I mean...'

'Who's that?' piped me and Shan in unison, whilst Mam looked ready to deck Nan.

The staff uniform at Go Your Own Way was not exactly funereal. Mr Papadopoulos said that to set them apart from other funeral companies, there would be no sombre black, and came up with a multi coloured jumpsuit which, quite frankly, would distress a lot of people, even if they weren't in mourning. Mr Papadopoulos had some weird ideas about the world of undertaking, but the residents of Lockley seemed to embrace the alternative approach, and whilst Mam never discussed her work, it was common knowledge that there had allegedly been some very bizarre celebrations. Apparently, according to Tommy the Tatt, someone is buried under the eighteenth hole at Lockley Golf Course. Suddenly though, I had one of those lightbulb moments. Mam might have a point. Just think of the stories I might get out of this experience. I could write a book. *Handy Hacks for the Dead* by Donna Dobbs sounds rather good. I could end up a massive influencer like Mrs Hinch, I mean not everyone cleans, but we all die, so I could make a killing, pardon the pun. I make a mental note to put the ideas in my journal for future reference and congratulate myself on my creative genius.

'OK then, Mam. As long as I'm not helping in the backroom, I'll do it.'

I know the backroom to be the nerve centre, the business-end where things you'd rather not know about happen. There is no way I am stepping over that threshold and crossing into the dark side.

'Donna, you will not be allowed in there so stop flapping. I'll bring your jumpsuit home, and just make sure you're ready for nine o'clock Monday morning, and your first bit of advice, do not wear any mascara for at least a year!'

At nine o'clock sharp on Monday morning, I nervously followed Mam into Go Your Own Way. I'd been in here loads of times and it hadn't bothered me before, but today felt different somehow. I was wearing the stupid jumpsuit and apart from suffering some verbal abuse from Brad Balls and his neanderthal mate, I got off lightly, probably because most of the scallies round here never get out of bed before lunchtime.

'You sit over there' said Mam, pointing me to a desk in the corner. A quick assessment of the room reassured me that it was the furthest one from the door into the dark side.

'You know where the tea stuff is kept, so why don't you go and put the kettle on? Mr Papadopoulos will be in soon, and I'll get this place sorted.'

I came back with the drinks. Robbie Williams was warbling 'Angels' out of the speakers, and the place stunk of something very pungent from oil burners dotted about the room.

'Mother! What's that dreadful smell?' I splutter, as it catches the back of my throat.

'It's cinnamon oil. Beryl made it especially for us, says it helps to jumpstart your appetite for life again.'

'Isn't jumpstarting life a little bit late for your customers? The smell of it is enough to put me off living. Is that why Mr Papadopoulos likes it; more customers for him?' Anyway, how come you believe anything Beryl Balls says? She's a fraud!'

Beryl Balls runs Aurora's Aura, an alternative health shop in the precinct, known locally as Zofloras. Beryl Zoflora is about as mystical as a banana, with a degree in holistic treatments from the University of Google, but the seniors of Lockley love her. They pile in for treatments swearing she's a miracle worker, but I know the truth as Nana goes and she told me it's the stinky tea and cookies Beryl gives them afterwards. I suspect there is more than cinnamon in those bad boys.

Mr Papadopoulos bounded cheerily into the shop, not really the demeanour expected of a funeral director. He is sporting the same jumpsuit as us. He's a short, rotund chap, with more than a hint of a resemblance to Poirot, and the uniform certainly doesn't do him any favours, but I'll keep that thought to myself. Wouldn't do to upset the boss on my first day, would it? Or there again...

'Ah, good morning, Donna. Thank you so much for offering to do your work experience with us.'

'Err offering? Work experience?'

'Yes, Donna is delighted to join us,' interrupted mam. 'Anyway Donna, put this on and wear it with pride.'

She handed me a badge which said *Donna, Trainee, Go Your Own Way - With me by your side.* I most sincerely hope not.

'Perfect,' said Mr Papadopoulos, as he disappeared through the gates of hell to the backroom.

'Got a special job for you this morning,' said Mam. 'Break you in gently and see what you are made of.'

'That's easy. Wobbly jelly today.'

'Well, this is something really important and I think you can do it – I have every faith in you Donna.'

Mam began to explain, and that's how I found myself in Nana's front room a short while later.

'Morning, Donna, thought you started work today?'

'I have, look,' I said, pointing to my badge.

'Ooh, very professional I must say. I'm watching *This Morning*, there's a feature coming on about finding love in later life, it's for Brenda by the way, not for me, before you think I've gone ga-ga. Apparently there's this woman, 84 years old, signed up to your computer whatsit malarkey, and is getting married to a 26-year-old next week. I've got older vests than him. It's truuuue lurrrrve you know, and if you believe that, you'll believe anything! Your Grandad is the only man for me,' she sighed wistfully.

'Pity you're not the only woman for him,' I mutter under my breath. 'Anyway Nana, you can see that on catch up. It's kind of about work why I'm here. I've come to ask you something. I don't want you to get upset or anything mind...'

She switched the telly off.

'Spit it out, Donna. What is it?'

'Well, er, Mam asked me to come. It's kind of like, well, sort of, about... like the Queen...' I mumbled, thinking on my feet.

'The Queen? What about her? She's not cold in her grave yet.'

'Well, that's just the thing. Mam thought it was about time that we discussed your, er, your... wishes.'

'Wishes? Eeh pet, I wish I was twenty-one again, but you're not the blooming Fairy Godmother with a magic wand.'

'I wish I was, Nana. I'd make you young and we could go out on the town together, that would be great fun!'

'That it would, pet. I was a bit of a girl in me time. Loved dancing and some hanky panky around the back of the Roxy.'

'Nana!'

'Anyway, Donna pet, why isn't your mother here asking me my wishes? Typical of Bernie passing it on to you.'

'Aw don't be unkind, Nana; she just loves you so much. She said she would get too upset. Even though she does this day in day out, it's different when it's family. Anyway, she said that you could be my guinea pig to see if I'm cut out for this line of work. Seriously Nana, I'm really not, so please just tell her I was rubbish!'

'And will you not get upset asking me awkward questions?'

'Of course, I will, but I'm tougher than Mam, and I think me and you are quite alike.'

'We are, pet. I do love your Mam dearly. I have no idea how she ended up working in a funeral parlour as she cries at the slightest thing. Sobbed her heart out when her stick insect died. I've had pencils with more personality, so the lord only knows what she's like with real people.'

'The customers love her because she is so kind, Nana. Anyway, err, back to this. Have you decided your wi... I mean what you want to do when, well, like the Queen. Do you want to be buried or cremated?' I blurt out.

'Here pet, have a hankie.'

'Thanks, Nana, I haven't got mascara on today thankfully,' I sniffed.

'Wouldn't you think after all this time we'd have another choice?' continued Nana. 'Quite frankly I'm not that keen on either of those. Do you think I might have a crypt like the Queen, and you could deck it out with all my ornaments? Save you going back and forwards to the charity shop.'

'I'm not sure, suppose I can look into that. What about cremation though? It's far more environmentally friendly.'

'You youngsters and your environment. Tell you what pet, by the time your turn comes around there will probably be no cremations because they won't be able to afford the fuel for the furnaces. Here pass me my cardi, I'm feeling a bit chilly, and I'm scared to put the gas fire on – that smart arse meter goes round quicker than Usain Bolt.'

'We'll come back to that decision then. Where do you want to have your, err, gathering?'

'Let me think. Maybe St Mary's where me and your Grandad got married. I've got a season ticket as I go that often to say goodbye to my friends these days, but it's a bit ordinary, isn't it? What about Hexham Abbey? Like a smaller Westminster. That would be nice.'

'I'm not sure how that works, Nana. I can check it out. Are you religious though? I know you sometimes go to church?'

'Listen, Donna, when you get to my age you keep your options open. Pays to pave the way, just in case. I'll do my best to come back and let you know. Mind, nothing as common as a feather or a butterfly. How about if you see a pink flamingo amongst the swans in the park then there will be no mistaking it's me!'

'And afterwards, for the tea?'

'You mean the funeral tea? Misnomer if there ever was one. Most of those things turn into excuses to get plastered. Funeral piss up more like.'

'Nana!'

'I'm not sure if I want one, but if I do I want it teetotal, it will be the last chance I get to annoy your Uncle Eric.'

'We can think about that later then. What about food?'

'Food? Do you think I'm made of money? I'm a poor pensioner, one step away from having to use the foodbank.'

'Now Nana, you know that isn't true.'

'OK lass, keep your hair on! I'm just messing, but they'll come out of the woodwork for a free feed, and I'd rather they were there because they come to say ta-ra to me.'

'Do you want a buffet, like the one that Auntie Jennifer had?'

'I might, but better, and posher. Our Jen was such a snob, so you make sure that mine is the best. Find out what the Queen had. I want those canapes; you know mini things that they have at posh parties. I bet they had them at the Queen's tea, so I want lots of them, like tiny Yorkshire puddings with beef, and teeny-weeny barbequed chicken skewers, stuff like that.'

'And what about vegetarians, Nana?'

'What about them? You can have cheesy things, but none of that toffee nonsense. Your Auntie Sylvie made a casserole with it, and I swear it was like chewing bits of old sand shoe.'

'What's a sand shoe?'

'You are funny, Donna!'

'Right, maybe we'll come back to food. Now then what about music?'

'I don't want hymns. Well, I don't think I do. Some of them were quite nice at the Queen's do. Maybe I'll go for more jolly stuff. I like Shirley Bassey. Alexa, play "Hey big spender".'

'Nana! Maybe that's a bit too jolly?'

'Alexa, stop. OK, how about this? I might have it as I leave the church. Alexa, play "Always Look on the Bright Side of Life".'

'I'm not sure they'll let you have that in Hexham Abbey, Nana. Maybe we'll come back to music. We're not getting very far, are we?'

'These things take time and shouldn't be rushed. You're a long time dead so we've got to get it right,' she said, winking at me. 'Now then, I know one thing, my mouth's as dry as the bottom of a budgie's cage so be a darling, go and put the kettle on and let's have a cup of tea. I've got a plan up my sleeve that I think you're going to like.'

I pushed open the door to Go Your Own Way. Robbie was still warbling 'Angels' on a loop, but the smell in the room was different. Mam saw my nose twitching.

'Antiseptic, you get used to it. Now then, sit down. Are you OK? Will I make you a cup of tea? After you had gone, I did think that maybe I was asking too much of you to talk to Nana like that. How did it go?'

'Fine,' I replied sitting down at my desk. 'Nana was OK and said I was doing her a favour and that you and Terri being her only daughters should have asked her ages ago, but she was happy to talk to me. Nana knew exactly what she wanted, and because you're in the funeral business it will be easy for you to arrange all her wishes, so job done. I told her she could have everything she wanted. Oh Mam, she was so delighted that she was going to have a send-off fit for a Queen.'

'What do you mean you agreed to everything? What does she actually want?' Mam's eyebrows were in danger of disappearing off the top of her head.

'Oh well, you know, just the usual. Kind of like what the Queen had. Nana is our Queen after all, so I knew you'd agree. She wants the full works; soldiers, pipers, horses with plumes, Hexham Abbey instead of St Mary's Church, a full choir, lots of bell ringing, a crypt with space for all the rest of us, including grandad if he ever decides to come back, a big funeral party at that posh hotel along the road... oh and a woman called Shirley Bassey to perform live.'

'Donna! You can't agree to those kinds of things, which would be impossible to organise, and we couldn't afford anything like that, even if it was possible...'

We were interrupted by the doorbell ringing. Mam went to answer and came back, her face even more contorted.

'That was Old Joe from the Knit and Natter Group. Said he'd come to pay his deposit on the plan you've just arranged with him. Something about being fired out to sea from a Canon?'

'Used to be in the Navy, makes perfect sense to me,' I replied.

Mr Papadopoulos came bursting through from the backroom clutching the phone.

'Donna, I've had an Edith Sims on the phone. Says she has decided on Elon Musk and not Richard Branson for her final journey into space?'

Mam looked ready to explode into orbit herself.

'Well, I may have just popped into the library on the way back, I thought you would appreciate my creativity, and I've got you loads of potential business.'

'I'm so sorry Mr Papadopoulos, I had no idea Donna was doing this. I'll put it right myself and tell them, including my mother, that we cannot possibly provide some of the requests.'

'Now don't be too hasty, Mrs Dobbs. I think Donna may have come up with a new and exciting initiative for Go Your Own Way.' I swear the pound signs were glinting in his black button eyes. 'Nothing is impossible, is that not right? Especially for Mr Papadopoulos,' he said proudly. 'We can improvise on anything they ask for, can we not?' he said, dashing into his office to make plans.

The next day I started my new paid job, albeit minimum wage, washing dishes in the local café. Mam had begged Betty the owner to take me on saying she couldn't stand any more stress, and that I would be perfect in a non-customer facing role. It wasn't exactly what I had in mind but there was no scary backroom at the café to contend with, and the banter would be good as most of Lockley congregated there. As I strolled by Go Your Own Way, it was impossible not to notice a huge new poster taking up almost the entire window. It featured a rocket launcher heading into space.

*Go Your Own Way to your Final Frontier.*

*Specialist funeral event organisers – nothing you request is impossible – challenge us!*

*Royal style funerals our speciality.*

I called in to see Nan on my way home.

'Well, I take it our little plan worked? Your Mam said you had been transferred to Betty's to wash up.'

'Promotion, Nana! Seriously though, I do want to help you with your wishes whenever the time is right for you.'

'Oh, that's lovely pet, and when we do, we can talk about it with your Mam and Auntie Terri as well. All us girls together. I've got something I want you to do for me now if you don't mind.'

'Anything, Nana.'

'Will you enrol me on that internet dating thingy? That 26-year-old turned out to be quite a hunk!'

'Eeh no Nana, anything but that! Tell you what though, seeing as we are both gap-year virgins, how do you fancy a fortnight in Skeggy with me instead? I can't think of anyone I'd rather go with.'

'Try stopping me, Donna. Life as they say, is for living. I'm telling you now though, I love you with all my heart, but you are not getting the lucky bingo dobber!'

# Nothing
# Compared to You

*Annemarie Cancienne is a former museum educator, ex-e-learning developer, and one-time teacher of drug and relationship issues via giraffe puppets. In 2016 she gave herself permission to take her writing seriously. Accomplishments since then include two unpublished novels, a Faber Academy course, script editing work, and a file called 'agents_contests_rejections.xlsx'. 'Nothing Compared to You' is her second short story.*

From: oui-its-audrey@yahoo.co.uk
To: rose1981@hotmail.co.uk
Date: March 4, 2004, 10:17:22 EST
Subject: Happy Friend-A-Versary!

Hey there, Rosie Lee! (Have I used Rosie Lee before? Apart from in my head? I keep losing track of my head conversations versus real-life conversations with you. So if I haven't said it: I've decided Rosie Lee is my new nickname for you. More fun than English Rose. I'm also auditioning nicknames for myself. Englishwoman in New York feels a little obvious. Audrey Golightly? It sort of works, apart from my non-Hepburn hips. Thoughts? Not on my hips, just on the nickname.)

More importantly I'm here to say HAPPY FRIEND-A-VERSARY (and RIP Mr Fluffy, world's best hamster). Fourteen years of being best friends. Crazy. The fourteenth anniversary gift is ivory which is a big 'No' from me, so please save your money for our fifteenth anniversary pressie: crystal. I'd like a crystal goblet because a) I don't have one and b) I want a glass called 'gob' that puts wine in my gob.

Even more crazy than our anniversary/the word goblet is that we haven't spoken since Christmas. That's probably my fault. I still haven't perfected the five-hour time difference (I have left voicemails, though – hope you got those?). If early in the UK-day is better for you, I can set my alarm for five am on some Saturday/Sunday (ouch – but you're worth it!). Email is good too, but (as you know) I have a habit of writing looooong ones – hahaha!

Miss you lots my Rosie Lee/English Rose/Rose by Any Other Name.

xx A

Audrey heard the familiar chord play under Derek Jameson's voice. She stopped, grey tights halfway up her calf. 'Oh my god, oh my god, oh my god,' she squealed, lunging for her tape recorder. She had been listening to the Radio 2 Breakfast Show for two weeks, waiting for this exact moment. Her fingers shook slightly as they mashed the 'Record' and 'Play' buttons. Audrey ran the few steps to the radio (left leg bare, right leg woollen, empty tight leg trailing behind like a deflated elephant trunk) and set the recorder next to it. She watched the reels revolve while, on the radio, Sinéad O'Connor counted the days and hours she had been alone. Audrey's heart squeezed and shuddered, Sinéad's pain becoming hers.

She knelt on the carpet and opened Mr Fluffy's cage. The hamster backed into a corner in a fruitless attempt to avoid Audrey's grasp. The girl's fingers closed lovingly, yet firmly, around the soft ginger fur. His heart beat rapidly against Audrey's cupped palms. She brought him to her face, nuzzled his nose, and sung about being able to eat in a restaurant.

Mr Fluffy's heart quickened, just like Audrey's. How she loved this pet, this friend, Mr Fluffy, the world's best hamster! Audrey raised him so his small-yet-big brown eyes were inches from her own. She took a deep breath and bellowed, 'NOTHING COMP...'

Mr Fluffy's body jerked. The fluttering in her palms stopped. His eyes – so wide, so shiny – dimmed. 'Oh my god,' she whispered. She placed the hamster on the corner of her desk. Mr Fluffy sat where he was put, entirely unmoving. Dead.

'Oh my god,' Audrey said once more, this time with a sob. She scooped up Mr Fluffy and dashed into the hallway. 'Mummy? Mummy?' No response came from her parents' room. Audrey ran down the stairs cradling her dead hamster, one leg bare, one leg woollen, deflated trunk trailing. She burst into the kitchen, shouting. 'Mummy? MUMMY?'

'Yes, Audrey. Yes. Yes. I'm right here.' Charlotte turned away from packing the lunch box. 'My god, so much commotion. You'd think someone died.' A silent tear wobbled down Audrey's face. She lifted her open palms toward her mother, Mr Fluffy the inert offering. 'Ah. Oh crumbs. Oh, darling,' said Charlotte. She spun Audrey ninety degrees to the side until the dead rodent was definitely not going to touch Charlotte's body, then wrapped her daughter in a hug. 'What happened? Did you just find him that way?'

'Yes,' said Audrey because it was more or less true.

'I'm sorry, darling.' Charlotte kissed Audrey on her head. 'These things happen. You finish getting ready for school and I'll... do something with Mr Fluffy.'

Audrey suspected the 'something' involved the bin. 'He needs a burial,' she sniffled.

Charlotte (just) supressed a sigh. 'Fine.'

'And a coffin,' Audrey added. 'Wood. With beautiful carvings.'

The sigh came out. 'Audrey, why do you always have to be so *much*?' Charlotte's eyes caught sight of something on the kitchen table. 'Here,' she said, picking up the margarine tub. 'Perfect.'

'It's not wood,' Audrey pointed out. She peered inside the container. 'And there's still margarine inside.'

Pink, manicured fingers ladled out the remaining Flora. A blob of spread coated Charlotte's upturned hand. 'There,' she declared. She held the mostly-empty container out for Audrey. Audrey didn't take it. 'Any spread left will keep him warm.'

'He doesn't need to be warm. He's dead!' Audrey wailed at this reminder of her loss.

All right, shh, come here,' Charlotte hugged her daughter with elbows since her hands were otherwise occupied. 'Pop him in the tub and we'll do the burial when you come home from school.' Audrey began to protest. 'Yes. Come on. You can make a lovely cross with lolly sticks later.'

Audrey wiped her nose across her cardigan and placed Mr Fluffy inside the plastic container. Clumps of yellow spread stuck onto the ends of his fur. He looked like the cheese and pineapple hedgehog she'd had at her last birthday.

Charlotte snapped the lid on. 'Go wash your hands and finish getting dressed. Quickly. And please do something about that hair, it's looking very puffy today. And change that cardigan now that you've used it as a tissue.' Glancing back as she left the kitchen, Audrey saw her mother place the Flora coffin on the window ledge and, with some grimacing, squirt a long dribble of dish soap into her palms.

Visions of Mr Fluffy haunted Audrey all day. Mr Fluffy, alive, trying to claw through the plastic. Mr Fluffy with specks of margarine on his unblinking eyes. Mr Fluffy slowly cooking in the sunshine and faux-butter. By the afternoon, Audrey's tummy hurt too much to concentrate. She was sent to the nurse's office where she curled up on the padded vinyl bench and considered the details of Mr Fluffy's funeral. She was in two minds over whether to play Sinéad O'Connor at the graveside, given the role the song played in his death.

The sound of quiet hiccupping interrupted Audrey's thoughts. An ashen-faced girl, her freckles so stark they looked like the work of a Sharpie, was placed on an empty chair. Audrey recognised her as the new-ish girl in the other year four class. Her left hand lay flat against her collarbone; its index finger stuck out at an awkward angle. Audrey swung her legs off the bench and sat up. 'What happened?' she asked.

'Ball,' the girl replied, her voice a squeak of pain.

Audrey stared at the purpling finger. First death, now a broken bone. What a day. 'Does it hurt?' Audrey asked. The girl nodded, spilling out the tears that had gathered in her wide brown eyes. Audrey came and sat in the empty chair beside her. 'I'm Audrey. From starling class.'

'Rose,' said Rose. 'Sparrow.' She inhaled a long shudder of breath.

Audrey did not know how to mend bones or take away pain. She did know how to distract people with conversation. Her mother said so all the time; 'Would you stop talking, Audrey, you're driving me to distraction.' Audrey employed this skill now. 'How come you arrived in the middle of the school year?' she asked.

It was exactly the wrong question. Rose was suddenly cushioned in sadness. Her head nodded down, heavy, blocking Audrey out through a curtain of copper hair. The shield of silence was so impenetrable not even Audrey had the skill to fight through it. Instead, she slid an arm along Rose's shoulder and pulled her into a hug.

'Ow,' whispered Rose. Audrey had bumped her hand.

'Sorry,' Audrey whispered back.

They sat like that – Rose with her head on Audrey's shoulder, Audrey holding Rose in place – until Rose spoke. 'My dad died last year. So, me and Mum moved into granny's house. She's coming to get me. My granny, not my mum. My mum can't leave work. She's the manager at Sainsbury's.'

'Does she bring you biscuits?' Audrey asked. 'From Sainsbury's?' she added for clarity.

'Sometimes,' Rose said. Then, after thinking about it, 'She'll probably bring some tonight.'

'My hamster died today,' Audrey said. 'Mr Fluffy.'

'I'm sorry,' Rose said.

'We have something in common. We both lost someone we loved.' Audrey took Rose's silence for agreement. 'Do you have many friends yet?' Audrey asked. Under her arm, she felt Rose's shoulders lift slightly to say, 'I don't know' or 'not really' which, Audrey knew, meant 'no'. 'I'll be your friend,' Audrey said. *Your best friend*, Audrey added in her head, certain Rose could use the huge amount of love Audrey was offering.

She buried Mr Fluffy under the apple tree in a ceremony that involved the scattering of pumpkin seeds (his favourite) and paper confetti from the hole puncher (elegant). On a lolly-stick cross she wrote in purple marker, 'Mr Fluffy, 4 March 1990'. It was sad and poignant and already, with the help of meeting Rose, Audrey could feel herself healing. It was true what they said: when God kills one best friend, he opens the door to another.


From: oui-its-audrey@yahoo.co.uk
To: rose1981@hotmail.co.uk
Date: Jun 24, 2004, 15:41:14 EST
Subject: Granny Violet

Dear Rose,
I just had an email from Sarah telling me about Granny Violet. I'm devastated. I can only imagine what you and

your mum are feeling. Please let me know when the funeral is. I don't know how many days I can take off but I want to try to make it back. All my love to you and your mum.

x A


Granny Violet stepped from the caravan holding the chocolate birthday cake. For her first few years of holidays with Rose's family, Audrey marvelled at the Miracle of the Cake. How did Violet produce such a perfect dessert on the caravan's two-ring hob? 'Sainsbury's, dear,' Violet said when Audrey finally asked. 'Bought with Lily's discount.' Audrey couldn't believe she'd made it to age fifteen without figuring this out. Just as disappointing was accepting that Violet, a gran she loved as much as her own, wasn't a little bit magical.

For seven years this four-berth caravan with views of both the beach and the Sellafield nuclear power station meant perfect happiness to Audrey. For seven years Audrey began the summer holidays by counting down to the second-to-last week in August. Seven years of travelling all day by train, from Oxford to London then London up to Cumbria just so she could sleep in a tin box on wheels. Seven years of Miracle Cake, ice-cold swims, and burnt sausages around the disposable barbeque.

Audrey also had holidays with her family, of course. The fire and ice in those were provided by her parents. Over the years, Charlotte's veiled hints about Simon's 'dalliances' had grown less veiled. Particularly once they started holidaying in France and the vin de table appeared alongside the morning's pain au chocolat. No academic publisher needed to go on as many business trips as he did.

What was he running from? Wasn't this family enough for him? Wasn't Charlotte enough? India, the United States, Australia – how many women were there, and in how many ports? Between the extra hotel room when Simon grew fed up with Charlotte's rages, and their fruits de mer dinners, their two weeks in France came with a hefty price tag.

Violet placed the chocolate cake in the middle of the fold-out table. From the picnic hamper Lily pulled out a knife, some napkins, and four small plates. Last year's candles came out of a Ziploc bag and were plunged into the frosting. 'Seventeen! It's hard to believe either of you are seventeen. A blink of the eye ago, you were both ten,' Lily said.

Audrey considered a blink as something easy and swift. Audrey would not have used either of those adjectives to describe adolescence. Up, out, around new bends; her body had expanded in ways that appalled her (and Charlotte, who had stopped buying biscuits 'out of kindness' to Audrey's hips). There was so much hair, all of it wiry and resistant to taming. And a voice that was too loud and too sure for most of what came out of her mouth. Audrey calculated she was fifteen per cent too much for most rooms that tried to contain her.

Lighting the candles, Lily half hummed, half sung 'Sixteen Going on Seventeen'. At the words 'innocent' and 'rose', she gave her daughter an exaggerated wink. A blush crept onto Rose's cheeks. Violet caught sight of it and laughed. 'Would you look at that, Lil! Roses are red!'

Audrey looked at the grass, afraid she would laugh her too-loud laugh if she caught her friend's eye. They still hadn't caught up after Rose's date last weekend. Rose's blush told Audrey there might be a lot to talk about.

Lily smiled at her daughter. 'Well, these are the days of wine and roses. And with a queue of university men asking our Rose for dates, why shouldn't she have some fun?' Rose, still quite red, stretched her mouth into a decent likeness of a smile.

After the birthday evening was packed away – the cake was eaten and Violet and Lily had finished their Babycham and then tucked themselves into their twin beds – Audrey and Rose were free to gossip. They lay in the dark in the convertible bed in the front of the caravan. 'Spill, Rose, spill!' Audrey was propped up on her elbow, staring down at her friend.

Rose rested serenely under the blanket, her hands folded atop her stomach. The moonlight melted through the thin curtains and bathed Rose in an ethereal whiteness. She reminded Audrey of a medieval tomb for some tragic child bride. In other words, silent and unmoving. 'Rose!' Audrey half-shouted. 'Talk to me!'

Rose's head snapped to the side. She glared at Audrey. 'Shh! They might hear.'

From the back of the caravan, snores drifted. 'Lily! Violet!' Audrey called.

Rose scrambled upright and slapped a hand over Audrey's mouth. 'You're so loud,' she lamented straight into her friend's ear. They held their breath, waiting for Lily or Violet to stir. The melody of snoring continued.

'See?' said Audrey. 'The Babycham worked. Now c'mon! Tell me about Giles!'

Giles had been coming into Rose's café for the past few weeks. 'Cup of tea and a slice of lemon drizzle' the girls had called him until he introduced himself and asked Rose for a date. Violet and Lily, who had met their husbands when still at school, were pleased Rose had a suitor. Though they themselves would have paired her with a local lad, they reckoned dating an Oxford University man brought them all one step closer to meeting the Queen.

'Giles met me at the bus on Magdalen Street and then we walked to the cinema.'

'What did you see?'

'*Con Air.*'

Audrey fell back laughing. '*Con Air*? That's a terrible date movie!'

'No, it's not.'

'Yes, it is! It's just explosions and testosterone.'

Rose bristled. 'Well, I liked it.'

'You only liked it because you were on a date. What was actually good about it?'

Rose's search for an answer took a fair few second. 'John Cusack was cute.'

'John Cusack is *always* cute. And *Con Air* is a terrible date movie.' Audrey waited for Rose to continue her story. There was nothing apart from moonlight and a background threat of nuclear fallout. It seemed Audrey had been too Audrey. Again. 'I'm sorry,' she said. 'Maybe it's good; I haven't seen it. Please tell me more. What did you do next? What was he like? What body parts did you touch?'

'Next we went to a wine bar. Giles knew one that would let me in. They didn't have any cider so he bought me a white wine. You've tasted wine before, haven't you?' Audrey's mother ordered her a glass when they went out in France but Audrey only ever had a sip. Which, conveniently, created a whole extra glass of wine for Charlotte to finish. Audrey nodded and let Rose continue. 'The wine was disgusting. I asked for sugar to stir into it but Giles just laughed.'

'So, what did you talk about?'

'Mainly philosophy? He talked. I listened. Or tried to. It was hard to follow, especially once the wine was in my head.' Rose stopped, seemingly at the end of the tale.

'That was it? You saw a movie and had some wine and learned about Nietzsche?' Was Nietzsche a philosopher? Audrey ploughed past her doubt. 'I know there's more. You weren't blushing at cake time because you couldn't explain Nietzsche.' Audrey committed to Nietzsche being a philosopher.

Rose groaned and pulled the blanket over her head. All that remained of her were ten ghostly finger stubs. This was bad. Something had gone wrong on the date. 'Rose? Rosie?' Audrey tried to lower the blanket but Rose held firm. Audrey slid herself under the covers so they were sheltered together, face to face. 'Rosie? What happened?'

Rose swapped from holding the blanket to covering her face with her hands. 'The wine made me dizzy and I didn't want to get on the bus like that. So, Giles said I could come to his room to sit down. So, I sat on his bed, and he sat next to me, and then he began kissing me.' Sensing Rose wanted to stop talking again, Audrey stroked her hair. 'And then, so we're kissing, and then, he sort of pushes the back of my head down toward… it.'

'His penis?'

'Don't say that word!'

'But was it his penis?'

'Yes.'

'What did you do? Did you go toward it?'

Rose's hands flew away from her face. 'What was I supposed to do? I didn't want to be rude.'

Audrey felt giggles bubbling up. 'So you sucked his penis because it was polite?'

A hint of a smile appeared on Rose's face. 'Stop saying penis.'

'How about "orgasm". Did Giles orgasm? Did you orgasm?'

'Ew. Stop. No.'

'The Big O?'

'Stop, Audrey.' Rose was laughing, but she was also serious. Audrey needed to stop.

'OK. So, things happened. Then what?'

'I just sort of... got the late bus home. He hasn't come into the café since.'

'Do you want to see him again?'

'I don't know. Mum and Gran keep asking. But I don't know.'

The blanket tent was making Audrey too warm. She flung her arms out and folded the cover off their faces. Rose didn't try to tug it back up. 'Look, it's done,' said Audrey. 'You met a mediocre guy for a mediocre movie and did some mediocre fooling around.'

'Giles is a nice guy.'

'This isn't nice guy behaviour.'

Rose thought about it. 'The fooling around was pretty gross. Even worse than the wine.' She made a face like a cat coughing up a furball.

'This is great – you've just expressed two opinions! And maybe next time, if a guy asks you to...' Audrey searched for the words Rose would find acceptable. She came up blank. 'To, you know, and you feel like it would be rude to refuse, ask for money. Either he says no and you don't have to do it, or you have something to show for your efforts.'

Rose's eyebrows came together in a questioning look. 'So, be a prostitute?'

'No, I'm just saying you should get something out of it too. If it's not pleasure, make it money.'

The look moved from simple-questioning to angry-questioning. 'You're saying I should become a prostitute.'

'I'm trying to make a joke. Obviously not a good one. Sorry.' The conversation felt finished. It would only be ambient snoring and then sleep if Audrey didn't find something else to talk about. 'Have you thought any more about university?'

'Mum thinks I should try. She says I'd make a good teacher.'

'Do you want to be a teacher?'

'I don't know.'

'Well, do you like kids? And school? And always doing times tables?'

Rose studied Audrey. 'You don't think I'd make a good teacher.'

'I didn't say that.' Though now that Rose mentioned it, a tiny piece of Audrey did think it. Rose didn't command authority, even over a bunch of seven-year-olds. 'You'd be a great teacher. I'm just wondering if you'd like it.'

'I don't know. I just… I don't want to leave Mum and Gran on their own.'

'If you went to Oxford Brookes, could live at home.'

'Maybe.'

'Promise me, Rose.' Audrey sat fully up. She tried to tug Rose up too, but Rose didn't want to budge. 'Please, my sweet Briar Rose, this is important.' Rose sat up. Audrey adjusted them so they were facing each other, cross-legged, knee-to-knee, both bathed in the bluey-white of moon-beams. 'Promise me we will get that flat in London one day.'

It was a promise sealed in spit and a handshake three years before. Charlotte had taken the girls on a Christmas trip to London. The lights and the shops and the dazzle of life's variety wove a magic over Rose. As Rose stared in wonder at the Selfridge's window, Audrey seized the moment (as well as Rose's palm): this could be their future, she said. Would she promise to make this their future? Audrey intermittently wielded their contract to stop Rose from slipping out of it.

'One year in London. We go to uni, you become a teacher, and we share a flat for one year. Then we can go off and have kids and live somewhere boring. But for the rest of your life you can look back and say, "I once lived in London".' Audrey hoped their time in London would stretch longer than a year. Forever would be fine. But she had to get Rose there first.

Rose looked uncomfortable. Like Audrey had said the word 'penis' again. Audrey swapped arguments. 'Having a flat would be like always being on holiday. This week with you is the best of my whole year. For you too, right?' Rose nodded. 'So let's have a whole year's worth of hol-idays by living in London together. We'll never get the chance again.'

'But why not stay in Oxford? Don't you find London a bit... scary?' Rose asked.

It was the staying that scared Audrey. Being stuck in a place too small to absorb her. Living with Charlotte, who never met a plate she couldn't smash in anger. 'London won't be scary,' Audrey said. 'I'll be there to protect you.'

From: oui-its-audrey@yahoo.co.uk
To: rose1981@hotmail.co.uk
Date: August 18, 2004, 09:08:48 EST
Subject: Happy birthday

Hi Rose,
Didn't want to let the day pass without wishing you a happy
birthday. Hope you find a nice chocolate cake for yourself.
  x A


From: oui-its-audrey@yahoo.co.uk
To: rose1981@hotmail.co.uk
Date: November 24, 2004, 11:32:04 EST
Subject: Giving thanks

Dear Rose,
It's Thanksgiving here. My American friends say this
is their favourite holiday. This is despite the fact no one
gives presents (and I thought Americans gave presents for
everything). It's simply a day of counting your blessings
and eating yourself sick.

It didn't take me long to figure out my biggest blessing:
you. (Sorry for how American that sounds.) You're my
oldest, steadiest friend. Your house has always been open
to me. I can't count the number of times I fled there just
to sit around the kitchen table laughing with you and your
mum and gran. You're more than just a friend to me; you're
family. And if I've not said it before, I love you.

I know I upset you last Christmas and I'm profoundly
sorry for that. I suspect your silence is about more than
Christmas, though. I'm pretty sure I've been an arse for

years. So what I'd be most thankful for today is the chance to talk to you, apologise in person, and hear how you need me to change. Because I can change. And I'd do it for you.

Love, Audrey

From: Mail Delivery Subsystem <MAILER-DAEMON@ hotmail.com>
To: oui-its-audrey@yahoo.co.uk
Date: November 24, 2004, 11:34:19 EST
Subject: Returned mail: User unknown

----- Delivery to the following recipients failed -----
<rose1981@hotmail.co.uk>

Error code 550 5.1.1. User unknown
Requested action cannot be taken: mailbox unavailable

Proving the adage wrong, Audrey not only led Rose to the metaphorical waters of London but also helped her drink. She found them jobs; a flat; a toilet brush shaped like a potted plant. They moved into Audrey and Rose's Honeymoon Suite (as Audrey's homemade banner dubbed it) the week after Rose turned twenty-one. A box of chocolates and bottle of prosecco waited for Rose on the Ikea bed Audrey had put together for her. The delicious happiness of playing at adulthood quickly filled Audrey.

Her misery, on the other hand, grew slowly, like the damp patch in their unventilated bathroom. Audrey sensed Rose didn't love London. *Yet*, Audrey qualified to herself. She took out a subscription to *Time Out* magazine. Onto the kitchen cork board went Audrey's handwritten roster of free events and the cheap restaurants that paired well with them. But jazz concerts did not woo Rose the way Audrey hoped, and Audrey only ever slurped her Wagamama noodles with a table of strangers.

Come winter, the London sunlight (or, what there was of it) barely touched Rose. She left for work in the dark. Came home in the dark. On the weekends, she took the tube to the train and journeyed to Oxford for time with Lily and Violet. She returned Sunday night, in the dark, to start a new week of the same pattern.

Their lives intersected at the point of bills. Once a month Rose had them work out, down to the penny, their shared costs. Rose brought out the carboard box dedicated to the exercise. There was a calculator. A special ledger. An envelope of receipts with household items highlighted. A highlighter.

Audrey silently, then not so silently, found it unbearable. 'Round it off and split by two, round it off and split by two,' she clapped and sang to the tune of 'Five little ducks went swimming one day,' hoping the daftness would amuse the schoolteacher in Rose.

'Audrey,' Rose chided. 'I can't think with your noise.' The song had indeed brought out the schoolteacher. But the strict, rather than smiling, one.

Audrey could ignore the truth no longer. She had led Rose to London but Rose wasn't drinking of it; she was drowning, and Audrey was holding her down by the neck.

She spotted a dignified exit for herself in New York, another city big enough not to be oppressed by her. Her father had used it as his escape from Charlotte, moving there to become the something-something executive of something publishing house. Audrey poked at the paternal guilt and the paternal guilt manifested itself in a job.

As their end of tenancy approached, Audrey's triaged her possessions by sentimental value. Necessities would go to New York. Ephemera, to the charity shop. Items she would one day dispose of after they had accumulated enough dust: Charlotte's house. The final thing she packed off was Rose, onto the train bound for Oxford.

Audrey put her friend's handheld suitcase down on the platform. All of Rose's life had fit into these two small cases, a feat that awed and confused Audrey (and perhaps explained why Rose declined taking the toilet brush. Or perhaps it didn't.). Audrey smothered her friend in a hug. 'I'm really going to miss you, Rosie,' she said, choking back the tears. 'But we'll be meeting for a Christmas pint before you know it.'

'That would be nice,' said Rose. She stepped out of the hug, tugged her rumpled dress back into place, and took her bags onto the train. With a final wave through the window, the friends said goodbye.

But December the twenty-second! 7 p.m.! The Star pub! Audrey set the date with Rose mere moments after buying her plane ticket home. After three months surrounded by strangers, the need to sit down with her best friend – someone she didn't need to ease into all her Audrey-ness – was an almost physical ache.

It was therefore a surprise to walk into The Star and find Rose already there, at a table with other friends. There were Sarah and Matt, Priya and Jon, Callum. All fine people, just not the people Audrey expected to see. Sarah leapt up and hugged her. 'Glad you could join us!' she said. And there was the second surprise given that it was them, in fact, who were joining Audrey's night out.

Audrey sat at the empty seat opposite Rose. Five smiling faces leaned in to hear tales of America. 'Tell us about New York!' Jon said. She was peppered with questions. Had she been to Ground Zero yet? (Yes.) Did everyone walk really fast? (Yes.) Had she seen anyone shot? (No.)

'I would take the risk of getting shot for two weeks in the California sun,' said Priya.

'You're probably safe in California,' Audrey said. 'Florida, on the other hand. My dad *actually* saw someone shot there. But I guess every holiday destination has its risks. In America it's getting shot. Here, it's freezing to death during your summer swim.'

Rose's rum and coke hit the table with a thud. 'I thought you liked our holidays.'

Audrey gave a good-natured laugh. 'I did! That didn't stop my lips turning blue.'

The table laughed along with her. Everyone apart from Rose. 'Cumbria has a beautiful coastline. And it's really near the Lake District.'

'Yes,' Audrey agreed. 'Florida is a mosquito rich bogland whose biggest cultural attraction is Mickey Mouse. It's still warmer than the north of England.'

'It's grim up north, is that what you're saying?' The hostility in Rose's voice was hard to miss.

Audrey was taken aback. Rose – quiet, agreeable Rose, who's opinion on most matters was 'I don't know' – couldn't be picking a fight over *this*? Trying to expedite whatever practical joke was in play, Audrey said, 'Well, the Sellafield Tourist Board isn't quite as busy as the Florida one, I reckon.'

Rose stood up, scraping her chair back. 'I'm getting another drink.' She turned and went to the bar.

Audrey looked to the table for answers. 'Is she OK? Did something happen before I got here?' But there were no easy answers, just bewilderment.

The evening carried on with Rose growing steadily drunker, Audrey staying decidedly sober, and the rest of the group stepping around the prickles in the conversation. By 10pm people were making their excuses and heading home. Audrey hung behind, hoping to catch Rose alone. She followed her weaving form over Magdalen Bridge. 'Rose, could you slow down?' It turned out a drunk Rose was a fast Rose.

'Going home. G'night, Audrey.' Rose carried on up the High Street.

'How are you getting there? Can I call you a cab?'

'Nope.' They walked on, sort of together, sort of apart. Rose turned up a quieter street, taking them past two Colleges. There were no lights apart from the occasional glow of a window, landing the lane somewhere between 'other-worldly and charming' and 'dark and foreboding'. Rose marched, hands shoved in pockets, feet slipping on and off the pavement.

'Rose,' Audrey tried again.

'Stop following me.'

They waited in silence at the bus stop until the bus came. Rose blocked the door, trying to stop Audrey from entering. 'I don't need help getting home.'

'OK,' said Audrey. 'It's my bus too, though.' This was true as long as Audrey was willing to walk twenty minutes out of her way. Which she was. She followed Rose upstairs and sat next to her, wondering how long the silent treatment would last. Audrey soon had her answer.

'So superior. You think you're so superior. You're a sneering, snooty snob who's so superior.' 'S' words were evidently feeling good in Rose's mouth. Her head lolled onto the window and she closed her eyes. 'If our holidays were so grim, why'd you keep coming?'

Audrey's throat grew thick with the threat of tears. 'I loved those holidays. They weren't grim. Please believe me Rose, I loved the time with you and your family.'

'Sssssssnooty,' Rose said into the pane of glass.

The bright bus sliced through the winter-dark roads. Audrey felt like she had stepped through one of Oxford's fantastical portals. To Narnia or Wonderland or Lyra's Oxford. Because in the Oxford of Audrey's reality, it wasn't controversial to say that Florida had more sunshine than Cumbria.

She rang the bell and helped get Rose off the bus. The journey (and, more accurately, the alcohol) had softened Rose into sleepiness. She did not resist when Audrey cradled an arm around her torso and walked/carried her to her door. Audrey fished Rose's keys from her bag and led her friend inside. Rose wove up the stairs without a backward glance.

'Rosie? Is that you?' Lily called from the living room.

'Hi, Mrs Hughes. It's Audrey. Rose has gone upstairs.'

'Audrey! Come in, come in.' Audrey hadn't expected Lily to be awake. She winced her way into the living room, ready to be told off for whatever she'd done to upset Rose.

Lily was sunk under a blanket on the soft navy sofa. A table lamp and a cathode ray TV – possibly the last in the country – lit the otherwise dark room. 'Did you have a nice evening? How is New York?'

'Yes, thanks. New York is good.'

'Is your father still out there?'

'Yes.'

'And your mother still in Oxford?'

'Yes.'

'Mmmm.' Lily packed a lot of opinion into the sound. 'So just a quiet Christmas with the two of you?'

'Yes.'

'Well, you must come around again before you fly away. Mum would love to see you. Maybe Boxing Day? I'll have the day off.'

'That would be really nice. Well, I should get home now.' There was a thud from upstairs. 'Uh, Rose may need some help getting into bed.'

Lily had a knowing smile. 'It was that kind of night, was it? Making the most of it while you're here, I suppose. I'll go up to her now. Goodnight, Audrey. See you soon.'

Audrey phoned Rose midway through the next morning. 'Hello?' Rose's voice sounded sandpaper rough.

'Hey. I just wanted to check and see how you're doing.'

'Yeah. Pretty terrible. How much did I have?'

'I'm not sure. You started drinking before I got there.' That detail preyed on Audrey as she lay in bed last night, not sleeping. Rose had buffered herself with other people, extra drinks, a different arrival time. Their argument felt frivolous because it was; there was something more going on. Yet Audrey couldn't figure out what the more was. 'Rose, do we need to talk?'

'About what?'

'You seemed pretty cross with me last night.'

'Did I?' Rose sounded instantly alert. 'What did I say?'

'You called me snooty.'

Rose gasped. 'What?'

'A couple of times. A "snooty snob", I think.' Audrey didn't need to 'think'. The denunciation was firmly in her head, word for sibilant word.

'Oh my god. Did I? Oh my god Audrey, I don't remember this.'

'Yeah. Do we need to talk about something?'

'I don't remember any of this! I have no idea where that came from. I'm so sorry.'

'If I've done something wrong...'

'Honestly, I can't remember a thing. I'm really sorry.'

A piece of Audrey's stomach untwisted. Another piece clenched tighter. 'You sure there's nothing I've done to upset you?'

'Positive.'

'OK.' Audrey gave Rose space to talk if she wanted to. There was only silence. 'Well, your mum invited me over on Boxing Day. So maybe we can talk then.'

Audrey had a text from Rose on Boxing Day morning. She was feeling a bit under the weather – it might have been the turkey – so wasn't up for a visit. Sorry she wouldn't see Audrey before she left. She hoped she had a safe flight back.


*Dear Rose,*

*I'm writing this letter on advice of my therapist.*

*(When Katherine – that's my therapist – suggested this exercise, she told me to write to you 'without judgement or censorship'. I can't even write a shopping list without judgement or censorship so I knew this letter would be difficult. Which is a long way of saying I don't love my opening line but*

*after many far worse introductions, I judge is to be adequate and will not censor myself further.)*

*For seven years I've had to tell myself you were dead. How else could I explain your sudden disappearance? The first two years were the hardest. A picture or a song could instantly set me off into tears and snot (so, so much tears and snot). In my dreams, I went to your funeral. When I came home to Oxford, I saw your spectre everywhere. Actually bumping into you would have been both the best and worst moment of my life.*

*The grief when my mother died was a lot blander. I felt sad and then OK with a shameful speediness. I decided there was something deeply wrong with me. Here comes Overblown Audrey, with her inappropriate words and incorrect feelings. I figured I needed a therapist to fix me.*

*Katherine assured me I didn't need fixing (thanks Katherine!), I just needed to sort out my feelings. She helped me see that when you died (asterisk – I know you're not actually dead) I loved you more than anyone in my life. Your death (I know) stunned me. Since I couldn't pour my love into you, it came out in tears and snot and confusion.*

*I loved you. That didn't mean we were right for each other. I think we were always gently incompatible. I hoped that being your friend meant I could claim your best qualities for myself. Kind, polite, loyal to her family. I thought keeping hold of you meant I wasn't the bad person I suspected I was. (Sidenote: do you know, in New York, I'm not overbearing? I'm considered thoughtful in an English way. It turns out I wasn't 'too much', I was just in the wrong place.)*

*I worry I treated you like a pet hamster. Frightening you with my excesses. Letting you out from your cage when*

*I wanted love. Katherine has helped me figure out two things. 1) You weren't a hamster and 2) I'm not a bad person. Sure, sometimes I'm an ass. A lot of the time stupid stuff tumbles from my mouth. Often, I'm pretty fun to be with.*

*If you hadn't already cut me off as a friend, I think this confession would do the trick: a part of me was relieved when my mum died. I was ashamed of her. What mother gets a new set of crockery every year because she smashed the old one to shit? I resented you for all those times I complained about her and you told me 'everybody' had to love their mum. Because sometimes, I couldn't.*

*But I appreciate you supported me in a different way. You opened your home and shared your family with me. You couldn't take away the bad from my life, but you tried to add some things that were good.*

*In my darker moments I wonder if I was any good for you. Did I help give you some boldness? Or was I a force who swept you along in directions you didn't want to go? (I still feel bad about that salsa dancing lesson I dragged you to during our second week in London. I don't think it sealed our fate, but I don't think it helped.)*

*Sometimes I wonder if I ever knew you at all. There is a lot of you I never managed to unlock.*

*So maybe you did us both a favour by friendship-breaking-up with me. I still would've preferred you did it in person. It would've been messy (and full of tears and snot and some very strong opinions on my part). You would have hated it. Which, I suspect, was why you ended things in the most Rose way possible: with silence.*

*I hear from Sarah that you got married last year. I truly wish you nothing but happiness. I hope he has found a way into all those rich pieces of yourself (that maybe even you didn't know how to get into).*

*I love you Rose, now and forever. Thank you for being the best friend I needed for so long.*

*Audrey*


With each carriage return the printer considered its options. It clicked, it paused, it swept some characters onto the page. It snapped, moved the reel, began again. Click, pause, sweep. Page one spat onto the desk. The machine gasped its way into a long stop then, in a chorus of clacks, loaded page two.

The rows of type were growing greyer. The ink was running out. Audrey tugged out the drawers, remembering, as they flew open, that she'd already cleared this room. Apart from boxed-up books, the empty desk, and the printer itself, there was nothing left here. Wait – there was the table lamp. A floor lamp, too. But after those, nothing.

The printer finished the job. The final few lines – the ones where Audrey expressed happiness, love, and thanks – were shadowy ghosts of ideas. She folded the pages into an envelope, reassured herself that it was the thought that counts, and went out to the garden.

A trowel and box of Sainsbury's Taste the Difference chocolate cake were waiting by the apple tree. As was a squirrel, eyeing up the cake. 'You'll just have to keep waiting,' she told the animal. Audrey guessed at the right spot (near enough to Mr Fluffy but not so close that she broke through the Flora lid) and started to dig.

Clearing her childhood home had been hard, emotionally and physically. Perhaps to save the annual cost of replacing the dinnerware she threw when angry, Charlotte had spent the last few years learning pottery. The house had been littered with asymmetrical plates and vases. Those were easy, albeit heavy, to get rid of.

The photos were harder. Audrey couldn't look through an album without her throat pulling tight. The joy of her parents' early years together leapt out from the faded prints. Charlotte the beaming bride, Simon the giddy father, Audrey the chubby toddler grasping each parent's finger for balance. Everyone smiling. It was impossible to pinpoint where it shifted into something sour. First there was happiness, then there wasn't.

Audrey's old bedroom became the loading bay for the things she would take to her London flat. A chest of drawers, Le Creuset pots, rolls of rugs from when her mother went through her kilim phase. The photo albums. Audrey felt ready to return to her native land now that she knew she wasn't overblown, over-wrought, just *too much*. She was simply Audrey, and could be Audrey wherever she lived, now. Plus, New Yorkers really did walk too bloody fast for her liking.

Audrey finished her digging. She knelt and placed the envelope into the shallow hole. From her pocket she took out a photo she found in an album: Audrey and Rose on their Christmas trip London. She lay this on top of the envelope. 'Goodbye, Rose,' she said. 'I love you.'

Audrey used the trowel to sprinkle the dirt back over the only copy of the letter she would print. Maybe she'd delete it from her computer one day. Maybe it would stay in her file folder until her own demise, and someone else would have to decide what to do with it when they did her death cleaning.

With the hole filled in, Audrey opened the cake box. She pulled out the cake, peeled away the cardboard edge, and grabbed a handful. It was very (very) tempting to take a bite of the chocolate resting in her fist, but she crumbled the cake and sprinkled the pieces over the ground. Audrey stepped back and bowed her head.

The squirrel hopped onto the letter-grave and snatched a lump of cake. 'You could at least wait until my back is turned,' Audrey told it. Her voice startled it; it darted back. But not away, as the main prize – the rest of the cake – was still in play. Audrey saw where it was looking and squeezed off another chunk. She threw it toward the squirrel. Suspicious of his easy victory, it didn't budge.

'Go on,' Audrey said, 'it's yours.' As if it understood, it walked over to the piece and picked it up. It was large in his tiny squirrel fists, and he seemed unsure what to do with it. 'Take it away and bury it somewhere,' Audrey advised. 'If you bump into Rose, maybe share some.'

The cake went into the squirrel's mouth, bulging out his cheek. He scampered across the garden. Little claws scrabbled up the fence. He hopped along the top for a few panels and then was gone. Audrey licked the chocolate from her fingers and went inside to finish packing.

# Shopping for England

*Kim Clayden has a Creative Writing (script) MA from the University of East Anglia and had a film script optioned after entering a competition run by The Script Factory. She has also completed the Curtis Brown Creative six-month 'writing your novel' course and is currently editing a draft of her first novel.*

The text notification came through just as the commentators reported the shock news: 'Favourite for the gold in the women's shopping race, American athlete Candy Battenburg, has withdrawn from the competition. She was rushed to hospital with a suspected beetroot juice overdose.'

The blonde announcer struggled to prevent her lip from curling as she continued. 'Problems were first noted when Candy gave a urine sample as part of the standard drug testing after the semi-final.' She whispered to her co-host, 'There is no way I'm saying pink sheen.' Then turned back to the camera. 'This throws the Shopping World Championship wide open and our own Tilly Ramsbotham could be in with a chance.'

The said Tilly Ramsbotham fist-pumped with her phone, which was accompanied by whooping, cheering and knitting needle clacking from her Nan and her friends at the over-sixties club. As was the norm at the club there was some vociferous effing and jeffing, followed by a lot of shushing. The over-sixties club met at the local bowls club, an agreement achieved by virtue of Nan's grand slam winning season of 2011/12 when she won ladies singles, pairs and triples. At the time there'd been a lot of grumbling due to the printing of her double-barrelled surname and Christian name on the club's honours board. Cynthia-Jane Ramsbotham-Kidd was almost too much for the ageing calligrapher, but it had the upside of someone noticing his excessively shaky hands; a symptom that led to a diagnosis of previously unrecognised diabetes.

The tables and chairs gathered around the TV looked like they'd been bought from a sell off of 1970s hotel conference furniture and the TV itself was a recent concession by the club's committee because of the BBC broadcasting live bowls from the Commonwealth Games.

A chant of 'USA, USA, USA' crept forward from the seats at the back. Nan glared at the woman responsible but rather than quieten the culprit down it only seemed to fan the flames.

'I bet she tampered with the urine sample,' came the accusation, prompting gasps from many of the old crones. Twelve pairs of eyes all turned to see the response from Tilly. The accusation was not without foundation. Tilly had only recently completed an eighteen-month ban from competing and her selection to represent England in the shopping category had been somewhat controversial. She had always claimed innocence on the charge of cheating at the European championships held in Paris. The problem had arisen with the amendment that the French board had made to the shopping requirements. As well as the usual criteria for the competition, they had refined the occasion dress to be from a *haute couture* fashion house only, whilst also increasing the limit on spend. Tilly was aware that to be termed *haute couture*, the fashion house would have to be a member of what she called the up their own jacksy club, more formally known as Chambre Syndicale de la Haute Couture.

What she didn't realise, having managed to fulfil the criteria of actually being able to wear the dress – which was a problem for some of the competitors and the French board were slammed for body shaming – was that Yves Saint Laurent was not a fully-fledged member of the club at the time of the competition. She had had to return the item, obtain a refund – which involved a lengthy argument with a thin-lipped couturier who wanted to allocate a credit note at best – and go through the whole procedure again with a so-called proper fashion house. She could have stuck with the dress but the time penalty she would have been given for an invalid purchase would have destroyed any hope at all of a medal or even a top ten finish.

Initially, she came second to the Chinese representative with the American competitor Candy Battenburg coming third. However, Candy's team then lodged a complaint that Tilly could not possibly have got from the first fashion house to the second without some sort of mechanical assistance, which was against the rules. There was a rumour that she'd used an electric scooter, but she hadn't been caught on CCTV nor by French TV. CNN and the BBC were so appalled by the coverage that they each devoted an hour-long special on the possible routes Tilly could have taken, CNN with the focus on the impossibility of the time constraints and the BBC with how it could have been possible whilst remaining impartial. Tilly could not confirm her route saying it was all such a blur and after an 'accidental' email was sent to the governing body showing an old interview of a UK prime minister saying that the French president had short man syndrome the ruling went in favour of the Americans and Tilly was banned.

Now Tilly addressed her wrinkly audience, 'I think you'll find that beetroot is not a banned substance.' There was a pause whilst this information was digested. She saw an opportunity to leave. 'She probably had an allergic reaction or something,' she said and bent down to kiss her Nan goodbye.

'Probably kidney stones,' smiled the woman next to Nan and winked at Tilly, who thought she was either having a stroke or she'd got something stuck in her dentures. Tilly mouthed 'ssh' to her and almost immediately got a text on her phone. It was from Aunty Pen, the same woman that was pulling the strange faces. God she could type quickly. The cannabis she was using must be working really well on her arthritic hands, but Tilly's worry was that it was beginning to loosen her tongue as well. Aunty Pen was no relation; it just seemed nicer to call her that as she was her Nan's friend and neighbour. Although it struck Tilly for the first time that perhaps they were more than friends.

Aunty Pen had done some research for her on Candy Battenburg's family history. People post all sorts of things on social media and Pen was an excellent stalker... well, detective. Candy had posted about her father's hospital experience with kidney stones on Instagram only a year or so ago and Pen had reported this to Tilly together with an article about potential side affects of excess beetroot consumption, one of which was kidney stones if there was a family history thereof.

Tilly couldn't force-feed Candy with beetroot nor be too overt in extolling the virtues of the underrated vegetable, most notably the improved physical performance and endurance. So, in the preparation areas before competitions, she would wait for Candy to see her and then secretly drink a shot of beetroot juice but visibly enough for other competitors to see. Or she would eat a beetroot salad or a beetroot and feta dip. It was enough to spark Candy's curiosity, her FOMO took over and she, also in secret, asked the other racers what was going on. It wasn't long before Tilly spied Candy surreptitiously drinking a deep red liquid out of her Chilly's sponsored bottle.

Aunty Pen's text was brief and to the point. 'What's next?'

Tilly gave a subtle shake of her head. Aunty Pen had done more than enough already. The rucksack she had with her, which Orla Kirby's 'bestie' bought on Vinted at a very acceptable price, had a large document wallet inside stacked with analysis of not only the top five of her competitors, but also statistical data on Tilly's own performances. Aunty Pen had done the research online using library computers to reduce the risk of discovery, then printed as paper could easily be destroyed.

Tilly walked home keeping an eye on her step length and stability as she was breaking in a new pair of trainers. They were provided to her free by one of her sponsors, Aldi, who were trying to expand and promote their special buys range. She was wondering if the logo on the trainers could be concealed at all, when a car blasted its horn at her as she was perilously close to stepping into the road. She saw her Nan and Aunty Pen waving at her from within. They were being driven by her Nan's new man-friend. Or perhaps it was Aunty Pen's. Or both. Whatever, he was a lucky man in Tilly's opinion. She hadn't yet been introduced to him but as far as she could tell from the glimpses she'd had of him he had a full head of hair and if that also was true of his teeth and his bank account then good for Nan and Pen. Just because he was driving a navy Honda Jazz didn't mean he wasn't minted.

When Tilly got home, she could barely get the key in the door she was so was eager to study the assessment of the Chinese competitor who she had previously lost to. She was aiming for her study, which she had created from a third bedroom that she'd had no desire to fill with a cot. Instead, she'd installed a corner desk to give her sufficient space to lay out maps and plan optimum routes and shops. She found it much easier to plot key landmark shops, colour-code and draw on paper first and then transfer her draft online to transfer to her smartwatch. These were for trial runs as until the race started the competitors wouldn't know the category of items required. There was a large monthly calendar stuck to one wall, with thick red crosses counting down the days to competition. There were occasional smaller orange blobs marking Tilly's menstrual cycle. In another corner sat an oversized paper shredder. Tilly didn't trust firms that offered confidential waste disposal. Unless you followed them, how would you know? There was shelving to display her trophies and medals. It also proudly showed off her most prized possession, a signed framed photo of Alexa Chung, fashion influencer extraordinaire. She wasn't sure what kind of love she felt for Alexa, perhaps it was a girl crush or maybe she just wanted to be her. Every day she looked at the photo and said, 'You are Alexa Chung and I am not,' channelling her idol's own attitude towards Jane Birkin. Out of respect Tilly had printed a small photo of Jane Birkin and placed it in the corner of the frame. She'd taken it from an old movie poster and it was there for a few months before she realised she'd printed Mia Farrow in error.

Tilly threw her keys in to a side table and gave a quick shout of 'I'm home,' before starting to climb the stairs. Her boyfriend of three years, Ryan, came out of the kitchen looking confused. It was a look not much different from his sex face and similar to his work face when he was battling with algorithms. Ryan was a man of few expressions. He was wearing his standard outfit of slightly loose taupe chinos, an Oxford shirt with the sleeves rolled up and rebellious socks. Today's were the colour of a baby's nappy. Not a fresh one. Tilly had always been unimpressed with his lack of originality or interest in fashion but at least he ironed his own clothes.

'Are you kidding me?' He fumed at her.

'What?' She looked down to make sure she'd not got her skirt stuck in her pants.

'I can't believe you,' he said. 'You shop for England but you can't manage to get onions, a tin of tomatoes and a tube of anusol from the supermarket!'

It was true. She'd totally forgotten his text.

'I can't make spag bol with half the ingredients missing, can I?'

'It could probably cope without the anusol.' She tried to win him over with a nudge of the elbow and a smile. 'At a push.'

He remained unmoved.

'I'll go out again. Sorry,' she said turning to leave. 'Ryan, we're still good for a shag later, aren't we? What with the anusol and everything.'

His sigh didn't put her off.

'I can't help it,' she continued. 'It's being an elite athlete. You know they all shag for England in the Olympic village.'

'Perhaps you and they should get their testosterone levels checked.'

'Well, you know I have to do that as part of being eligible to compete. And I'm allowed to compete so there's your answer. A high libido is part and parcel as I say of being a super elite athlete.'

He sighed. Then perked up, 'Unless we're trying for a...'

Tilly was shaking her head. 'No, well we just need to be careful. Wouldn't want you to get injured.'

She laughed and rubbed his shoulder. 'I don't think we'll get into too much trouble doing missionary.'

He gave her a defeated look. 'As long as we get it over with before Corrie.' Ryan had a penchant for 1980s *Coronation Street* and quite often Tilly didn't have to ask for sex; all she had to do was don a pair of Deirdre Barlow spectacles. If anyone could source an authentic pair of Deirdre glasses it was Tilly.

After Tilly had had her fill, including dinner, she went to her study, unlocking the door as she did so. It wasn't that she didn't trust Ryan per se but if his mates came round or more specifically his mum, they might not be able to resist the temptation to look inside her den. Ryan had resisted the request for his friends and mum to list any known relationships with any shopping championship competitors. This refusal had led her to take more extreme action. She placed three Maoams in a triangular formation behind the door so that if someone opened it, they would push the sweets out of the way. Tilly had to start taking a photo on her phone of the layout so if someone had spotted the Maoams and replaced them she could tell if they'd done it wrong. But nine times out of ten she would forget and open the door fully herself and send the sweets flying. Today she pushed the door slightly ajar and was happy that her creation was intact. So much so that she decided to eat them.

Tilly opened her rucksack as if it was a Christmas present. The file was weighty and thick. Aunty Pen had clearly surpassed herself. Her anticipation turned to a frown as it wasn't the Chinese competitor's analysis that was first in the file. It was that of her own. She flicked the pages to zip forward but a chart caught her attention. It was a summary of Tilly's times for the year by date. There were some repetitive dips in form. Tilly pulled her calendar off from the wall. She had a theory that the dips in form might coincide with the orange stickers and lo and behold she was right. She performed more poorly during her period. Tilly used the contraceptive pill and had been known to carry on taking it through the week that you're supposed to stop. She hadn't done that recently for fear of what the hormones dancing around in her uterus might do. But now she thought, what trouble could a little extra progesterone get into? Maybe reduce her libido. Ryan would probably be grateful for the respite. She revisited her calendar and counted forward to competition day. That couldn't be right. She counted again. She's three days overdue. Her eyes start to get sore from staring at the calendar. She blinks quickly, snapping herself out of it. Three days? Hardly anything at all. It's the gap between hair washes. Barely time for her leg stubble to grow. God, sometimes it's been longer than that between poos. Stress was probably to blame.

'Tilly?'

'Jesus Christ!' She jumped. Seeing Ryan at the door she quickly folded the calendar and tucked it in the back of the folder. 'You're like bloody Feathers MacGraw spooking me out.'

'I did knock,' he said. 'Brought you this.' He offered a mug of tea which she accepted. Then as though he was a magician pulling the proverbial rabbit out of a hat, he produced a packet of Maoams from his trouser pocket. 'To keep your strength up. You know, for your race.'

Tilly tapped the packet on her desk, what was that all about? Keeping her strength up and then giving her the very sweets that she used to check entry into her room. They had had the baby conversation quite early on in their relationship. Tilly didn't feel at all maternal and Ryan had said he wanted at least one each of a mini-Ryan and a mini-Tilly. The 'at least' made her want to go to the pharmacy *tout suite*. She thought she'd get away with it by saying they needed to wait until she'd achieved all she could as a competitive shopper. Could Ryan really have done something to scupper her contraception? Perhaps he'd developed sperm with superpowers. Or maybe put something in her food that counteracted the hormones. Or tampered with her pill packet and substituted them with placebos. That would be quite a challenge, to open replace and then reseal a blister pack. She was being ridiculous. She dipped into the sweet packet, which was already open, Ryan must also have succumbed to temptation, and started unwrapping. Of course, he didn't need to do all that opening and sealing, he could simply replace the whole packet. Was he trying to sabotage her shopping career? She texted Aunty Pen, 'please can you check if Ryan has any friends or relatives in the race this year xx'.

The reply came back quickly: 'l8r am out with your Nan + Bo.' Bo must be the new man.

'Stop it, Tilly,' she told herself and went back to the folder. She really needed to focus.

The Chinese competitor's pack was an eye opener for Tilly. Her name was Vera Ng and she had been either first or second in each of the last five competitions. Other competitors thought themselves hilarious when they dubbed her as Miss Dry Eyes, her being a 'Wa' short of being a fashion designer. That wasn't her plan when she had chosen an anglicised Christian name, she loved TV crime drama and Vera was her favourite. She often turned up to competitions wearing an oversized Mac and bucket hat, before stripping off to reveal a size four, five-foot-one inch body.

Tilly didn't need Aunty Pen's folder to tell her all this, but there was a little bit of background as to her parents. Vera was the daughter of a businessman and an accountant. She'd had a very strict upbringing and had been expected to follow her mother into a financial profession. She clearly knew how to balance the books in her races, she always fulfilled the spending criteria of the Shopping competition. However, there had been some sort of scandal surrounding her mother, a casino and a missing fifty thousand pounds. Her parents had subsequently separated and Vera lived with her father. Rumour had it that her mother now worked for a race course bookie and was very good at communicating odds using tic-tac. Or TikTok. Or both. Vera herself was sponsored by a Chinese betting company. The shopping championship board considered long and hard whether this was the kind of message they wanted the competition to send. But after they all received impressive fake apple watches, Xboxes and large packs of low-quality face masks they quickly rubber stamped the sponsorship.

Tilly studied Vera's performance charts. She was consistent over all five categories whereas Tilly was faster for three and slower for two. One of the categories that Tilly was faster at was the dress buying. Usually there was a stipulation like the *haute couture* one in Paris but a bit simpler, such as a specific colour or pattern or fit. Skater was a popular one with the competitors as was A line. Bodycon not so much. Whatever the style the dress had to fit. Tilly was a size ten and there was usually something available in her size. She did everything she could to retain her advantageous shape to the extent that after a Christmas binge she would do the whole body wrap in cling film exercise. She assumed that as Vera was a size four it took her more time to find a dress to fit her depending on what area the race was in. Tilly decided that the dress category was a tick to her.

Another category that Tilly was fast in was skincare and make-up. This could be anything from bronzer to bikini wax. She didn't know why she had a knack for this element but it looked like Vera was slow in the previous race because she bought foundation that didn't have sun protection when the criteria had been at least SP15. Tilly doubted Vera would make such a mistake again so couldn't consider this particular category as a given.

Tilly needed to look at where she was slower and why the deficit was so much bigger than the ones she was better at. She was OK at handbags but weak at shoes. Perhaps

Vera had the advantage with having sufficiently small feet that she could buy children's shoes thus saving money and increasing her budget for other categories. But Tilly's nemesis was the 'answer and find'. It was what it said on the tin: a question would be set, the answer to which would give the final item to purchase. It would be something like, 'What brand of shoes is Carrie from Sex and the City renowned for'? Or 'What was the most popular style of jeans in 2022'? The extra twist being that competitors didn't know how much money to leave for this purchase and yet they couldn't hold back too much because there were penalties for having more than five percent of the budget left at the finish. There's a lot of difference in price between a pair of Manolo Blahniks and a pair of mom jeans. They couldn't plan before the race because the budget is changed each time. Tilly often fell foul of having kept too much money back. She wanted a much better method of allocating her budget but short of finding out the question in advance she didn't know what to do. A different approach was necessary in one of the other categories to create a bigger advantage in the ones she excelled in. She needed Ryan's help.

The ride to the start was rocky. Tilly retched at each bump in the road. God, was this morning sickness? A few drops leaked from her mouth on to the Manolo Blahniks she was wearing. The cobalt blue stung her eyes. She'll struggle to get anywhere quickly in those, she thought. Why didn't she put her Aldi trainers on? The minibus stopped and the other competitors jumped out all sporting supermarket trainers. They lined up on the start line and a laminated sheet was given to them, with a map of the boundary they had to shop within on one side and the list of items required, final question and budget on the other.

Aunty Pen handed out the sheets, which was odd, and she winked at Tilly as she passed it to her. Tilly turned it over and over. It was blank. She turned it over again. Nothing! She looked up but everyone else had started the race. 'Noooooo,' she screamed, took off a shoe and attacked Aunty Pen with it, stabbing her repeatedly with a Manolo Blahnik heel. The resulting blood soaked through Pen's clothes forming the shape of a stiletto.

'Ouch, get off.' Ryan fended off Tilly's fist that was pounding him in his chest. 'Wake up.'

She sat up woozy and nauseous. 'Sorry. Pre-race nightmare.' She belched loudly. 'Bit gruesome to be fair.'

The actual journey to the start was less troublesome. One poor girl was the colour of Kermit the frog, so Tilly felt reassured that others were more nauseous than her. She was sat opposite Vera and had a go at who blinks first. Tilly didn't consider it a bad omen that she lost, she told herself that she'd winked first and that was a totally different vibe. As they drove along, they could see boundary tape being placed on the pavement. It was the brightest of rainbow stripes so the competitors couldn't claim they hadn't seen it if they went out of bounds.

Quite a crowd was gathered at the starting line. Ryan stood with Tilly's Nan and Aunty Pen. He gave her an encouraging thumbs up, whilst tapping on his mobile with his other hand. Nan and Pen started a cheerleader chant with crocheted pom-poms from the over sixties club. The competitors lined up, the top ten in the front row. Tilly wore a cropped top and leggings, her Aldi trainers and had an oversized rucksack on her back for her purchases. It was the standard uniform for them all. They all checked their smartwatches. It was there that the message would be sent with the list of shopping requirements, there was no lamination involved at all. They also paid and logged their purchases on their watch and once they'd completed the four standard purchases, they would receive the final question.

The official starter appeared. There was a cumulative gasp from the crowd and two competitors fainted. It was Alexa Chung. Tilly's heart was racing but she managed to stay upright. Two fewer people to beat. Vera began another stare-off with her, but Tilly simply winked and checked her watch. She had the psychological high ground. All that studying of Anne Robinson was paying off.

Wrists vibrated, Alexa Chung shouted 'Go!' and they were off. Off to the extent that they all meandered forward whilst reading the message. Tilly noticed Vera's wrist vibrate for a second time. She glanced at Ryan who gave her a dou-ble thumbs up this time. Vera stumbled after the second message, zigzagging away from the start line. Tilly resisted the urge to follow her, sticking to her own plan. The bag category was a satchel, requiring an inside pocket and large enough to carry an eleven-inch tablet. She knew exactly which shop sold the much-coveted Cambridge Satchel. Even though there was a sale on, it was a big spend out of the budget, and a large item to go in the rucksack. She'd rue the extra weight to carry from such an early phase. It was a rookie mistake and she needed to sharpen up. Tilly let the shop door close just as another competitor ran towards it.

'Sorry!' She shouted, not meaning it, while double checking the skincare requirement. She would do that next, then dress and finally shoes. That would help her with weight distribution in her rucksack. It was a tough choice as it meant a little doubling back on her route, but she didn't know what distance she was going to have to cover on the final question category and the satchel was already rocking about and upsetting her rhythm. Balance was the name of the game.

Sweat was already forming on her upper lip when she got to Superdrug. She was going cheap on an anti-wrinkle serum that needed to have hyaluronic acid as an ingredient. As if that was a thing. There was a queue at the checkout including two competitors who'd had the same idea as her. By the way their rucksacks hung off their backs Tilly was fairly certain this was their first purchase. She jogged on the spot whilst waiting to make sure she didn't stiffen up.

The next item had to be a strapless cocktail number and a photo of it on was required. It wasn't party season so was unlikely to be in many of the cheaper high street shops. A concession in John Lewis was the only answer. She ran up an escalator and started a second until she saw Vera waving a bag at her on the down escalator. Tilly couldn't stop staring and landed flat on her face at the top. As she laid stunned on the floor a saleswoman from the perfume counter bent down so close to Tilly's face that she could see the contours of her foundation and said 'Would you like to smell like Kylie?' whilst brandishing a perfume atomiser.

Tilly put on the black cocktail dress as quickly as she possibly could, tucking in her boobs for the photo. She didn't want to be disqualified because of a rogue nipple. Sweat accumulated on her face and she felt weak. There was no CCTV in the changing room so she took the opportunity to retrieve two Maoams from the lining of her trainers to boost her sugar levels. Job done she sprinted down escalators, flipping the bird at the perfume counter as she went, and out of the shop back on to the high street.

Vera was in the same shoe shop that Tilly had chosen and was struggling. Vera had dozens of shoes scattered over the floor in a pattern that on another day could form part of a modern art installation. She'd never shopped in the adult section previously and it had blown her mind. Tilly did a little fist pump. Her evil mastermind plan had worked. She'd asked Ryan to hack into the competition system and send Vera a second message, that she was forbidden from buying children's sized shoes. Tilly had had to agree to have a baby but given she thought she was up the duff in any case, it didn't seem to much of a hardship. It had worked a treat. Although Tilly had sweat beading on her upper lip and an uneasy twitching in her stomach, she calmly picked up a red pump in her size and asked for its partner. This spurred Vera on to complete the requirement of a pair of pumps the same colour as the satchel.

They both logged their shoe purchase at the same time and stood nervously next to each other for the final question, each edging towards the door whilst being wary that the answer might be a shoe. Tilly particularly so since she thought her nightmare might have been a kind of premonition. She urgently tapped on her watch to see how much money she had left. Sixty-five pounds. She needed to spend at least fifty on the final item.

Both watches beeped.

Tilly let out an excited involuntary burp.

'What kind of hat does Alexa Chung have in her collaboration with Barbour?' was the final item.

Tilly was first out of the blocks. A bucket style rain hat was what she was after. Fifty quids worth. She'd not spent enough on other items; at that price she would have to buy from Barbour. So back to John Lewis. Tilly could see that Vera was taking a different route. Pressure was on. She dived into John Lewis, the perfume saleswoman raised her atomiser, saw Tilly's expression and thought better of it, shoppers parted to let Tilly through and the checkout guy didn't even have time to say 'have a nice day'.

Tilly turned into the street for the final run in. Her heart was pounding, the rucksack beating her back, a blur of people cheering along the pavement. And a glance behind her revealed Vera struggling under the weight of her shopping. Tilly's stomach flipped with increased adrenaline. Or something.

She could see the finish line. Ryan jumping up and down cheering her on. Nan and Aunty Pen, not cheering her on. Odd. Her stomach was really flipping now and sweat cascaded down her face. She felt so sick. The finishing line was now almost in touching distance. Vera was practically breathing down her neck. She could find a drain cover and try to discreetly get it over with, like Paula Radcliffe having a poo in the street in the London marathon, or she could fall to her knees and projectile vomit semi-digested Maoams over the finishing tape and Alexa Chung's feet.

Later she would claim that she won because part of her crossed the line before Vera. But the board turned down her appeal on the grounds that the contents of her stomach weren't actually in her body at the time they crossed the line.

Ryan hugged her, despite the mess she was in. Tilly gripped onto him more tightly when she saw Vera being lifted up and swung round by Nan and Aunty Pen's new man. There was an uncanny resemblance between him and Vera. Worse still, Nan and Aunty Pen joined in the celebrations.

Realisation came to her. 'You know that pack of sweets you gave me,' Tilly asked Ryan. 'I don't suppose Aunty Pen gave them to you?' He nodded to confirm. 'Oh my god, is that what's been making you sick? She poisoned you. Deliberately sabotaged your race!'

So, it wasn't morning sickness after all and Tilly doubted she was pregnant. She would have to speak to Nan and Pen, she didn't know if Bo had targeted them specifically or whether their friendship was real.

She squelched away from the crowds, hand in hand with Ryan. 'Don't suppose you fancy a shag, do you?'

# Acknowledgments

We are grateful to the following for permission to reproduce copyright materials in this collection.

'Sorry, Delivery' © 2024, Paula Lennon. Printed by permission of the author.

'Double Date' © 2024, Lucy Vine. Printed by permission of the author.

'Unbound' © 2024, Jean Ende. Printed by permission of the author.

'Jenny Bean, Calamity Queen' © 2024, Julia Wood. Printed by permission of the author.

'You Can't Get There From Here' © 2024, J.Y. Saville. Printed by permission of the author.

'Fake It Till You Hate It' © 2024, Sadia Azmat. Printed by permission of the author.

'Glue' © 2024, Clare Shaw. Printed by permission of the author.

'Care Home Capers' © 2024, Wendy Hood. Printed by permission of the author.

'Hapless' © 2024, R. Malik. Printed by permission of the author.

# Acknowledgments

'Poets Rise Again' © 2023, Josie Long. Printed by permission of the author and Canongate Books. This story comes from Josie Long's book, *Because I Don't Know What You Mean and What You Don't.*

'Ways With Mince' © 2024, Kathryn Simmonds. Printed by permission of the author.

'The Art of Genital Persuasion' © 2024, Kathy Lette. Printed by permission of the author.

'Go Your Own Way' © 2024, Kimberley Adams. Printed by permission of the author.

'Nothing Compared to You' © 2024, Annemarie Cancienne. Printed by permission of the author.

'Shopping for England' © 2024, Kim Clayden. Printed by permission of the author.

##  COMEDY WOMEN IN PRINT PRIZE

Comedy Women in Print (CWIP) is the first UK prize dedicated to comedy writing. Our aim is to create a platform for content by witty women authors. Launched in 2019, the awards are the brainchild of comedian, author and actress Helen Lederer.

Women have long been underrepresented as drivers of wit, but CWIP has changed the conversation. Many long- and short-listed CWIP writers have gone on to have writing careers, gain agents and become part of the writing community. We also provide a platform for underrepresented stories to be told.

Categories of the prize include Published Novel, Unpublished Novel and Short Story. Judges have included Marian Keyes, Loli Adefope, Joanna Scanlan, Llewella Gideon, Gloria Hunniford, Thanyia Moore, Paula Wilcox, Susan Wokoma, Steph McGovern, Shazir Mirza, Maureen Lipman and Kathy Lette. Honorary Awards have been given to Jilly Cooper, Ruth Jones, Mavis Cheek, Meera Syal, Debora Frances-White, Jo Brand and Sharon Horgan.

For more details and full terms and conditions visit www.comedywomeninprint.co.uk

'Wit is the way we make friends and the way we make revolution' Meera Sayal at the CWIP awards.

'Winning the CWIP flash prize gave me the confidence to keep writing' A.J. Morris, winner Comedy Cringe Flash Fiction partnering with Black Girl Writers and People in Harmony.

'The CWIP Awards have truly changed my life and made my lifelong dream of being an author come true. I urge everyone to support, cherish and nurture this very important prize' Hannah Dolby, Unpublished Novel runner-up 2021.

'My phone never stops ringing! I'm thrilled to have won a CWIP award but more than that, it's been a joy to be involved, right from the start' Nina Stibbe, CWIP published novel winner 2020, *Reasons to be Cheerful* (Penguin).